More Praise for Terrill Lankford

"Lankford writes gripping and amazingly sustained action. He provides a tense noir, roller-coaster ride for those with a taste for wryly twisted imaginings and the darker side." —*Santa Barbara News*

"If you read three pages of *Angry Moon* it will grab you by the cojones and not let you go until the end."
—Eddie Bunker, author of *Straight Time*

"This is Lankford's second novel after *Shooters* and it establishes the author as a first-class storyteller, a master of spine-tingling excitement and unexpected plot twists." —*Booklist*

"*Shooters* cooks! This is a blood thriller that will vibrate your vindaloo! Will keep you up nights howling at the moon! Read it or be deprived!"
—James Ellroy

"*Shooters* is excellent. It grabs you on page one and won't turn you loose." —Robert B. Parker

"Lankford breathtakingly tosses the reader into a Hollywood snake pit that is at once compelling and repugnant."
—*Dallas Morning News* on *Shooters*

"Violent, gritty, cynical, and provocative, *Shooters* takes you on a wild ride through seamy, narcissistic L.A., where the threatening pall of smoke from fires in the hills hangs over everything."
—*The Detroit Free Press* (four stars)

"When you crack this book, make sure you've cleared your schedule for the next twelve hours. This is an absolutely superb read."
—Douglas Preston, coauthor of *The Relic*

"Wizard! A witty, bawdy, staccato, suspenseful, and very hip update of Nathanael West's *Day of the Locust*. Not just an exposé of the L.A. scene, the wacky fashion world, the porn world, the recreational-druggie culture, but also a perceptive look into all of us inhabiting the 1990s." —Gary Jennings, author of *Aztec*

Also by Terrill Lankford

Shooters

angry moon

TERRILL LANKFORD

TOR ®

a tom doherty associates book / new york

This is a work of fiction. All the characters and events portrayed in this novel are either products of the author's imagination or are used fictitiously.

ANGRY MOON

Copyright © 1997 by Terrill Lee Lankford

A Tor Book
Published by Tom Doherty Associates, Inc.
175 Fifth Avenue
New York, NY 10010

Tor Books on the World Wide Web:
http://www.tor.com

Tor® is a registered trademark of Tom Doherty Associates, Inc.

ISBN: 0-812-54834-5
Library of Congress Card Catalog Number: 97-14500

First edition: October 1997
First mass market edition: March 1999

Printed in the United States of America

0 9 8 7 6 5 4 3 2 1

For Martha Lee McCoy,
who taught me to appreciate the moon.

acknowledgments

No book writes itself. And no writer truly writes alone. So I would like to take this opportunity to thank the following friends and family who have put up with me over the years it took to crank this sucker out. Many of them offered wisdom and vital criticism: Jeffrey Falls, David Pecchia, Sandra Petersen, Dale Jaffe, Lisa Joyner, Cynthia Rothrock, Lisa and Samantha Bergener, Fred Olen Ray, Alan and Hilarie Ormsby, William Peed, the Garsons—Paul, Illona, and Grant, Mary Bruyere, Mac Ahlberg, Alvin Sargent, Laura Morton, Jan and John Alonzo, Dani Imura, Steve and Kit Picard, Jennifer Goodman, Diana and Bill Shaffer, Ken Mitcheroney, Steve Collins, Susan Petricone, Lisa Hubler, Jill and Arden Burrows, Sheldon McArthur, Richard Brewer, Steve Vascik, Paul and Mara Jaffe, Onita Bazauri, Mark Ruszczyk, Carol Weigel, Kriss Turner, John "the Devil" Vogel, Joey Ito Farina and his brood, and, of course, Sterling Hayden.

Special kudos to Alexander Braddell, who provided intense editorial assistance at a crucial early stage of the book; Andrew H. Zack, who delivered a needed kick in the teeth toward the end of the long journey; Rick Bazauri, who supplied chilling technical advice on weaponry; Steven de las Heras, troubleshooter without peer; Breene Farrington, the sweetest publicist in North America; Carol McCleary, the first agent to take the book on; Bob Gleason, my editor at Forge, who had the weird courage to publish the thing; and Tom Doherty, who gave him the bread to do it. And last, but certainly not least, Nicholas Hassitt, whose initial interest and assistance in this work (way back when) rescued it from the filing cabinet. His contributions to this book were invaluable.

There will come a day when bad men outnumber good,
When wrong seems no different than right. . . .
And then there will come an angry moon,
To show the righteous a new light.

prologue

"Tequila," the stranger said with a wicked grin.

The bartender, a fat guy named Jesús, poured a shot of Cuervo Especial and slid it in front of the ugly gringo.

Every eye in the room watched the stranger as he downed the tequila in one gulp, slammed the shot glass down on the bar, and said, *"Uno más, amigo."*

"Jesús," the bartender corrected as he poured a second shot. He was not this stranger's amigo. The man sipped the shot and seemed to be contemplating the distinction.

The stranger was tall and gaunt. His silver hair, slicked back tight against his head, revealed a high forehead and widow's peak, giving him the look of a greased-down mountain lion. The skin of his face seemed to be wrapped tightly around his skull, as if at any moment the flesh might tear and bone would come poking through. His prominent cheekbones highlighted a thick white scar on the right side of his face. His teeth were sharp and pointed, as if they had been filed into little knives. His age was hard to determine. Perhaps he was in his mid-fifties. He was thin, but there appeared to be muscle on his bones where most men his age would be fat, or at least soft.

He wore a dusty black leather bomber jacket over a white cotton shirt and a pair of dark dress slacks. The tattered jacket had the words *Night and Fog* across the shoulders in faded white paint. It looked a good three sizes too large, as if it had once belonged to a much bigger man. His boots, made of fine Italian leather, were worn thin from abuse.

The stranger was ugly, but no uglier than any of the other men in the bar. It was the kind of ugly that often appealed to women. They mistook it for intensity.

Everyone in the darkened bar had laughed at him when he'd first entered the place and rather arrogantly asked the bartender if he could make change for an American hundred-dollar bill. This was not a part of Mexico where gringos walked alone. Not safely at least. Especially gringos with an attitude and a wallet full of cash.

If the stranger had been aware of his gaffe, he certainly hadn't seemed concerned. He had immediately positioned himself at the bar next to the most attractive señorita in the place. The *only* señorita in the place. Now he was stepping over a very dangerous, yet invisible, line. The señorita belonged to Savage Jack, the only gringo that drank at this bar on a regular basis.

Savage Jack owned a spread near the lagoon. A major farmer in the area, he had come down to retire and grow weed for his buddies, the Hell's Angels of Oakland, California. Many of the men seated around the bar worked in his fields. They considered him an honorary Mexican. They *had* to.

Once a month a pack of Angels would descend on this little town for an orgy of drunken debauchery. The rest of the month the locals would take revenge on any non-Angel gringo that stumbled into the area. Savage Jack didn't mind the subtle racism; he was usually the first one to start the stomping. He didn't care much why someone was being stomped. Stomp or be stomped, that was his motto, and it had served him well.

Jesús poured another shot of tequila for the stranger. He realized it would probably be the last thing the man ever tasted, except maybe some of his own blood. The stranger had entered the bar at an opportune moment, or an unfortunate moment, depending on the relative perspective of all involved. Savage Jack had just gone into the head to "tap the lizard." Savage Jack had been downing tequila and Indio beer for the better part of three hours without a piss break, so he had quite a lot of tapping to do. This was giving the stranger just enough time to set himself up for disaster.

"Thirty pesos, please," Jesús said to the stranger.

"What's the rush, barkeep?" the stranger hissed. "I'm not going anywhere for a long, long time. Let's run a tab, shall we?" The stranger turned his head and smiled at the pretty little señorita next to him. Teresa. Savage Jack's girl.

Teresa was small in stature but she had large breasts, a sweet face, and jet black hair that went all the way down to her impossibly thin waist. She had been a prostitute before Savage Jack took possession of her. He wasn't her first regular man, but he had lasted the longest. He still screwed anything that came along, but *her* extracurricular sex life had ended when he moved her into his shack. Once, one of Jack's buddies, a nice, handsome guy named Matt, almost managed to slip Teresa one on the sly, but Jack caught them and Matt was no longer handsome. Teresa still had a thin red scar on her left cheek from Jack's switchblade.

Scars.

Her scar was small compared to the ugly white one that marked the stranger's face, but a scar meant more to a woman than a man. It wasn't enough of a scar to make her ugly, just enough to make her remember. And the look on the stranger's face was making her remember very well.

She touched the scar and turned away from him. He might

want to die, but she did not. She started to get up off her barstool, but the stranger put a hand on her arm, stopping her.

"What's the problem?" the stranger asked pleasantly.

Teresa's first instinct was to run, just pull away from this madman and get the hell out of there, but something about the way he touched her made her stay. The man's grip was firm and strong, but he did not seem to want to hurt her. Something about the stranger attracted her. Teresa had always been uncontrollably drawn to danger, and in this man she sensed something very dangerous indeed. She thought it might only be his impending death that she was sensing, but then again maybe it was something more. Maybe this gringo was to be her liberator. The man who would finally manage to take her away from Savage Jack.

She decided to play her hand.

"Problem?" she asked with a laugh. "The problem is you are a dead man and you don't even know it. You're crazy to come into this place. *Loco en la cabeza.*"

"What's wrong with this place?" the stranger asked, downing his tequila. "I think it's rather sweet." A hint of German accented the man's voice.

"Sweet?" Teresa said in horror. "Look around. Do you see those men? Do you think any of them are going to let you out of here? You are one dead gringo."

The stranger looked around the room. It was a dinky little rat-trap of a bar. The walls were disintegrating where they stood, rotting from the corrosive sea air outside. A thin white crescent moon shimmered over the dark night ocean through the sole window in the front of the joint. The window was cracked in three places. Years of dirt and grease appeared to be all that held it together. Fifteen Mexican men of various sizes, shapes, and ages sat around the smoky room. None spoke. They just stared at Teresa and the stranger in total silence.

"I don't think these men want any trouble. I feel fine. Very safe." The stranger motioned with the shot glass, requesting a re-fill. Teresa shook her head in amazement.

Jesús filled the glass again and said, "Señor, I must insist on col-lecting your tab. It is now forty pesos."

The stranger fixed an icy stare on Jesús.

"Your lack of faith is really beginning to annoy me, barkeep." The stranger smiled a smile that was not a smile. "I'll tell you what," he said in a pleasant tone. "Why don't you sell me what's left in the bottle plus my tab so far for that hundred I mentioned, and then you can just get the fuck out of my face, how would that be?"

The stranger reached into the breast pocket of his jacket and pulled out a wad of hundred-dollar bills. The tension in the room swelled audibly. It took the form of rustling as men shifted in their seats to get a better look at the dough. Teresa stopped breathing at the sight of all that cash.

The stranger peeled off one of the bills and stuffed it into Jesús's shirt pocket. Jesús was so shocked by the move that he of-fered absolutely no resistance as the stranger pulled the bottle of Cuervo out of his sweaty hand.

The stranger filled Teresa's highball glass to the brim. *"Salud,"* he said with a smile.

Teresa raised her glass and said, "To crazy, dead gringos every-where. They will soon have company." She sipped off the floating top of the tequila, then tipped the glass and drank half the hot liq-uid down. She wanted to get numb quick—for medicinal purposes. Maybe Savage Jack would just kill this man and that would be enough. Maybe it wouldn't. Maybe *she* would be punished as well. Whatever happened, she wanted to be deep drunk before the hurt-ing started.

"I will tell you something," Teresa said. "There is a man in the bathroom. His name is Jack. He likes to be called Savage Jack, and he is just that. *Muy salvaje.* I belong to him."

"I was under the impression Mexico was a free country," the

stranger said solemnly, as if someone had just popped his balloon. Maybe it was an act. Maybe, Teresa considered, everything this man said or did was just an act. He had the air of a mischievous little boy, playacting and putting everyone on, only he didn't seem to understand that punishment for this behavior would not be going to bed without supper or getting spanked with a hickory switch. It would be death.

"Mexico may be free, but I am not," Teresa continued. "I am his property and he is going to kill you."

"Why are you telling me all this?" the stranger asked sadly.

"I don't know," Teresa answered. "Maybe because you bought me a drink." The hooker in her was beginning to boil to the surface. Buy her a drink and she owed you something.

The door to the john opened and out stepped Savage Jack. He'd been in there a long time. He had timed his daily dump to go with his piss break, and Jack was known to suffer from constipation. A man sitting near the bathroom door waited politely until Jack passed him, then moved to another part of the bar to avoid the noxious fumes emanating from the john.

Savage Jack was almost as wide as he was tall. The day he stopped riding his Harley and traded it for a truck with which to haul weed was the day that bike groaned a silent sigh of relief. He was as thick-skinned as he was thick skulled. He had a pig's face and a killer's mind, and he'd abandoned what little morality he ever had a very long time ago.

Upon seeing Jack exit the bathroom, Teresa immediately turned away from the stranger and acted as if she had never taken notice of him. She finished her tequila in one gulp and began to sweat profusely.

The stranger took one look at Savage Jack, calculated some information, then turned and filled Teresa's glass with tequila again. She looked down at the glass in terror. This crazy gringo wanted to get them both killed. She looked up at the stranger in quiet desperation. He just smiled and winked at her.

Savage Jack grabbed the stranger by his jacket collar, jerked him off his barstool, spun him around, and slammed his back against the bar.

"What in *motherfucking hell* is going on here?!" Savage Jack bellowed.

"Well, you see," the stranger said, "it's sort of like a party. We're all just drinking and carrying on and having a great time. Aren't we, honey?" He looked at Teresa. Tears were beginning to well in her eyes. She was terrified.

Savage Jack brought a meaty, ham hock of a hand up and slapped the stranger on the side of his face with enough force to rip many a man's head clean off his shoulders. The stranger almost lost his footing, but he grabbed the bar at the last second and kept his balance. He looked dizzy.

Regaining his composure, the stranger stood straight up on his feet. Savage Jack was amazed, as was everyone else in the room. This scrawny creep could take more punishment than the average man his size and age.

The stranger looked up and down Savage Jack's bulky body with false admiration. "Gosh, you're a big man," he said in a fey voice. "Big and strong. I don't want any trouble from you."

Savage Jack stared at the stranger for a moment, trying to figure him out. Then he began to laugh. It was the laugh of a diseased jackal. "Seems you've picked yourself up a faggot here, Teresa," Savage Jack spit out between chuckles. The other men in the bar joined in the raucous laughter.

Teresa lowered her eyes to the floor and watched a teardrop fall and mingle with the sand and dust. She was in deep shit and she knew it. She had overestimated the stranger out of blind hope and now this skinny gringo was going to get both of them killed.

Savage Jack grabbed Teresa by the back of the hair and jerked her viciously off the barstool into the air. "So, you got yourself a boyfriend while I was off taking a shit?" he snarled. "I can't leave your side for one goddamn second, can I, you fucking whore?" He didn't give her a chance to answer. He slammed her, face first, into the side of the stranger's head. Teresa lost consciousness and crumpled on the floor in a heap. The stranger, amazingly enough, stayed on his feet.

"You shouldn't have done that," the stranger said. He wiped blood from his ear where Teresa's forehead had smashed into him. "That's no way to treat a lady."

Savage Jack stared at the stranger in disbelief. The rage building in his heart was uncontrollable. He didn't know what to do to this creep first, there was so much punishment to be dealt out. He was going to break this old fucker's skinny neck, then dance on his bones, but he wanted to be careful not to kill the guy right away. He wanted him to suffer for a very long time. And then Savage Jack would take care of that ball-busting bitch Teresa.

Savage Jack began to bring a fist up to deliver a punch to the stranger's head. The punch never arrived. The stranger made a lightning-quick move with his right hand, so fast that most of the men in the dark room didn't even see it darting up to Savage Jack's face and removing something from it. Savage Jack immediately stumbled backward, clawing at his face, at the empty sockets where his eyes had been a moment before. Now there was nothing, except blood and dangling optic nerves. The stranger turned toward Jesús and with a snap of his wrist threw Savage Jack's eyes onto the bar in front of him. The bloody orbs rolled over and came to rest by the bottle of Cuervo like dice on a craps table.

"Snake eyes!" the stranger yelled with a crazy laugh.

Jesús backed away in abject horror from the terrible sight. He wanted his shotgun and it was all the way at the other end of the bar. He inched toward the weapon, trying not to let on to what he was doing.

A low, terrifying sound filled the air. Savage Jack, finally comprehending what had just happened to him, was beginning to go mad. The scream started softly and moved through the scales of insanity to a hideous shriek. He flailed about, trying to get hold of the asshole that had taken his eyes. His mind cleared for a mi-

crosecond and he reached under his belt for the .38-caliber Smith
& Wesson he knew he would find there. If he was going to be blind
a lot of people were going to die. The stranger watched with quiet
fascination as Savage Jack flailed about. The rest of the men in
the bar were paralyzed with surprise. Most of them didn't like
Savage Jack very much anyway. He'd be easier to deal with minus
his eyes. They were glad to be rid of him. But this other man, this
crazy gringo with the fast hands and the big wad of hundreds, he
would have to be dealt with now.

Savage Jack got his gun out from under his belt and fired it in
the general direction where he thought he would find the stranger.
The shot missed by two feet and hit the giant mirror behind the
bar. A large chunk of the mirror fell and shattered on the floor, taking a row of liquor bottles along for the ride. Dust and glass flew
everywhere.

"I'll get you, scumfuck!" Savage Jack yelled. "I'll blow your
fuckin' brains out!"

The stranger took a few steps to the left, positioning himself
directly between Jesús and Savage Jack. Then the stranger laughed.
Savage Jack aimed the pistol in the direction of the laughter and
fired. The stranger sidestepped with lightning speed and allowed
the shot to go past him. The bullet hit Jesús in the arm, shattering
his elbow. He screamed and ran from the bar, forgetting all about
the shotgun and the stranger's money, terror overriding his pain
and greed.

The stranger reached over and grabbed the .38 out of Savage
Jack's hand. Savage Jack took a step forward, but the stranger pistol-
whipped the bigger man on the crown of his skull with three sharp
blows. Savage Jack fell backward onto an empty table. The table
gave under the weight of the big man and he crashed to the floor,
his face a crimson wash, a blind giant among the splintered tooth-
picks.

The stranger turned and looked at the men who remained in
the room. A few of the barflies had taken off when Savage Jack

began firing his gun, but eight or nine were still left, the roll of hundred-dollar bills burning in their minds.

"Show's over, fellas. Relax," the stranger said with feigned innocence.

Two men to the right of the stranger drew guns from under their belts. The stranger moved his arm and shot them both cleanly between the eyes with the .38, blowing their brains out onto the wall behind them. The stranger did this without looking at them, like a trick shot at the circus. He lowered the gun to his side and looked at the other men in the room.

"Don't make me kill the rest of you, okay?" he said with a smile that revealed every one of his pointy teeth. The remaining men ran for the front door. They wanted no part of this madman, for any amount of money. The bar was empty in five seconds flat.

Teresa started to come around. The stranger placed the .38 on the bar and helped the girl to her feet. She was young, but she had lived a hard, desperate life. The stranger thought how merciful it would be if he just killed her now and put her out of her misery. Then he tossed those thoughts away. Mercy was not his business.

"What happened?" Teresa asked through her daze.

"We had a bit of trouble with your boyfriend," the stranger replied.

Teresa focused her eyes and looked around the room. She saw the two dead men in the corner and then she saw Savage Jack amid the rubble of the broken table, his face covered with blood, his optic nerves hanging out of his vacant eye sockets. He was either unconscious or dead. Either way he was definitely no longer a threat to her.

"*Caramba!*" Teresa muttered to herself, making the sign of the cross in front of her body in good Catholic fashion. Then she rubbed the bump that was swelling on her forehead.

The stranger dumped broken shards from the mirror out of their glasses and poured two tall shots of tequila. Savage Jack's eyes rolled into the sink behind the bar when the Cuervo bottle moved. A cockroach resting in the drain skittered out to greet the new arrivals.

The stranger raised his glass in a toast.

"To freedom," he said jubilantly.

Teresa stared at him for a moment, trying to figure out what to do. She picked up her glass with a shaky hand and drank slowly, trying to put the image of all that was lying around her out of her mind.

They sat drinking until the bottle was empty. Maybe it was an hour, maybe more. No one returned to the bar to disturb them. There was no local police force in this little hovel of a town on the Mexican coast, and none of the locals wanted to die.

Though they didn't talk much, Teresa *did* manage to tell the stranger every pertinent fact that she could come up with about herself. But that's why the stranger preferred the company of young girls over older women. Their life stories were shorter.

When they finished the bottle of Cuervo the stranger picked Teresa up and laid her out on the bar. He positioned himself on top of her without saying a word and slipped his hand under her dress, ripping her panties off with one quick jerk. Then, amid the bottles and glasses and blood and broken shards of mirror, he thrust into her angrily, like a wild animal.

Teresa had never been ravaged this way before. Her previous lovers had just been men. But this one was different. This man tore into her in a way that told her she had never really *had* sex until now. That everything she had experienced up to this moment had just been play from little boys.

Now, with this stranger, Teresa found her true species. It was painful, but the pain soon turned to pleasure. She came after five minutes and she kept on coming for another twenty, until the sweating, drooling beast on top of her had finally spent his last load of the night. The stranger collapsed on top of Teresa and she stroked his sweat-soaked hair.

"I belong to *you* now," Teresa said between gasps as she tried to catch her breath.

The stranger brought both arms up along Teresa's body, caressing her gently as his hands traveled over her curves and crevices. He stroked the egg-sized bump on her forehead, then placed his hands on either side of her face and wrapped his fingers in her long black hair. He jerked her head a few inches off the bar and slammed it back down with all the strength he could muster. The back of her skull shattered and her body began an immediate death rattle. She shook and vibrated violently on the bar for a full minute, the stranger hugging her tightly as if they were sharing one last, great orgasm. And then she was still, her dead eyes gazing vacantly out the bar window at the crescent moon hanging over the black ocean.

The stranger looked at Teresa's pretty face and noted the small scar on her cheek. "You're free," he whispered to her. Then he rested his head between the girl's lifeless breasts and closed his eyes for a short, peaceful nap.

one

Nate Daniels coughed up a gob of blood into a Burger King napkin and lit another cigarette. He looked around the darkened motel room, somewhat in awe of where his life had led him.

A green-shaded desk lamp provided the room its only source of illumination. Ugly vinyl furniture dominated the decor. Cardboard boxes, suitcases, magazines, and stacks of faded newspapers, mostly tabloids, further cluttered the landscape. Even from the distance of the desk Nate could clearly make out the headline on the top newspaper on the stack closest to him: HIT MAN TALKS, FRIES MOB. His ulcer may have been acting up, but his eyes still worked fine.

HIT MAN TALKS, FRIES MOB. You better fucking believe it, Nate thought. He wanted all those bastards to fry. Every last one of them. Short Nate Daniels thirty grand and you're looking down the barrel of a grand jury indictment, that's what you're doing. Yes, sir.

He took a drag off the cigarette, then pressed the PLAY button on the mini–tape recorder that sat on the desk in front of him. His own voice floated out of the tinny speaker to greet him.

"The first hit is the one I remember the best. The rush of adrenaline as I coiled the wire around his throat. . . . I relished this, dragged the moment out as long as possible . . . slowly tightening the wire and watching my victim's life ebb away."

Nate smiled to himself. A best-seller in the making if he ever heard one. He hit the RECORD button on the tape machine and picked up the microphone. He rubbed his throat a few times before continuing. He was thirsty again, but he wanted to wait awhile. There was work to do and he knew his inspiration would melt into fog if he continued drinking.

"The later hits run together like a series of one-night stands. All I remember is the blood and the occasional explosion. . . ."

Nate paused for a second. It was no use. He couldn't stop thinking about that next drink. Just a little swig. That's all he'd take. Just enough to keep the fire going. He could handle it. Nate dropped the microphone and reached for the bottle of Jack Daniel's. He tipped it back and got half a sip. Then it was empty.

"Shit."

Jack Daniel's was Nate Daniels's favorite drink in the whole world. He lived for it. He loved it so much that he had long ago convinced himself that his family was related to the creators of the spirit. After all, they *did* share a last name . . . practically. When he was younger, running in the streets of Munster, Indiana, he would tell his teenage drinking buddies that he was actually heir to the Jack Daniel's fortune. A fortune he would collect on his twenty-first birthday, along, of course, with a lifetime supply of the finest premium whiskey in the land. He told the story so often that he actually grew to believe it himself. He was quite upset when the big day came and went and the Jack Daniel's people failed to contact him.

The humiliation he felt at the hands of his friends inspired Nate to seek his fortunes out west. It was a long, twisted road that had led him to this motel room, but in a way that road had been paved by his affection for Jack Daniel's.

Getting too late to send out for a bottle, he thought. Besides, he didn't appreciate the way the delivery kid looked at him last time. As if he knew more about Nate than he wanted him to know.

Nate suddenly stiffened up, his ears sensing something out of tune with the norm.

Trucks rumbled by outside the motel room window, but Nate had long ago grown accustomed to their random melodies. This had been something else, but he couldn't tell exactly what.

From the darker side of the room came a faint rustle. Nate got up and looked around nervously. He checked the locks on the front door for the two hundredth time that night. He returned to his chair and the tape recorder. Nothing appeared to be out of order. The building must have just been settling. Paranoia, he thought to himself. Sheer paranoia, plain and simple. All this waiting was taking a toll on his nerves.

Then the coughing began again. Heavier this time. He felt mucus and blood crisscrossing in his throat and he ran into the bathroom to spit into the sink. He ran the water for a good two minutes, spitting and gagging, stopping every now and then to stare at his face in the mirror, all red and flushed. He noted how his looks had changed in the last six months under the twenty-four-hour-a-day care and scrutiny of the Justice Department. His short red hair was thinning, his eyes had dark bags under them, his face looked puffy and unhealthy; he reminded himself of a swollen rodent. The initial interrogation period had been grueling. It had taken a long time for Nate to convince Justice that he had enough information to warrant immunity and protection. Part of Nate's deal with the Justice Department included his relative freedom while waiting to testify. He was sick of the jail cell and he didn't trust the bulls. He felt he could protect himself better on the outside than they could on the inside. Anyone could be bought for the right amount of money. Prime witnesses had been killed by agents on the take on more than one occasion. Nate was on his own now, more or less, until the grand jury could be convened. They were watching him, of course, *protecting* him, but he had been allowed to take precautions of his own for his peace of mind. He felt safer with his fate in his own hands. His ulcers had all developed *after* he cut his deal with the Feds. Once they were in control of his life he became a nervous wreck. Now that he had a taste of freedom again he was in the mood to get healthy. They were delivering a tread-mill in the morning.

After his stomach settled he splashed cold water on his face, then soaked a washcloth and rubbed the back of his neck until it was nice and cool.

Nate returned to the motel room proper, sat down at the desk, picked up the tape recorder, and began to gather his thoughts for another run down the literary hill. An armchair on the far side of the room made a creaking noise. Nate looked up with a start. This wasn't his paranoia creaking.

The brown back of the armchair turned slowly. Despite the chill of the night, sweat began to bead on Nate's forehead. His pulse started to race and he felt short of breath. He considered going for the .45 he kept taped under the desk, then thought bet-ter of it. A sudden move on his part could bring chaos from any corner of the room. Better to wait and see how the hand would be dealt.

The chair finished its turn and Nate's desk lamp reflected off the blue-black muzzle of a long-barreled 9mm automatic. A black suppressor was attached to the muzzle. The gun was held by a gloved hand. Nate felt his ulcer brewing up a good broth of bile and blood.

Something about the calm way that the gun was being held seemed familiar to Nate. He spoke, trying not to spit up, his voice a choking whisper. "Caulder?"

The chair turned another inch and stopped. Ry Caulder leaned into the light. Caulder could have been considered handsome, if the lines of life had not bitten so deeply into his face. He looked a good ten years older than forty-four, his actual age. Steely blue eyes swam sharply in a sea of crow's-feet. His nose was small, but leaned to one side, having been flattened out by a baseball bat when he was young. Thin lips covered straight, white teeth. His chin was hard and square, marked with three small scars received in a knife fight. Wavy hair, the color of wet sand, went to his collar in the back, but was well away from his eyebrows in the front. When Ry Caulder spoke, which was as rarely as possible, his voice sounded as if his throat had been scraped by a thousand razor blades. He said simply, "Hello, Nate."

"How did you find me?" Nate asked, choking back some blood.

Caulder fixed an icy stare into Nate's eyes. "Don't insult me."

Nate fidgeted nervously with his hands. He was stalling for time, but he knew how careful he had to be about what he said and did. He didn't want anything to set Caulder off before he could reach the .45 under the desk.

"I didn't think they'd send you," Nate said.

"Professional courtesy. You were good . . . for a while."

"I heard you retired . . ." Nate said with a mixture of curiosity and hope.

"That's folklore," Caulder replied. His voice sounded bored, as if the actual physical act of killing Nate Daniels would be just a matter of detail. Tedious. Just this side of unnecessary.

They sat staring at each other for what seemed a very long time. Nate realized that the end could come at any moment. There would be no warning. One moment he would be there, sweating and breathing, the next moment there would be nothing. Only destiny.

Ry Caulder was the consummate professional. The very best in the business. His marks rarely suffered. To Caulder, killing was something akin to a magic act. He wanted the people he killed to be totally unaware of his sleight of hand. He would never "drag" a death out and "relish" it as Nate had bragged. That was an obscenity in Caulder's book. Nate realized that his death would be quick and painless. Somehow Caulder would make sure he didn't feel a thing. That was the upside of the deal.

The downside of them sending Caulder was that Nate was going to die. Absolutely, no question about it. If they had sent almost anyone else Nate might have had a chance. There were only two or three assassins of Caulder's caliber and experience still in the business. Only two or three other guys that Nate had actually been worried about. Stegman. Pecchia. Fredrickson. Although rumor of late had it that Fredrickson was dead. Killed down old Mexico way. The rest of the men working the circuit were slobs, ignorant brutes, cherries, or lame mercenaries that had lost any hope of finding a country full of peasants to slaughter. The second-stringers wouldn't have had the wherewithal to nail Nate Daniels.

No, Ry Caulder was one of the very few hitters that Nate feared. Hell, most guys couldn't have even *found* Nate, holed up in a rattrap motel in a lower-class suburb of Baltimore, let alone gotten past his security measures and alarms. Nate had positioned himself at the end of a cul-de-sac hallway and then booby-trapped the corridor with warning systems that were silent from outside the room. How Caulder had bypassed them, Nate would never know. To ask Caulder would only further insult him. Besides, that was all moot now. The fact was that Caulder was sitting in front of him with a pistol and it came as no shock at all to Nate Daniels. He'd seen Caulder get around the best security systems in the world to enter other people's houses as freely as he might walk through the front door of the Aladdin Hotel in Las Vegas.

Nate had heard through the grapevine that Caulder was going soft, that he wanted out of the business, that he didn't have the stomach for it anymore. Nate prayed that it was true. The man who was staring him in the eye looked as if he had no qualms about committing murder, at least one more time.

Nate reached for his cigarettes on the desk, more as a gentle test of Caulder's tension level than from an actual need for a smoke. He wanted to see how close he could get to the gun under the desk before Caulder got riled.

Caulder immediately made a very slight but serious motion with the pistol.

"Keep your hands away from the desk."

"I just want a cigarette."

"Later." Caulder spoke with a severe finality that caused a shiver in Nate's body. It also convinced him to retract his hand.

"You're making me very nervous, Ry."

Caulder just stared silently at him.

Nate stood up slowly and began pacing nervously in front of Caulder. Caulder allowed it. If Nate was going to do something stupid it would just make the whole thing go easier.

"The cop gave me no choice," Nate tried to explain. "I had to do it! The guy pulled me over with the stiff in the car."

"You had the makings of a good technician, Nate. But you blew it. You lost the edge. What's worse, you started to get a kick out of it."

Nate stopped pacing and looked at Caulder accusingly. "Tell me you don't get off on it."

"I'm a professional."

Nate could tell Caulder was getting angry. It wasn't like Caulder to engage in conversations with his marks, but he seemed to want some answers before he did his job.

Maybe that was a chink in the armor, Nate hoped. Maybe this time Ry Caulder *wouldn't* be the consummate professional. Maybe the wily Nate Daniels would find a way out of this situation.

Caulder had introduced Nate Daniels to the business. He had schooled Nate in the ways of being a "proper" assassin. They had spent time together, gotten drunk together, gone whoring together, even done a job together. Or at least been in the same house when the job went down. Caulder did the actual killing. Nate had just been along as an observer. A test to see if he had the kind of nerve the job required. Of course Nate *did* kill the dog on that trip.

They had been sent to eliminate an attorney that had pulled a particularly nasty double cross on one of Caulder's employers. Not only had the attorney embezzled over half a million dollars from Caulder's client, he had also managed to have his way with the man's wife while he was pulling the scam.

"Never kill anyone who doesn't have it coming." Caulder had said that to Nate Daniels over and over again. But Caulder drew a very odd line as to when a person became eligible for elimination. It had little or nothing to do with morality. There were just certain kinds of contracts that were beneath his abilities. Insurance scams, vengeful spouses, cop killings, or anything involving children. This was the stuff of tabloid journalism and Caulder wanted nothing to do with that kind of nonsense. Sleeping with another man's wife would not necessarily qualify you for a spot on the hit parade, but being an attorney just might, on general principles alone. Being the *wrong kind* of attorney certainly would. Being the wrong kind of attorney and using that power to rip off half a million dollars from one of Caulder's paying customers while banging the man's wife would put you right on top of the hit list.

Nate had been working as a bodyguard for Mike Del Monaco, the man who had been ripped off by this particular attorney. Mike Del Monaco wanted to promote Nate higher up in the ranks of the organization, so he paid Caulder a bonus to instruct Nate in the finer aspects of the elimination game. Caulder worked freelance. He didn't like company. He knew it could put him in a compromising position. When he needed one or more partners on a job, he preferred to choose them himself. But Mike Del Monaco was one of Caulder's better clients so he decided to help him out, against his better judgment.

Caulder had spent months with Nate before finally taking him along as backup on a job, and Nate had served him well when the time had come.

Yes, Nate and Caulder went back a ways. Caulder had rarely been unkind to Nate. Of course Nate had never really seen Caulder be unkind to anyone, unless you counted killing them as an unkind gesture. Maybe, Nate thought, he could parlay their past relationship into a reprieve.

"I *had* to roll over, Ry. Imagine being a cop killer inside! Every swingin' dick in the joint trying to make points with the bulls. . . . I'd be turned out and sliced up within twenty-four hours."

Caulder slowly stood up, revealing his six-foot, two-inch stature to the much shorter Nate Daniels. Caulder had a prison lifer's body, lean and sinewy.

"I trained you," Caulder said. "I taught you the code. I told you I'd kill you if you ever broke it, and you know I never lie."

Caulder leveled the pistol at Nate's face. Nate flinched and backed away. He suddenly realized he had overcalculated their friendship. A new shade of fear washed over his expression. He looked at Caulder imploringly. "Come on, Ry . . . we were friends . . . we were friends!"

"You're a punk, Nate. I never trusted you." Caulder's finger tightened on the trigger of the pistol.

Nate was frozen with terror. He just stood there, simpering, whining, softly pleading, whispering "Please Ry, please Ry . . ." over and over like some kind of death row mantra.

"You made me look bad," Caulder said.

Something snapped inside Nate Daniels. Sudden religion flooded over him. He abruptly realized that there were many angry souls waiting for him on the other side. He got down on his knees, slobbering and crying.

"Oh God, Ry, anything . . . I'm sorry. . . . Oh please, please . . . anything . . . Just don't fuckin' kill me!" Nate's voice was high and shrill.

"You can't even accept death with dignity. You disgust me." Caulder lowered the pistol and walked toward the door.

Nate wiped his forehead with relief. Could it be that Caulder had only come here to scare the hell out of him? To teach him some kind of bizarre lesson, but not to kill him? Doubtful, but Ry Caulder was not predictable. Maybe he *was* getting soft.

Caulder opened the door. The faint scent of sulfur accompanied the sound of drizzling rain outside. Caulder started to leave. Then something seemed to occur to him. He turned and walked back into the room, past Nate and over to the desk. Nate flinched as Caulder passed him.

Caulder flipped the tape out of the recorder, pocketed it, and moved toward the door again.

"I hate killing people I don't respect. It makes the job seem cheap," Caulder said with all the joy of a mortician.

"Oh God, thank you, Ry," Nate squeaked. "I won't testify. I'll disappear, I promise.... The outfit'll never know. They'll think you wasted me. Thank you! Thank you!" Nate was babbling now. Something had melted in his brain the moment he truly contemplated eternal oblivion. Now that it looked as if he might be spared he was too far gone to get back on track.

Caulder stopped at the door and looked at Nate, who was still on his knees in the middle of the room.

"Good-bye, Nate."

The phone on the desk rang loudly, startling Nate Daniels. He looked over at the phone and then back at Ry Caulder.

Caulder had the gun up and aimed point-blank at Nate Daniels's head. Nate had only a split second of recognition before Caulder fired. A small flash emanated from the end of the suppressor. It was accompanied by a *pop*. The shot caught Nate squarely in the face and his astonished expression exploded. Caulder had used a Black Talon shell. It entered Nate's flesh fairly small, but it expanded and flattened out upon making contact with Nate's skull and took most of his brain along as it exited the back of his head, thus ensuring immediate death. Nate's body slumped over backward and convulsed a bit, but Nate Daniels's consciousness had already vacated. If there was a heaven or a hell, Nate was checking in.

Once Ry Caulder had decided to end Nate's life, it was as quick and painless a hit as any he had ever performed. He *had* been the consummate professional after all.

Not that there had ever really been any doubt that the job would have to be done. Nate had broken every rule in Ry Caulder's book. But Caulder had still wanted to see Nate face-to-face, to hear what he had to say. Maybe Nate could explain why he had done the things he did. Maybe there was a side to the story that Caulder hadn't heard or understood. There wasn't.

Nate had performed a hit on a man, gotten pulled over for speeding while transporting his victim's body to a desolate location for disposal, killed the cop who pulled him over, and got caught on videotape by a camera on the cop's dashboard used to record drunk drivers taking sobriety tests. By the time Nate had buried the body of his initial victim, every cop in the state had the make and model of his vehicle and a complete description of him. Nate had been surrounded by a half dozen patrol cars before he got halfway back to the city. His employers understandably had refused to make contact with him or his bank account after the bust, so Nate felt that he had not only been abandoned, but stiffed as well. They had thirty grand of *his* money in *their* pockets.

This had been Nate Daniels's justification for rolling over and turning rat on "the boys." That the Justice Department had granted him full immunity in return for his cooperation was only incidental in his rationalization. As far as he had been concerned, *he* had been victimized. Used. Abandoned. Ripped off.

If Nate Daniels had had his way many people would have gotten hurt and Ry Caulder would have been one of them. Caulder had done it for himself as much as he had for the man who had hired him. The man Nate would have eventually been testifying against if he and the Justice Department had completed their business arrangement. But that was not to be.

The phone on the desk was still ringing. Caulder walked over and picked it up with a gloved hand. He listened for a moment. It was a man from the Justice Department calling to check on Nate Daniels. They had been watching him, but not closely enough. Ry Caulder had slipped chloral hydrate into the coffee of the two men in the plain sedan parked in front of the motel, and they were sleeping peacefully.

It was simple enough to arrange. A waitress from the Denny's across the street delivered two large cups of black coffee to the agents every hour on the hour. Ry Caulder went into the restaurant at seven minutes before the hour, ordered two large cups of black coffee to go, slipped in the juice while the waitress wasn't looking, then asked her if the coffee was decaf as he was paying her. She said she hadn't heard him ask for decaf, but she promptly poured two decafs for him. She was very obliging. She then delivered the drugged coffee to the two agents across the street. They were asleep in five minutes. Now Nate Daniels was beyond their protection and the Justice Department had been denied an important informant.

Caulder listened silently to the agent's voice growing more and more desperate as he tried to get an answer out of the telephone. Caulder dropped the receiver on Nate Daniels's dead body and walked out into the drizzling rain.

two

The flight from Baltimore to Los Angeles was abnormally rough. Caulder slept through it anyway, getting the first good sleep he had had since the whole business with Nate Daniels began.

Nate had posed a very real threat to Caulder's existence. Nate had already spilled his guts to the Feds, but subpoenas are hard to come by if the star witness is dead before the suspects can be brought to trial. Indictments would not be handed down on the word of a dead man. But more importantly, just how much had Nate Daniels said in the six months the Justice boys grilled him? How much did Nate know in the first place? Could they track Caulder down using Nate's information? Caulder hoped that Nate had been disposed of before any irreparable damage had been done. Only time would tell for sure, and he didn't plan on being around that long.

As he slept, Caulder dreamed of dogs and lawyers.

* * *

Ry Caulder and Nate Daniels had studied the offending attorney's life patterns for a full three weeks before they made their move. Nate grew anxious during that time but he controlled his impatience as best he could. He knew that Caulder would do what had to be done when the time was right and not before.

When the job went down they were in the attorney's home for less than ninety seconds. Caulder had already disconnected two of the three security systems earlier that afternoon, but the third system had a safety beep that sounded when anyone entered the house, to prove that it was operational. Caulder couldn't risk the attorney noticing a faulty alarm and calling out a repair team, so he left the third alarm functional. Caulder did not want to be in the house, waiting, when the attorney arrived. The man might have someone with him. That would complicate things.

"No innocents will be killed" was Ry Caulder's most adamant commandment. An "innocent" was anyone not targeted for a hit. It had nothing to do with the individual's actual personal guilt or innocence in any way. A person might be guilty of heinous crimes against humanity, but if he or she was not specifically targeted for a hit, that person's life was sacred to Ry Caulder. There was a time and place for everything.

Caulder solved the third-alarm problem by timing entry to the house to coincide with the attorney's shower, which he always took in the upstairs bathroom within ten minutes of arriving home. The bathroom window could be seen from the backyard and the test beep of the alarm could only be heard clearly on the first floor of the house. The owner then had thirty seconds to punch in a code to disconnect the alarm before a loud bell would go off and the local police department would be contacted via telephone line. Caulder knew all this because he and Nate had spent almost as much time in the attorney's house over the last three weeks as the attorney himself had. They had cased the place thoroughly and were ready to go. The one thing they had not counted on was the dog.

The dog was a large German shepherd that the attorney had

purchased on the very same day that Caulder had decided to perform the elimination. The attorney must have sensed something different about his house in the last week. Caulder had always made sure that everything was exactly the same when they left as it had been when they entered, but the attorney must have felt a change in the place nevertheless and, getting a little spooked, had decided to purchase the dog as an extra measure of safety. After all, there were a lot of bad people out there and some of them were very angry with certain attorneys.

Caulder was disappointed when he saw the attorney pull up with the dog in his car. Caulder liked dogs. Nate thought for sure that Caulder, being the meticulous planner that he was, would postpone the hit until further preparations could be made for the animal. Instead, Caulder simply handed Nate a butcher knife and a roll of plastic kitchen wrap and said, "The dog is your problem."

Nate later said, and he had been half right, that Caulder used the dog to test him. The whole truth of the matter was that Caulder had been overly cautious in planning the hit because of Nate Daniels's novice presence and he was tired of waiting. He was ready to do the job, dog or no dog. If Nate could handle himself, the dog would be no problem. If he couldn't, Caulder would put a bullet in both of their skulls. Nate couldn't have been trusted after a mauling. There was too great a possibility of him babbling like an idiot while they sewed him up at County General.

Caulder and Nate waited until they saw the attorney in the upstairs shower. It had taken more than fifteen minutes that night. Feeding the dog for the first time, Caulder figured.

They entered the house swiftly, effortlessly, Caulder's familiarity with the front door lock now almost embarrassing. No sound occurred save the soft safety beep of the alarm. The dog did not make an appearance at the sound of the beep. The experience was all too fresh for him to comprehend what the beep meant.

Caulder moved to the control panel of the alarm and went to work. Nate spread long sheets of plastic wrap on the floor, then stood with his back to Caulder, holding the knife out, waiting for the dog to hear them and attack. The dog could be heard in the kitchen, eating. He was new in the house and didn't fully understand his duties yet, another benefit of making the move now instead of later.

Caulder finished with the alarm and headed for the stairs. He glanced briefly at Nate, then over at the kitchen door. Nate knew what he meant. If the dog finished eating and came out of the kitchen it was Nate's job to see that the animal never made it to wherever Caulder was at the time.

Caulder went upstairs, found the bathroom door unlocked, entered quickly, reached into the shower, grabbed the attorney by the ankle, and pulled his feet out from under him. The attorney slammed his head sharply against the bathtub faucet, shattering his skull. Caulder thought a second blow might be required to finish the job. It was not, for the attorney died upon impact. It had gone even easier than Caulder expected. He turned and went down the stairs just as quickly, just as calmly, as he had gone up. There was absolutely no difference in his demeanor.

It had taken less than thirty seconds.

When Caulder saw Nate Daniels again, the dog was already dead. The dog had finished eating, come out of the kitchen, and seen Nate standing there, knife in hand. The irony of the matter was that the dog probably wouldn't have attacked Nate at all if he hadn't been carrying the knife. The surroundings were new and the dog had not yet determined who was friend or foe on the property. Even a trained German shepherd will quite often give a guy a chance under those circumstances. But Nate had a knife. That identified him instantly as an enemy. The dog charged quietly, emitting only a low growl, and leaped for Nate's knife arm. Nate had been ready for that. At the moment of the dog's leap Nate tossed the knife into his other hand, allowed the dog to grab his now empty hand at the wrist, and sunk the knife deep into the animal's stomach, ripping a two-foot gash along his chest as gravity pulled the dog back to earth. All bleeding was done over the plastic wrap. Not a drop hit the floor.

Nate had been proud of himself. He did his job and did it well, receiving only minor bite marks on his arm in the process. Besides, unlike Caulder, Nate Daniels hated dogs.

They encased the dog in more plastic wrap, then removed it from the house. Caulder left a side door slightly open so the police would assume that the dog, being new, had run away after his master failed to return from the shower. They reconnected the alarm systems and cremated the dog at a funeral parlor that their employer owned. It had all been very simple, very clean. An accident, the papers said. The man fell in the shower and hit his head. Nate Daniels used to joke that everyone came out of that one clean, even the attorney.

Clean. An accident. A good clean hit. That's what Ry Caulder was put on earth to do. It shouldn't bother him. It certainly shouldn't be in his dreams. But it was.

Caulder slept so deeply that a flight attendant had to wake him after all the other passengers had departed the plane. Caulder had a lot of catching up to do, but it was unlike him to sleep so soundly anywhere, even in his own home, let alone in public. Once awake, though, he appeared perfectly lucid and in control, as if he hadn't been deeply unconscious only a moment before.

Caulder walked purposely through Los Angeles International Airport. The sleep hadn't been enough. His head was throbbing and the hundreds of people moving about around him in the airport weren't helping matters any. Caulder threaded through the crowds, skirting huge immigrant families, with their mounds of baggage, and slicked-down businessmen, late for their flights. The Krishnas were out in force, dancing for handouts. A Moroccan woman at a check-in counter screamed and passed out from exhaustion, frustration, or a combination of the two. It was LAX in all its glory.

As Caulder wound his way through a maze of Chinese tourists, he began to get an odd feeling in his neck. Over the years he had developed a sixth sense that watched his back and warned him of trouble. And this sixth sense was telling him now that something wasn't right.

Caulder glanced over his shoulder. He saw nothing unusual, but he felt he was being watched or followed. He walked casually into the men's room. There were three people visible in the bathroom, an elderly man washing his hands at the sinks and two teenagers working the urinals.

Caulder bent down and looked under the doors of the toilet stalls. No legs. He went into the second to the last stall and locked the door. He had no weapon on him so he pulled the toilet paper roll off its dispenser and dismantled the spring-loaded cylinder. He bent the sharp end of the spring outward, fashioning a crude knife. He stepped up onto the toilet seat and crouched low so neither his feet nor his head would show. If they came for him he had a fair chance of getting at least one of them. Caulder had to rely on his hearing from this point on. He could see only a sliver of the bathroom through the crack in the door.

It was not unusual for an inexperienced hit man to have a contract placed on him to finalize the silence after completing a job, but an assassin of Caulder's caliber was rarely in danger of this occurring. Pros always had backup contracts standing for anyone that would place a hit on them. They called it "insurance." Perhaps that was who was after him now, he thought. Men contracted by Nate Daniels in anticipation of his possible demise. But how could they know so much so soon? Nate Daniels was barely cold. No, this had to be coming from a different source. The only people who would even suspect Caulder would be at LAX at this time would be Mike Del Monaco or James Baxter, the men who had hired him to eliminate Nate Daniels. If a contract had been placed on Caulder, it would probably be originating from Baxter Industries.

The old man finished at the sink and left, replaced by the two teenagers, who were talking a mile a minute. Something about the relative splendor of Pearl Jam compared to Nirvana before Kurt Cobain sucked the shotgun, but Caulder wasn't able to follow the lingo. There was an abrupt silence. The kids quit speaking in midsentence and left the bathroom. Other voices could now be heard communicating in whispers. Two or more men had entered the room and whoever they were, they had scared the hell out of the teenagers.

Caulder made himself as small as possible and braced against the back wall of the stall, preparing to thrust forward. If they fired through the door he had little chance of surviving, but if he could surprise the first one, get him in the eyes with the spring, he might be able to come up with a gun and get out of the thing altogether. It was a long shot but he had no other options. He could hear movement, clothes rustling, leather soles on the cold tile; they were coming closer. The whispers were getting angrier, as if they were considering the possibility that they had lost their quarry.

Suddenly dozens of voices filled the bathroom. Happy voices. Foreign voices. The Chinese tour group had found the men's room. Caulder took his first breath in two minutes. His chance of survival had increased marginally. Stalls opened and closed, urinals flushed, discussion was rapid-fire and multilingual. A shadow played across the crack in Caulder's door and someone pulled on the handle. Caulder braced for action. Chinese curse words came from the other side of the door and the man moved to the last stall and entered.

Caulder stayed in his crouched position for fifteen minutes as the Chinese did their business and freshened up. When the bathroom was relatively empty he went on full alert once again. If the men who had come looking for him knew he was in there, they were waiting to work in anonymity. Some hitters would have come right through the door, tour group and all. Some guys don't care about witnesses, especially witnesses that don't speak English. But whoever was following Caulder wanted to work clean. The interruption had either frightened them off or confused them. Caulder considered a variety of possibilities: 1) The men who were after him decided the men's room at LAX would not be the proper place to make the hit; 2) the men left believing that Caulder was not in the room; 3) the men were not sent to hit him at all, but only to follow him, in which case they had done a very sloppy job; 4) the men weren't following him at all and he was merely having a paranoia attack; 5) the men were still in the bathroom waiting for Caulder to leave the stall; 6) the men were waiting for him outside the bathroom and would wait until a more opportune time to make the hit.

Caulder had a long time to consider these possibilities. He crouched painfully on the toilet seat for over an hour listening to the traffic in and out of the bathroom before he felt he could safely attempt to leave. Finally he bent forward and looked under the stall across the expanse of bathroom floor. There appeared to be no one in the bathroom. Of course there were nine other stalls in the place that could conceal other men the way Caulder had been hiding. He could no longer be a prisoner of his own fear. He lowered his legs to the ground and painfully took a stretch. He had to rub his thighs and calves to get circulation back into them. Once he felt ready to move, he did it swiftly. He pocketed the toilet paper dispenser, opened the stall, and made for the exit. The door opened as he got there and two men in business suits entered. Caulder stepped to the side and watched them with wide-eyed caution as they passed. One of the men looked over his shoulder at Caulder as he backed out of the bathroom. Caulder's behavior had to be considered odd, even for Los Angeles.

* * *

Ry Caulder saw no one suspicious from the time he left the men's room at LAX and got a taxi in front of the terminal to the time that the cab dropped him at the American Express office in downtown Los Angeles. From there he walked home. Caulder began to feel foolish. If a contract had been put out on him it would take a lot more than a bunch of Chinese tourists to interrupt the hit. Perhaps the Feds were trailing him or maybe even a couple of clueless pickpockets had targeted him without realizing what they would be dealing with. Whoever it was had given up, at least for now.

Caulder lived in a one-bedroom apartment on the seventh floor of a crumbling tenement in the heart of downtown Los Angeles. The location was deliberately cheap and anonymous. In the middle of the city he was hiding in plain sight. He was lost in a sea of humanity, yet accessible to the underworld connections that sought his services.

Caulder entered the building via the parking garage. There were locks on the walk-in gates to the garage but they'd been broken long before Caulder had taken up residence. The iron gate that slid open automatically allowing residents to drive in and out was a mere formality. None of this offered the slightest bit of protection. Caulder went to his car, a light brown 1988 Buick Skylark. Obscure enough to blend with traffic without drawing undue attention, powerful enough to do what it was asked to do. Caulder checked under the vehicle. He checked the wheel covers, the doors, the windows, the undercarriage. He finally felt safe enough to try the hood. It came up with no problems. He surveyed the engine, then checked the trunk, even pulling up the carpet and opening the hidden compartment built into the floor where he occasionally stored weapons. He opened the car and looked under all the seats and in the glove compartment. The car was clean. No bombs, no tampering.

Caulder collected his mail from the rusty box in the lobby, then took the stink cage of an elevator to the seventh floor. It creaked and groaned painfully as it ascended. Every kind of food imaginable could be smelled cooking in the various apartments, from tandoori chicken to couscous to fish tacos. The building housed a diverse cross section of races, but the neighbors kept to themselves. Ry Caulder wasn't the only tenant with something to hide in this place.

Once in front of his apartment, Caulder checked the hairs he had glued on three sides of the door to see if the seal had been broken since he'd left. They were all intact. He entered the apartment tentatively nevertheless.

Caulder's apartment consisted of a smallish living room, which led to an even smaller kitchen adjacent to a tiny bedroom that fed into a practically nonexistent bathroom. A few windows allowed ventilation, light, and a view of the alley and apartments behind the building. Venetian blinds ensured Caulder's privacy. The place was built in the late thirties and the architecture had remained the same ever since, withstanding earthquakes and riots and petty vandalism. No landlord had ever seen fit to renovate. Calder's apartment was fastidiously clean but lacked any personal touches. The walls were bare and the furniture was a sparse collection of non-matching stuff found at the local Salvation Army. There were a couple of makeshift bookshelves that housed an eclectic collection of secondhand books. A visitor could guess nothing about the owner of these books by the range of subjects covered, other than, perhaps, that he was easily bored. The entire apartment was as plain and drab as a bachelor could imagine. Caulder had no personality invested in this place, which suited him fine.

Ry Caulder had been told more than once that he had no personality whatsoever. Of course, the people telling him were always women who felt left out of his world. Women who said Caulder was unable to share his personal feelings with them. Women who would have puked their guts out if he *had* shared the truth with them. Caulder *was* aloof with the women in his life. He had to be. For his own protection and theirs.

Caulder slid a pile of junk mail addressed to Resident onto the kitchen table and poured himself three fingers of Glenlivet. He picked the latest copy of the *Wall Street Journal* from the mail, went to his recliner in the living room, eased down into it, and started checking the stock listings. He was home at last. He nodded contentedly to himself as he reviewed his portfolio and sipped the Scotch. His investments were doing well. Not that Caulder was surprised. His investments usually did well. He only put money into enterprises with which he had solid connections. He always knew long before the majority of the stockholders when it was time to bail out. Just another fringe benefit of the profession. His offshore accounts were swelling with retirement funds. Soon he would be ready.

Ry Caulder's life was a schizophrenic thing. He would go long months without activity, during which time he felt it necessary to keep a low profile. Television, books, and magazines would occupy most of his time during these periods. He would exercise extensively while watching TV. He had an intense isometric routine worked out, requiring no fancy Nautilus equipment; he merely worked various muscles against others. He was his own gym. He did not subscribe to cable nor did he own a VCR. He preferred network television to prerecorded movies. The commercials made him feel less isolated, more a part of society. The knowledge that thousands or hundreds of thousands of other people were experiencing what he was experiencing at the very same moment gave him some sort of mild comfort. His reading tastes were eclectic. He'd read anything, from technical journals to corny romance novels. Books and magazines about travel were his favorites.

Caulder's sex life was kept to a minimum. Occasionally he would go to bars or clubs and pick up a one-nighter, but he would always go to the woman's place. He would never bring them to his apartment. He kept complications to a minimum. Once in a great while Caulder would meet an exceptional woman. He would see this woman until she became too inquisitive, then he would vanish into the night. Normal existence was generally a tedious experience for Ry Caulder.

And then, every few months, he would be hired to kill someone.

three

"A case like yours can get very complicated," the portly man said to the woman. "Expenses can get out of hand, go right through the roof. I see it happen all the time."

The man was sweating through a Brooks Brothers suit that had seen better days. He was in his early forties. He had thick jowls and a big gut and a bad toupee that was starting to loosen up in the late afternoon heat.

"I understand, Mr. Hertzberg," the woman said. She brushed his hand from her knee for the third time that day. "If you don't want the case, I understand perfectly. I won't waste any more of your time."

The woman was in her late twenties, five-foot-seven, brunet, a little on the thin side, but still quite a looker. She had curly dark hair down past her shoulders and a winning smile when she would use it, which wasn't often as of late. Her hazel eyes could appear a variety of shades from light brown to dark green depending on how the light caught them. She wore a simple yellow flowered sundress. She knew when she put it on that it was probably a mistake, but it was the only thing she had that was remotely nice and relatively cool. Now it was causing trouble.

"I didn't say it was impossible," the man said. "It's just that I'm used to receiving a large retainer up front in a case like this and with your limited resources, well I just thought that, you know . . ." The man started to reach out for her knee again. The woman sprang to her feet and moved into the kitchen.

"Mr. Hertzberg, I think you are trying to take advantage of my situation," the woman said as she poured herself a cup of coffee. She still had half a cup on the dining-room table but she wanted to be doing something with her hands.

"I'm trying to help you," Hertzberg continued. He came into the kitchen and crowded in on her. "But I'm a professional, not a charity worker. If you can't pay me in cash, why should I get involved?"

"I told you I would pay you." She took a step back and eyed the rack of carving knives on the sink, calculating how quickly she could pull one if need be.

"Yes, but you do not have enough money," he said. He followed her sight line and realized what she was considering. He decided not to crowd her any further. He was here to negotiate, not wrestle with knives.

"How much is enough?" the woman asked.

"Considering expenses and the hourly, with your discount of course, I'll need at least five thousand to get started."

The woman looked stunned. "Five thousand? But you said yesterday you could start for fifteen hundred."

"That was before I realized that the case would take me out of state."

"I told you that my husband lived in Portland when I spoke to you on the phone the very first time."

"That didn't mean I would have to *go* to Portland. But once I heard all the details, I realized I would have no choice, seeing that you and your son are fugitives from the law. You've got a very complicated set of circumstances going. Very complicated. I could get disbarred for even being here with you."

"I wanted to meet in your office. . . ."

"Are you crazy? You go to my office again and we'll both end up in jail."

The woman looked down at the floor of her ratty little apartment. She was trapped. Not just by this fat pig of a lawyer, but by her entire situation. She no longer knew what to do. Had things gotten so bad that she would have to resort to sleeping with a creature such as this just to survive? No. There had to be another way.

The portly man leaned forward until his face was only an inch away from her downcast forehead. She could smell his sweat through his cheap deodorant.

"Listen, Stephanie," the man continued. "I don't want you to think I do this all the time. I'm not some kind of creep. I've never done anything like this in my life. But I *like* you. I really like you. I think I could be good for you. You need a friend when you're in a big town like L.A. and I can be a hell of a friend."

Stephanie Taylor looked up at the portly man who wanted to be her "friend." "I'm sure you mean well, Mr. Hertzberg, but I feel you're putting pressure on me that I'm just not ready for. I just escaped one relationship. I don't want to jump into another one yet."

"We can take it slow. I understand how these things go." Hertzberg put a clammy hand on Stephanie's shoulder and she backed away again and grunted, unable to disguise her revulsion any longer. Sensing her disgust, Hertzberg became incensed. He rushed forward and pinned her up against the refrigerator.

"Listen, bitch," he slobbered, "I've had it up to here with your bullshit! Stop with the queen-for-a-day act. We both know who you are and what you are. You're a two-bit, scheming tramp that stole a kid away from his dad. You're on the lam and you're asking for favors like you're Mother Teresa. You're no better than anyone else, so quit looking down your nose at me. I don't owe you a fucking thing and if you want something you're going to have to earn it. You got two choices now. You put out and maybe you get to keep your kid and your freedom. You don't play ball, you're going to jail and the kid'll go back to his old man or end up a ward of the state."

Hertzberg reached under Stephanie's dress and made a grab for her crotch. She felt his thick stubby fingers pull against the elastic of her panties and she almost vomited. She shoved him aside and scrambled for the living room. He was between her and the knives so they were no longer an option. Now she wanted to get to the front door.

"Jason!" she yelled as she shoved a dining chair at the big man coming up behind her fast.

A six-year-old boy with curly blond hair came out of the bedroom in a hurry. He'd been waiting breathlessly for some kind of signal and finally it had come. He got the front door open just as the portly man untangled himself from the chair and grabbed a thick clump of Stephanie's raven hair.

"Get back in your fucking room, kid," Hertzberg spit, "or your mother's gonna be sorry!"

The boy paused for a second and looked at Stephanie for a command.

"Get Ry!" she yelled, and the boy was out the door.

four

Ry Caulder's tranquillity was shattered by the sound of a door slamming down the hall. Caulder looked up briefly, then returned to his *Wall Street Journal*. A few moments later there came a frantic knock on his door.

Caulder got up and opened the door. A small boy stood in the hallway, crying. It was Jason, the next-door neighbor's son. Caulder liked the kid as much as any other kid, which wasn't very much, but he liked the kid's mother enough to make up for it. Not that he was about to do anything about liking the kid's mother, even though she was a knockout. Caulder firmly believed in the old adage "You don't shit where you eat."

"What's wrong, Jason?" Caulder asked, hoping it would be nothing that would call for his involvement, but suspecting otherwise.

The little boy tried bravely to fight back tears as he pointed down the hall. "He's hurting her," the kid sobbed.

Caulder walked past Jason without saying another word. Whatever the problem was, he wanted to be done with it quickly.

Caulder tried the door of the apartment across the hall and one door closer to the elevator than his. It was locked. Behind the door he could hear scuffling sounds. Caulder took two steps back and planted a boot in the center of the door, kicking it open, practically off its hinges.

Stephanie, Jason's mother, was struggling with a slimy-looking guy in the center of the apartment.

The guy took one look at Ry Caulder and froze. "It's okay, it's okay," the man pleaded. "I'm her lawyer."

Another fucking attorney!

"Just business, huh?" Caulder said sharply.

"Yeah, ah, that's right. . . ." The guy was terrified and he didn't even *know* Caulder or what he did for a living. "And actually I was just, uh, leaving."

"You said it. . . ."

The attorney grabbed his briefcase and nervously stumbled to the door. Caulder blocked his passage.

"Not so fast," Caulder said.

"Listen," the attorney stammered, "I've got a six o'clock appointment and I'm late already."

Caulder ignored the attorney and looked at Stephanie. "What happened here, Steph?"

Stephanie was suddenly concerned with the attorney's physical well-being. She didn't know what Caulder might do and she didn't want to get him into any trouble over a piece of crap like Hertzberg. "Nothing, Ry," she said. "Mr. Hertzberg and I just had a misunderstanding."

"Looked like a big one." Caulder stared into Hertzberg's eyes. For some reason this gave Hertzberg a burst of indignation and bravery. He didn't like being threatened. *He* was accustomed to being the bully.

"The lady said it was a misunderstanding," Hertzberg said in the toughest voice he could muster. "Let's just leave it at that, okay pal? Unless you want to bring the authorities in on this. I don't think she'd like that very much, considering her situation. Know what I mean?"

Caulder grabbed Hertzberg by the throat and pinned him against the wall, completely cutting off his oxygen. Hertzberg dropped his briefcase and punched Caulder in the stomach twice. Caulder pulled the man toward him, then shoved his head hard against the wall, stopping the attack.

"Ry!" Stephanie yelled. "Stop it!" She grabbed Jason and turned him away from the violence. He resisted and managed to watch through her fingers.

"I'm going to say this once," Caulder said to Hertzberg. "You better hear me and believe me. If anything happens to these people I will find you and I will hurt you very badly. Understand?"

Hertzberg did not respond. He just stared at Caulder, terror in his eyes. Caulder gave the back of his head another rap against the wall.

"Understand? Let me hear you!"

"I understand," Hertzberg mumbled. He was beginning to weep with fear.

"Get out of here."

Hertzberg gathered his briefcase and stumbled out of the apartment, wiping tears from his eyes and avoiding Stephanie's gaze.

Caulder closed the door and stared at Stephanie. Stephanie looked down at her son. "Jason, go play in the bedroom."

"Awww, Mom . . ." Jason groaned. He didn't want to miss the good stuff.

"*Please* . . ." Stephanie asked in the familiar tone that was actually a demand. Jason disappeared into the bedroom.

"Don't you think you went a little far?" Stephanie asked Caulder.

"Probably not far enough. How'd you get into this one?"

"He offered to help me."

"Looks like he was helping himself."

Stephanie scratched the scar on her right wrist. The scar always itched when she got nervous. It was as if her tension gathered at the spot symbolizing the lowest point in her life, a time even worse than now. A time when she'd contemplated ending it all. But that was many years ago. She'd been young then. And alone. Very alone. Before Jason came along and gave her a reason for being. Now there was no turning back. No easy way out. No razors promising sweet nothingness. She had a child now. Someone who depended on her. She was in it for the long haul whether she wanted to be or not. But this was still a man's world and she resented being at the mercy of the "kindness" of men, strangers or otherwise. Even men like Ry Caulder.

"I told you I'd loan you money for a real lawyer," Caulder continued.

"He *was* a real lawyer."

"Real lawyers don't have to perform complete physicals before taking on a case."

"I know . . . I know."

"Stephanie, why won't you go home? You could stay with your mother for a while . . . get your act together. Why don't you just go home?"

"So what do I do? Go back to Portland? Let him take Jason? Admit I can't look after my own son?"

"Him" was Stephanie's ex-husband, a used-car dealer named Alexander, who thought he was God's gift to Portland in general and the women of Portland in particular. He also liked to give his wife a look at his knuckles when she asked stupid questions like "Where were you?" His own son had seen the back of his hand more than once for annoying him. Stephanie had been locked in a custody battle with Alexander for two years before she left Portland. When it looked like she was going to lose the fight, she packed up Jason and their meager belongings and fled. She had a distant cousin who got her an under-the-table job in the Los Angeles garment district. The cash was minimal, but it came tax-free with no traceable records. They were managing to make ends meet—barely. Stephanie and Jason were fugitives from justice and reality every bit as much as Ry Caulder. Only Caulder's face wasn't on milk cartons all over Oregon.

"This is no place for either of you," Caulder said, pointing out the window.

The sun was setting over Los Angeles. The street below was filled with beat-up old cars, many of them abandoned, some of them residences. In a trash-filled vacant lot across the street two young kids conducted a mock knife fight with plastic picnic knives. The homeless were clustered outside the Korean market on the corner. Somewhere a couple argued, their threats and curses blending with the sound of screaming sirens in the distance.

Stephanie looked at Caulder. "I can't take money from you."

"That's all I can offer you, Steph."

"That's not true."

"I'm afraid it is."

Caulder fixed his stare on Stephanie. He couldn't explain anything more to her and wouldn't even if he could. He wanted her. But not enough to screw up his life and his plans. He'd be out of L.A. soon and he didn't need any baggage, certainly not a bratty kid and his oversexed, underloved mother, even if she was a stone-cold fox wrapped in innocent sheep's clothing.

There was a long, awkward silence before Caulder moved quietly toward the door. Stephanie knew it was useless to say more. They had been playing this game for six months now and it always turned out the same.

Caulder left the apartment without another word and Stephanie turned her attention back to the window. One of the kids across the street had a big gash on his chin where his buddy had made contact with the plastic knife. The gangs were starting to come out for their nighttime activities. A shotgun went off somewhere nearby and the sounds of sirens just kept getting louder. Stephanie leaned on her windowsill and grimly reveled in the tapestry of scum in the streets.

five

Ry Caulder went into his bathroom. He unscrewed the faceplate of his medicine cabinet and pulled it free. In a hollowed-out space behind the cabinet he found a Glock 17 9mm pistol and three boxes of ammo, all wrapped in individual Ziploc bags. The gun was clean and free of all fingerprints. It was legally registered to Forrest Sabine, the last tenant of this apartment. Forrest Sabine had no idea that he was the owner of a Glock 17. If Caulder was ever busted and the apartment searched there could be no legal connection made between Caulder and the Glock.

Caulder went under his sink, peeled back a piece of plastic tile paneling, and removed two driver's licenses. One was in the name of Richard Alton, and the other was listed as Francis Quinn. The face on the licenses was that of Ry Caulder.

Caulder pulled the tile back further and found a plastic bag containing five one-thousand-dollar bills, circa 1934, the last year they were printed. They were each worth well over a thousand dollars at the current premium, but he would end up spending them at face value. He took three of the bills from the Ziploc and replaced the plastic tile. He loaded the bills into the hidden compartment in the lining of his leather belt with the rest of his money. He always kept between five and ten thousand dollars in his belt for emergencies—bribes, payoffs, sudden munitions purchases, etc. He used thousand-dollar bills because there was only so much room in the money belt, but he'd also fold in as many hundreds as space would permit. They were much easier to pass.

Caulder dressed in a black turtleneck, black jeans, and a black sport jacket. He looked like he was ready to read poetry in a coffeehouse. He removed a pair of black evening gloves from his dresser and stuck them in his pocket. Caulder went through black gloves like other men went through cigarettes. He discarded any pair of gloves that he used for anything, even cursory scouting missions. He wanted no fiber to be able to jail him. Forensic detective work had grown frighteningly microscopic over the years. If Ry Caulder was ever pulled in for anything he felt sure that the FBI would have some speck of dust or flake of DNA on file somewhere that could pin a murder rap on him, but he wanted to reduce his risk whenever possible. So far he had been incredibly lucky. He had never been busted for so much as jaywalking. He was the invisible man. So far.

Caulder loaded shells into two clips. He slapped one of the clips into the bottom of the Glock and chambered a shell. Then he reached for the yellow pages.

It was after two in the morning by the time Peter Hertzberg entered his house. He considered it a modest house for a man of his talents. Three bedrooms and a pool in the Miracle Mile district, a two-story Tudor affair. Hertzberg hated Tudor, but he had gotten the place for a song when one of his clients had to file bankruptcy. Hertzberg planned on moving into one of the minimansions in Hancock Park the moment real estate turned around and a couple of his "big" cases came through.

Peter Hertzberg was basically a loser. An ambulance chaser in a town full of ambulance chasers. Personal Injury was his forte. And he wasn't even very good at that. But insurance companies like to settle most PI cases with a minimum of fuss, whether the case is being handled by a good attorney or not, so Hertzberg had done better than he had any right to in this life, owing to the parasitic nature of his profession. If you were in serious legal trouble you had to be either desperate or naive to contact him. The woman he had attacked earlier in the day had been both.

Hertzberg went into the den, dropped his coat on the floor, and poured himself a drink from the wet bar.

"Fucking bitch," he muttered drunkenly. "She has no idea. No idea. She's fucking with the wrong man. One phone call. That's all it takes. One phone call. I'll lock 'em all up. Her and her junkie boyfriend."

Hertzberg drained part of the drink, then took a half step and spun to the floor. He ended up in a partial lotus position and his drink splashed all over the room.

"Motherfucker . . ." Hertzberg mumbled. He fell backward and hit his head on the hardwood floor. For a moment he thought he was going to lose consciousness, then he saw stars and lights. He lay on the floor and played the afternoon debacle through his brain for the ten thousandth time that night. The woman thought he was a joke. The man humiliated him. Something had to be done. He had discussed it with his cronies at the Lucky 13 until closing time. He altered many of the details of course, so that he would not appear so much the fool. He was careful not to get too specific about the woman's identity. He didn't want any of his good colleagues beating him to the negotiating table. But now he was beginning to put blackmail out of his mind and settle for revenge. One call downtown and that apartment building would light up like a Christmas tree. Just one call. That's how powerful Peter Hertzberg was. *Didn't she know that?*

Hertzberg struggled to get to his feet. He half crawled, half walked to his desk. He got into the swivel chair and felt the power surge in his body. He was a man of action and he was about to cut loose. He reached for the telephone. It did not work. He played with the various parts of the phone with no response. He would have to go upstairs.

There were two other phones in the house. Both were upstairs. One was in his bedroom, the other was on the landing at the top of the stairs. Hertzberg had a small workstation positioned on the landing because it offered a great view of his neighbor's pool. His neighbor was a low-budget exploitation movie director. Hertzberg liked to work the phones in the afternoons and watch the bimbos sunbathe down below.

Hertzberg painfully made his way up the flight of stairs. He was starting to get a hangover already. He hadn't even slept yet. He would have to make his call fast, if he could make it at all, then go eat some Advil.

Hertzberg got to the workstation and picked up the phone. To his mild surprise, it was in perfect working order. The problem wasn't on the line. The phone downstairs was broken. This one was fine. He began to dial the number.

Gloved fingers suddenly pushed the posts down on the phone's cradle, disconnecting the line. Hertzberg looked up and saw a man dressed completely in black, including a black ski mask. Hertzberg started to run, but he didn't get far. The man in black snatched the phone receiver out of Hertzberg's hand and wrapped the cord around his neck two times fast. Hertzberg got about four feet before the cord went tight, sending the portly man into the air and onto his back for the second time in the last half hour.

The man in black leaned over and spoke into Hertzberg's face.

"Who have you told about Stephanie Taylor?" the ski mask demanded in a growl.

"Nobody . . ." Hertzberg said, gasping for breath. "I swear to God. I never told a soul. I was going to, but I didn't."

"That'll have to do," the man in black said. He hoisted Peter

Hertzberg to his feet and shoved him through the banister of the landing in one fluid movement. The banister gave easily and Hertzberg plummeted headlong toward the floor, telephone and all. The masked man held one end of the telephone line in his gloved hands and pulled before Hertzberg could hit the ground. Hertzberg jerked in midair and his neck broke immediately. Then he crashed to the floor, his head and neck suspended two feet off the ground, held fast by the phone cord. It looked like he was trying to sit up but had forgotten his backbone somewhere. A Ma Bell marionette.

The masked man surveyed the workstation for evidence, then went down the stairs and looked at Peter Hertzberg. The attorney's eyes bulged out of his purple face. His toupee had torn loose in the fall and dropped to the floor near the body. Hertzberg appeared to be reaching for it, even in death.

Peter Hertzberg had leaned against the banister on the second-story landing and broken through while trying to make a call. Caught in the tangle of cords while falling, he had hanged himself. Another household accident to add to the statistics.

The man in black went into the den, unscrewed the box on the telephone jack, and reconnected the line. He scanned the house for anything that he might have overlooked, then went out the back door, locking up behind himself.

Ry Caulder walked for half a mile before he found a public trash can to dump the ski mask into. He held on to the gloves and the lockpicks. He'd need them to get in and out of whatever car he would be stealing. This one was a dream. It was a 1969 Mustang parked in the shadows of an apartment complex. No alarm. He was in the vehicle and had it hot-wired in thirty seconds flat. Ten minutes later he abandoned the Mustang six blocks from where he had left the Buick. After walking a few blocks, he discarded the gloves and most of the lockpicks in another trash can. He kept his tension wrench and one multipurpose lockpick hidden in a pocketknife for future emergencies.

Caulder never took his own car anywhere near a job. Stolen vehicles were the best form of transportation. Caulder was always in and out of them before the owners even realized the vehicles were missing. He would abandon them many blocks from the job site, then steal a fresh car after the job went down. If the stolen cars and the hits were ever connected, which was highly unlikely, there would still be no tie to Ry Caulder.

Caulder had left the Buick a few blocks from Shelby's Tattoo Parlor. Shelby was one of three men in the city that had a way to reach Ry Caulder if someone wanted to hire him for a kill. Shelby took the standard agent's commission, 10 percent off the top. Caulder bought the lockpicks, tension wrench, and ski mask from Shelby. Caulder had purchased a set from a fence in Baltimore for the Nate Daniels job, but that set had been tossed immediately after Caulder left the motel room. It didn't pay to carry anything more incriminating than a nail file on your person unless you were certain you'd be needing more sophisticated tools.

Caulder had had no idea what the layout was going to be at Peter Hertzberg's house. He had no time to plan this one. If he didn't eliminate the attorney immediately, Stephanie and Jason were going to be picked up and there was the distinct possibility that he himself would be asked more than a few questions by the local authorities.

After gathering what he needed from his house and the tattoo parlor, he'd stolen a Mazda and gone to Hertzberg's office downtown. He had gotten the address out of the yellow pages. He had only heard the man's last name used in conversation by Stephanie, but it was a simple process of elimination to find the only attorney named Hertzberg with an office within ten miles of the apartment building.

If Caulder had found Hertzberg in the office he might have needed to use the Glock to make it look like a robbery, but the man hadn't been there. Caulder found Hertzberg's home address on some IRS correspondence in the office. He then stole another car and parked it a mile from his destination. It was still early and a brisk walk through this neighborhood would cause little suspicion. Caulder had located Hertzberg's house and entered from the terrace. He'd been disappointed to find the place empty, but he had used the time to formulate a plan.

Caulder was fairly certain that Hertzberg had spent the night whining about what had happened to him. The question was, Whom did he whine to? The authorities or just his drinking buddies? Caulder couldn't go around killing all of Hertzberg's friends. The whole incident was ludicrous. He should have never gotten himself into the middle of the thing. But he had and it was too late to do anything but try to rectify the situation. If Hertzberg had mentioned details to anyone who counted, Caulder could be in a world of trouble by morning. The fact that Hertzberg mumbled what he mumbled in the den gave Caulder hope. It appeared that Hertzberg's night had been spent drinking up the courage to make the call that had been interrupted on the landing. If that was the case, he and Stephanie might be safe.

The smart move would be to pack and leave immediately, and to tell Stephanie and Jason to do the same. But there was still unfinished business for Ry Caulder in Los Angeles and he would need a few days to sort things out.

He started the Buick and headed for home.

six

Caulder was asleep on his couch, buried deep under the covers as the harsh sun burned its way through his windows. The stench of whiskey and cigarettes hung thickly in the air. He had passed out watching TV early in the morning. As he tossed and turned furiously, the covers slipped to the floor. Caulder was half dressed and fully hungover. He lay there, bathed in sweat, in the throes of a terrible nightmare.

A gun barrel pressed against Caulder's right cheek.

Caulder immediately grabbed his assailant's gun hand at the wrist, twisting the muzzle away from his face. He pulled the Glock from under his pillow and jammed it under the gunman's chin. Caulder did all this in the split second before he opened his eyes. When he saw who it was, he sat up in shock.

"Jesus, kid, don't ever stick a gun in someone's face!"

Jason, terrified by Caulder's ferocity, backed away, dropped his plastic machine gun, and began to cry. He wasn't as afraid of Caulder's anger as he was hurt that Caulder would speak to him in the tone of voice that he had used. Ry Caulder was the only adult male influence he had encountered since he and his mother had arrived in Los Angeles eight months earlier, so what Caulder said and did affected the boy deeply. He looked up to Caulder like a surrogate father.

Stephanie appeared in the open doorway of the apartment. Jason ran over and hugged her skirt. "What happened?" she asked, noticing Caulder had a pistol in his hand.

"Nothing. Jason just gave me a start," Caulder said.

"So you pull a *gun* on him?" she asked with all the incredulousness she could muster.

"I was asleep. I didn't know who he was. I thought I was being attacked!"

"I've heard of paranoia before, but that's ridiculous!" Stephanie was trying to maintain her temper, but her voice was now approaching a shriek.

Caulder brought himself down a few notches, trying to get a grasp on the situation.

"The boy is carrying a plastic Uzi," Caulder said with steely calm. "We're in downtown Los Angeles. I'd hate to think of what might have happened in any other apartment in this building."

A scowl twisted on Stephanie's face. She remained mute for a few moments, acknowledging the truth in Caulder's words. Caulder understood her silence and tried to ease her guilt or at least distract her from those thoughts. "What was he doing here anyway?" he asked.

"I sent him to see if you wanted something to eat. He didn't mean to scare you."

"How did he get in?"

"The door was open some," the boy said.

The door was open some? Could Caulder have been so tired and drunk last night that he forgot to secure the door? If he was truly at fault then it was sheer uncontrolled folly on his part. The Uzi could have easily been a real one and in the hands of a killer instead of a little boy. Then he remembered. He had left the door open last night so that he could hear any activity in the hallway. He had not anticipated passing out, but alcohol and exhaustion had combined to send him into unconsciousness. He had been foolish in his paranoia.

Suddenly two men appeared behind Stephanie: Gordon Quinn and Hal Mativich, enforcers for Baxter Industries, Ry Caulder's most recent employer. They looked like linebackers in designer suits. Quinn, the larger of the two men, gave Stephanie a rough shove into the room.

"Oh look, the whole family's here," Quinn said to Mativich.

Caulder tried not to reveal his alarm at seeing the men in his doorway. They weren't supposed to be there. They weren't even supposed to know where he lived. He subtly moved the Glock so that it was pointed at Quinn as if he didn't really mean it, but he did.

Quinn patted a spot under his right arm and eyed Stephanie and Jason with meaning. Stephanie held Jason tightly against her skirt. "Get dressed," Quinn said to Ry Caulder.

Hal Mativich cautiously walked over to Caulder and took the Glock from him with a gloved hand. Caulder offered no resistance. He didn't want to start any fireworks with Stephanie and Jason in the room.

"Let's just put this thing away before someone gets hurt," Mativich said. He placed the gun on a bookshelf far out of Caulder's reach.

"Ry, who are these people?" Stephanie asked.

"It's okay," Caulder replied as cheerily as possible. "They're friends of mine."

Caulder put on the black turtleneck shirt that he had dropped on the floor the night before and reached for his jacket. Draping it casually over his shoulder, he moved toward Quinn and Mativich.

Quinn eyed Caulder suspiciously and moved to one side. Caulder walked straight past the two men into the hallway. He turned and smiled pleasantly. It was far from genuine.

"Come on, guys. . . . What are you waiting for?"

Quinn and Mativich were confused. This was going too easily. What was this guy trying to pull? They followed Caulder out into the hall.

"Why . . . What should I do?" Stephanie asked.

"Don't do *anything!* Just lock up on your way out. I'll be back soon."

The three men moved down the hallway, leaving Stephanie and Jason bewildered in the apartment.

Gordon Quinn and Hal Mativich followed Ry Caulder to the elevator at the far end of the hallway. Gang graffiti on the door let everyone know that the Rolling 60s were currently claiming this building as an extension of their turf. At least until the next gang came along and painted over their *placa.*

Caulder pushed the call button. Almost a full minute passed before the elevator door opened. The three men entered the elevator and Quinn pushed the down button. The door did not move.

Feeling uncomfortable, Quinn tried for some light conversation. "It's good you didn't give us shit," he said to Caulder. "I don't like shit. I don't like having to fuck people up. It's ridiculous, this day and age." It was his crude way of attempting friendliness.

Caulder did not respond. Instead he turned and spoke to Hal Mativich. "Nice suit," he said.

Mativich looked down at his Armani and grinned. He had picked up the suit wholesale, of course. "You like this?" he asked.

"Very much," Caulder replied as the elevator door slowly ground shut.

By the time the elevator door opened in the lobby, Caulder was standing over the bloodied bodies of Gordon Quinn and Hal Mativich. Caulder held both of their pistols, standard-issue Colt .45s, one in each hand. He had one aimed at Quinn's forehead. The other fit snugly into Mativich's mouth.

"Next time you invade my privacy, you're dead," Caulder said as calmly as he could. He scanned the lobby to see if it was empty. It was.

The close quarters had made the violence simple. A few aikido strokes and both men had found the elevator floor rushing up at them like some bad home movie where the camera got dropped. Their pistols had been removed from under their jackets so skillfully that they weren't really sure Caulder had taken them. Through the pain and fog both Quinn and Mativich shared exactly the same thought: *Where the fuck did he get those guns?*

Caulder removed the pistol from Mativich's mouth and motioned with both the guns. "Get up," he said with no trace of malice. They got to their feet. Caulder picked his jacket up off the floor and slipped it on; then he put the guns in the pockets of the jacket and aimed one at each man through the fabric.

"Where's your car?" Caulder asked.

"In front," Quinn replied.

"Let's go."

Caulder guided them out of the building and they went down the stairs to a brand-new red Cadillac parked right outside the front door.

"You guys are subtle," Caulder said.

"Hey, we were just supposed to pick you up," Quinn replied. "We got nothin' to hide."

"Keys," Caulder demanded. "Slowly."

Mativich produced a set of keys.

"Drive," Caulder said to Mativich.

Mativich slid behind the wheel. Caulder and Quinn got into the backseat, Caulder directly behind Mativich. Once they were in the car Caulder pulled the guns from his pockets and aimed one at the back of Mativich's skull and the other at Quinn's chest.

"Go easy, Mativich," Caulder said. "I've got your pistol aimed at your head. Anything strange happens and you'll get a bug's-eye view of the windshield."

Mativich shifted uncomfortably in his seat and started the car.

"You guys really stank up the airport yesterday," Caulder said. "You can't tail for shit."

"We weren't at any goddamn airport yesterday," Quinn said.

Caulder struck Quinn on the side of his face with the butt of the .45.

"You don't listen," Caulder said. "Let's move it, Mativich."

Mativich put the car in gear and pulled out into traffic.

Quinn rubbed the welt growing on his cheek and looked at the floorboard.

They rode for a few minutes in silence, until finally Mativich broke the tension. "May I ask you something?" Mativich flinched as he posed the question, thinking he would take a blow to the head, like Quinn.

"Sure," Caulder said, without striking the man.

"Are you going to kill us?"

Caulder laughed without smiling, then said, "Not yet."

"Then where am I driving?"

"We're going to go see your boss."

seven

Century City came into being in the mid-sixties, when the film studio 20th Century Fox was forced to sell most of its back lot to pay for the losses of its megabudget, megaflop film, *Cleopatra*. The resulting business area became one of the most profitable centers of commerce in Los Angeles County. A cleaner, more sterile downtown than downtown itself. Century City contributed heavily to the degeneration of downtown Los Angeles and the decentralization of Los Angeles in general. Many businesses had relocated to this area long ago. Many more grew directly out of the fertile environment. Even more took the cue and realized that Los Angeles did not have to be like other big cities, rotating around a central hub. There could be many central areas, many downtowns. Up sprang competitive power centers in Westwood, Beverly Hills, Santa Monica, West L.A., Marina Del Rey, Hollywood; and in the valley, Sherman Oaks, Burbank, Glendale, Canoga Park, and Woodland Hills, to name a few. Los Angeles was just too big for *one* downtown. This was a contributing factor to the city's diversity and its schizophrenia. Century City was the place to be if you wanted to be in business with the upscale elite.

Ry Caulder escorted Gordon Quinn and Hal Mativich across the cobbled promenade toward the Twin Towers of Century City. They drew stares from black-suited men clutching attaché cases rushing to their next appointments and street vendors hustling the lunch-hour crowd. Bored secretaries and legal assistants on benches looked up from their flirtations to stare at the bruised pair of thugs as they were hustled along by the taciturn man with his hands in his jacket pockets.

Caulder, Quinn, and Mativich emerged from the elevator on the penthouse level. The entire top floor of the 2029 building was owned by Baxter Industries. The urine-tinted Los Angeles skyline showed through filthy windows to the right of the elevator.

The three men went down a long hallway lined with offices. Caulder produced one of the pistols from his jacket and held it tight against Quinn's back as they walked, to maintain more control. He was pulling a ballsy move and the thought that it might backfire began to trouble him.

The operation looked like a busy and successful brokerage or real estate firm. Secretaries chattered, adding machines clicked, computers hummed, serious-looking men and women worked their way through mountainous stacks of paperwork. They looked up briefly as the bizarre troop walked past. Some of them spotted Caulder's gun, but chose to ignore it and went quickly back to work, as if the sight of a gun in the office was as common to them as a cup of coffee.

A sign on a door at the end of the hall marked the offices of James Vincent Baxter, president and CEO of Baxter Industries. Caulder shoved Mativich and Quinn into Baxter's outer office, a large room occupied by two secretaries seated behind art deco desks and one giant ape of a man, impeccably dressed and reading *Vanity Fair* on a couch to the left of the doorway. The man fit oddly in his Rick Pallack three-piece, as if he were going to bust out at any moment and start swinging on the rafters.

The younger of the secretaries looked up and saw Caulder, Quinn, and Mativich standing in the doorway. "Uh . . . Mr. uh, uh . . ." she stammered. She knew Quinn and Mativich, but for some reason their names escaped her.

The ape and the older secretary looked the scene over. The older secretary took it all in stride. The ape stood up, casting a large shadow over Ry Caulder.

"Where do you think you're going?" the man asked in a much higher tone than Caulder expected to hear.

"Baxter wants to see me," Caulder said, trying to remain unimpressed by the big man's size and attitude.

"I'll announce you," the older secretary said.

"I'll announce myself," Caulder replied.

"I have to ask you for your weapons before I buzz you in," the woman continued pleasantly.

"Of course."

Caulder placed the .45s on the secretary's desk. She looked at the two battered men with scorn, realizing the guns had once belonged to them.

"What about your own?" the secretary pressed Caulder.

"Not carrying today." Caulder raised his arms in the air, indicating he was willing to stand for a frisk.

"I'll take your word for it," the woman said, and she hit a button on her desk that released the lock on a set of double mahogany doors behind her. "They're in a meeting, but I know Mr. Baxter wants to see you immediately. It's a matter of utmost urgency. I'm sure he won't mind the interruption."

The woman had a smile going that unnerved Caulder. He couldn't tell if he was being set up or if she was just getting some form of perverse joy from all the fun and games. Caulder moved for the doorway nevertheless.

eight

Jimmy Binanchi had changed his name to James Vincent Baxter shortly after his arrival in Los Angeles in the mid-seventies. A "made man" at twenty-two, Jimmy was nearing thirty at the time, a lieutenant in the Carmine Mercante family. Jimmy had taken a crew into the home of one Ernst Salerno and split the man down the middle. They strangled and stabbed five other people in that house, two of them children, in what the New York City P.D. called the most heinous act of Mob violence since the St. Valentine's Day Massacre.

Ernst Salerno was not Mob. He had nothing to do with the outfit. But that was the point exactly. Ernst Salerno owned a strip of stores on a block in Greenwich Village that Carmine Mercante was trying to buy for a real estate developer friend. They were going to tear the whole thing down and put up a nine-story parking garage. Money had already changed hands downtown to clear the zoning; everyone else on the block had sold their businesses to the outfit no later than the third offer, the one that included physical pain, and now the only problem was Ernst Salerno. He was a stubborn old bastard who actually pulled a gun on Jimmy Binanchi and his men when they dropped by to make him the third offer. This was not going to fly. Jimmy Binanchi took great joy in putting the ax to the old man after they woke him up so he could watch himself die. The garage now sits in the heart of the Village, some of the choicest real estate in Manhattan.

As a reward for a job well done, and a way to keep the crew out of the heat of the subsequent investigation, Carmine Mercante sent Jimmy Binanchi and his men out to Los Angeles in a brand-new Lincoln Continental. They were to oversee Mercante's West Coast drug operation, centered in Los Angeles. At the time things were being run by a lowlife named Renny Cartier. It was chaos. Cartier was using. Tossing freebie parties all over town. Runners were carrying kilos of coke out of his house like they were dime bags of grass. Everyone was stealing. The nonsense had to come to a halt. One night they hung Renny Cartier by his heels off the roof of the Playboy Building on Sunset Boulevard for an hour and a half until he swore to God and the baby Jesus that he would get his act together. He didn't last six months. The cops eventually found him in Dumpsters from Pacoima to Arcadia. Jimmy Binanchi took charge then. He changed his name to James Vincent Baxter, a gentrified, almost regal name to suit his new position. Business moved differently in Los Angeles than in New York. It was much harder to put the fix in here, and a lot tougher to square things if you got popped. The Feds were a big presence in Los Angeles and the Feds were not purchasable as a rule. Too many other Feds were watching over their shoulders. Everybody was taping everybody else. Attorneys were running the show. It just wasn't civilized. Jimmy Binanchi was a thug, but he wasn't stupid. He realized that L.A. was going to have to be cracked from the inside. Brute force wouldn't do it alone. He told Joe Gates, "When in Rome, do as the Romans do." He told him that in the lobby of the law offices of Bender, Cohn, Cohn, Sterling, and Rothman as they waited to have their first meeting with the group of sharks that would show them the way to commit crime as legitimately as possible. When it came to manipulating the law, la Cosa Nostra had nothing on Bender, Cohn, Cohn, Sterling, and Rothman. They taught Jimmy Binanchi what money could *really* do.

That was almost twenty years ago and Los Angeles was looking a lot more like New York now. Joe Gates was long dead from prostate cancer; Carmine Mercante had a heart attack in prison and died while awaiting trial on racketeering charges, but James Vincent Baxter was still alive and kicking and he was in charge of the entire West Coast now. The Mercante family was merely an occasional annoyance. Other than the money that was shipped back east, there was little communication between the two entities. The difference in the two business styles was night and day. While the Mercantes still ruled by a mixture of fear and respect, Baxter was vying for legitimacy and corporate power. He wanted to be sophisticated, but deep down he was still just a hood. His methods often lacked the panache he coveted. Baxter had all the heart, charm, and bluster of the old-time beasts from whom he had inherited his position. He was the missing link between the petty-thugs-turned-mob-bosses of the old days and the techno-attorney-run-scam-artists of today. A throwback to a more brutal way of doing business that was doomed to obsolescence, but not before causing a great deal of trouble for anyone who interfered with his grand schemes.

Sixteen hardened executives sat around a huge redwood table inside the main conference room of Baxter Industries. James Vincent Baxter himself stood at the head of the table, a large, imposing man of fifty. When he smiled it was the smile of a dog. Baxter smiled frequently, but not for the same reasons most people smiled. His smile usually indicated displeasure. Everyone in the room sported Brooks Brothers suits except for Baxter, who was decked out in an oversize Hugo Boss outfit that made him look like he had inherited Al Capone's wardrobe and was slowly growing into it.

Baxter pointed to a series of computerized graphs and flow-charts on the wall behind him as he addressed his staff. "I don't know how much you guys are putting in your pockets, but when I find out, heads are going to roll!" he bellowed.

It was the weekly greed sermon. It was a scene that was being repeated in corporations all over the country. But most corporate production did not include cocaine and heroin. These were the subsidiary businesses of Baxter Industries. They were the high-profit items on a business sheet that would otherwise be dominated by red ink. Illicit drug sales accounted for 45 percent of Baxter Industries' gross receipts and a whopping 92 percent of its profits. The wide variety of other businesses that Baxter Industries owned were there mainly for money-laundering purposes. A sideshow to keep everything looking legit.

"I'm serious, people," Baxter continued. "This bullshit has got to stop."

"My sentiments exactly," Ry Caulder announced as Baxter came up for air.

Caulder was leaning against a coatrack near the mahogany double doors. No one had noticed him enter the room. They had no idea how long he had been there. The interruption infuriated Baxter, but he stifled his anger. "Mr. Caulder . . . welcome back," he said in even tones. Baxter liked to call everyone "Mr." or "Mrs." He thought it gave him an air of professionalism and sophistication.

Caulder didn't like Baxter. The man represented to him all the worst elements of the "old guard," the wise guys, the gangsters. Baxter considered himself a businessman, but to Caulder he was just a two-bit thug in a three-piece suit. Baxter reminded him too much of Hollywood and B movies.

"I didn't come here for pleasantries," Caulder said. "You owe me money."

A meek-looking guy at the table spoke up: "Uh, accounts

payable has a problem verifying that the merger has been achieved." In spite of the fact that Baxter had the place swept for electronic listening devices daily, most of the employees preferred euphemisms to direct, prosecutable conversation.

"Are you calling me a liar?" Caulder asked dispassionately.

Baxter spread his arms wide in an all-encompassing gesture of trust. "No, Mr. Caulder, I'm sure you did a wonderful job. We just need to receive verification."

"How about a little privacy?" Caulder looked over the room full of "executives."

"Everybody out," Baxter commanded. "Except for Mr. Clark."

The executives grumbled, shuffled papers, and made for the double doorway.

"We'll continue this meeting at two o'clock," Baxter continued. "Mr. Courtney, please ask Mr. Del Monaco to join us in my office."

A thick guy with glasses and a limp said "Yes, sir" as he exited the room and closed the double doors. Caulder was left in the conference room with Baxter and Clark, the meek-looking guy who had challenged Caulder's completion of the Nate Daniels job.

"Did you put a contract out on me?" Caulder asked Baxter directly.

"Of course not," Baxter said with genuine horror. "What gives you that bright idea?"

"Couple of guys were on my ass at the airport. They were waiting for me. Not many people would be looking for me at the airport, but *you* knew I'd be coming through LAX sometime soon."

"Why would I put a contract on *you?*"

"Who knows? I'm sure you could come up with plenty of reasons. You wanted me to take care of Nate, maybe you wanted someone else to take care of me. That kind of nonsense used to be standard procedure around here."

"I'm not the only person that might have a beef against you. I'll check around. If there *is* a contract, I'll buy it off."

"Don't do me any favors. What's with the two goons showing up at my place patting their underarms and all?"

"I needed to get you in here quick. We didn't have time to go through the channels."

"How did you find me?"

"You have your way of doing things, we have ours. Like I said, we needed you in here fast."

"What are you talking about? I want my money and I'm gone."

"We need verification before we can release that amount of petty cash," Mr. Clark piped in from his seat at the table.

"Bullshit! I left the job in plain sight, per your request and against my better judgment. Police verification will be fully accessible by now. You're stalling me."

"Well, actually, Mr. Caulder," Baxter said, "we do have a new problem to discuss."

Caulder fixed his gaze on Baxter again. "The only problem we have is that you owe me money and I am here to collect it."

"And we fully intend to pay you, but we have one more assignment—"

Caulder slammed his fist down on the conference table, interrupting Baxter. *"Listen to me! I'm out!"* I'm retired, quit, resigned. I'm through. . . . I only did the last job as a favor to Nate."

"If you've done your job, Nate Daniels got the company's 'golden handshake,' " Baxter said. "That's the only way you retire from this organization."

Caulder looked at Baxter as if he were insane. "I'm a freelancer. I'm not part of your three-ring circus. And you don't have anyone *good* enough to give me a 'golden handshake.' "

Baxter stared at Caulder for a moment, trying to decide how to handle him. Finally he smiled that canine smile.

"I assure you it could be done."

"Your life won't be worth a week afterward either and you know it."

"You're going to stand in the middle of my office and threaten me with *insurance?* You got balls, mister! I didn't bring you here so we could piss on each other. Let's get down to business."

"Pay me. That's our business."

This wasn't working. Baxter softened and decided to appeal to Caulder's curious nature. "Why don't we step into my office and discuss the situation in detail with Mr. Del Monaco? I'm sure you'll find our problem interesting. If not, then we'll pay you and part company as friends, okay? No more strings."

Caulder looked at Baxter's concerned face, thought the situation over, then smiled at the CEO condescendingly.

"Sure, Jim," Caulder said with only the slightest hint of irony. "Anything for a friend."

James Vincent Baxter's private office was vast and lavishly decorated in nineteenth-century Italian. Baxter sat behind a sprawling desk made entirely of Sicilian marble. He could have easily passed for the president of General Motors or the head of a movie studio. Ry Caulder took a leather chair across the desk from Baxter. Michael Del Monaco, Baxter's junior partner, entered the room. Caulder stood and shook his hand.

"I trust you had a profitable trip, Ry," Mike Del Monaco said. He had a smooth, silky voice and strong features like a soap opera actor. He was the only contractor that called Ry Caulder by his first name.

"It went just fine," Caulder replied.

Mike Del Monaco was the man who had introduced Nate Daniels to Ry Caulder those many years ago. Mike Del Monaco had merged his company with Baxter Industries a few years later. Caulder hadn't worked as much for Mike Del Monaco after the merger. Caulder didn't like Baxter and was surprised that Mike Del Monaco would go into business with the man. Caulder rarely worked for Baxter Industries, except in special cases where Baxter's needs were in line with his own, such as the neutralization of Nate

Daniels. Caulder wanted the job done as much as Baxter did and he was not above taking money from Baxter to achieve the common goal.

Baxter hit a button on his desk; the shades dropped, the lights dimmed, and a wall panel slid back to reveal a projection screen at the far end of the room. It was all very melodramatic.

Baxter flicked another button and an image projected by a slide projector built into the wall appeared on the screen. The slide showed a tall, slim, well-built man of about fifty-five with slicked-back silver hair. He had a stern face with high, well-defined cheekbones. Sunglasses covered his eyes, but the face was unmistakable to Ry Caulder.

"Fredrickson," Caulder whispered, almost to himself. Caulder looked as if a cloud of gloom had descended around him.

"Your buddy . . ." Mike Del Monaco said.

"A long time ago."

"What happened between the two of you?" Baxter asked.

"You know damn well what happened!"

"The Jameson contract?" Baxter pressed, even though he knew the answer. He was playing an angle.

Caulder stared at Baxter coldly.

"Come on, Ry. You know that situation was unavoidable," Mike Del Monaco said. "It was an honest mistake."

"Any time the wrong people get killed it's more than an 'honest mistake.' That operation was a twenty-four-carat fuckup."

"So that's why you won't work with Fredrickson anymore?" Baxter asked.

"That's why I won't do this *at all* anymore," Caulder replied, revealing more personal information than was the norm for him.

"Which is also why you are perfect for this job." Baxter was smiling widely now. He was growing confident, in spite of Caulder's obvious reluctance.

"For some time now," Mike Del Monaco said, "Fredrickson has been freelancing for us in Latin America. Mopping-up operations, quick extraditions, unleveraged buyouts . . . That sort of thing." Mike Del Monaco was a thesaurus of euphemisms. He would never say anything that could clearly be used in court against him. "But recently we've been experiencing major difficulties in his territory. Shipments were sent but never received. Operatives began disappearing. Our entire operation in Panama was systematically wiped out in less than a month after Fredrickson severed contact with us. . . . We think he's gone over to Varga's side."

"What gives you *that* bright idea?" Caulder asked. Camilo Varga was Baxter's number-one competitor on the West Coast. His operation originated in Colombia, but he was cutting deep into Baxter's business in California with a string of drug boutiques and distributors that was growing by the day.

Baxter clicked the remote control and the slide changed. The photo was dark and blurry. Caulder could barely make out the hazy shape of a man. There was something eerie about him. Something unsettling.

"This photo was taken by a surveillance camera outside our warehouse in Ensenada . . . moments before everyone in the place was slaughtered," Mike Del Monaco said. "We think this is Fredrickson."

"What do you think, Mr. Caulder?" Baxter asked. "Could that be Fredrickson?" Baxter seemed to know the answer to this question as well.

Caulder took a few moments to answer. *"Could* be *anybody,"* he finally replied.

"We believe whoever is in this picture is at least partially responsible for what you are about to see," Mike Del Monaco said.

Baxter touched the remote again.

The next slide showed a long warehouse gallery filled with vats and bailing machines. The photo was a wide shot and at this distance it looked as if several very messy packages had exploded inside the warehouse.

"These photographs were taken approximately five hours after the attack," Mike Del Monaco said. "The surveillance cameras inside the warehouse were all destroyed. We didn't get one shot of the incident as it was happening."

The next shot was tighter. It was now apparent that the packages were human and there were many of them. Or at least many *pieces* of them. It was hard to distinguish where one body ended and another began.

"Fucking savages," Baxter said.

The following shot was an even tighter close-up on one of the bodies. What was left of this person's flesh was a hideous map of crimson lines, brutally carved designs, some so deep that they revealed a hint of white bone. The body lay in a thick puddle of dark blood. Black blood.

"As you can see, the crew was overly thorough," Mike Del Monaco said. "They didn't just want to kill. They were making a statement."

The next slide was another nauseating crisscross of blood-encrusted channels. Straight slashing lines ran down the legs, shredding through cloth and then proceeding even through the hard leather of cowboy boots. All the toes on one foot were missing.

"Mutilation was widely varied from victim to victim," Mike Del Monaco said. He was beginning to have trouble holding down lunch.

The next slide showed a wider angle that revealed the carnage in full; hideous mounds of bloodied flesh were everywhere. More than a dozen men had been rendered lifeless by a force of incredible savagery. They hadn't just been murdered. They had been torn to bits. There were what appeared to be bite marks on some of the bodies.

"The bastards chewed on them," Caulder said in awe.

"There were some cases where it looked that way," Mike Del Monaco said, trying to make less of it than it was.

The lights came up in Baxter's office. The three men sat for a few moments, not saying anything. Even the world-weary Ry Caulder looked slightly nauseous. "Jesus," he finally muttered. He'd seen worse, but not lately.

"Our entire Ensenada crew, fourteen men, wiped out in one assault," Baxter said.

"Varga?" Caulder asked.

"Probably . . . But with help."

"We think Fredrickson's gone over," Mike Del Monaco said. "Varga got to him. We sent two men down to look for Fredrickson. He sent us back their decapitated heads. We think he's tied in with a truckload of Colombians and they're working their way north, trashing our operations as they come. . . ."

"There's one problem with all this," Caulder said.

"What?" Baxter asked.

"Fredrickson is dead. Word is he was killed down in Mexico a few months ago by the Sanchez brothers."

"We wish," Mike Del Monaco said. "We've had reports of him spotted everywhere from Tijuana to right here in town. We've sent crews out looking for him but they either come up with nothing or we never see them again."

"You guys are having real problems."

"No shit," Baxter snarled.

"Fredrickson's one thing," Caulder said. "But if it's Colombians you're after, send your torture squads. I don't conduct suicide missions."

"Are you afraid of Colombians, Mr. Caulder?" Baxter asked out of the corner of his mouth.

"There's a big difference between fear and self-preservation. I don't like fucking with Colombians. Besides, I don't need to get in the middle of some half-assed gang war. This is juvenilia."

"All you need to worry about is Fredrickson," Mike Del Monaco said. "It's *his* inside knowledge that's crippling us. You stop him and we'll take care of the Colombians. Fredrickson trained you. You were his friend. You know his habits, where he goes, what he does. You *think* like him. You can get close enough to tag him."

Caulder couldn't believe what he was hearing. He had just killed one hit man for them, a man whom Caulder had trained; now they wanted him to go out and kill his *own* mentor. The cannibalism was going too far. Sooner or later, he figured, they were going to ask him to kill himself.

"This is all none of my business," Caulder said. "I'm quite unconcerned about the problems this company has with its competition or its employees. What makes you think I'd want to go after Fredrickson? What's my incentive?"

"Paul Shepfield was your uncle, wasn't he?" Mike Del Monaco asked.

"What do you mean, *'was'*?"

"He was one of the fourteen," Mike Del Monaco said, with what appeared to be earnest sadness, even though this was obviously a button he had been waiting to push.

Caulder's jaw tensed; the news visibly upset him. Paul Shepfield was, indeed, his uncle; Caulder's only known living relative. Shepfield had raised Caulder from the time he was seven, when Caulder's mother, Shepfield's half sister, committed suicide. Caulder had never known his father. For that matter, Caulder's mother was not so sure of his identity herself. There had been a number of possible suspects and they all conveniently moved on at the announcement of her pregnancy. Shepfield was the only father Ry Caulder had ever known. Caulder had not seen Shepfield in many years, but he still felt a deep kinship to him. Hard times and coincidence had led Shepfield to a position with one of Baxter Industries' "underground" companies. Now he was dead.

Caulder sat in silence for what seemed a very long time. "All right," he finally said. "I'll find Fredrickson. I'll watch him. I'll verify your story. If I'm convinced he's responsible, I'll take him out."

"We're already convinced," Baxter said.

"That means nothing to me." Caulder added a slight wave of his hand for effect.

Baxter took a picture out of a file and tossed it across the desk. The photo was of one of the less badly maimed victims. The man's arms were outstretched and there was a bullet hole in the center of both palms.

Caulder's jaw went slack.

"That's Fredrickson's signature, isn't it?" Baxter asked.

Caulder stared at the photo. Yes, that was Fredrickson's signature all right. A little symbolism stating that the owner of these hands would not be needing them any longer, that whatever crime the condemned had perpetrated against Fredrickson or his employers would never be repeated.

"He signed them all that way . . . even Paul Shepfield," Mike Del Monaco said.

He reached into his jacket, brought out an envelope, and handed it to Caulder. "Here's the first payment on the balance of the Daniels job. Half now and the other half when you get Fredrickson, plus an extremely substantial bonus."

"You're blackmailing me into working for money that I've already earned? That's not like you, Mike. You've picked up some bad habits around here."

"We really need you on this one, Ry," Mike Del Monaco said. "So much so that I'm willing to bend my principles to ensure that the job gets done."

Caulder's brow furrowed. "If I move against Fredrickson the price will be four times my standard fee."

"That's outrageous," Baxter said.

"It's an outrageous request," Caulder replied. "And it will be very dangerous."

"I'm sure we can come to terms," Mike Del Monaco said.

"That's right. It will all work out to your advantage," Baxter added. "You'll have even more money for your *retirement.*" Baxter said "retirement" in a tone that carried something distinctly mocking, as if he knew Ry Caulder would never manage to retire. Caulder was growing more irritated than usual with Baxter.

"I told you I'd check it out," Caulder said. "I still haven't said that I'd *take* the job."

"You'll take it, Mr. Caulder. It's what you do," Baxter replied.

"We have great faith in you," Mike Del Monaco added.

Caulder tapped the envelope with his knuckles and stared hard at the two men. "Faith," he said, "is for children and grandmothers."

nine

A group of young black girls were singing and skipping rope on the sidewalk in front of the crumbling apartment building. The lyrics were distinctly Janet Jackson.

Stephanie sat at the top of the steps watching Jason play with a plastic fire truck down below. Stephanie and Jason were generally accepted by the neighborhood as poor white trash and, even though they weren't an official couple, people assumed that Stephanie was under the protection of the dangerous-looking guy who lived down the hall from her, so the harassment, sexual and otherwise, was kept to a minimum. Stephanie felt relatively safe on these mean streets, at least for a one-block radius or so.

Stephanie smiled as she spotted Ry Caulder getting out of a taxi on the corner down the block. Caulder paid the driver and disappeared into Rhee's Market.

Stephanie had been wound up in knots since the incident with the two men that morning and she was glad to see that Caulder was all right. Something always relaxed within her when he was around. Despite the fact that she could get almost no sign of true affection or even minor commitment out of him, his mere presence nearby made her feel safe, secure, and right, as if some primordial instinct within her was saying that this was *the* man, her other half, the other piece of the puzzle. Unfortunately, Caulder didn't appear to be receiving the same signals, or if he was, he was choosing to ignore them.

Caulder came out of the store carrying a small bag containing a liquor bottle. He crossed the street and approached the apartment building. He didn't notice Stephanie sitting on the stoop until he was already halfway down the block, and by then it was too late. He got by Jason without the boy looking up from his toy and noticing him, then made his way up the stairs.

Stephanie stood to greet Caulder. She noticed how slowly he was moving. He looked worn-out. "I've been worried about you," she said.

"Do us both a favor—*don't*," he said without emotion. He didn't want anyone worrying about him, thinking about him. He didn't need the hassle, the responsibility. He wanted to end this farce *now*.

Caulder entered the building. Stephanie was stunned. He had cut her to the quick. When they first met, Ry Caulder had been all the quiet gentleman. Very sincere, very helpful. He gave freely of his time and advice, and there was even the occasional surprise like the pizza and ice-cream cake he brought home for Jason's birthday when Stephanie was near destitute. But Caulder gave nothing of himself. He never shared his personal feelings or motivations with them. Not even the minor details of his life—what he did for a living or in his spare time, or who his friends were. He was very closed off about that type of thing. Stephanie had known for a long time that he wanted her. She could tell by the way she caught him looking at her when he thought she wouldn't notice. But he never made the move. Something kept his actions in check and it frustrated the hell out of her. She had opened up to him repeatedly, exposed her full femininity, her sensitivity, her feelings and emotions. It should have been obvious to him that she would be receptive to his advances. She had done everything but jump his bones. All she got in return was apathy, and now, rudeness. No more, she resolved. That was the end of it. She was closing up shop.

ten

Caulder parked the Buick Skylark a block away from Alvin's Alcove. A decaying neon sign announcing topless delights sputtered violently on the roof of the joint. The outside of the bar itself looked every bit as exhausted as the neon. Gang graffiti was layered so thick on the walls it rendered all the *placas* indiscernible, providing a poor man's paint job in dingy brown and black spray paint.

As Caulder approached the place he noticed a man puking on the sidewalk just outside the entrance. The man wiped his mouth with his sleeve and stumbled into the bar, only to be tossed back out into the street by a short, burly bouncer with long blond hair and a silver ring through one nostril. The drunk rolled against a parked car and lay there, staring up at the sky with dilated pupils.

The bouncer held the door open for Caulder, who did not recognize the guy.

"Welcome," the bouncer said.

Caulder nodded and entered.

The interior of the Alcove delivered all the wonderful attractions its exterior promised. A long runway surrounded by rails dominated the center of the room. Poles were spaced along the runway so the two aging strippers who were competing to see who could take her clothes off in the least provocative way could do gymnastics when they got bored. Mick Jagger serenaded them from the jukebox. He was singing "Brown Sugar" for the thirtieth time that night.

The place was half full, but except for one short bald guy to whom any female flesh looked good, the rest of the customers had their backs to the stage and were focused on serious drinking.

Caulder approached the bartender, a big guy with a buzz cut and twenty-two-inch biceps. Caulder knew this man only as "Dutch," his biker name.

"Alvin in?" Caulder asked.

"He's out back settling somethin' in the parking lot," Dutch offered in an unpleasant tone. "Should be back in a sec."

Dutch rummaged around under the bar and produced a bottle of Glenlivet. "You still drinking this stuff?" he grumbled.

Caulder nodded. The bartender set the bottle and a glass in front of Caulder.

"Rough night?" Caulder asked.

"Every fuckin' crazy in the city been here tonight," Dutch said. "We been tossing 'em out the front and the back at the same time. Dude even pulled a gun on our new guy, you know, Goldilocks over there. Boy that motherfucker can fight. He looks like a girl and all, but get him started and you're sorry quick. He took that gun away from that poor sumbitch and broke his arm in three places quicker'n I can open a beer. We had cops in here for an hour and a half. This whole fuckin' town's losin' it. I don't know what the fuck is going on anymore. Everybody's got a piece and they're all dyin' to play Dirty Harry. It's crazy."

"Uh-huh," Caulder muttered sympathetically. He poured himself a tall Scotch and settled in to watch the freak show.

The bald guy at the runway appeared to be falling in love with one of the strippers. She was brunet and had a distinct advantage over her blond counterpart: she had all her teeth. The bald guy had gotten into the habit of laying dollar bill after dollar bill on the railing in front of himself so that the brunet would bend over to pick them up, giving him a clear look at her sagging breasts and that shiny, full set of capped teeth.

Apparently the man ran out of dollar bills because he abruptly left his seat along the runway and sidled up next to Caulder at the bar. He waved a twenty at the bartender with his left hand. His right hand was busy somewhere under the bar, out of sight. The bartender snatched the twenty out of the bald man's hand and headed for the cash register. No words were exchanged. None were needed.

Caulder kept watch on the bald man out of the corner of his eye. The man was obviously drunk and incompetent, but Caulder knew trouble could come from any source at any time. The man had a penguinlike head and body: tiny chin, hawk nose, hairy ears, rotund stomach, and bald head. He was horny as a tomcat. The man appeared to be Armenian in descent. Not that Caulder was prejudiced or judgmental. Other nationalities might have produced this birdman, but there was something specifically Armenian about this fellow.

Caulder had a lot of experience with Armenians. When he was young he had dated an Armenian girl for quite some time until her family put a stop to it. Theirs was an old culture trying desperately to hold on to its roots. The elders frowned heavily on mixed marriages. Once the girl's father identified young Ry Caulder, then known by his birth name, Keith Milton, as the problem, the girl was conveniently sent to Europe for rest and protection among other relatives. The girl's father looked very much like the bald guy standing next to Caulder now. Thinking about all this, Caulder began to hope for trouble. He wouldn't mind exorcising some old demons at the expense of an obnoxious drunk.

The bald man sensed Caulder's attention. He leaned closer to Caulder and decided to share a secret with him.

"These women!" the bald man groaned in a distinctly Armenian accent. "They're *killing* me!"

The man squeezed whatever he was holding below the safety of the bar and moaned like an animal.

"Kit's my favorite," he said as he pointed at the brunet up on the stage. "She's got great teets."

Caulder looked over at the stripper and checked out her breasts. They were big, loaded with silicone, and suffering from the effects of gravity. Mercifully, the bartender arrived and shoved twenty singles into the bald man's free hand. The man jettisoned himself from the bar and bounced back into his seat at the runway. Dutch looked at Caulder and shook his head. Caulder sipped his Scotch and tried to relax.

After a few more minutes had passed, Alvin appeared at the back of the bar carrying a bloodied baseball bat. Whatever he had been settling in the parking lot was obviously a done deal. Alvin made Dutch and Goldilocks look like pygmies. He weighed in at just over 340, most of it old muscle, spread over a hulking six-foot-five frame.

Alvin spotted Caulder at the end of the bar and let out a war whoop that startled everyone in the place. Alvin loved Caulder like a brother. He wasn't sure why, but something about Caulder appealed to him. Alvin sensed that Caulder's presence on this planet made *his* existence seem almost decent by comparison. They were friends, but Alvin occasionally worked for Caulder, whenever a second set of hands was needed in a nonlethal situation. Caulder had never asked Alvin to kill for him, but the big man would without asking questions. Alvin was as trustworthy and loyal as he was crazy.

As Alvin walked along the front of the bar the customers eyed him and his Louisville Slugger nervously.

Caulder got up to greet Alvin. They shook hands and Caulder felt as if his arm were being jerked out of its socket.

"How's it going, buddy?" Alvin roared. "Haven't seen you in a month of scumdays!"

"Been busy, been busy."

"What's up?" Alvin asked good-naturedly.

"I'm looking for Fredrickson. Have you seen him?"

"No, but I hear he's back in town. Bobby ran into him over at Boardner's a couple of nights ago. Said he was acting real weird."

"What do you mean?"

"I don't know. Bobby tried to talk to him, but Fredrickson just gave him the brush and told him to fuck off. Aaaaah . . ." Alvin made a motion as if he was brushing a gnat away from his face. "He always was an asshole anyway."

Caulder looked somewhat offended by the comment. Even though there had been a bad parting of ways between he and Fredrickson a few years earlier, the man had once been numbered as one of Caulder's few comrades. It was a tight clique, and getting tighter by the moment. Nate was dead. Alvin was nuts. And Fredrickson was a marked man. So much for Ry Caulder's circle of friends.

"Yeah, well, I need to find him," Caulder said, trying to subdue his indignation.

"Have you tried his crib?" Alvin asked.

"You mean up on Mulholland?"

"No, man. He hasn't lived there in years. He's got a spread in Malibu now, up in the mountains. I went up there a couple'a months ago to score coke for some friends of mine. The place was freak city. He's got a fucken castle, man. It's weird."

"Where in Malibu?"

"If I tried to tell you how to get there you'd never find it. But I can take you there."

"When?"

Alvin shrugged. "How about now?"

Caulder downed the last of his drink and slid the bottle onto the back rail of the bar so Dutch could store it again. "Now," Caulder said, "is the only time we can count on."

"You said it, brother." Alvin went around and placed the baseball bat in its resting spot behind the bar. He tapped the cash register, opening the sliding drawer, and withdrew a .357 Colt Python. Many eyes around the bar tensed as Alvin opened the cylinder, checked to make sure the gun was fully loaded, then slapped the cylinder back into place. Alvin did it so matter-of-factly one would have thought he was alone in his own bedroom. Satisfied, Alvin looked up and grinned at Caulder.

"Just to make sure we have more 'nows' in our futures," Alvin said.

eleven

Other than the occasional road direction, there was little conversation as the two men drove toward Malibu. Alvin knew better than to ask for too many specifics. If Caulder felt he needed to know details, he'd tell him. They took Sunset all the way out to the Pacific Coast Highway and turned right. When they reached Kanan Dume Road, they turned right again and headed up into the Santa Monica Mountains.

They had taken the Buick. Caulder no longer worried about using his own vehicle. Circumstances were closing in on him and he knew that he would be leaving town sooner than he planned. The Buick would have to be junked. He'd sell it to Joey Farina for three hundred bucks and call it a day. Joey ran a chop shop for hot vehicles. The Buick would be parted out and cut to pieces in two hours flat. It would vanish from the face of the earth.

They did have a short discussion about the Justice Department. As they went through a tunnel carved through a mountain, Alvin said, "Couple of JD guys came by my place last week."

"Yeah?" Caulder said. He knew what it was about before Alvin said another word. Nate had ratted them all out and the Justice Department had begun looking for confirmation of the facts. Unable to find Caulder, they were working his connections.

"I didn't tell 'em shit."

"You don't have to tell me anything."

"Yeah, but I *want* to tell you. You should know all about it. They don't have dick on me. That little rat bastard didn't know shit about me but that I had a bar and all and that I knew *you*. You was the one they were looking for. I told 'em to go fuck themselves. I didn't know where the fuck you lived and I didn't hardly see you around anymore. They can kiss my goddamn ass those Justice boys."

"They're just doing their jobs."

Alvin laughed. "That's got to be a first. Ry Caulder defending the Justice Department."

"There are worse people out there. Speaking of which, you didn't get a visit from any of Baxter's boys in the last couple of days, did you?"

"Hell no."

"I didn't think so."

"What's with that?"

"Couple of his guys found my place. I asked Shelby and he swore he didn't tell anybody where I was." Caulder had stopped by the tattoo parlor on the way to the Alcove to find out if Shelby had told Baxter's men how to find him. Shelby did a fair job of convincing Caulder that the information had not come out of the tattoo parlor.

"And you think *I'd* rat you out?" Alvin asked, insulted.

"No. I just wanted to hear it from you direct. Sorry."

"It's okay. You gotta do what you gotta do."

"That leaves only one person."

"Dawson?"

Dawson was a bail bondsman and underworld connection extraordinaire. He was the third man trustworthy enough to know how to locate Ry Caulder.

"Have you seen Dawson lately?" Caulder asked.

"About a week ago. Stopped in for a drink. Didn't seem nervous or anything."

"I think they got to him recently. Maybe even this morning."

"Did they try to hit you?"

"That's the strange thing. They just wanted to talk. They could have gone through the channels and done it right, but they were in a hurry."

"A hurry like that can get a man killed."

"This is true."

They didn't say another word to each other until Alvin told Caulder to turn left onto a dirt road that was so overgrown with trees and brush that it was barely visible from Kanan Dume. They wound their way up the twisting dirt road, over a rickety bridge spanning the creek that ran along the mountainside. Fruit trees lined both sides of the road. The air smelled heavily of rotting citrus.

Alvin had been fidgeting in his seat for the bulk of the drive. His nervousness made Caulder feel heavy and light at the same time. It was humorous to think of Alvin being afraid of anything, but it was unsettling for Caulder to realize he would soon be encountering the source of that fear.

As he rounded a curve, Caulder saw a piece of something metallic reflect his headlights in the distance. An old Chevy van sat tucked away in a clearing behind a grove of trees to the left of the dirt road. He only got a glimpse of it so it was impossible to tell if it was an abandoned derelict or something stashed away deliberately. He considered investigating the vehicle, then decided against it. The business at hand was more pressing.

The dirt road went almost a mile up and around the mountains. Finally it fed into a circular, cobbled driveway leading up to Fredrickson's mansion and back.

"I can't believe you remembered how to get here," Caulder said.

"It's not exactly somethin' you forget," Alvin replied.

The light of the half-moon dimly illuminated Fredrickson's mansion, a huge, baronial monstrosity. Roughly hewn stone walls swept up to a long parapet. At both ends of the parapet there were turrets, replete with arrow loopholes. The architecture was right out of twelfth-century England.

The Santa Monica Mountains loomed darkly in the background. The house stood all by itself in a minivalley. No neighbors. Just a television broadcasting relay tower sitting up on a distant hill, small red lights twinkling in the night to warn off low-flying aircraft.

"I hate this place," Alvin said. "Gives me the creeps."

"It's just a house."

"Looks like Bela Lugosi's crib—but the worst part of it is, I know who *really* lives here."

Caulder decided to zone out Alvin's fear vibrations. They could only serve to jam him up if there was trouble.

On the way over, Caulder had selected a course of action. The direct approach. Right. Just go up to your old buddy, whom you now despise, ask him to his face if he's double-crossing his employer and if maybe he killed your uncle along the way. If he answers yes, pull out a piece and blow him away. It seemed like the logical course of action to take with Fredrickson. No need for cat-and-mouse games between friends. A long prep time used against a pro of Fredrickson's caliber would just increase Caulder's chances of being taken out himself.

Of course, for Alvin's sake, Caulder wouldn't actually kill Fredrickson at this first meeting. He didn't want to involve his friend any more than necessary. If Fredrickson's answers justified his death, Caulder would leave with Alvin, take him back to the city, then return to do the job in the early hours of the morning, when Fredrickson would be most vulnerable to attack. Even though Fredrickson would probably suspect that trouble was on the way, he might not expect such a quick turnaround period.

The entrance to the house was under a huge carriageway, a roofed area, open at both ends, supported by granite pillars. Caulder pulled up and parked under the carriageway. He looked at Alvin and noticed that the big man had a case of the shakes.

"You don't have to go in," Caulder said. "I can handle it."

"I'm sure as hell not staying out here."

Caulder nodded and said, "Let's go."

They got out and approached the massive front door. A huge knocker in the shape of a gargoyle's head occupied the center of the door. Caulder reached out and rapped the gargoyle three times. The retort of the knocker reverberated through the house loudly.

Nothing happened.

"Oops," Alvin said. "Not here, let's go."

"Someone's in there," Caulder said.

"I don't hear anything."

"I do."

"Shit."

"I left the key in the car. If there's trouble and you can make it out, don't wait for me."

"I'm not leaving you here."

"At least you'll have the option."

Caulder gave the door a push. It creaked open slowly. There would be no need to play with the locks. They entered the house and passed through the vestibule into a large hallway. Moonlight cast enough ambient illumination to reveal that the stone walls were covered with weapons of all shapes, sizes, and intentions.

"See? The guy's crazy," Alvin said.

They walked through the corridor looking at the weapons, an entire history of man's desire to slaughter man: from primitive clubs and spears to exquisitely manufactured crossbows and knives to supersophisticated machine guns and rocket launchers. All carefully mounted and strategically placed on the walls. Occasionally an ancient painting broke the monotony.

Caulder called out Fredrickson's name a few times. The only reply came in the form of Alvin's heavy breathing.

Turning to their left, they went down a short flight of stone steps into a large parlor.

Darkness filled the parlor. The drapes had been pulled across the floor-to-ceiling windows, cutting the moonlight by 80 percent. The room was vast, with a high-vaulted ceiling and a sunken floor. The walls were lined with sabers, muskets, dueling pistols, machine guns, antitank weapons—an arsenal for a time traveler. The five stone steps that led down to the floor were flanked on either side by Civil War–era cannons. A few pieces of antique furniture dotted the sparsely decorated room. A baby grand piano was the most modern item in the parlor and it looked at least sixty years old.

The two men moved through the dark room. They could make out very little detail, but Caulder's hearing and sense of smell had already told him everything he needed to know. They weren't alone in the parlor. Caulder wasn't sure exactly how many there were, but he knew he and Alvin were outnumbered. He said nothing, trying not to alarm Alvin prematurely. Caulder had to assume that the others in the room couldn't see Alvin and himself much better than he saw them. He stayed low and pretended he didn't know they were there. He was waiting for someone to make the first move.

With Alvin's next footstep there came a soft splashing sound. He looked down. A black pool of liquid on the floor shimmered faintly in a sliver of moonlight that escaped the heavy drapes.

Alvin whispered in a sickened tone, "I just stepped in something wet . . . and sticky."

A match fired up on the north side of the room and illuminated the lean, rugged face of Camilo Varga. The kind of man who could run a revolution or a drug empire, Varga had opted for the latter. He lit a fat cigar with his match and rotated it in his mouth to engineer an even draw.

Caulder immediately pulled the Glock 17 from his shoulder holster and aimed it between Varga's eyes.

Varga tossed the dead match to the floor and clapped his hands twice.

The overhead room lights came up, revealing that Caulder and Alvin were surrounded by eleven tough-as-nails-looking Colombians, nine men and two women, holding a variety of weapons, from machetes to Ingram Mac 10 submachine pistols.

Caulder and Alvin looked at the hostile faces surrounding them and then back at each other.

"This is the last time I go anywhere with you," Alvin said dryly to Caulder. He seemed to be taking this more calmly than he did the prospect of encountering Fredrickson again.

Varga pointed at a wooden chest to the right of a large fireplace. "Who are you and what do you have to do with *that?*" he demanded.

One of the Colombians walked over to the chest and opened it, revealing the mutilated remains of a man. He had been quite literally torn to bits.

Alvin looked down at the black liquid that flowed out of the chest to form a puddle around his feet. It was blood. *A lot* of blood.

"Shit, I had a feeling that's what that was," Alvin deadpanned.

Caulder stared at Varga, keeping the gun trained squarely between his eyes. If Caulder was going to die, he'd make sure to take Varga with him.

"Looks like the same kind of mess you left in Ensenada," Caulder hissed, thinking about his dead uncle, about how Paul Shepfield and thirteen other men had been turned into ground meat by an army of savages. The wounds on the men in the warehouse were not unlike those on the dead man in the chest.

"What are you talking about, *pendejo?*" Varga's curiosity sounded genuine.

"Word on the street is that you and Fredrickson are working together to wipe out Baxter's operation."

Varga snorted. "Fredrickson working for *us?* We came here to *kill* him. The man you see *there,* in the box, worked for me. Señor Fredrickson murdered him. We have come here to put Señor Fredrickson in a box of his own. Now tell us who you are and why you are here."

"We came to find Fredrickson as well," Caulder said.

"You are friends of Señor Fredrickson?" Varga asked.

"Far from it," Caulder responded. He lowered his pistol in a vain play for Varga's confidence. If he could find a way to defuse the situation, he and Alvin might get out of it alive.

That move was exactly what Varga had been waiting for. Varga produced a .44 Ruger Blackhawk from his lap and aimed it at Ry Caulder, the fear of catching the first shot of the exchange finally free from his thoughts. "I don't believe you," he said matter-of-factly. "I think you are his partner. Now my men will do to you what you and Señor Fredrickson did to their brother."

The three men to the left of Caulder tapped thirty-inch machetes against their palms with anticipation.

Three more Colombians, standing on the other side of some furniture from Alvin, slowly drew similar weapons from sheaths on their belts and grinned at him.

Alvin studied the situation carefully and said, "Fuuuuuuck."

Caulder considered opening fire on Varga, but Varga had the draw on him. Caulder would probably lose the shoot-out. His pistol carried a large clip, one of the largest standard clips available for a pistol—seventeen rounds—which would be more than enough to kill everyone in the room if they would just hold still for a minute or so. A very unlikely prospect. He had to bank on the Colombians' desire for eye-for-an-eye revenge and hope that the men with the machetes would be the first wave of attack. During the fracas Caulder might be able to get a bead on Varga and surprise him with sudden death.

Varga made a small gesture with his hand. The men with the machetes swung into action.

Caulder jumped back, raised his pistol, and fired, point-blank, into the first Colombian's face. The report from the pistol echoed throughout the room like cannon fire. The man instinctively reached for his face before realizing that most of his brain was gone. He was dead before he hit the floor.

The second Colombian lashed out with his machete, striking the barrel of Caulder's gun, knocking it out of his hand. Caulder stepped in on the Colombian and brought his elbow up into the bridge of the man's nose, sending bone fragments into his brain. The man collapsed on the floor.

The third Colombian dove forward toward Caulder, swiping at him with the machete. Caulder sidestepped and got the man in a headlock, punching him repeatedly in the face, but the Colombian was tough and held on to both consciousness and Caulder's rib cage, which he attempted to crush.

Caulder looked over at Alvin, who appeared to be too stunned to move. The initial attacks had focused on Caulder because of his closer proximity and the fact that Alvin had not produced a weapon yet.

"How 'bout a hand?" Caulder gasped. He could feel his rib cage starting to give.

Two of the Colombians behind Alvin came flying over an art deco chaise longue, screaming and waving their machetes, which only served to startle the big man out of his daze.

Alvin drew the .357 Colt from his back pocket, grabbed the first Colombian in midair with one hand, and fired the pistol into his stomach with the other. He smashed the man down into the middle of an antique table, but as this happened the man's loose shirt tangled around the Colt, wresting it from Alvin's grip and flinging it onto the floor a few feet away. Alvin, ever the adept improviser, scooped up the man's machete and imbedded it deep into the gut of the second Colombian, who stood impaled, unable to move.

A big guy with a shaved head took advantage of Alvin's turned back and cut a slice out of his shoulder.

Enraged, Alvin jerked the machete out of the impaled Colombian's stomach, spun, and neatly decapitated the bald man. Alvin found himself caught between two gushers of blood.

Once he got started Alvin was a force to be reckoned with.

Caulder continued struggling with the Colombian he had in a headlock. The guy was much stronger than he looked. The tighter Caulder squeezed the man's windpipe, the harder the man squeezed Caulder's rib cage, making it more and more difficult for Caulder to breathe. Realizing he wasn't going to win a contest of sheer strength, Caulder brought his knee up into the man's face, stunning him, then delivered a crushing elbow to the back of his neck, putting him out permanently. Caulder dropped to all fours next to the unconscious Colombian, trying to catch his breath.

The violence in the room had taken less than thirty seconds.

Alvin stepped over two inert bodies and helped Caulder to his feet.

The five remaining Colombians gathered around Varga on the other side of the room. The two women stood guard directly on either side of him. None of them carried machetes. They had submachine guns. And their boss looked very unhappy.

Caulder and Alvin stood in the middle of the room, drenched in blood and surrounded by the dead and the dying.

Caulder looked at Alvin's profusely bleeding shoulder wound. Alvin noted Caulder's concern, flexed his weapon arm, and shrugged. He was still ready and rarin' to go, machete and all.

Varga had wanted these two men to die properly, the way he imagined they had killed *his* man, but he had underestimated the gringos and now he was forced to fall back on technology. He signaled to his people and said, softly, *"Mátenlos."*

Both Caulder and Alvin knew enough Spanish to realize Varga

had said, "Kill them." They began to move in opposite directions immediately.

Spent brass danced across the floor and the smell of burned gunpowder filled the room as the five Colombians opened fire with their submachine guns.

Alvin grabbed the baby grand piano and tipped it up onto its side for cover. A hail of bullets created a horrible cacophony of plucked strings and splintered wood.

Caulder sprinted for the southernmost door in the room. A line of bullets chased along the wall behind him. Some made sparks off the ancient weapons hanging there. Caulder dove up the stairs and through the doorway into the hall, inches ahead of the line of death.

Varga motioned for one of his men, an older, seasoned-looking vet, to go after Caulder. "Gabriel, he's yours," Varga yelled in Spanish over the din of the gunfire.

Gabriel crossed the room fearlessly and disappeared into the hallway.

The other Colombians continued to riddle the piano with bullets. Alvin held on to the back of the piano tightly, trying to wait out the metal storm. From the Colombians' vantage point, Alvin could not be seen behind the baby grand.

Varga motioned for his people to stop firing and waved the remaining two men forward. They moved cautiously toward the bullet-ridden piano. They didn't know what kind of weaponry Alvin might be concealing. The women stayed next to Varga to protect him.

Alvin pressed even more tightly against the bottom of the piano, trying not to breathe. Sweat was now working hard to dilute the blood that covered his body. The Colombians drew closer. Alvin saw the .357 Colt glistening on the floor a few feet away. Getting to it without being killed would be almost impossible. He had nothing but the machete with which to defend himself. Not much against a Mac 10 unless you got *very* close. He was hopelessly outnumbered and outgunned.

Suddenly a sound made the Colombians freeze in their tracks. It emanated from the hallway; a hideous rasping, gagging, choking sound that signaled either Gabriel's victory or his death.

"Gabriel?" Varga called out. Everyone in the room looked at the doorway.

Gabriel staggered into the parlor. An idiot's grin on his face competed with a dark red smile slit across his throat.

Gabriel fell forward onto the floor, revealing Ry Caulder standing in the doorway behind him. Caulder held a LAWS rocket launcher, a light antitank weapon that fires a rocket used primarily to pierce heavy armor, balanced on his shoulder. Fired in this room, everyone, probably even Caulder, would be incinerated. Caulder aimed the rocket launcher at Varga and his associates.

"Fly or fry," Caulder said sternly.

Varga and his people stared with disbelief at Caulder.

Alvin sighed with relief. The Colombians were only a few feet away from having a clear shot at him.

"I suggest you leave," Caulder told the Colombians.

"You are not going to kill us?" Varga asked. Caulder could easily pull the trigger, disintegrating the room. Varga himself would not have hesitated if the roles were reversed, even at the risk of his own safety.

"Not unless you force me," Caulder said.

"What game do you play, *hijo de puta?*" Varga snarled with a level of contempt that was impressive.

"We came to see Fredrickson. Your life doesn't interest me, one way or the other. Drop your weapons and back out of the room."

The four remaining Colombians looked at Varga for instructions.

"We lay our weapons down for no one," Varga said.

Caulder flipped a button on the side of the rocket launcher, arming the weapon. "Then you die," he said calmly, without emotion.

Caulder took careful aim through the rocket launcher sight, centering it on Camilo Varga.

Varga, his people, and now even Alvin became very nervous.

"You will not do it," Varga said. "You will not kill your friend."

"He's not a friend. He's an *employee.*"

This broke Varga's calm facade. To him, there was a big difference between a friend and an employee. A friend you would die for. An employee must die for you. Workers were property, and generally low-priced property at that. Varga now believed that the gringo was capable of blowing them all away.

Varga looked at Caulder, calculating. There was still Fredrickson to deal with. It would be hard to get revenge from the grave.

"We will do as you say," Varga said, stunning his fellow Colombians.

Varga motioned for his people to lay down their guns. They could not believe that he was backing down. Secretly each of them felt relieved, but Varga's stature in their hearts dwindled slightly nevertheless. They carefully placed their weapons on the floor.

Alvin took his first breath in two minutes. Caulder had pulled it off.

"Go," Caulder commanded.

The Colombians began to back out of the room, still not exactly sure what to do. They were not used to retreating. They *were* used to being on either end of a double cross. They expected Caulder to blow them away at any moment.

"Move faster," Caulder snapped.

Alvin stepped out from behind the piano, waving his bloody machete, suddenly filled with new confidence. "Yeah . . . Get the fuck out of here!" he yelled. He scooped up the Colt and fired it once over their heads for effect.

Plaster and wood from the ceiling rained down on the frightened Colombians, who turned and ran through the northern doorway, out of the room. Caulder stepped back into the hallway and followed their progress with the rocket launcher until they were through the vestibule and out the front door.

Alvin glared at Caulder. "Absolutely *the* last time I go anywhere with you!" he reiterated, only half joking.

Dawn had yet to break when the Buick pulled up in front of Alvin's Alcove. The two men hadn't said a word to each other during the entire drive back to the city.

Alvin's wounds weren't as severe as they had first thought, so he decided to skip the hospital. There would be too many hard questions there.

Caulder found some electrical tape in Fredrickson's kitchen and used it to temporarily close Alvin's wounds. They both knew a doctor in town who prided himself on his apathy toward police reports. Alvin would visit him in the morning for some of the old S&S—sterilization and stitches.

They left the dead Colombians for Fredrickson to deal with. It was his fault that they had been there in the first place. Caulder and Alvin had probably saved his life. They had, however, done their best to eradicate all other traces of their own presence: fingerprints, footprints, shell casings, etc., in the unlikely event that the police ever arrived. The house was isolated enough for the small war that had taken place to have escaped notice. Fredrickson certainly wouldn't report the murders. He would find a way to dispose of the bodies. And why not? Caulder and Alvin had contributed their services at no charge. The least Fredrickson could do was clean up.

Caulder and Alvin looked up at the darkened bar. It had been closed for hours. Even the neon had gone to sleep for the night.

Alvin got out of the car. "Something's very screwy about this whole setup, partner," he said.

Caulder nodded.

"What next?" Alvin asked.

"I know his habits; I'll find him."

"I'd offer to come along, but . . ."

"I understand."

Alvin hesitated a second. "Ry, you didn't really mean that shit about me just being an employee, did you?"

Caulder looked at him like he had asked a crazy question. "Course not," he said.

Alvin smiled.

Caulder revved the Skylark's engine and pulled away.

"Be careful, bro," Alvin hollered, but Caulder was long gone.

Alvin turned and walked into the Alcove. It had been a weird night, but not the weirdest in his life. Although the last time he could remember a body count that high was back in the war. It would take half a bottle of Everclear to cleanse his thoughts of the night's events, but that was just fine. After all, Alvin *did* own a bar.

twelve

The first orange glows of early dawn were spreading on the horizon by the time Caulder got to the firing range just outside the city limits. A large, ominous sign to one side of the road leading up to the gate announced that Survivalists, Incorporated owned the land. A high chain-link fence reinforced the message. One of the few outdoor shooting ranges in Los Angeles County not owned by the police, the range had a very exclusive and very expensive reputation. Membership was extremely selective.

Caulder pulled up to the gate. He wound his window down and inserted a plastic membership card into a small metal box standing to the left of the driveway. The gate opened slowly.

Only three vehicles occupied the parking lot in front of the clubhouse: a stretch limousine, a Corvette, and a Jeep. Caulder pulled around behind the clubhouse and parked between two large delivery trucks near the service entrance. It might be only a hunch on his part that Fredrickson would be at the club for some early-morning target practice, but Caulder didn't want his car to be parked in plain sight, regardless. After the encounter with the

Colombians Caulder had had second thoughts about the head-on approach. Fredrickson was obviously in the middle of something more complex than Baxter understood or had communicated. Caulder decided to slow down and do things properly. He wanted to get a look at his man from a distance and see what he was up to before confronting him face-to-face.

Survivalists, Incorporated was all but deserted. The night manager was half-asleep at his desk. No one else was about. Caulder went to the roof of the clubhouse and looked out over the range. Soon the early-morning risers would fill the landscape down below.

Fredrickson had introduced Caulder to the club over a decade ago. Caulder had found it to be a good place for information and contacts during its active hours and for quiet, meditative gunplay in the early morning. Fredrickson and Caulder would meet there often in friendlier times to discuss "business" and hone their shooting skills.

The clubhouse sat at one end of the firing range. Stretching out in front of it, an expanse of grass led to a series of cardboard human targets sixty to one hundred yards away. Directly beneath Caulder ran a walkway where the shooters would stand to fire at the targets. Thick concrete dividers safely separated the shooters from one another.

Caulder scanned the range. He found it empty, save for a lone figure in the shadows at the far end of the walkway.

The figure was kneeling on the ground, crouched over a weapon, making some kind of adjustment. After a few moments the figure stood erect and fired at a target in the distance. The figure moved casually along the walkway, turning and firing between the dividers at each target as he passed them. On each turn there was a muffled *pop*, the sound of a silenced shot.

Caulder looked through one of several observation scopes positioned on the roof and examined the targets. Even in the blue haze of early-morning light he could see that each target had been neatly punctured with one shot through the center of the forehead. Caulder turned the scope and looked down at the approaching figure.

Fredrickson. Tall, slim, well built, in his mid-to-late fifties. Prominent cheekbones highlighted a thick scar on the right side of his face. Silver hair, slicked back off his forehead, revealed a widow's peak. His skin looked tight, as if it had been wrapped around his bones. Muscle showed where other men his age would have had wrinkled, dangling flesh. His posture and walk were Germanic in their precision. He wore a light-colored windbreaker, a white cotton shirt, tan chinos, and black Nikes.

Caulder couldn't believe his good fortune. He had found his man on his very first stop. It seemed *too* easy. Fredrickson wasn't on the lam. He wasn't hiding from anyone. He was right out in the open, going about his normal business, seemingly without a care in the world.

Fredrickson fired another shot. Another target was neatly punctured through the forehead.

Fredrickson now stood almost directly below Caulder. He seemed to sense something and began to look up. Caulder dropped behind the wall, below eye level. When he looked over the wall again, Fredrickson was gone.

Caulder made his way back to his car and pulled out just in time to see a black Mercedes stretch limousine leaving the compound. Caulder followed the Mercedes at a discreet distance. They were heading into town.

The black Mercedes stopped outside Chuck's Steak House on Hollywood Boulevard. A sign out front proudly announced that Chuck's never closed. Not as long as the health department got their payoffs on time.

Caulder pulled the Buick to a halt on a side street across the way from Chuck's. He removed a pair of high-powered binoculars from the glove compartment and hunkered low in his seat to try to watch Fredrickson without being spotted.

Hollywood Boulevard was slowly waking up. A street-cleaning machine rolled along, leaving a trail of flattened wet trash in its wake. A bag lady rummaged through a garbage can, looking for breakfast. An early-morning drunk entered a bar called the Frolic Room for first call. Stray people and animals wandered up and down the wide city street. Survivors of another night in Hollywood. The victorious.

A chauffeur got out of the limousine. A tall blond man of apparently Swedish descent, he wore a name tag on his chest that read Dove. He opened the rear passenger side door for Fredrickson. Dove kept his head tilted toward the ground, avoiding eye contact with his employer as he climbed out of the limo.

Fredrickson entered Chuck's Steak House. An aged hostess guided him to a padded red vinyl booth directly in front of a large plate glass window. Caulder had eaten in this place with Fredrickson on more than one occasion in the old days. He never understood the appeal. The checkerboard tablecloths were covered with grease stains. The silverware didn't match and the creamers were cow figures that vomited milk. It was dirty and tacky and Fredrickson loved it. He said it was very American.

Fredrickson sat down in the booth and immediately motioned to a waiter. The waiter tried to hand Fredrickson a menu but Fredrickson waved it away and said something that seemed to puzzle the man. The waiter shook his head and left for the kitchen.

Fredrickson polished his knife and fork with a napkin, then held the silverware up to the light, looking for spots. Satisfied, he reached for a clean napkin and tucked it under his chin.

Fredrickson turned to the window and looked directly, yet absently, at Caulder's car parked far in the distance. Fredrickson couldn't possibly see Caulder with his bare eyes, but it made Caulder nervous nonetheless. Fredrickson just kept staring at him through the plate glass window of the restaurant, smiling and tapping his fingers on the tabletop.

Caulder crouched even lower in the car, hoping Fredrickson hadn't actually spotted him. He couldn't tell if Fredrickson was looking *at* him or merely through him at a point in infinity. Fredrickson had a dazed, bored look on his face. Certainly not the look of a man who had discovered he was being followed, or at least not the look of someone who cared about such news.

The waiter returned to Fredrickson's table with a large, covered tray. He set the tray in front of Fredrickson and looked away as he removed the lid, revealing a huge slab of dripping, half-cooked beef. Fredrickson dabbed gracefully at the sides of his mouth with his napkin and then tore into the meat with his teeth, shaking it, ripping and shredding the slab, splattering blood everywhere. Fredrickson devoured the thing in less than two minutes.

Caulder watched in astonishment. He had dined with Fredrickson often and had never witnessed anything remotely like this.

The waiter looked around desperately for an escape route. This was too much for him at 7 A.M., even in Hollywood. Fredrickson wiped his mouth with the napkin, then crooked his finger and, with a voracious grin, summoned for the man again. He was still hungry.

The waiter covered his mouth and ran toward the kitchen, not quite making it before his own breakfast came up, spurting from between his fingers as he went through the spinning doorway.

Fredrickson sat staring at the kitchen door for a few moments, as though hoping the waiter would return; then he stood up, dropped some money on the table, and exited Chuck's Steak House.

The chauffeur waited with the limo door open and his eyes pointed at the ground. Fredrickson slid into the back of the car and they were off.

Caulder started the Buick and thought about what Alvin had said when he dropped him off a few hours earlier. Something was, indeed, very screwy about this whole setup.

* * *

Caulder followed the Mercedes out to Malibu. Once they were on Kanan Dume Road, he let the limo get far ahead of him. He knew Fredrickson's destination and he didn't want to be spotted on the sparsely trafficked road leading to Fredrickson's home.

When Caulder reached the dirt road he turned, went over the rickety bridge, and then found the trail that led to the clearing where he had spotted the Colombians' van parked the night before. The van was gone. Caulder went a bit deeper into the grove of trees and parked. He got out and looked around. Dozens of fresh footprints leading to and from the mansion covered the ground.

Caulder followed the tracks to a trail through the brush and found a shortcut up the mountain to Fredrickson's mansion. He wanted to see what the reaction was going to be when the dead Colombians were found in the parlor. When Caulder reached the edge of the grove he saw that the limousine was parked in the middle of the circular drive leading to the mansion. The driver had not made the final curve to go under the carriageway. From this angle Caulder could only see the rear of the car. He hunkered behind a lemon tree and watched the limo. The engine was still running, but no movement could be seen behind the opaque windows.

After about five minutes the chauffeur got out and opened Fredrickson's door. Fredrickson climbed out and said something to the driver, who listened intently, never raising his eyes from the ground. The Swede got behind the wheel, drove the rest of the circular drive through the carriageway, and headed back down the dirt road.

Fredrickson stood silently in front of the mansion and stared at it for a few minutes, contemplating something, and then, as if he had reached a sudden decision, he turned and walked down the driveway away from the house.

Fredrickson stopped and peered over the edge of the driveway into a deep gully. Suddenly he froze. His pupils dilated and his nostrils flared. He appeared to be smelling something on the air. A smile of recognition played on his lips as he seemed to identify the scent; then he started to make his way down the mountainside.

Caulder went to the edge of the gully a few moments later and looked down, crouching low on the ridge to avoid being seen. He watched Fredrickson scramble and claw his way quickly down the steep hillside. Fredrickson seemed extremely agile for a man of his age. He reached the bottom of the gully and walked along a narrow trail to a small cave dug out of the opposing mountainside.

Fredrickson lifted some branches off the ground, revealing a gigantic steel bear trap that had been set in front of the mouth of the cave. Using one of the thicker branches, Fredrickson sprung the trap. The branch practically exploded. The effect on a human limb would be devastating.

Once on the cave side of the trap, Fredrickson wrestled with the contraption. He pulled the rusty metal jaws back and inserted the central plate into its groove, securing the mechanism. Then he covered the trap with branches and brush again and disappeared into the cave. It would be almost impossible for anyone to enter or exit the cave without springing the trap first.

Caulder stared down at the cave, baffled. It occurred to him that he didn't know Fredrickson at all. They had been "friends" for over twenty years before their falling-out, but Caulder had never really *known* Fredrickson, never really understood the man. Caulder was a very private person, but Fredrickson made Caulder look like a publicity hound by comparison. In conversation he said nothing of his past, his heritage, how he started in the business, or anything else of a private nature. Caulder didn't even know what country Fredrickson came from. He suspected Germany or Austria, but he'd never been sure. Fredrickson lived in the now and shared nothing with his acquaintances, no matter how long or how well he knew them.

Caulder had tried to emulate Fredrickson's "professionalism," but part of him stayed human. Vulnerable. Caulder tried to blanket that part of himself, but lately it had been poking through, unsettling him, causing him to make errors in judgment he wouldn't have made in younger, cooler days.

The hairs on the back of Caulder's neck were on end. Something was wrong all the way down the line on this one. Every instinct in his body cried out for him to leave. Screw the money Baxter owed him. He had enough stashed away already. So what if his uncle had been killed? The man knew the risks involved in what he was doing. He had played a tough game and lost. That was his problem, not Ry Caulder's. Dead was dead.

Revenge was not sufficient reason for Caulder to put his neck on the line. He knew he should just get in the Buick and blow out of this place. Out of town. Out of the whole damn country.

Caulder marched back down the dusty road. The day was already turning into a scorcher. He could smell a dead snake cooking in the sun somewhere nearby. He entered the grove of trees and opened the door of his car. He stopped for a minute to listen to the cicadas. He didn't get to hear sounds like that in the city. Strange, he thought, how nature still managed to hold her own so close to all the steel and concrete. Perhaps the facade of civilization wasn't going to win the battle against nature that the environmentalists constantly whined about. Caulder felt certain that Mother Nature still had a few tricks up her sleeve.

Caulder lowered himself into the car, put the key in the ignition, and turned it with great deliberation. The Buick rumbled to life. He revved the engine, no longer concerned with whether or not he was discovered. He was going home. It was over.

And then he did something that he realized could be the biggest mistake of his life. He reached back up and turned the key to the off position. The engine sputtered and grew silent. Caulder sat in the car and waited. He waited for his destiny.

thirteen

Stephanie Taylor was frying chicken when the knock came at the door. She had already left a plate of it in front of Ry Caulder's door with a nasty note attached basically telling him to fuck off and stay out of their lives, so she figured it was Ry coming over to make peace. That was the true intention of the note, whether she wanted to admit to it or not. She didn't want Ry out of her life. Not really. But she couldn't allow the situation to remain as it was. Something had to give. If *he* wasn't going to change tactics, then *she* would have to take the initiative. Maybe if she told him to go away he would realize what he was losing.

She knew the risk she took, putting pressure on a guy like Ry Caulder, but she figured she'd rather lose him now than continue pining like some pathetic old maid. She had to know if there was any possibility of a future for them, and if there wasn't, then it would be time to move on.

When she opened the door she found two men dressed in rumpled, sweat-soaked suits, holding badges. *Busted,* she immediately thought. *Now I will go to jail and they are going to take my son away.* She tried to stay calm, tried to hold back the terror and the heartbreak. She couldn't say anything for fear of bursting into tears. One of the men spoke, the tall one with the mole on his lip.

"Ms. Brandt?"

Stephanie stared at him, her mind racing, not knowing what to say. What had Rosa told her to do if this happened? Yes. Volunteer *no* information. Make them work for it all. They may not have you cold. They may not have you at all. Just *answer* them. Say *something*, for God's sake.

"What?" she stuttered.

"Are you Stephanie Brandt?" the man with the mole said.

"Uh . . . yes." Stephanie was jarred. Brandt *was* the last name on her California ID card, the phony one that had cost her fifty dollars down on Olvera Street. It was the name she had been living and working under since she arrived in Los Angeles. If they were using that name, maybe they *didn't* have her after all.

"I'm Detective March and this is Detective Hayworth."

"Afternoon, ma'am," the shorter man said. He had curly hair that was thinning on top. His underarms were five shades darker than the rest of his suit.

"We're with the LAPD Robbery-Homicide Division," Detective March continued. "We were wondering if we could ask you a few questions."

"Homicide?" Stephanie said with horror. "Who's dead?"

"A man named Peter Hertzberg," March said.

"Mr. Hertzberg? The attorney? Oh my God!"

March and Hayworth looked at each other, measuring the sincerity of Stephanie's reaction.

"May we come in, Ms. Brandt?"

"Oh, yes, yes, I'm sorry. Please come in." Stephanie stepped aside, still reeling from the news of Hertzberg's death.

The detectives put their IDs back in their pockets and entered the apartment.

"I think something's burning," Hayworth said.

The sudden squeal of the smoke alarm snapped Stephanie out of her daze. "Oh, no, the chicken! I'll be right back."

Stephanie ran into the kitchen and turned off the burner. She pulled the skillet off the stove and set it in the sink, running cold water next to it to take some of the heat off the bottom of the pan. She held herself up against the sink and caught her breath. They *didn't* have her. Not yet. Not for sure anyway. This was about something completely different. She tried to stop shaking and then she heard Jason's voice in the living room over the sound of the smoke alarm. He was telling the cops how to get the thing to stop shrieking.

Stephanie entered the living room to find both detectives frantically waving magazines at the bottom of the smoke alarm. "Faster! Faster!" Jason was commanding.

The alarm went silent and Stephanie opened the window wider to provide better ventilation.

"Sorry about that," she said to the cops.

"We're the ones that should apologize," March said. "I hope dinner isn't ruined."

"It's a little burned, but it's edible."

"I like it burned," Jason said.

"I know, honey," Stephanie replied. "You'll *love* this. Why don't you go fix yourself a plate and eat in the bedroom? Mommy's got to talk to these nice men."

"Awwww, Mom . . ." It was the same old story. Adults in the place, the kid is sent to solitary.

"C'mon, baby," Stephanie said. "Be careful, the pan's still hot."

Jason reluctantly moved into the kitchen and began rummaging for his dinner.

March and Hayworth sat down on Stephanie's plaid couch. Stephanie took a seat in an oversize cotton chair across from them. She tried to look comfortable.

"How well did you know Mr. Hertzberg?" March asked, trying to get the interview back on track.

"Oh, God, I almost forgot. . . . Mr. Hertzberg? You said Mr. Hertzberg is *dead?*"

"That's right, ma'am."

"How? What happened?"

"That's confidential at the moment, Ms. Brandt. It *may* have been an accident, but the circumstances were odd enough to warrant an investigation."

"I can't believe it. I just saw Mr. Hertzberg day before yesterday. He was right here in this apartment as alive as you or I."

March and Hayworth shared another look.

"What was your business with Mr. Hertzberg?" Hayworth asked.

"He, um, well, that's confidential, isn't it?"

"Not anymore. We have a possible murder case. You can either talk to us here, or we can go down to the station and discuss it officially."

"That won't be necessary." Her mind was racing, trying to come up with a likely alternative to the truth. "See, I'm just a little embarrassed about my business with Mr. Hertzberg."

Hayworth and March leaned forward involuntarily.

"I wouldn't want you to think I was one of those kinds of people," Stephanie continued. "You know, the kind that sues for every little thing."

"Could you elaborate?" March said.

"I fell on the stairs in front of the apartment building a few months ago. You probably saw they're all chipped and cracked down there. I hurt my back and I haven't been able to work without pain. I'm a freelance seamstress, you see, and I have to sit up straight most of the day. After a while it begins to really get to me. Anyway, I was discussing the possibility of suing the owners of the building with Mr. Hertzberg."

"What was his advice?" Hayworth asked.

"He sounded interested in the case."

"Why didn't you meet him at his office?" March asked.

"He didn't want me to travel unnecessarily."

Hayworth pulled a steno pad from his jacket pocket and referred to some notes. Electricity crawled up and down Stephanie's spine.

"Was there any trouble while Mr. Hertzberg was in this apartment?" Hayworth asked.

Stephanie felt her face flush with blood. She couldn't speak.

"What happened?" March asked.

"I'm so embarrassed." *Stay as close to the truth as you can, without implicating yourself,* she thought.

"Just tell us the truth. There's nothing we haven't heard. We're cops."

"Mr. Hertzberg tried to force himself on me." Stephanie scratched at the scar on her wrist. "But I didn't *kill* him, for God's sake."

March laughed. "Of course you didn't. No one said anything like that. We're just tracking Hertzberg's last hours and trying to dig up some leads. *You* were the last meeting in his appointment book, but we know he spent the rest of the night at the Lucky Thirteen getting plastered before he went home. He did a lot of talking at the bar and we're just seeing if there's anything to what he had to say."

They didn't have her. All she had to do was stay calm and it would be over.

"Who's the guy?" Hayworth interjected.

"What?" Stephanie asked. They meant Ry. *They were trying to implicate Ry.*

"Who's the guy? The guy that messed with Hertzberg when he was here?"

"Oh, just a neighbor or someone visiting a neighbor, I guess. I never saw him before that afternoon. We must've been making so much noise that he heard us out in the hall. I'm glad he did.

He saved my neck. If you talk to him, thank him again for me."

"This man who 'saved' you," March continued. "Was he violent with Hertzberg?"

"No. If anything, he was **very** restrained. He merely asked Mr. Hertzberg to leave and they both left. That was the last I saw of either of them."

"Can you describe the man?"

"Oh, he was about your height, brown hair, okay-looking but nothing special. I really don't remember. He was only here a few minutes."

"And you don't know which apartment he's in?"

"Like I said, I'm not even sure he lives here. He was probably just visiting. I'd never seen him before and I know most of the neighbors by sight. Maybe he's new."

March and Hayworth looked at each other again. Hayworth folded his notebook and put it away. The two men stood up.

"Thank you for your cooperation, Ms. Brandt. If you have anything else to add this is my number at the shop." March handed Stephanie a business card with the address and phone number of the LAPD Robbery-Homicide Division.

"Thank you," Stephanie said weakly.

"We may want to ask you more questions in the future."

"Sure. Whatever you want. Poor Mr. Hertzberg."

"Mmm-hmm," Hayworth muttered.

March opened the front door.

"See you soon," March said to Stephanie with a smile.

Stephanie smiled back and said, "See you." She closed the door behind the two detectives and put her hand over her heart to stop it from racing.

Outside the apartment, March and Hayworth looked at the door, studying the stress fractures that Ry Caulder's size twelve boot had put there.

"Strong guy," March whispered.

"This is bullshit," Hayworth whispered back. "The drunk fucker fell and strangled himself."

"Maybe."

March looked down the hall and spotted the plate sitting on the floor in front of Caulder's apartment across the way. They walked the fifteen feet and looked down at the plate of cold chicken with the nasty note attached to it from Stephanie to Ry Caulder.

"What do you make of it?" Hayworth asked.

"Trouble in paradise."

fourteen

As the day progressed, Ry Caulder realized he had picked up a cold in his travels. Probably from the airplane air-conditioning on the way in from Baltimore. Caulder was susceptible to drafts; his lungs were badly scarred, the result of a pneumonia he had suffered when he was a child. He had almost died. Sometimes a simple cold would come on him and lay him out for a month. Sometimes it would be worse.

He had been so busy that he hadn't noticed just how bad he felt until he had time to relax while waiting in the grove of trees. He pulled a medicated inhaler out of the glove compartment and took a couple of hits. He felt better, but the glands in his neck were beginning to swell. This was going to be a bad one. Maybe Nate Daniels *would* end up killing him after all.

Caulder tried to sleep throughout the day, but always with one eye open. He didn't want Fredrickson slipping away from him. A brief rain fell at about four. Just enough to get a light steam out of the ground and increase the humidity. As the sun started to dip in the sky Caulder got restless and decided to take a look around the grounds. He stayed close enough to the dirt road to be able to hear any vehicle that came along.

Caulder wandered among the wild fruit trees and dried scrub. The land appeared to have been a thriving, if eclectic, orchard long ago. But now it had grown wild. Dead brown trees mingled among the green, living specimens. Orange, lemon, and grapefruit trees fought it out with oaks, palms, and pines for the best turf. Nature was deciding now.

Caulder went down by the creek and studied the prints in the mud leading to the water. There were deer in the area and coyotes and raccoons. He came upon a wide patch of smeared dried mud that appeared to have blood mixed with it, as if something heavy had been dragged either to or from the stream. The tracks were thick around this area. Men had been here. Some wore shoes, some had bare feet. Their tracks mixed and mingled with the animal tracks, leaving all kinds of weird impressions.

Caulder made his way up the narrow trail to the mansion. The place was deadly quiet save for some crickets preparing for night. He couldn't tell if Fredrickson had ever entered the house. It appeared totally undisturbed.

Caulder ducked low behind an orange tree as the black Mercedes limousine came up the dirt road again. The limo pulled directly under the carriageway this time. Dove, the chauffeur, got out and opened the rear door of the vehicle, then stood there, waiting patiently. He stood for a very long time, not moving a muscle, barely breathing. He looked like a blond statue.

After ten minutes Fredrickson came out of the mansion, dressed in a full-length black kimono embroidered with dragons. There was no sign of concern on his face related to the dead Colombians. Dove averted his eyes as Fredrickson entered the waiting automobile. No words were exchanged. Dove closed the door gently, then went around to his side of the car, got into the driver's seat, put the car in gear, and headed down the long driveway.

Caulder turned and scrambled down the narrow path. He ran as fast as he could until he got to the Buick. Halfway down the hill he saw the limo make Kanan Dume Road and turn right. His breath was coming in gasps by the time he got the Buick started. He took a hit off the inhaler and pulled out of the orchard onto the dirt road. Soon he could see the Mercedes a half mile ahead of him on Kanan Dume. He kept his distance, though, losing the limo every now and then around the twisting, winding road that hugged the mountains, but eventually seeing the car again whenever the nature of the curves allowed.

Caulder wondered what Fredrickson had done when he saw the Colombians. Had he disposed of the bodies sometime during the day, or was he just going to leave them to rot in the parlor while he went out on the town?

They traveled along Kanan Dume Road to the ocean and then turned left onto Pacific Coast Highway. Caulder narrowed the distance. There were a lot more options for the limo now and traffic was thick.

To Caulder's right the golden orb of the setting sun glowed brilliantly over the metallic blue water of the Pacific Ocean. Atmospheric conditions were creating an odd phenomenon he had never seen in a sunset before. The sun was a bright orb that contained an internal intensity far greater than the amount of light it was casting. It was like a brilliant lightbulb that he could stare directly into without harming his eyes, a postcard or a picture of the sun in a magazine. But this was real, and it looked so close that he thought he could reach out and touch it. The orb hung suspended just above the water, a giant, greedy, glowing ball of energy that was slowly sinking into oblivion, taking its life-giving warmth elsewhere.

When they got to Sunset Boulevard they turned left and headed into the city. Night had fallen by the time they made it to the Strip, that part of Sunset Boulevard that trails out of Beverly Hills and feeds into Hollywood.

Darkness had transformed Sunset Strip into a ribbon of neon lights and flashy cars. Men and women clad in black leather strutted up and down the boulevard like the mutant offspring of a bizarre bovine/peacock experiment. Cops cruised the Strip slowly, checking out the meat. Overhead, expensive billboards hyped current and future movies and records. This night was no different from ten thousand others on the Strip. It was all very status quo.

Fredrickson's Mercedes prowled along Sunset Strip, a shark searching for prey. Traffic had snarled in front of the Roxy, a famous rock and roll joint. Dove stuck his head out the window to see what the commotion was all about. A band called Smashing Pumpkins had decided to drop by the club for a few cocktails and their limo was being mobbed by fans.

Dove shook his head and looked up into the sky. The brief rain that afternoon had rendered the sky unusually clear. A light breeze was blowing and the air smelled fresh. Silver-blue clouds passed in front of the half-moon, a bright chunk of yellow cut against the night sky.

Fredrickson's hand rapped on the window separating the back compartment from the front. Dove slid the window down. Fredrickson reached into the front of the vehicle and snapped his fingers. Dove handed him an electric razor and he withdrew his hand.

"Mr. Fredrickson," Dove said tentatively. "There seems to be someone following us."

"Don't worry about it." The voice in the back was rough and hostile.

Fredrickson plugged the razor into the cigarette lighter and the car was filled with a furious buzzing sound.

Dove tried hard not to look into the rearview mirror. At his very first meeting with Fredrickson, Dove had been given all the instructions he would ever receive, other than specific locations to drive to, and the rules had not changed to this day. Rule number one was the "no look" policy. Dove was never to have eye contact with his employer. He was not to stare, look, or even glance at his face. Ever. Fredrickson had told him that he hated to be watched. Once Fredrickson dropped something on his way out of the limo and Dove picked up the item and handed it to him. They made accidental eye contact and Fredrickson slapped Dove, hard. That was the last time Dove recalled actually seeing Fredrickson's face full on. He had not made the same mistake twice. But the suspense was unbearable. Every now and then he simply *had* to steal a glimpse.

After a few minutes the buzzing ceased and Fredrickson held up a hand mirror to examine his cleanly shaven face. Dove took a quick look out the corner of his eye into the rearview mirror.

Fredrickson's features had changed dramatically since Dove had last looked at him. His cheekbones were much more pronounced now and pulled the skin on his face even tighter than usual, making him look younger, but almost bestial. His mouth seemed larger and more toothy. His top lip curled under as he stroked his smooth cheeks and smiled into the hand mirror. It could not be called a warm smile. Saliva gathered involuntarily in the right corner of his mouth.

Dove looked away quickly as Fredrickson lowered the hand mirror. Dove could sense that he was being watched from the rear compartment. He began to get nervous. Luckily it was time for the nightly booze run.

Dove pulled the limo into the parking lot of Abraham's Liquor and parked. He got out and disappeared into the store, fully aware that Fredrickson was watching his every step.

Caulder drove past the liquor store and pulled over a block away. He stared at the Mercedes, waiting for some movement, something. If the limo pulled out and went in the opposite direction,

Caulder would have to make a U-turn on busy Sunset Boulevard.

A police car pulled up in front of Caulder's car, but Caulder was so busy watching the Mercedes over his shoulder that he failed to notice until the officer tapped on his window. Caulder looked at the cop with a start, then over at the fire hydrant he had parked next to and swore under his breath. He handed the cop the driver's license with his picture and Richard Alton's name and pulled a registration from the glove box that had the same name listed as the owner of the Buick.

Caulder had been taken totally by surprise. A sloppy, careless, potentially terminal mistake. He chalked it up to his cold, which seemed to worsen by the hour, and his fascination with Fredrickson's new lifestyle and peculiar behavior. Nevertheless, dead would be dead. No excuses would change that.

The chauffeur came out of the liquor store bearing a full case of Crown Royal. He opened the back door of the Mercedes and set the case on the floor in front of Fredrickson, careful not to make eye contact with his employer.

The Mercedes pulled out of the parking lot and drove past the Buick just as the cop was handing Caulder his ticket. Caulder's paperwork was in order and he didn't argue with the cop, he simply signed Richard Alton on the ticket and wished the cop a good night.

The stretch limo headed into Hollywood, where the Strip simply became Sunset Boulevard again. Here, furtive hookers lined the street. Many of the girls clustered in doorways, waiting to dart forward when a customer pulled over. The bolder ladies stood around the lit pay phones or lingered provocatively near the bus stops, ready to make a run for it if a john turned out to be a cop.

The Mercedes pulled up in front of two young hookers. The girls were conservatively dressed in identical outfits: white leather

jackets and thigh-high leather boots connected to red velvet hot
pants by black garter belts. These two knew that it paid to adver-
tise.

The rear passenger-side window of the limo lowered slowly
and a hand came out, a bony, muscular hand, covered with coarse
hair. The fingernails on the hand were abnormally long, sharp, and
clean. The hand beckoned to the two hookers.

The girls looked at each other with smiles, then approached
the limo. They spoke to the occupant for a few moments before
climbing in. The Mercedes pulled out slowly and continued its
predatory cruise through the area. Caulder followed as discreetly
as he could.

The only light in the back of the limo came from a small color
television. The volume was all the way up, blasting out the screams
and groans of a late-night horror movie, an early-seventies zom-
bie flick entitled *Children Shouldn't Play with Dead Things*. It was the
kind of movie that *TV Guide* described as "lurid."

Severely violating the "no look" rule, Dove glanced into the
rearview mirror and peered through the smoky glass partition. In
the eerie light from the television he could see Fredrickson making out with one of the hookers while the other girl tied off his free
arm with a tourniquet fashioned from one of her garters. The boss
was lighting up again. It was going to be another long night.

Dove adjusted his mirror down so that he would not be drawn
to the activity in the back of the vehicle, even by accident. He'd
need his concentration focused to navigate the hazardous city
streets while Fredrickson partied. Dove used his side mirror to
keep an eye on the traffic behind him. Every now and then he
would spot the headlights of the Buick trailing them. He occasionally wondered what the driver of the car wanted, but Fredrickson had told him not to worry about it. That was good enough for
Dove. He didn't like complications.

* * *

Caulder followed the Mercedes around town for the better part of three hours before the chauffeur finally pulled over to let the girls out. They hadn't stopped anywhere during the entire trip. They simply cruised slowly around Hollywood and its environs in ever-widening circles while Fredrickson and the girls did their thing in the smoke-filled seclusion of the limousine.

It had been quite monotonous for Caulder. The most exciting part of the night was a brief jaunt along Mulholland Drive during which the Buick had almost been hit head-on by a pair of racing MGs.

The Mercedes stopped at exactly the same spot where the girls had been picked up. The chauffeur got out and opened the rear door. The two hookers emerged from the limo. They were blasted to the gills and looked a trifle mauled, but not unhappy. Dove handed each of them three crisp hundred-dollar bills and got back into the car. The hookers watched the taillights disappear as the Mercedes sped away. Caulder pulled up and stared at the two girls. For some reason he was surprised to see that they were unharmed.

The hookers thought Caulder was another john and shook their heads. They'd had enough for tonight, thanks. The girls were strawberries, young hookers that trade their wares for drugs. They would have turned the tricks for the narcotics Fredrickson had given them alone, but the chauffeur had thrown cash into the deal as well, and their will to work had temporarily evaporated.

Caulder sped up, once again in pursuit of Fredrickson. The Mercedes headed into East L.A., through the badass barrios, deep into neighborhoods where even the cops were reluctant to venture. Caulder followed the limo past a group of winos circled around a trash can fire sharing bottles of screw-top wine, then by a cluster of gangbangers prepping for an assault on the hood. He noticed a family of six huddled together in a giant cardboard box that had once housed a refrigerator.

The black limo stopped in front of a row of abandoned buildings. Condemned by the city and converted to crack houses by the local entrepreneurs, their shattered windows stared in mute testament to just how bad things had gotten. Small firelights could be seen where the denizens of the night were firing up crack pipes in the houses. This shambling strip of buildings could have been Dresden in 1945. Except in Dresden there probably would have been intelligent life stirring within the bombed-out walls, fighting for survival, not begging for oblivion.

After a moment, two young men came out of one of the crack houses and approached the limo. One of them leaned down and spoke through the rear window of the Mercedes. The other man stood with his back to the car, keeping watch on the neighborhood.

Caulder parked behind the rusted hulk of an abandoned '84 Maserati Bi Turbo, picked clean by scavengers. He leaned his head out his window to see around the Maserati and watch the meeting at the limo's side in the distance.

A light mist was in the air, marine layer being blown in off the ocean some twenty miles away. The weather was turning out to be as unpredictable as Fredrickson himself.

After about a minute and a half, the man standing watch went back into the crack house. A few minutes of conversation later, Fredrickson handed something to the remaining man. Maybe money. Maybe a small package of dope. Caulder couldn't be certain. The man then returned to the crack house, but the limo didn't budge. They were waiting for something. But why would Fredrickson be buying drugs in a place like this? He certainly had access to the finest quality narcotics available on the market, wholesale. And if he was *selling*, why would he be selling in such small quantities? Maybe he had handed the man a sample of a larger shipment to be delivered later. But if that was the case, what was Fredrickson waiting for? His business here should be done.

The hairs on the back of Caulder's neck started tingling. He checked the rearview mirror on the door of the Buick and saw a young Latino about forty yards back, slowly making his way closer and closer to the car. The man had something cradled in his hand. Probably a Saturday night special, a cheap .38-caliber pistol.

Caulder knew how it would go down. Once close enough, the assailant would start running. He would fire into the car as he sped past, wounding or killing the occupant before the attack could even register. Then the assailant would return, finish off the job, and pick the victim clean of all cash and valuables. Even if it was a hit for hire, the robbery would take place to provide a legitimate motive for the police. Simple diversionary motives often took the edge off investigations.

Caulder didn't have a gun. He had disposed of the Glock after the conflict with the Colombians. It was a murder weapon now, not something he wanted to have on him if the police were to search him. He had wiped the gun clean, pulled the ammo clip, and dumped the weapon in a drainage ditch off Kanan Dume Road on the way back to Alvin's bar. He had not accessed another gun yet, but that did not mean he was weaponless.

Caulder eased his head back into the car slowly and reached down beside his seat for the Equalizer. The Equalizer was a three-foot length of sharpened pipe that had come in handy on more than one occasion when Caulder had to work close in and quiet without the use of a gun. The pipe fit perfectly into a section of steel along the base of the driver's seat. If the car was searched the weapon would probably not be found. If found, it would be a difficult piece of admissible evidence.

The moment Caulder's head disappeared into the car, the Latino began his run. Caulder had only a moment to wonder if this was one of the men that had been talking to Fredrickson or a new assailant of anonymous identity, a coincidental attack from someone who knew the Buick was out of its element. As the young man rapidly approached the car, Caulder thrust the Equalizer out the window at an angle. The speed with which the man was running served to fully impale him on the pipe and pole-vault him away from the side of the Buick. Caught a split second away from firing, the pistol discharged into the air, alerting the population that something was amiss.

Caulder lost control of the Equalizer on impact and he had to get out of the car to retrieve it. He knew this would blow his cover and allow Fredrickson a visual ID on him, but he didn't care. Caulder figured Fredrickson had been aware of his presence the entire night anyway. A moment after Caulder stepped out of his car the limo pulled away and disappeared down the street.

Either Fredrickson had been spooked by the gunshot, which was highly unlikely, or he wasn't waiting for anyone to come back out of the crack house after all. Perhaps he had been waiting to see what the outcome of the attack on Ry Caulder would be, which would verify his involvement with the incident. This would indicate that Fredrickson was aware of Caulder's presence and wanted to kill him. Or at least slow him down.

Caulder looked down at his assailant. The Latino couldn't have been older than seventeen or eighteen. Just a kid. Acne scars marked his face and he wore a yellow tank top that exposed needle marks on his muscular arms. His breathing was heavy and his eyes stared up at the foggy night sky. Steam drifted out of the pipe imbedded deep in his solar plexus. A wet, wheezing sound came from somewhere within his body, amplified by the hollowness of the pipe.

"Who ordered you to kill me?" Caulder asked quietly. The kid didn't reply. He didn't even look at Caulder. Caulder took the end of the pipe and added a small amount of pressure and a twist. The kid groaned and finally gave him the courtesy of some eye contact. Still he would not speak. It occurred to Caulder that the kid might be physically incapable of speech because of the nature of his wound, so he gave the pipe a quick jerk and removed it from his body. This produced a gusher of blood from the kid's chest. He would bleed to death in the next few minutes.

Caulder shoved the pipe against the kid's Adam's apple.

"Speak," he commanded. The Latino clutched his guts and spat up at Caulder. Caulder dodged the spittle and grinned down at the kid.

"Enjoy hell."

Caulder's sadistic side had boiled to the surface. Nate Daniels's words came back to haunt him. *"Tell me you don't get off on it,"* he had said to Caulder. And Caulder had replied that he didn't, but of course that wasn't entirely true.

Nate had brushed against the secret Ry Caulder tried to keep in a hidden corner of his heart. Part of him *did* enjoy what he did for a living. There *was* a rush, a thrill to it. Something deep and predatory that Caulder tried not to acknowledge over the years. He had tried to remain as cold and detached as possible, hoping that it would actually keep him more human, but there were times when a sense of ecstasy accompanied the kill.

Forget laws. Forget morality. There were people that just simply *deserved* to die. The planet was overpopulated with vermin and Caulder *liked* exterminating them. The man in front of him might be young and misguided, undereducated and neglected. Probably abused or ignored by his parents, if he had any. He may have been screwed by the system and all around him from day one. His life had quite possibly been shit, a lousy hand dealt him by fate, but the fact remained that if Ry Caulder had been someone else, someone a little less alert, a little less prepared, then *he* would be the dead one now and this kid would be going through his wallet looking for spare change. All the questions of social injustice melt under that spotlight. No amount of empathy would change the fact that this kid, this *punk*, was a victimizer, pure and simple.

The day of the professional killer was coming to an end. The sport was being overrun by amateurs. Anyone with an attitude and a weapon was into it now. Kids were killing other kids for tennis shoes. Chaos was sweeping the land and Caulder had no sympathy for those that victimized randomly.

A crowd of the stoned and curious was gathering down the

street. No one stepped out of the rock houses, which was odd, but Caulder did not want to push his luck. He decided not to wait for the punk's death. He picked up the kid's gun. It *was* a Saturday night special. Just a cheap .38. A very untrustworthy weapon, but at this point it was better than no gun at all.

Caulder climbed back into the Buick and hauled ass out of the neighborhood. He knew it was risky carrying around another man's gun, but he felt it would be even riskier to go unarmed this night. He wiped the Equalizer with a rag and tossed the pipe into a pile of rubble as he sped past. Then he tossed the rag into a burning trash can that had been abandoned as the fire had waned.

It took Caulder less than a minute and a half to catch up to the limousine. At first he thought he had lost track of his quarry, but he spotted the big Mercedes in the drive-through of an all-night Burger King only a mile or so from the crack houses on the exact same street. If Fredrickson wanted to lose Caulder, he wasn't trying too hard.

The limo pulled out as if on cue and proceeded into the industrial district of downtown Los Angeles. Caulder felt certain that he was being set up for some kind of trap. He had the distinct sensation that Fredrickson was leading him around by the nose.

The Mercedes stopped in front of a two-story brick warehouse situated in a valley of warehouses. This building occupied a triangular island of land all its own. Street access was available on all three sides of the warehouse. The windows of the big building had been painted an opaque yellow from the inside. Security cameras were placed strategically around the exterior of the building, affording the occupants complete knowledge of all activity outside their little fortress.

Caulder quickly turned off his headlights and parked under a broken streetlamp two blocks from the warehouse.

The limo flashed its headlights three times in rapid succession, paused, then flashed twice more. Obviously a signal of some sort to let those who dwelled within the building know that friends, not foes, were outside.

Caulder killed his engine and watched Fredrickson's car. His cold was getting worse. Every bone in his body ached and his lungs were getting congested. Driving around all night long would not be the cure.

Caulder stared for what seemed an eternity at the limo sitting in front of the warehouse. The Mercedes sat quietly, totally stationary. Then the muffled sound of breaking glass came from within the car. Caulder leaned his head out of his window, straining to hear more of whatever might happen next.

Fredrickson got out of the Mercedes by himself and looked up at the half-filled moon in the night sky. Something seemed different about him. He looked bigger, huskier. Could it be the way he was dressed? Fredrickson had lost the kimono. He now wore only an oversize Los Angeles Lakers sweatshirt and loose white pants. He didn't appear to be wearing any shoes, but his feet seemed swollen and large. And there was something weird about his face . . . something . . . *different*. Caulder couldn't see clearly enough from his vantage point through the fog. He reached into a metal box under the passenger seat and withdrew a pair of night-vision binoculars. By the time he got them up to his eyes, Fredrickson was gone.

Caulder scanned the area and found Fredrickson walking up a flight of stairs leading to a heavy security door on the side of the warehouse. Fredrickson put his hands on either side of the door and lowered his head meditatively as if he were sensing something from within the building. He stayed like that for forty-five seconds and then he suddenly started pounding violently on the security door.

A muscular man armed with an Uzi opened the door. He looked mildly surprised to see Fredrickson. He apparently knew Fredrickson, but he seemed uncertain whether Fredrickson should be there or not. While the muscular man's brain processed the information, Fredrickson's hand whipped out and grabbed him by the throat. With a brutal jerk, Fredrickson snapped the man's neck and dropped him onto the floor inside the warehouse, a puppet without strings.

Fredrickson entered the warehouse and closed the door. The street grew quiet again, as if nothing had happened.

The sudden violence stunned Caulder. He sat straight up and grabbed the steering wheel with his free hand to steady the binoculars. His head throbbed and he knew he had a fever; he even thought for a moment that he might be hallucinating. The whole thing seemed surreal. Fredrickson had acted in such a calm manner, as if he were merely shaking the muscular man's hand. He seemed to have no fear, no tension, as if what he did was the most natural, normal thing in the world, from which there could be no repercussions. A cool act, even for a professional killer.

Caulder picked up the .38 and checked to make sure it was fully loaded. It was, except for the one spent round. He slowly got out of his car, feeling puzzled and confused. He wiped cold sweat from his forehead and eased his way toward Fredrickson's limo, keeping a paranoid eye on the windows and rooftops of the neighboring warehouses as he moved. He paid almost no heed to the Mercedes. He was fairly certain of what he would find inside. The chauffeur was the least of his worries. The real danger had already left the vehicle.

Caulder sidled up along the limousine and flung open the driver's door. The chauffeur's body tumbled out onto the street. The back of his head had been ripped open. Caulder looked inside the car. The dividing window was shattered and the front compartment was splattered with the chauffeur's blood. Large chunks of grayish brain matter from the interior of his skull clung to the windshield. Caulder felt a deep sickness well in his stomach. He had expected the man to be dead, but not like that. It was as if someone had taken a jackhammer to his head.

A hideous sound suddenly filled the night, a fierce, high-pitched shriek. The shriek was quickly drowned out by gunfire and a series of brutal screams emanating from within the warehouse.

Caulder decided enough was enough. He would meet the challenge head-on. He ran to the warehouse, up the stairs to the door. Locked tight. The screams and gunfire persisted within. Then new sounds joined the cacophony of bedlam—sounds of men gagging and choking. Sounds of flesh being torn and bodies being slammed against brick walls. The building literally vibrated with the conflict.

Caulder aimed his pistol at the doorknob and fired. The knob exploded, but a massive dead bolt held the door in place. Fredrickson had double-locked the door behind himself, possibly to keep Caulder out of the building. But why? To keep Caulder from interfering with whatever was happening inside or to protect him from the violence? There was only one way to find out. Caulder raised the pistol and fired, blowing the dead bolt out of its socket.

Caulder pushed the splintered door open and warily entered the warehouse. The sounds of battle had stopped as abruptly as they had begun. The lights were out in the building. An eerie silence pervaded the darkness. Caulder stepped over the muscular man with the broken neck and peered into the large darkened room. Cool air from the overhead fans blew a stench into his nostrils. Death was in the air.

Caulder pulled a small flashlight from his pocket and scanned the room. The warehouse was filled with scales, packing material, chemical stations for drug cutting and processing, and dead bodies. Dead bodies everywhere. Mutilated corpses dripped blood onto reddening piles of cocaine. Some of the men had been killed by gunfire. Others had been cut to pieces. The scene was very reminiscent of Baxter's slide show. Fredrickson was nowhere to be seen.

Caulder walked over to a body slumped on the floor and flipped it over with his boot. The dead man looked as if someone had run his face through a paper shredder. Neatly through the center of each of the corpse's palms was a fresh bullet hole.

Caulder crossed over to another dead man and looked down. This man's palms had also been shot. The smell of gasoline penetrated Caulder's clogged sinuses, overriding the heavy scent of death in the warehouse. Caulder moved closer to the central storage area. Millions of dollars worth of cocaine was stored here. Gasoline had been poured across the bags of coke in a trail that led through the warehouse out another exit, the door now standing open in the wind. Caulder walked briskly toward the door, gun at the ready. Flame suddenly shot along the floor through the doorway and sped past him, along the trail of gasoline, toward the cocaine. A full can of gas, left behind as a mortar, exploded as Caulder dove for cover. Flames quickly engulfed the warehouse.

Caulder was sure that there were chemicals stashed throughout the warehouse. He wanted out quick, but he couldn't go back the way he'd come; the fire was already too intense in that direction. He had no choice but to rush through the doorway that the fire had come through, even though he knew whoever set the blaze would probably be waiting outside that door, waiting to kill anyone that came out of the building.

Caulder raised his gun high over his head to avoid heat making contact with the bullets in the weapon, then ran as quickly as he could through the flaming doorway. He stumbled and fell to the ground outside the warehouse and did two quick rolls to extinguish the flames that had caught on his clothes. He came up on one knee, leveling the pistol and scanning the area for Fredrickson or whoever had lit the fire. He found himself alone.

There was a loud hiss followed by a violent *whomp* deep within the warehouse and suddenly the windows became glass shrapnel as explosions rocked the building. The fire had reached the chemical stations and the gas lines. Caulder covered his head as best he could as the windows sprayed broken glass all over the place.

Flames were actually shooting out of the warehouse now. The big brick building was going up quick.

Sirens wailed in the distance. The orchestra of death that had played here was loud even for this neighborhood. Someone had finally called the cops.

As Caulder came around to the other side of the warehouse he noticed that the Mercedes and the dead chauffeur's body were gone. Someone, presumably Fredrickson, had loaded the body back into the limo and driven away.

The sirens were growing closer. It was time to leave.

fifteen

When the phone rang, James Vincent Baxter was sitting in his favorite Eames chair in the den of his rambling Bel Air abode, listening to Bartók and reading the sports section of the *Los Angeles Times*. He thought of this as his special time of the day, the winding-down period that would eventually bring him a calm and guiltless sleep. The last thing he wanted to hear was the ringing of the telephone. Especially the work line, the number given out to top aides or important subcontractors who handled complicated jobs for the company. He picked up the receiver, knowing that at this hour it would probably not be good news. "Yes?" he said irritably.

"You've got some cleaning up to do," a gravelly voice spoke into Baxter's ear.

"Caulder?"

"Yeah, it's me," Caulder said. Baxter could hear sirens screaming in the background. "Looks like you were right about Fredrickson. He hit your Tracton Street warehouse. You're gonna have to write it off."

Baxter sat up and tossed the paper to the floor. "The whole fucking thing?"

"It's a total loss."

"What happened?!" Baxter hollered, thinking more about red ink than blood.

"Fredrickson got into the warehouse, then he either had people on the inside already or he let his accomplices in the back way. By the time I got inside, all your people were dead and whoever was responsible had split. They torched the place on the way out. It was done *very* quickly."

"And you just stood around and watched?" Baxter asked, starting to lose grip on the modicum of patience his parents had bequeathed to him.

"There wasn't much I could do about it."

"Goddamn it, Caulder, are you going to let him wipe out my entire operation before you do something?"

"No, I'm going to—"

Suddenly there was interference on the phone, a great electronic buzzing, and then the line went dead.

"Caulder? Caulder? Are you there? Fuck!" Baxter slammed the phone down and hoisted himself to his feet. The time had come to get personally involved.

Ry Caulder stood in a phone booth at an all-night gas station. Police cars and fire engines streamed by, heading for the flaming warehouse two miles south.

Caulder was trying to tell Baxter what he was going to do about the situation when he was cut off and a new voice took over the line in Baxter's place.

"What *are* you going to do, Ry?" Fredrickson demanded, his voice a growling rasp. "Tell me what the plan is."

Caulder was astonished. He took half a step out of the phone booth and studied the area. Parked at a distant corner under a streetlamp was Fredrickson's black Mercedes limousine. How he'd tapped into the line, Caulder did not know. Caulder stepped back into the phone booth and spoke into the receiver.

"Fredrickson?"

"Yes, Ry ... Did you enjoy the fiesta? I'm sorry you arrived after all the piñatas had been broken."

"What the hell is going on?"

"Game time, Ry. Time to quit following me all over town and get down to business. You and Alvin left quite a mess at my place last night."

Caulder considered denying the accusation, but realized it would be futile. He stared at the Mercedes on the corner, wanting to *see* Fredrickson. The interior was pitch-black. He could see nothing through the opaque glass.

"How did you know it was us?" Caulder asked.

"I could smell your sweat on the bodies. You really shouldn't leave corpses lying around the house. We could have gotten into a lot of trouble over that."

"You're one to talk. What did you do to those guys in the warehouse?!"

"Well, I *killed* them, Ry," Fredrickson growled. "We used to do a lot of killing, you and I. I still do as a matter of fact. How about you? Kill anyone good lately? I mean, of course, anyone I don't know about."

"I'm trying to cut down," Caulder said flatly.

"Really? I'd say you've racked up quite a body count in the last twenty-four hours, judging by the look of my living room and the young man you spiked a few minutes ago."

Caulder's suspicions had been correct. Fredrickson had complete knowledge of all the night's activity. He had been aware, and probably in control, of every event that had taken place.

"You're to blame for the kid," Caulder said. "You sent a child to do a killer's job."

"There's a killer in every child, Ry. You know that. Everyone is fair game on this planet. I just wanted to test you. To see if you still had the stuff ... Obviously, you do." Fredrickson's voice was getting harder to understand. He seemed to have something stuck in his throat. His speech was becoming increasingly punctuated by growling, hacking coughs. "But I see you still feel the need to justify your actions. Why can't you just accept what you are and enjoy it, like I do?"

"I've been developing a conscience."

"That will be your downfall," Fredrickson hissed.

"You should try it sometime. Might be good for you."

"I'm beyond that business."

"Why did you kill your driver?"

"Sometimes I get carried away. Besides, I caught him staring at me...." Fredrickson let that hang for a moment before continuing. "As for the warehousemen, they had it coming ... but that was nothing compared to what I'm going to do to *you*, Ry. The only difference is that *you'll* have a fighting chance. It'll be nice to have a little challenge in life again. What great sport this will be!"

"What if I don't want to play your game?" Caulder asked.

"Oh, you'll play. I'll make you...."

The phone went dead.

Fredrickson had confirmed Caulder's deepest fears. In spite of what he told Baxter, the men in the warehouse did not look as if they had suffered from a group attack. As hard as it was to believe, it appeared to be the work of one man. It seemed impossible, but the slides in Baxter's office had been Caulder's first clue that Fredrickson was working alone. There seemed to be no evidence of more than one assailant in either of the warehouse slaughters. But how could this be? Fredrickson was good, but no one was *that* good.

Fredrickson's car started to pull away from the curb in the distance.

Caulder dropped the phone and chased after the Mercedes, all rational thought gone from his fevered brain. He needed to see

Fredrickson, to give tangible life to what was happening so that he would know he wasn't simply going mad. Caulder ran as hard as he could, but as he got closer to Fredrickson's limo the vehicle sped up and left him in the dust.

Caulder couldn't stop himself. He ran and ran until there was nothing left in him to run with. Then he collapsed in the middle of the street, panting and wheezing, his lungs on fire, a clammy sweat oozing from every pore in his body. His eyes were wild and his temples were throbbing with dull pain. What the hell had he gotten himself into?

sixteen

On the way home Caulder decided to stop in and visit Alvin. He felt the need to see someone real. Someone tangible. He also wanted to find out how Alvin's wounds were healing. The big man had acted as if the deep cuts were only scratches. Anyone else would have gone straight to a hospital.

Alvin considered wounds a personal thing. Too personal for strangers to deal with. In Vietnam he had almost lost his right hand when a minor cut became infected and he refused to be bedridden. Ironically, his stubbornness probably saved his life.

Not wanting to let his buddies down, he humped through the jungle with a hand that was twice its normal size until fever laid him out. Finally they had to chopper him into Saigon for bed rest and drainage.

While he was in the hospital the Tet Offensive began and most of his company was killed near Hue. To this day Alvin had never reconciled himself with the fact that he hadn't been there when he was needed most.

Caulder had been one of the few in the company to survive.

He *liked* Vietnam the first few weeks he was there. It was beautiful country and the service provided him with a sense of freedom and abandon he had never experienced in his life. He was a wild kid with a machine gun. There were few rules in the field, other than "Try to survive" and "Don't fuck over your buddies." Laws were meaningless. He thought he had stumbled onto nirvana. He never expected anything like the Tet offensive. *None* of them did. Wave upon wave of Vietcong and North Vietnamese soldiers swept over the land, like an ocean of hostile red ants in a shoot-the-wad effort that was extremely costly to all sides. Bodies piled on bodies. Fire and blood filled the rice paddies. Napalm and concussion bombs leveled forests. He was only a teenager when Tet began, but by the time it was over Ry Caulder had danced with the devil under an angry moon and eaten death for breakfast. He would never again be comfortable with the living.

Alvin missed it all, sweating Tet out in the ICU. He got to see plenty of frantic action in Vietnam, but he had missed what he considered the Big One and always regretted it, almost as much as Caulder regretted having been there.

Not long after Tet, Ry Caulder met Fredrickson. Caulder was under observation in a psych ward on the outskirts of Da Nang. Fredrickson was a "technical adviser" to the CIA looking for a recruit that could be molded for some "special" work. "Wet work," as he called it in private. He took one look in young Ry Caulder's coal black eyes and knew that he had found his man. Of course he wasn't known as Ry Caulder at the time. That was thirty years and a thousand lifetimes ago.

It had all started out legally enough.

Caulder made his first official kills during the Tet offensive. He had killed soldiers, men trying to kill him and his platoon. But with Fredrickson he began eliminating civilians. Undesirables. Undercover Communists. Intellectuals. Political activists that hadn't seen things the U.S. of A.'s way. The silent war. The line had blurred.

Still Caulder thought he was being a good patriot. Fighting for God and Country. An already fragile brain solidified into a killer's tool. By the time the show was over and everyone packed their toys and went home, Ry Caulder had acquired a very marketable skill.

Fredrickson helped him make the transition to the private sector. He set him up with his third official identity, "Ry Caulder," and introduced him to all the wrong people. They worked together for many years before the trouble began in earnest. The trouble was Ry Caulder's humanity. A small piece of it had surfaced unexpectedly. From that moment on it was only a matter of time before he and Fredrickson had to part company.

The fact that neither man had killed the other by now was somewhat surprising to both of them.

Alvin's Alcove had closed hours earlier but the back door was unlocked, as usual. Alvin never slept at night. He hadn't since he was a teenager. He would sleep only after the sun was up and high in the sky. He left the rest of the day for the "noncoms," as he liked to call them. The normal folk with the nine-to-five schedules.

He left the back door unlocked for friends that shared his nocturnal instincts and needed an after-hours drink. It was a select club and anyone not in it had the good sense not to come to the back door after closing time.

State law prohibited drinking in the bar after 2 A.M., but Alvin had a small apartment upstairs and it was there that he and his cronies would drink and get high until all hours of the morning.

Caulder entered the back of the bar and called out Alvin's name. Sometimes when he was alone and drinking Alvin would take a shot at noises in the dark. Occasionally he would hit something. It was always a good idea to shout out your ID nice and loud so that he would know you weren't Charlie.

The bar was empty. Caulder made his way up the stairs to

Alvin's apartment. The door was wide open. Every light in the place burned bright. The TV flickered silently in a corner, showing an old black-and-white Alan Ladd movie. Caulder recognized it as *The Blue Dahlia*, a late-night perennial. It usually played well after midnight. Night owls knew it by heart.

Caulder called Alvin's name again and still got no response. He went into the bedroom. The place was a wreck, but no more so than usual. Magazines, from *Soldier of Fortune* to classics like *Beaver* and *44 'D' Cup Honeys*, were strewn about the floor amid a litter of empty beer bottles and dirty clothes.

Caulder entered the bathroom. There was dried blood on the sink and a few drops on the floor that were still wet. The dried blood he chalked up to the morning when Alvin first dealt with his wounds. The wet stuff, Caulder figured, must have dripped during a recent redressing of the bandages. But where was Alvin?

Maybe the man decided to go to the hospital after all. Doubtful. No, it was more likely that he just got claustrophobic and decided to cruise the city or go down to the beach for some cool breezes and the cacophony of crashing waves.

Caulder knew Alvin liked to hit the beach on nights when he felt the city was closing in on him, but it was unlike him to leave the bar unlocked when he went out. It just wasn't something the man would do if he had his wits about him.

The hairs on the back of Ry Caulder's neck began to bristle.

seventeen

Caulder stepped out of the graffiti-smeared elevator and walked down the hallway toward his apartment. He unlocked his door and a blast of cold air hit him in the face as he swung it wide.

The windows in the apartment were all open. He had closed them before he left. Caulder drew the .38 and entered cautiously. The blinds were slapping against the windowsills, blown into the air by the cold night wind.

Caulder went into a defensive crouch. Someone was sitting in the recliner, hidden in shadow, not moving. After a few seconds Caulder realized the person in the chair was not breathing either.

Caulder got up and turned the recliner toward the window, allowing red neon from the *Tecate* billboard on the roof of the building across the alley to light the figure in the chair.

Alvin was slumped down in the old recliner, eyes closed, a peaceful expression on his face. The *Wall Street Journal* lay open on his lap, as if he had fallen asleep reading.

"Alvin?" Caulder's voice cracked as he spoke.

Caulder nudged Alvin. Alvin rolled forward onto the floor, his right arm outstretched on the rug. A bullet had bored a hole through the center of his palm.

Caulder checked Alvin's left palm and found a similar bullet wound, but the bullets had not killed Alvin. The cause of death was a small hole located on the back of Alvin's neck at the base of his skull. The puncture had been made by an ice pick or something of similar dimensions.

Caulder speculated that Alvin had been killed in the bathroom of the apartment above his bar. That would account for the fresh blood found on the floor. It appeared that Alvin had been taking a leak when his assailant snuck up behind him and slid the sharp instrument into his brain. Alvin, probably drunk, would have been distracted while urinating. The lack of struggle in the bathroom indicated the attacker had an easy time of it.

"Fredrickson . . ." Caulder spoke under his breath. "You bastard . . ."

Caulder bent down and touched Alvin's neck in the hope that there was some spark left. There wasn't.

eighteen

Caulder opened his refrigerator to see if he had anything cold to drink. He was dehydrated and the task of disposing of Alvin's body would take a lot out of him. He found a plate of fried chicken covered with cellophane sitting in the otherwise barren fridge. A note was taped to the cellophane:

> *Dear Ry,*
>
> *You get your wish. We won't bother you anymore.*
> *Thanks for everything. . . .*
>
> > *Fuck off,*
> >
> > *Stephanie*
>
> *P.S.—Here's some cold chicken.*
> *Consider us even.*

Stephanie didn't have a key to Caulder's apartment, so she either broke in, or she left the chicken and the note in front of Caulder's door. That would indicate that Fredrickson had been kind enough to place the plate in the refrigerator upon his arrival with Alvin's body. There was only one Stephanie in the building, and her name was clearly marked on the postal box down in the lobby.

Caulder's heart began to race. He left his apartment and went to Stephanie's door. There was a white card stuck in the doorjamb. Caulder removed the card and looked at it. It was the size of a business card, blank except for two words written in a childlike scrawl in what appeared to be red ink.

The card said simply, "She's pretty!" Caulder recognized the ink for what it was—blood. He pounded on the door in extreme panic. *Not again. Not another innocent!*

It took a while, but the door finally opened just as Caulder was about to kick it down. Stephanie, dressed in a slinky blue night-gown and still half-asleep, looked out through the three-inch, chained gap.

Caulder's pulse began to slow. The card had been a warning, a flag to tell him Fredrickson knew who Stephanie was and that he could access her if Alvin's murder was not sufficient motivation to enter the game. A good poker player always left something on the table to keep the suckers interested.

Stephanie wiped sleep from her eyes.

"Get your stuff together," Caulder said. "You're getting out of here."

"What?"

"You and Jason have to leave this place immediately."

"Are you crazy? Just because I wrote a nasty letter to you?"

"It's got nothing to do with that," Caulder said, exasperated by the complexity of the situation. "You're in danger. We've got to get out of here, now!"

Stephanie was at a loss for words but she was beginning to wake up. "Is this about Hertzberg?" she asked.

"Hertzberg? What about him?"

"The police came by today and asked me about him. They said somebody killed him."

"It's got nothing to do with that," Caulder said, feeling the noose grow tighter around his neck.

"Well, what is it then?"

"Just open the door," Caulder demanded. "I'll explain on the way."

nineteen

Stephanie Taylor slipped on a pair of tight jeans and a loose pullover blouse. She tried to rouse Jason, but he wouldn't have it. She packed what she could into the suitcases she had brought with her from Portland and finally got Jason moving by telling him they were leaving and it was up to him whether or not he was bringing his toys. Jason scrambled about the apartment piling his things into two large grocery bags and a suitcase.

They had accumulated more than she realized. When she had come down here eight months ago everything had fit snugly in her sister's Volkswagen. Now she had built up a collection of knickknacks, photo albums, cheap clothing, and tastefully selected yard sale furnishings that had transformed her dinky little rattrap of an apartment into a home. She was determined to take as much with her as she could. Caulder had told her that they might not be coming back. She had worked too hard for her meager belongings to leave them behind on Ry Caulder's whim.

Caulder didn't help her pack. He spent the entire time standing in her open doorway, alternating looks down the hallway with studies of the windows inside the apartment. It was as if he expected an army to attack without warning. His intense concentration convinced Stephanie that there was method behind his madness, so she complied with his bizarre request. He still hadn't told her any more than that she was in danger, and she was taking him at his word. She knew that trouble could come in many forms and strike without warning. She was willing to act now and ask questions later. But she had better get some damn good answers from Caulder when she started asking those questions.

Stephanie finally ran out of suitcases and boxes and paper bags with which to pack things. Caulder went into his own apartment and found one large suitcase, an overnight bag, and two cardboard boxes that he had brought a bulk of paperbacks and magazines home in a couple of weeks earlier.

Finally she had packed all she could. The rest was unimportant. If she never got back to this apartment she would just consider this an early spring cleaning. In spite of Caulder's protests she packed most of the food in the refrigerator into the cardboard boxes. Caulder said he would give her money for food and she responded that she would not waste so much when so many had so little.

Caulder brought the elevator up and hit the STOP button. They loaded everything into the elevator so they could do it all in one trip. The elevator groaned louder than usual as it dropped toward the parking garage. As they loaded the Buick, Stephanie noticed that Caulder was sweating profusely despite the cold night air. His eyes constantly scanned the open areas of the garage. He seemed on the verge of panic. She had never seen him so nervous, and it frightened her.

The picture created by the car packed with suitcases, boxes, and grocery bags loaded with junk, its trunk crammed with stuff and the lid tied down half-open, might have been funny, until one looked at the grim expressions on the faces of the occupants of the vehicle.

Jason was asleep on Stephanie's lap before they got to Wilshire Boulevard. When she asked Caulder where they were going, he simply replied, "Someplace safe," and continued driving. He had promised to explain to her once they got in the car, but he was so busy watching the surrounding traffic, heavy for this time of night, that she decided not to press him. He seemed certain that disaster would strike at any moment. Finally Stephanie relaxed into her seat, shifted Jason to a more comfortable position on her lap, closed her eyes, and decided to enjoy the ride.

The Buick pulled up to the front of the Beverly Hills Hotel. Big and pink, it reeked of old money, vacuous movie stars, and corrupt business deals.

Caulder turned off the car and looked at his passengers. Jason was still asleep, curled up on Stephanie's lap. Stephanie looked at the oppressive hotel.

"Are you crazy? I can't afford this place," she said indignantly, fed up with the arrogance of Caulder's behavior.

"I can," Caulder stated flatly.

A valet opened Stephanie's door. Stephanie stared at Caulder for a few moments, but his rigid features told her nothing. She stood Jason up outside the car and he slowly started to awaken. His legs were wobbly, but he finally realized he had to stand up on them and he shifted into the subconscious autopilot that a child will kick into when he or she really wants to stay asleep but is forced by the adult world to stand and move about.

A bellboy approached the car with a luggage cart.

"Bring it all in," Caulder said to the bellboy. "Everything. Leave the car right here. I'll be down in a few minutes." Caulder spoke in a tone that allowed for no defiance.

"Yes, sir," the bellboy said, and he immediately began loading the luggage onto the cart.

Caulder left Stephanie and Jason standing just inside the entrance of the hotel while he made the booking arrangements. Neither Stephanie nor Jason were fully awake. Stephanie looked around her. The Beverly Hills Hotel was a big, luxurious dinosaur of a place. It had the stuffy air of arrogant wealth and hostile attitudes reserved for those that didn't belong.

The bellboy rolled two luggage carts crammed with the Taylors' belongings into the entryway. Stephanie clutched Jason's hand tightly. Jason leaned against her leg and went back to sleep.

The cavernous lobby was empty except for an elderly bellman slouched in a chair and the night clerk behind the registration desk who was talking to Ry Caulder. The bellboy stood at the ready next to the carts, waiting to be told where to go. He was young and full of himself. He gave Stephanie the once-over and threw in his best gigolo smile. Stephanie ignored him with intensity. She knew his kind. He was a young dog that liked anything in a skirt and she was the only woman in the room.

Of course disliking that kind of behavior was a great way to spend your life alone. Stephanie didn't care. She'd rather be alone with her son than spend time with dogs. Ry Caulder was not a dog. He was a serious individual and did not do things in a shallow or common fashion. He *meant* what little he said or did. This was why Stephanie loved him. It was why she was trusting him on this strange adventure. It was also what kept them apart. A less intense individual would have succumbed to her charms long ago. Caulder had always managed to control himself.

Caulder had no girlfriend that Stephanie knew of; he wasn't gay and he certainly cared for Stephanie and Jason, but for some reason he had always kept his distance from her, sexually. They were close without being intimate. He knew everything about her that he would allow her to tell him, yet she knew practically nothing about him. When she probed him about his life he always changed the subject, saying there was nothing to tell and that he didn't want to talk about himself. It had been a frustrating one-way street.

Caulder walked over to Stephanie and handed her the room key. "You're in three-oh-two," he said.

"What's going on?" Stephanie pleaded.

"It's a suite," Caulder answered, as if he hadn't understood the actual meaning behind her question.

"I don't care what it is! I want to know what's going on!" Stephanie was beginning to make a scene.

Caulder signaled to the older bellman, who slowly got up and began a ritual of cracking and snapping his sleeping bones to get them moving.

"I can't tell you," Caulder said to Stephanie. "I'm not even sure myself. But there's something I have to deal with and I need to know that you're safe."

The bellman took the key from Stephanie's hand and trundled away with the first of the luggage carts. The younger bellboy stood by the second luggage cart watching the interaction between Caulder and Stephanie as if he were part of the family.

Caulder turned to the bellboy and asked him if he had a problem.

"No sir!" the bellboy replied nervously, snapping out of his fantasyland. He pushed the second cart after the old man.

"Just tell me one thing, Ry," Stephanie continued.

"What?"

"Did you hurt Mr. Hertzberg?"

"No," Caulder lied. His response was immediate and believable. He had mastered the art of guiltless lying decades ago.

"Thank goodness. I was so frightened when the police came. I thought they were going to take us away. And then when they started asking questions about you . . ."

"What did they say?"

"They just wanted to know what happened while Hertzberg was at the apartment. They wanted to know who *you* were. How long I had known you. I lied and said I had never seen you before.

I didn't want you to get in any trouble on account of us if you didn't do anything."

"That was smart."

Caulder reached into his pocket, produced a thick roll of money, and handed it to Stephanie.

"Where did you get this?" Stephanie had been under the impression that Caulder lived the way he lived because he could afford nothing better. He didn't appear to have a job. She even thought he might be on disability of some sort. He seemed to be living on a very small, fixed income. Obviously she had been wrong. The bankroll contained nearly five thousand dollars.

"I've been saving it . . . for an emergency. Take it."

"No! What is this? Some kind of payoff to be rid of us?"

"Don't be ridiculous and don't argue with me. There's no time for it."

He had never spoken to her this way before. It suddenly occurred to Stephanie that Ry Caulder might actually be dangerous. Maybe she had mistaken pathological behavior as emotional distance and eccentricity. For a split second she considered the card Detective March had given her. Should she call him before whatever was happening escalated out of control? The scar on her wrist began to itch. Jason shifted against her leg, still managing to remain asleep standing up, like a horse. Deciding it was safer not to argue with Caulder, Stephanie pocketed the cash, not intending to keep it.

It was impossible for Stephanie to suspect the reality of the matter: that Ry Caulder avoided her to protect her from the truth, the truth about his profession and his past. He knew that if she ever found out what he *really* did for a living she would despise him, fear him, never want him to come near her or her son. Caulder kept the other side of his life a dark secret from Stephanie and Jason to keep them far from the loop, and now even that wasn't enough. His business had finally intruded on their lives. Just living near him had endangered them. Now he had to do everything in his power to correct the situation and then, once he was sure they were out of danger, he must never see them again.

Once Fredrickson was eliminated, Caulder would leave Los Angeles and start over somewhere else. A different life, a different profession. Different friends . . .

"Are you coming back?" Stephanie asked.

Caulder studied her. A wisp of hair dropped in front of her eyes. He gently moved it out of her face. Stephanie clutched his hand. Caulder moved forward to kiss her, then stopped himself. He stroked her cheek lightly with his fingers and took a step back, away from her.

"I hope so," he said.

twenty

Ry Caulder, dressed in a raincoat, rain hat, and galoshes, pulled a heavy blanket from his closet, spread it out on the floor, and rolled Alvin's body onto it. Caulder wrapped the body in the blanket, hefted it over his shoulder in a fireman's carry, and exited the apartment.

Caulder rode the elevator to the parking garage without incident. He carried the body out into the alley behind his apartment building. A light rain was coming down. It was a little after 5 A.M. The sun would be up soon. He only had a few minutes to accomplish his grisly task.

Keeping to the shadows, Caulder made his way down the alley carrying Alvin's body. The rain made good cover for the business at hand. Even if anyone was up at this hour, he or she wouldn't be able to tell what Caulder was carrying. He watched the surrounding windows scrupulously nevertheless.

After a couple of blocks, Alvin's body began to weigh heavily on Caulder's shoulders. Another block and they would be there. Alvin had begun to get ripe, but Caulder didn't want to think about that. Finally they arrived at their destination. Two bums sat passed out under the awning covering the rear entrance of Ray's Liquor, snoozing it up until the store would open an hour later. Caulder quietly lowered the bundle, unwrapped Alvin, and positioned him next to the bums. He was concerned about leaving Alvin so close to the apartment building, but the risk of taking him farther or moving him in the car would be even greater.

Caulder had already removed all of Alvin's personal belongings and had considered removing his hands as a final precaution, but he couldn't bring himself to do that. If the police made the connection between the bullet holes in Alvin's hands and the wounds on the warehousemen, there would still be no tie to Ry Caulder. He had worn gloves in the warehouse and while handling Alvin. They couldn't connect him to either incident. Besides, most dead transients got little inspection before being tossed into the state trash heap.

It would be an anonymous burial, paid for by the taxpayers. Alvin wouldn't mind. There were plenty of anonymous American bones left in Khe Sanh and Da Nang and the gullies along the Hi Van Pass and the Ho Chi Minh Trail. Alvin wouldn't have wanted his pals slobbering over his corpse anyway. This way people would just think he had gone off on one of his adventures, never to return, like a modern-day Ambrose Bierce. They'd talk about him for years to come, until they were all mindless or dead. Then it would matter even less than nothing.

Caulder picked up a discarded liquor bottle and placed it in Alvin's hands, making him look like just another dude who had passed out with his drinking buddies.

Caulder stared down at his dead friend for a quiet moment, then picked up an old cigarette butt and stuck it between Alvin's lips.

"See you, buddy."

Neither of the bums stirred. They looked as dead as the corpse sitting with them.

Caulder turned and walked away. He staggered slightly as he moved down the alley. A drunk act for anyone who cared to watch. He folded the blanket tightly and tossed it into the sewer system. He'd let the rain wash his only tie to Alvin out to the ocean. He tossed the Saturday night special into the drain for good measure. He wouldn't need it anymore. He pulled the rain hat tight over his eyes and entered the parking garage of his apartment building.

In one corner of the garage sat a large Dumpster. Above the Dumpster, a communal trash chute led up into the building. Caulder pushed the Dumpster to one side, pulled a medium-sized convex mirror from his pocket, and attached it to the corner of the Dumpster, turning it at a very precise angle. There was double-sided electrical tape on the bottom of the mirror, so once it was situated properly it did not move. When Caulder decided he was happy with the angle of the mirror, he climbed on top of the Dumpster, then up into the trash chute.

The chute was a square shaft of rusty, sticky, garbage-encrusted metal. Caulder pushed his back against one side of the chute and his knees against the other and slowly shimmied up the tube.

From above came the sound of a metal door squeaking open. A shaft of light from the fourth floor filled the chute. Caulder protected his head with his hands. There was a ferocious clatter of cans and trash hurtling down the chute as Caulder was bombarded by garbage. Then the door closed and the light disappeared.

Brushing off as much of the garbage as possible, Caulder continued up the chute, every now and then looking down at the mirror on the Dumpster below. The mirror was curved outward to give the widest viewing spectrum possible. It was the kind of mirror that convenience stores use to keep an eye on the customers, wherever they may be in the store. The mirror provided a fairly complete, if distorted, view of the garage. Caulder would know if anyone entered the area and he would halt his activity until they were gone.

Caulder stopped sixteen feet up in the chute. He reached into

his raincoat and withdrew the pocketknife/lockpick. He opened
the knife and stuck the blade between a gap in the metal sheeting
that lined the tube. A small panel about two feet square came loose.
Caulder pocketed the knife and removed the panel, revealing a
hollowed-out space in the side of the chute. He reached into the
space and pulled out three canvas-wrapped packages of varying
sizes. The packages were connected by rope so Caulder could hang
them from his shoulders, leaving his hands free to work.

Caulder replaced the panel, checked the mirror, and started to
shimmy back down the chute with his load. Above him there came
the sound of another door opening, this time on the sixth floor. He
couldn't believe that two different people had chosen this early
hour to dump their garbage.

Caulder quickened his pace, desperately trying to get out of
the chute before the garbage fell. He reached the bottom of the
tube and jumped down onto the edge of the Dumpster. Quick, but
not quick enough.

A deluge of slop showered him from above. He dropped to
the ground and shook wet coffee grounds and discarded stew from
his raincoat.

Caulder pushed the Dumpster back into place. He took off
the raincoat, hat, and galoshes, rolled them up, and tossed them
into the Dumpster. He picked up his packages, removed the convex mirror, and headed for the elevator.

Light from the morning sun was beginning to creep in through
Caulder's windows by the time he got back to his apartment.

Caulder put a pot of coffee on and started unwrapping the
canvas packages. The first package was a plastic case containing a
customized F.N.F.A.L. .308 sniper rifle, in sections, complete with
high-powered day and night telescopes and a suppressor. The second package was a wooden box containing three guns secured in
a velvet-lined mold: a .380 Colt Mustang Plus II palm gun, a 9mm

Browning Hi-Power, and a Heckler & Koch MP 5 machine pistol. The third package was a foam-padded plastic case containing enough ammunition to arm a terrorist assault squad. There was also a large wad of C-4 plastique explosive, a radio detonator, and a small radio transmitter in this container.

Caulder removed a panel under the sink and placed the MP 5 in a cubbyhole dug out of the wall. It was unlikely he would be needing a machine pistol, but one never knew. He didn't want to take a bust for carrying an assault weapon, but he was willing to risk a search of the apartment for the mild comfort the gun would give him over the next hours.

Caulder poured a cup of coffee and scarfed down some of Stephanie's cold chicken. He reread her friendly note telling him to fuck off. He had been getting about as much food into his system lately as sleep, and that wasn't very much. The cold chicken hit the spot, even if the note caused his stomach to rumble.

After finishing the coffee and chicken, Caulder washed his hands thoroughly and began to inspect and clean the sniper rifle. He was, officially, back in business.

twenty-one

After prepping his weapons and contemplating a plan of
attack, Ry Caulder lay down in his bed for a nap. He hadn't slept
in almost forty-eight hours, other than the brief catnap while waiting outside Fredrickson's house the first full day of surveillance.
But Caulder had remained half-awake even then, sensing all surrounding activity in case Fredrickson tried to leave the property.
Now it was all catching up to him. His immune system had taken
a beating and the cold had the best of him. His eyes needed rest.
His body needed sleep. Just a few minutes, that's all . . .

   Caulder's dreams were never simple, but rarely did he dream
of his youth. His subconscious was working overtime this afternoon. Maybe it was his sixth sense trying to clue him to something, but this time Caulder's sleep took him places he had not
ventured in many years. Caulder dreamed of a time when he was
not Ry Caulder, but simply a young man, innocent and naive,
known as Keith Milton, his true name given at birth. His first official identity.

   It was the late sixties. Life was free and easy then for young

Keith Milton. Flower power, hippies, Nehru jackets, Hendrix, Joplin, Morrison and the Doors, Vietnam, Lyndon Johnson, Tricky Dick Nixon, *The Beverly Hillbillies,* Dylan, pot, acid, the Chicago Seven, the Who, Tim Leary, *Laugh-In,* the Velvet Underground, the Black Panthers, the Man with No Name, *Route 66,* Lava Lamps, Bobby Kennedy, uppers, downers, swingers, the Beatles, the Beach Boys, Dr. Martin Luther King, Jr., the March on Washington, the My Lai massacre, draft dodgers, Playboy bunnies, James Bond, Hunter Thompson, Neil Armstrong's walk on the moon, Allen Ginsberg, Andy Warhol, Malcolm X, Hubert Humphrey, Peter Max, the cold war, Jefferson Airplane, *Easy Rider,* Walter Cronkite, Steppenwolf, Woodstock, psychedelic lights and Day-Glo colors, the Stones, the Hell's Angels, Altamont, free music, free love, free sex, no AIDS. It was a wild time to be young.

Even wilder if you were living in San Francisco.

As far as Caulder was concerned the "sixties" began in 1967 and ended with the fall of Saigon in May of 1975. It started building in the fifties with the beatniks and swelled in '63 when Kennedy got shot, but 1967 was the official "Summer of Love" that really kicked it all into gear, crystallizing what the whole thing was about. At that time, Keith Milton was hanging with a group of the disenfranchised in the heart of the City by the Bay. They were soldiers of nonconformity that looked exactly like half the rest of the population. Individuality was their uniform, poverty their code of honor. They had been sleeping on the rooftop of an old warehouse for a few weeks during the Summer of Love when the incident that changed the course of Keith Milton's life occurred.

Early one morning Keith was awakened by strange sounds down in the warehouse. His zoned-out friends slept through it all. They had been up late trying out the most recent batch of Dr. Tim's magic acid, but Keith decided to pass on the substance abuse for a change, just in case anyone went on a bad trip and a clear head was needed. Keith Milton awoke that morning to the sounds of struggle.

It was light out, but the sun was not quite visible yet. The city seemed unnaturally quiet. Keith had heard the warehouse door down below open and shut a few minutes earlier, but he didn't think anything of it and went back to sleep. The warehouse was a distribution center for a free weekly tabloid that was circulated throughout the city preaching the new gospel of love and understanding. Drivers picked up bundles of the stuff three days a week, Mondays, Wednesdays, and Fridays, and circulated the paper to any business that would display it. Advertising paid for it all, and the young man who started the good-natured rag was quickly becoming a millionaire.

This was a Sunday morning, not one of the standard workdays, but Keith Milton was not in the habit of keeping track of the days during the Summer of Love. It was not unusual to hear early-morning vehicles pull into the warehouse during the week. What *was* unusual was to hear moaning and crying coming from the warehouse proper. This brought Keith to total consciousness. It sounded like two people were in pain, a girl, definitely, and maybe a boy.

Keith tried to rouse a few of his friends but they would have none of it. They wanted to sleep it off. He was on his own.

Keith made his way down a rickety staircase to the top floor of the warehouse, which was basically just an extended service walkway and a series of catwalks that went around the inner frame of the building. The sounds were clearer now. They were coming from the ground floor, somewhere at the far end of the warehouse. Keith found a loose board and pulled it out of the walkway banister. A cluster of bent nails protruded from one end of the board. Keith had been attacked by a group of unbelievers earlier in the Summer of Love and had gotten trampled pretty badly. He did not want to repeat the incident.

Keith made his way cautiously down the treacherous stairs to the ground floor and moved stealthily toward the rear of the warehouse. Then he saw a sight that would burn in his memory forever.

A police car was parked inside the garage. The car was turned off, but the headlights were on, harshly illuminating the back corner of the warehouse. Two cops had two teenagers, a freckle-faced, red-headed girl and a boy with long blond hair, facedown on two different bundles of newspapers. Both cops were raping their victims from the rear. Service revolvers were jammed against the back of each victim's head and their hair was being pulled by each of the policemen's free hands. Tears were streaming down the kids' faces and they were moaning and sobbing in pain and humiliation. The two cops said nothing, but they shared almost identical expressions of ecstasy. Their faces glowed with a perverse mania in the glare of the headlights.

Keith sensed the cops were not in it for the sexual aspect of the act, but that they were teaching these dirty young hippies a lesson. There's no such thing as free love, any more than a free lunch. Get a bath, get a haircut, get a job. Tell your friends.

Nausea overcame Keith Milton as he watched the cops pound into the backsides of the two young, innocent people. He knew this could just as easily be him taking a raping, or any of his friends. He could stand it no longer.

Keith rushed forward with the plank of wood raised over his head. The two cops noticed him, but not soon enough. As the cop nearest Keith lifted up off the girl, Keith planted the piece of wood squarely in the back of his head. The nails held firm. The cop's revolver went off four times as he struggled to reach the board in his skull. The first shot put out a skylight, finally waking the sleeping kids on the roof. The second shot went into the side of the young man that was being raped by the other cop. The third shot went into a stack of newspapers. But it was the fourth shot that proved to be the lucky one. It caught the other cop in the forehead as he was raising up off the boy to get a bead on Keith Milton with his service revolver.

Both cops fell to the ground. The cop with the bullet in his skull was dead. The one with the wooden hat was not so lucky. It took him almost five minutes of brain spasms to die. The boy who had been shot was screaming in agony and losing a lot of blood. The girl was a sobbing, heaving wreck.

Keith Milton's friends finally made it down to the ground floor. Panic was the name of the game as Keith tried to explain what had happened. The true nature of love and friendship got tested that day and Keith's pals failed the test miserably. They all split. No one wanted to get busted for murdering cops. The red-haired girl proved to have the most composure. Once she caught her breath, she used the police radio to call for an ambulance for the young man, who, it turned out, was her brother. The kid would live. The bullet hadn't struck anything vital. The girl thanked Keith and told him to take off. She and her brother would bear any legal consequences incurred by the incident. They had both been raped and they could prove it. Even a conservative, hippie-hating jury would have to find them guilty of self-defense at worst. Hopefully.

Keith left and called his uncle, Paul Shepfield, who was, at the time, working a numbers racket out of San Diego. Paul arranged for Keith's first new identity. A totally new, completely legal identification. Then Keith Milton, alias Erik Price, signed up for military service to lose himself even deeper. He wanted out of San Francisco, out of America. He got his wish. Vietnam. Right in time for the Tet offensive. And then along came Fredrickson.

With Fredrickson came a string of murders for hire that would shape history. They were *the* team. Their exploits were whispered legend. They had done a number of big jobs, some of which had the world scratching its collective head to this very day. Jimmy Hoffa, for example. A notorious elimination, meticulously planned and carried out. Not many could have pulled that one off and stayed alive, let alone anonymous. After a high-profile hit like that contracts are traditionally put out on the assassins to keep them quiet. This was where Fredrickson had taught Caulder about "insurance." After accepting the job, Fredrickson let it be known to their employers that a subcontract had been put out on them, to be executed if either Fredrickson or Caulder got hit by any contract emanating directly or indirectly from the employers after the hit went down. The employers had been enraged, but Fredrickson and Caulder had performed the elimination and survived. Caulder never did another big job without insurance. It was usually a gentleman's agreement with one or more of the other top pros, payment coming in the form of the same arrangement for like services. A trade-off of protection.

Hoffa was a coup for Fredrickson and Caulder, but one that existed only as speculation in the underworld. No one except those directly involved knew for sure and none of them had ever spoken about it. Rumors ran rampant, but the truth had not come out. The trail was cold now; nobody would ever be able to prove anything. Even if the men who had commissioned the job confessed on their deathbeds, it would all be considered hearsay and conjecture.

The Hoffa job was a textbook hit, but it was the size and scope of the little jobs, the jobs that never made much news, that built a legend around the team of Fredrickson and Caulder in the underworld. The fact that they even *survived* as long as they did in a business with a notoriously high attrition rate was enough to create a mystique around them. They were legends in their own time and after a while the legendary status made survival all the easier. No one dared cross them.

At their best they were magicians, making problems disappear with the wave of a hand. Federal probes rarely followed their jobs. They worked so clean they left nothing to investigate. People simply died or vanished. It happens all the time. Hoffa, of course, was an exception. A cottage industry of speculation had built up around that one. And it had been one of the quickest, cleanest, easiest hits of their careers. Hoffa had been sitting alone in his car waiting for them, practically begging to be hit. They obliged him. The fee was large and the risk was great, but they pulled it off without a hitch.

Hoffa was the first time Ry Caulder experienced intense dissatisfaction with the job. He had known Hoffa through his uncle, Paul Shepfield, while he was growing up. He always thought Hoffa was a stand-up guy. A lot of people did. Many others thought he was a thieving, two-bit scumbag, but Caulder had always liked him. When the job came in, he wanted to turn it down. But Fredrickson went for it. He *had* to have it. The fact that Caulder didn't want it made Fredrickson desire it all the more. He pushed Caulder, with perverse glee, into accompanying him on the assignment. Once Caulder knew about the contract, Fredrickson couldn't pull it off without him and leave him alive. It was all or nothing. It was fairly early in Caulder's career as a professional killer in the States, and the first time he considered that he and Fredrickson might actually try to eliminate each other, but he went along and did the job, like a pro. Hoffa had smiled at Caulder with recognition moments before Caulder put a slug into his brainpan. Caulder could still see that smile in his mind if he closed his eyes the wrong way. It was a warm and friendly smile, filled with acceptance, thoroughly devoid of condemnation.

The job would be a high-water mark in the career of any professional assassin, but Caulder had taken no satisfaction from the experience. It formed the foundation of his discontent. He didn't realize it at the time, but it was actually the first step on his road to recovery. It would be a very long road, lined with corpses, but it was a road Caulder traveled nevertheless. A road back to his humanity. Something he had left behind in that warehouse with the two dead cops.

Caulder never placed the full blame of his choice of profession on the incident in the warehouse, but that, coupled with his experience during Vietnam in general and the Tet offensive in particular, definitely did something to his metabolism. It shaped the way he felt about right and wrong. About the nature of life and death. About authority figures and the plight of the underdog.

Ry Caulder's philosophy solidified after a few years with

Fredrickson. He understood that murder for hire was a fact of life on this planet. He justified his actions by acknowledging that his targets would be killed by *someone* anyway, even if he didn't do the job. If he *did* do the job he would be the controlling factor. He could actually *help* people, by making their exit from this world as quick and painless as possible and preventing incidental or accidental victims of sloppy hits. His precision was his license, his professionalism his badge. This was the way he faced the mirror every day. But over the last few years that had not been enough. He began to fully grasp how deeply he had lied to himself. All his rationalizations melted away under the vacant gaze of the Jameson girl's dead stare. And now Stephanie and Jason were injecting *life* into his existence. Guilt over the Jameson girl and his affection for Stephanie were combining within his psyche to totally fuck him up. Stephanie's noble struggle against the odds brought out the knight-errant in him. He wanted to help her, protect her, *be* with her. But the goodness that Stephanie and Jason represented to him just magnified the evil that he had become. His only recourse was withdrawal. Avoidance.

Ry Caulder was two warring sides of a very tarnished coin. A coin that had been minted during the Summer of Love.

twenty-two

Caulder sped along Kanan Dume Road much faster than he should, trying to make up for lost time. He wanted to get to Fredrickson before the man left on his nightly rounds, and the sun had already dropped below the horizon. The day had been spent checking and readying his weapons and then he made the mistake of resting his eyes for a brief time that became less brief than he wanted. Because of his level of exhaustion, Caulder slipped out of consciousness for almost three hours. He awoke in a panic and got on the road immediately, but still late and afraid he would miss Fredrickson's exit from his home. Los Angeles was a big town and there were too many liquor stores and hooker corners for Caulder to be cruising around all night in search of his man. So Caulder pushed the pedal to the floor, speeding to the point of being dangerous on the twisting mountain road. This behavior was unlike him. He was usually methodical and calculating, especially with a target as deadly as Fredrickson. But the business with Alvin and the threat against Stephanie and Jason had combined to produce a determination to end it all that could prove fatal for a man in his position. He no longer cared. One way or the other, it would all be over soon.

Twice the car skidded dangerously close to the edge of the canyon road. An eighty-foot drop beckoned both times. But Caulder's need for speed was rewarded. He spotted Fredrickson's limousine as it appeared around a bend up ahead. Caulder had made it in time to intercept his target.

Caulder slumped low in his seat as Fredrickson's limo zoomed past the Buick. Not that he didn't fully expect Fredrickson to notice the Buick, but he felt his quarry deserved the courtesy of the charade. Maybe Fredrickson wouldn't notice or care that Caulder was following him. It hadn't bothered him the night before, that was for sure. As Caulder sped past the limo he got a brief glimpse of Fredrickson behind the steering wheel. He was driving himself for a change. Of course he *had* killed his own chauffeur the night before and good chauffeurs were hard to come by these days, especially if you were as peculiar a customer as Fredrickson appeared to be. Caulder watched his rearview mirror until the Mercedes disappeared around another bend in the road; then he slammed on the brakes and did a 180-degree spin in the middle of Kanan Dume Road. Once stabilized, Caulder floored the pedal and burned rubber after the limo.

Caulder kept his distance as the black Mercedes cruised toward downtown Los Angeles on the Santa Monica Freeway. Fredrickson took the Pasadena Freeway north, turned off on the Sixth Street exit, and cruised the surface streets looking for action. It was almost nine o'clock by the time he pulled the limo into a parking lot full of expensive cars, most of them imported and racy. The parking lot was an appendix to a crumbling hotel that sported a sign out front that read THE TOMB in bright green neon.

Caulder's car moved past the club slowly. He parked in a burned-out restaurant's parking lot across the street from the club and surveyed the scene. A big crowd and lots of noise. Not a very good place to conduct business. But if he was going to confront the man face-to-face it would be better to be in public, where Fredrickson would be less likely to just open fire on him.

Caulder knew he was going to kill Fredrickson. Or at least *try* to kill him. The smart thing would be to do it from long range and be done with it. But the anger he felt over Alvin's death and the implicit threat to Stephanie and Jason had brought out the sadist in him again. He wanted to look the man in the eye. He wanted Fredrickson to know what was coming. Even if it would make the job more dangerous.

The entrance to the Tomb was already swarming with the trendy late-night set, all desperately trying to convince the doorman that they were "hot" and wealthy enough to be admitted to the newest "in" club.

Fredrickson swept through the crowd, looking even more bestial than he had the night before. He was decked out in a black Kenzo suit. His brutal features were a direct contrast to his fashionable attire. Fredrickson didn't touch anyone, but his presence seemed to form a natural path through the mob. People assumed he was *somebody.*

The beefy doorman working the entrance of the club took one look at Fredrickson and immediately ushered him inside. He had obviously had run-ins with this strange-looking man before and wasn't interested in contesting him tonight. It took a twenty in the man's palm to get Ry Caulder through the same door.

The interior of the Tomb was filled with bizarre artwork of all kinds. Nude statues, some of them half-swathed in mummy rags, embraced a variety of objects, from animals to tools to weapons to other nudes. At the far end of the room the great jackal god Anubis sat regally, surveying his flock. Nude male and female statues lay crushed under his mighty paws. The lamp shades were stretched with what appeared to be dried flesh of some kind. Brown and frosted white neon strips dimly illuminated the place, allowing only so much to be seen, which was a very good idea indeed.

Kitsch seemed to be the interior designer's principle inspiration.

Fredrickson was dancing with a tall, beautiful woman wrapped in an open-backed black dress. They were punking it up pretty good to the tune of loud seventies disco. Fredrickson had some good moves for a man of his age. The dance was a brutal display of passion and lust. Fredrickson ran his long fingernails down the woman's back, leaving light, bloody scratches. She loved it.

Fredrickson looked over the woman's shoulder and saw Ry Caulder standing at the bar, staring at him. Caulder sipped a Scotch and watched the dance floor. He raised his glass in a toast to Fredrickson. No more charades. It was nose-to-nose time in the big city.

Fredrickson left the woman stranded in the middle of the floor. She danced for a few seconds before realizing that she'd been abandoned. She dejectedly watched Fredrickson's retreating form for a moment before moving on to another candidate.

Fredrickson sliced through the crowd toward Caulder. Caulder was astonished by Fredrickson's features. His face was that of a beastman. His entire head seemed bigger than Caulder remembered. Too large for his body. His brow looked swollen, his jaw distended. Caulder thought that it might be the grotesque lighting in the club playing tricks with his eyes. One thing was certain: this man did not look like the same person that Caulder had known those long years ago when they were partners.

"What happened to your face?" Caulder asked incredulously.

Fredrickson reached up with his index finger and touched the scar on his face with a three-inch-long fingernail. The scar was new to Caulder, but it couldn't account for the rest of the change in Fredrickson's appearance.

"I had an accident.... Had to have a bit of plastic surgery...."

"Yeah? Well, they really fucked you up."

"Did you come here to tell me that I'm ugly?" Fredrickson asked.

"No. I came here to kill you."

Fredrickson looked around the room. "Right here? In front of all these good people?"

"Maybe."

"Have another drink and think it over."

Fredrickson motioned to the bartender, waving two fingers, then pointing at Caulder's empty glass.

"What's your game, Fredrickson? Why have you been messing with Baxter?"

Fredrickson gave Caulder a cold smile. "Money, drugs, fun . . . Revenge."

"Revenge? For what?"

"Baxter set me up. Had me killed. He's still killing me. He kills me every night. But that's not good enough for him. Now he sends *you* after me."

"Have you completely lost your mind?" Caulder asked.

Fredrickson laughed and tapped the side of his own head. "It's not lost. Just rearranged."

The bartender set two Scotches on the bar in front of Fredrickson and Caulder. The men picked up the drinks and downed half of each immediately, their eyes never leaving each other.

"Why did you kill Alvin?"

"I knew it would be the quickest way to get you to play."

"Well . . . you got me and you're not going to like it. You're going to die," Caulder said matter-of-factly.

Fredrickson grinned and clicked his glass against Caulder's. "That's the spirit," he said cheerily, and then he tipped the glass up and drained it.

Caulder stared at Fredrickson and his thoughts raced from the Jameson girl, to his murdered uncle, Paul Shepfield, to Jimmy Hoffa's smile as he was about to take the bullet, to Alvin, sleeping it off forever behind a liquor store, to the card that Fredrickson left in Stephanie's doorjamb and the lack of future he planned for her. Suddenly Caulder was filled with rage against all killers, competent and incompetent, everywhere, including, and especially, himself. Caulder thought about all this in a microsecond, while Fredrickson finished his drink. Absolute and total loathing overflowed in Caulder like molten lava seeking an escape route. It chose Caulder's fist. Before Fredrickson could lower his hand, Caulder snapped his right arm through the air and punched the glass, shattering it in Fredrickson's face. Fredrickson fell backward into a table of eight, knocking drinks and appetizers everywhere. The table smashed to the ground under Fredrickson's weight. The people jumped to their feet, shocked and angry, a few of them ready to fight.

Fredrickson started to get up. His face was covered with broken glass and blood streaked the corner of his mouth.

"Now you're cooking . . ." he said to Caulder with a toothy, crimson-coated smile.

Bouncers emerged from every corner of the club. Caulder turned and stormed out of the place, avoiding them. He had blown it. He had lost control. Even though the club was dark, there were now witnesses that would remember him. The best move now was to get out of there as quickly as possible and maybe no one would be able to properly describe him if the police were to connect this incident to Fredrickson's eventual murder. It's hard to retire if your likeness is on WANTED posters in post offices all across the country.

Caulder scoured the parking lot outside the club, searching for Fredrickson's limousine. He spotted it in the far corner of the lot and walked over to the big shark. Caulder looked around to see if anyone was watching him. He was in the clear. He removed the large wad of plastique explosive from his pocket, dropped to the ground, slid under the Mercedes, and attached the bomb near the gas tank. Plastique was a marvelous thing. Nitro loaded into a stable clay base. The French came up with it in World War II. It was easier for the underground to smuggle than dynamite and much more lethal.

Once the plastique was secure, Caulder slid a radio-controlled detonator pin into the heart of the bomb. Then he stood up, dusted himself off, took another look around, and headed for his car to wait for Fredrickson to exit the Tomb.

Caulder sat in his car in the parking lot across the street from the Tomb, watching the club for hours; still Fredrickson didn't come out. He must have been having quite a time in there, in spite of the glass that had exploded in his face.

The Tomb finally started to empty out around quarter to two. Fredrickson was one of the last to leave, almost an hour later. The place couldn't serve alcohol past 2 A.M., but there was no law against the customers taking their sweet time getting their shit together enough to get on the road.

As Fredrickson stood in front of the club, waiting for the valet to bring his limo from the parking lot, he took the opportunity to chat up a couple of the girls who were also waiting for their cars. He paid particular attention to two blonds who were either sisters or vying for roles as the Doublemint Twins. They did not look totally alike; one was at least twenty pounds heavier than the other, but they were both tall and busty. They wore matching red dresses and they had done their hair in identical fashion, teased out in what was commonly referred to as the freshly fucked look. They were out to draw attention to themselves and that they had done.

Caulder began to get nervous. It appeared that Fredrickson had a thing for women who came as a matched set and it would not do for the man to have company riding in his car. There could be no innocents lost this time. But Caulder was anxious to get this over with. The longer it took before he threw the switch, the more that could go wrong. He was hoping that neither of the women would take Fredrickson up on whatever offer it was that he was making them.

Fredrickson's Mercedes pulled up to the entrance of the club. A valet got out and held the driver's door open for him. Fredrickson made one last proposal to the Doublemint Twins. They looked at him, they looked at his car, they looked at each other, and they talked it over. The less attractive of the two wanted to go, but the other one nixed it, which convinced the first girl to change her mind as well. They were not to be separated. Fredrickson shrugged and walked away from the girls. He tipped the valet, got into the car, and drove away.

Caulder breathed a sigh of relief, waited the proper amount of time, then pulled out and followed the limousine.

Surprisingly, Fredrickson headed straight for his home. Maybe he had gotten all he needed in the Tomb. Plenty of sex and drugs went down in the bathrooms of clubs like that and if you knew the right people you could probably even get a giant slab of beef served perfectly raw.

The limo cruised to the end of the Santa Monica Freeway and then headed north on the nearly deserted Pacific Coast Highway. It was that very rare time of the morning when almost no one was on the streets. That twilight zone between the time when things wind down and other things start up. Even the late-night drunks had all either been arrested, made it home, or passed out on the side of the road.

Caulder followed the Mercedes at a distance until he got a feel for the environment. The timing couldn't have been better. Fredrickson had stayed in the club long enough to seal his doom. Caulder had originally thought he would have to follow Fredrickson all the way back to his house before he threw the switch, so as not to endanger any other motorists, but this would be even better. He would blow the car up on the Pacific Coast Highway, thus ensuring quick and immediate press coverage that would convince Baxter that the job had been done. Caulder could be out of town by that afternoon, cash in hand, with Baxter off his back forever.

The subsequent police investigation of the bombing would be no more intense this way than if the explosion took place on a private road. The conclusion would be the same no matter what— *terrorism!* That's why Caulder had chosen C-4, terrorism's plastique explosive of choice. It would take quite a while, but the police would eventually find some link between Fredrickson's travels and a possible terrorist plot: arms shipments, drug deals, etc. A man of Fredrickson's talents would provide multiple motivations and suspects for the investigators. The Feds always loved a good terrorist yarn. And the boys in the news media were right with them on that one.

Caulder sped up, pulled alongside the Mercedes, and looked over at Fredrickson. He was sitting behind the wheel of the limo, window down, humming to himself. He looked over at Caulder and showed absolutely no surprise. He gave Caulder an evil grin and a wave, as nonchalant as could be. He acted as if Caulder were just racing him home so they could share a few prearranged drinks, like in the old days. Caulder stared at Fredrickson perplexedly, but looked closely into the car so he could be absolutely positive that no one else was aboard. He should have been certain already, but with Fredrickson how could he be sure of anything? The man might have slipped a girl up his sleeve for all he knew.

Satisfied that Fredrickson was alone in the vehicle, Caulder floored the pedal, pulling the Buick quickly ahead. Fredrickson tilted his head back and laughed like a madman. He was having a great time.

Caulder studied his rearview mirror. Fredrickson's car was now thirty yards behind him and the distance was growing. No other vehicles were visible anywhere on PCH and they were about to hit a stretch of road barren of houses. This time there would be no witnesses and no accidental deaths. It was almost *too* perfect.

Caulder reached over and picked up a small black box that had a red button in its center and an extendable antenna at one end. He pulled the radio transmitter's antenna out with his teeth and pointed it over his shoulder, toward the limousine. He checked his rearview mirror again. Fredrickson appeared to be waving and smiling at him. Caulder pressed the proverbial red button and the Mercedes exploded.

The limousine lifted into the air as if kicked from behind. The initial blast was immediately followed by another burst of fire as the fuel tank went up while the Mercedes was still in midair. The limo windows became a million glass projectiles. Metal bent, melted, twisted, and tore away from itself in every direction possible. Shrapnel rained down on the highway. A lone door landed in the ocean twenty yards away with a steamy, fizzling crash.

Caulder eased up on the gas, slowing to about twenty-five miles an hour. He looked over his shoulder. The Mercedes was a fiery, twisted ball of molten metal in the middle of the Pacific Coast Highway. Caulder felt pained but relieved.

Caulder took the long way home, up and over the Santa Monica Mountains, past that huge monstrosity of a house that no longer had an inhabitant. He turned onto the Ventura Freeway and went south until it fed into the Hollywood Freeway and then dumped him off downtown. It was an extra hour out of his way, but it was better than going back past the fiery chunks and scraps of metal, leather, and flesh that were creating an early-morning traffic jam on the Pacific Coast Highway.

twenty-three

Ry Caulder sat on his couch cradling a steaming cup of coffee and watching a local early-morning news report on TV. He would never sit in the recliner again. The memory of seeing Alvin dead in the chair was too depressing. There had been a few blood-stains on the chair, but Caulder had torn them loose and burned them in an ashtray. He would have dumped the chair if he was staying longer, but he wasn't.

Caulder's cold had gotten worse. His lungs were filling with fluid and he was coughing up phlegm. He had been participating in far too much strenuous activity of late and his adventure in the rain certainly hadn't helped matters any, to say nothing of the mental and emotional stress he had experienced over the last few days. He had killed two "friends" and been indirectly responsible for the death of a third. He had endangered the lives of an inno-cent woman and her young son. He had risked identification on numerous occasions. He had participated in the slaughter of seven soldiers in the employ of a noted Colombian drug lord and killed an attorney who had been unfortunate enough to cross his path at the wrong time. Caulder had behaved erratically and irrationally. The Justice Department was looking for him, the local cops were asking questions about him, and the Mafia felt he had outlived his usefulness to them. His world was falling apart just when he thought he had everything under control.

Ry Caulder. The consummate professional. The iceman. If the cops, the Colombians, the Feds, or Baxter's thugs didn't kill him, his own lungs probably would. Well, his work was done and now he could go about the business of nursing himself back to health. He wouldn't be able to leave town as soon as he had planned, but he'd have to leave the apartment as quickly as possible to avoid the police. He was going to need bed rest before his long journey. He'd check into a hotel under a new alias for a few days, after he collected his money from Baxter, and there he would recuperate, far from the pressures of his current identity. A week or two healing up at the Holiday Inn registered under the name of Smith or Jones and Caulder would be as good as new. Then he could get out of Los Angeles permanently. He could go someplace where no one knew him. Where no one would ever ask him to do the things he used to do. Where he would never be called upon to kill again. Where he could become one of the normals and enjoy the simple pleasures they enjoyed. A Xanadu for retired hit men. Spain, maybe?

Deep down he knew it was impossible. It was merely a fairy tale he had been telling himself to keep going. But he was too far gone already. He was burned out. The years of self-protective stoicism had taken their toll on Caulder. He had one gift for the world—his little magic act. If he stopped doing that he had nothing left to give anyone. There was no other life for him, but he could not continue to live as he had been living. His contact with Stephanie and Jason had perverted him. Softened him. Shown him the other side of the coin again. He was caught between two worlds. He didn't fit into either. He never had. But he never fully realized it until now.

The news returned from station break. A rather buxom young woman named Marsha Blake commanded the screen. An icon depicting an exploding stick of dynamite occupied the upper right corner of the screen. "A bizarre explosion rocked Malibu early this morning," Marsha Blake said. "Christopher Boden is *live* on the scene. . . . Christopher . . ."

The scene shifted to Christopher Boden, a man in his late thirties doing a tough-reporter-in-a-trenchcoat-in-the-field act, standing amid the flashing lights of police cars, ambulances, and fire engines at the site of the explosion on the Pacific Coast Highway.

"Well, Marsha," Christopher Boden said in a deep baritone. "All police have determined at this time is that a car in the northbound lane of the Pacific Coast Highway exploded at around four o'clock this morning. It is not clear whether the explosion was due to a malfunction of the automobile or perhaps some act of terrorism. . . . The police are not sure yet whether the vehicle was occupied at the time of the blast, since no bodies have been found at or around the accident site, though they are fairly certain that the vehicle was in motion when it blew up, owing to the pattern made by the debris. The rest, as of now, is a mystery. A mystery that is going to make the morning commute an adventure for the residents of Malibu."

Caulder was stupefied. He jumped up off the couch and spilled hot coffee down the front of his robe, scalding his legs. *No body!* How could there be no body? He stared blankly at the set, ignoring the burns on his legs. He was beyond pain. Something was terribly wrong.

It occurred to Caulder that the body could have been thrown into the ocean. They had been close enough to the water for that to have happened. At least one of the doors had flown that far.

Maybe the body hit the water too. Or maybe the police *had* a body and they just didn't want to release the information to the press or the public at this time. That had to be the case, because Fredrickson certainly couldn't have walked away from that blast. Nobody could have survived what Ry Caulder had done to his old buddy. Fredrickson had to be dead. He just *had* to be.

twenty-four

Caulder crossed Century Plaza, entered the 2029 building, and ascended to the penthouse level. It was Sunday, so most of the employees of Baxter Industries were home with their families. Only a skeleton crew manned the massive office suite. People with things to prove and jobs to protect.

Mike Del Monaco's secretary informed Caulder that Mr. Del Monaco was away on business, but Mr. Baxter would meet with him on the roof of the building. Caulder didn't like the sound of that. He was directed to a private elevator, but he opted for the stairwell. In his line of work it didn't pay to do as you were expected.

A large tennis court took up a good portion of the rooftop. Baxter, dressed in tennis whites, was playing fiercely against two attractive teenage girls. Baxter was holding his own, even though he was playing solo against a pair of opponents who were in excellent condition.

Five of Baxter's "executives" stood on the sidelines, watching the game. Gordon Quinn and Hal Mativich were among them, enjoying the spectacle of the two nubile young women bouncing around, chasing the tennis balls.

Caulder watched the game for a few moments from the shadows of the stairwell before stepping onto the roof.

Two of Baxter's men approached Caulder and began to frisk him. Caulder raised his arms over his head in mock compliance. One of the men, an unfortunate fellow named Blanchard, found the 9mm Browning in Caulder's shoulder holster and started to pull it out from under his jacket. Caulder brought his arm down and pinned the man's hand to his chest, painfully bending back his wrist. With his free hand, Caulder waved a finger in a negative gesture. The other man tried to grab Caulder. Caulder turned Blanchard and slammed the back of his head into the other man's forehead. The man stumbled and fell to the ground, unconscious, out of the game. Blanchard was dazed, but remained on his feet. Caulder locked Blanchard's wrist in a paralyzing grip that allowed him to move Blanchard at will like a puppet. He pulled the Browning from under his jacket and placed it against Blanchard's cheek.

The "executives" noticed the activity by the stairwell and rushed over, producing guns from under their jackets and aiming them at Caulder's head. Baxter stopped playing tennis and approached Caulder. One of the two girls went to the other side of the net and they began a game of their own. They had no interest in anything other than tennis, at least not at the moment.

"What do you want?" Baxter asked Caulder.

"My money."

"For what?"

"You saw the news this morning, didn't you . . . ?" Caulder still had Blanchard in the painful wrist lock, the pistol against his face. Baxter didn't seem to notice. The other "executives" were now circled around Caulder, but any time one of them would get too close Caulder applied pressure to Blanchard's wrist. Blanchard's yelps and cries convinced them to give Caulder his space.

"Are you referring to the car that blew up in Malibu? The car that no one was riding in?" Baxter asked.

"Believe me, Fredrickson was in that car. He was driving. The cops must be suppressing information for some reason."

"Sure . . . sure," Baxter said. "I got guys all over the state looking for this guy. They can't come up with spit. You say you found him right away and popped him just like that." Baxter snapped his fingers.

"He *allowed* himself to be found," Caulder said. "He wanted it."

"And why is that?"

"I have no idea. I think he wanted to kill me. Or he wanted me to kill him. I don't know."

"Bullshit. I've got Varga on my ass threatening to wage open warfare against us. He's claiming that you and Fredrickson are working for *me*. Maybe he's only half wrong. . . . Maybe you and Fredrickson are trying to start a gang war and take over both our businesses."

"It doesn't wash, Baxter," Caulder said. "You got me into the middle of this nonsense. I didn't want any part of it. What happened with the Colombians was unfortunate, but unavoidable. Varga gave me no other option. His people tried to kill me. Anyone that does that is fair game. *Anyone.*"

"Don't start with the threats, Caulder."

Quinn whispered to Mativich out the side of his mouth, "Ten bucks says he breaks Blanchard's arm."

"Make it twenty and you're on," Mativich whispered back.

Quinn nodded.

"Where's my cash?" Caulder asked Baxter again.

"What are you going to do? Call the Better Business Bureau? Or maybe the police?"

"What if I just kill you?"

The men around Baxter tensed. Baxter just smiled canine smile.

"Then you'll never get paid and the company will eliminate you."

Caulder knew Baxter spoke the truth. If he killed Baxter,
his life would be over as well. Baxter was part of a big machine,
and the machine always sought vengeance when one of their
own was eliminated. The Japanese called it "keeping face."
These guys just considered it an open warning to anyone who
fancied themselves a Brutus or a Judas. Preventive medicine
after the fact, so the disease would not spread to other members
of the family. They would find Caulder and they would kill
him. No matter how good he was. No matter how well he
hid. Sooner or later they would find him, just as he had found
Nate Daniels. One day Caulder would start his car and get
blown through the roof like Fredrickson. Or he would be in the
shower and end up like the attorney that he and Nate Daniels
had eliminated. Or he might be reaching for the phone like Peter
Hertzberg. Or taking a leak like Alvin. Or a million different
ways that it could come. But come it would. The company would
make a point of it.

"You've talked a lot of shit and you've slapped some guys
around," Baxter said. "I've allowed it because you've demonstrated
how pathetic the help is around here, but I'm running out of patience with you. You've got twenty-four hours to prove to me
Fredrickson is dead."

"Or what?"

"Then we come after *you*."

Caulder stared at Baxter for a few moments, not really knowing what to do next. He didn't know what was worse, being threatened by a scumbag like Baxter, or the nagging feeling that the
Fredrickson affair wasn't over. The fact that the body had not been
found troubled him, frustrated him, angered him. He decided to
take his angst out on the person closest to him. He snapped Blanchard's wrist. Blanchard screamed and fell to his knees. Tears

streamed down his face and he fell forward and rolled around on the ground nursing his broken wrist.

Quinn grinned and slapped Mativich on the shoulder. Mativich frowned.

Caulder and Baxter looked each other over. The "executives" tensed up another notch, ready to pull triggers.

"You've got a bad attitude, Caulder," Baxter said.

Caulder lowered his gun and backed into the stairwell. He started the long walk down to the street, the sweet sounds of Blanchard's screams echoing in his ears.

twenty-five

Caulder parked just off of Kanan Dume and walked through the woods to the orchard at the base of Fredrickson's property. He brought his binoculars but left his guns behind in the off chance that he would encounter the police. He climbed high up into a large oak tree and scanned Fredrickson's mansion through the binoculars.

Caulder could only see a small portion of the grounds from this vantage point, but what he *did* see made his heart skip a dozen beats. The veins in his temples expanded and throbbed as if they were going to explode.

Fredrickson was standing in front of his mansion, watering the lawn!

Fredrickson was dressed in a black robe and appeared to be perfectly healthy. His face looked even better than it had the night before, as if the explosion had been good for him cosmetically. Fredrickson looked more like the way Caulder remembered him. Almost normal. He certainly didn't look as if he had been in any exploding limousines lately.

"Son of a bitch . . ." Caulder muttered to himself. "How the hell did you pull that stunt off?!"

Caulder watched Fredrickson in utter amazement. Fredrickson appeared to be just another wealthy eccentric out watering his lawn. Caulder lowered the binoculars and scanned the valley. There were no other houses visible anywhere. Fredrickson had chosen his property well. Privacy had obviously been a big selling point for him.

Caulder studied the television relay tower on the far hill across the valley. He wondered if Fredrickson was going to go on his nightly hunt. Fredrickson had no car, so he would have to make new arrangements for transportation, and Caulder had a feeling that it wouldn't happen tonight. Fredrickson would either lay low or skip town altogether, and he certainly didn't look as if he was going anywhere in a hurry. You don't usually take time to water your lawn if you feel an urgency to skip town. Fredrickson must have been clear of identifying ties to the limousine. If it had been rented or registered to him the police would have been all over his place like ants. Maybe he had rented the limo through a third party, a shill of some sort. Perhaps the chauffeur himself. Or perhaps that's how he *got* the chauffeur in the first place, through some mysterious third party, because no one seemed to have missed the chauffeur yet either. There was no word of his disappearance or murder on the news. Just as there had been no mention of the dead Colombians or Alvin's body being found behind the liquor store. Maybe this was all a dream. Maybe none of it had happened. As far as the police were concerned it hadn't. But that situation was probably temporary.

Fredrickson watered his circular lawn for an inordinate length of time for such a small patch of grass. He appeared to be enjoying the outdoors. He would stretch out his arms every now and then and breathe deep and thump his chest. A Tarzan for the geriatric set. At one point he even laid down on the wet grass and stared up at the sky for almost five minutes, like some kind of crazed schoolboy hustling a girl on the mysteries of life and the magnificence of nature. Only Fredrickson was alone out there. He didn't have a girl to hustle. He just seemed to be hustling himself.

Then Caulder considered the possibility that Fredrickson might be aware that he was being watched. Maybe it was Caulder that was being hustled, jerked around by Fredrickson's nature-boy act.

As the sun started to dip behind the mountains, Fredrickson meticulously coiled his hose and put it back in his garage. He jumped into the air and clicked his heels as he entered the mansion. He seemed thrilled to be alive.

Night fell and Fredrickson made no attempt to leave his house. Caulder went back through the woods and got the large duffel bag out of the hidden compartment under the floor of the Buick's trunk. There had been no cops anywhere to be seen so he felt more comfortable carrying the weapons now. Caulder hiked through the woods along the stream to the television relay tower on the far hill.

A chain-link fence topped with coiled barbed wire surrounded the tower. Aside from the faint baying of coyotes and the rustle of the wind, quiet ruled the hills surrounding the area.

Caulder went to work on the padlock on the main gate. The lock was old and rusted, but it eventually came loose. Caulder set the duffel bag down and opened it. He withdrew a phone company utility belt and strapped it around his waist. Then he brought out the sniper rifle, attached the nightscope, and walked over to the tower.

The relay tower was about 150 feet high and trimmed with flashing red lights to warn off low-flying aircraft. The service ladder at the rear of the tower was not positioned ideally for Caulder's purposes so he shimmied up one of the tower's metal legs until he reached the first crossbeam. Then he climbed the tower using the crossbeams as rungs on a ladder of his own design.

Caulder stopped when he got about a hundred feet up the tower. He took the carabiner attached to the front of the utility belt and snapped it around a crossbeam. The carabiner held Caulder securely in place and permitted him to move both hands freely. He could see the front of Fredrickson's mansion from here. The angle was better and the view less obstructed than from the grove of trees.

Caulder shouldered the rifle and looked through the night-scope, switching on the infrared beam. Everything appeared as a muddled green through the scope, but far brighter than normal vision would produce. Details in the darkness could now be seen, even in some of the shadows. Illumination was provided for the scope wherever the infrared beam penetrated. Scanning the area, Caulder looked down toward Fredrickson's mansion, sitting alone in the small valley below, almost seven hundred yards away. It would be a long shot, but Caulder could handle it. He *had* the technology.

The house was dark save for one room on the left side of the uppermost story. This room was lit by flickering candles that caused the infrared to flare in places, but did not render the scope useless. Caulder refocused the scope and he could clearly make out Fredrickson standing in the window, smoking a cigar and staring out into the night. It was almost as if he knew Caulder was out there, as if he was waiting for him. Fredrickson was wearing a burnoose. His face looked odd once again, but different even from the night before. It seemed somewhat misshapen, and he looked like he was wearing a fake beard and mustache. He reminded Caulder of Fidel Castro. A master of disguise Fredrickson was not. It was quite obviously him. No five o'clock shadow could conceal that fact. Even if it had been glued on with spirit gum by some Hollywood makeup man.

Caulder braced himself and took deliberate aim with the rifle. "I've got you this time, you slippery fuck . . ." he muttered. Then he coughed violently and spit out a gob of phlegm. He watched the thick fluid drop the hundred feet to the ground below before turning his concentration back on his target.

Caulder adjusted the scope to compensate for the drop from what he estimated to be 683 yards of distance between him and his target. He chambered a shell and focused the crosshairs of the nightscope on the center of Fredrickson's forehead. He steadied himself and slowly squeezed the trigger. A flash and a loud bang accompanied the bullet's high-velocity exit from the gun.

The window in front of Fredrickson spiderwebbed and Fredrickson's head promptly exploded. Caulder had used a shell tipped with fulminated mercury to increase his odds for a one-shot kill.

Fredrickson stood headless behind the shattered window for a few moments, his hands flailing about wildly as if they were looking for his head; then he toppled over and fell backward onto the floor.

All was silent save the distant baying of coyotes.

Caulder looked at Fredrickson's dead body through the nightscope with a mixture of sadness and relief. From this vantage point Caulder was actually looking slightly down into the room, so the floor where Fredrickson lay could be clearly seen. Fredrickson's headless torso looked pathetic sprawled out like that. It was hard to believe that he had been a living, breathing human being only moments before. The magic act brought Caulder no dark joy this time. He had killed one of the most influential people in his life. Good or bad, Fredrickson had been a force in Caulder's existence for a long time. Now he was gone. And this time Caulder did not have the anonymous nature of an exploding limousine to protect him from personal involvement in the murder. This time Caulder had seen the sparkle in Fredrickson's eye as he pulled the trigger. This time there was a sense of responsibility that struck him deeper than he thought possible. It seemed so much more final than it had the night before. A part of Ry Caulder was dead now, for better or worse. Caulder bit his lower lip and shook his head slowly.

"That was embarrassing . . ." he muttered to the wind.

"Fredrickson's history," Caulder said bluntly into the pay phone. "Get my package ready. I want it tomorrow morning. No more bullshit. No more intrigues."

"When we have proof, you get paid," Baxter said on the other end of the line.

"Tomorrow morning—or else." Caulder hung up.

The Santa Monica pier was jamming with Sunday night visitors. It was hot for October, even for Southern California. The natives had migrated to the beach to put a bow on the weekend. Caulder had come here to get lost in the crowd. He didn't want to go back to the apartment yet, but he knew he must return eventually. There were things there that he needed.

His cold now verged on pneumonia. He needed to lie down. He sat on a concrete bench and breathed the sea air. Dead fish mixed with the salt smells, but it felt good to get relatively clean air into his lungs. Families and lovers mingled with the teenagers and the fishermen on the pier. They had all gathered at the same place with completely different agendas. The pier was a melting pot within a melting pot.

Caulder felt his chest heave and pain shot along his ribs, still sore from the conflict with the Colombians. His breathing was labored and he felt dizzy. He thought he might pass out and then he considered that maybe he wouldn't wake up. That this could be it. He could think of many worse ways to die and many worse places that it could occur. He slumped on the bench and fell asleep listening to the sounds of children playing on a nearby carousel.

* * *

Caulder could feel them watching him as he slept. The normals. The people with lives, jobs, families, homes. He could feel their judgments, their disgust. Finally it was too much. He awoke to find that he had slumped all the way over on the bench and was sleeping like some bum in the middle of the night. His hair was stuck to the bench by old soda that had spilled there. His clothes were matted to his body by his own sweat. He sat up and pulled his hair back and blinked like a junkie getting a methadone shot. He tried to find his bearings and ignore the eyes staring at him. He got to his feet and went to the Buick, which was parked in the five-dollar lot.

Caulder sat in the car for a few minutes, watching the lights of the pier, before deciding to go home.

•

Caulder found a business card on the floor just inside the door of his apartment. On one side was the address and phone number of the LAPD Robbery-Homicide squad and the name of a Detective Bradford March. On the back there was chicken-scratch writing in blue ink—*Mr. Caulder, please give me a call at your earliest convenience. Thank you.*

Caulder laughed painfully, locked his door, and collapsed on the couch. So this is how they do it, he thought. They just slide a card under your door and you turn yourself in. Obviously they didn't have much if they were this carefree about talking to him. If they *really* thought he had done something they would never have left the card. They would have been more patient and waited to catch him off guard. And if they already had him cold the place would have been staked out by SWAT and he'd be nailed now.

No, these guys either weren't sure or they just didn't give a damn. They didn't want to keep coming back here trying to catch him at home just to chat and they had no leads on how to find him when he wasn't home since he didn't really exist outside of this building. They wanted him to do their work for them. Just come on down to the station and confess to the murder of Peter Hertzberg so the file can be closed. He thought he might call them one day.

From Bangkok.

twenty-six

James Vincent Baxter embraced Ennio Garibaldi warmly, then turned to the one called Franco and shook his hand. "It's a pleasure meeting you, Mr. Franco."

"And it is an *honor* meeting you, Mr. Baxter," Franco said with a thin smile. He was smaller than Ennio Garibaldi, lean and muscular, with intense dark eyes.

Baxter motioned for the two men to sit down at the big round table meant for twelve. They were in the back room of Cafe Roma. The front of the restaurant had closed, but the kitchen staff was still in the back, awaiting orders. *Don Giovanni* played on the sound system just outside the room, allowing for more private discussion within. Four of Baxter's bodyguards sat at two smaller tables in the room, watching quietly. Another had positioned himself in the curtained doorway, looking into the front room. Quinn and Mativich sat at a table in the front room, sipping espresso and watching the entrance to the restaurant. They were on point as punishment for their recent failures.

Tony Marsala, Cafe Roma's night manager, entered the back

room with a bottle of Amerone. The waiters and waitresses had left long ago. Baxter motioned for him to pour without going through the charade of sniffing and tasting. If the wine wasn't up to par, the boys could have it. Tony Marsala asked if he could be of further service. Baxter ordered two antipasto platters as appetizers. Tony thanked Baxter, sidled past the bodyguard, and disappeared through the curtain.

"You guys want to look at menus or you want to talk business first?" Baxter asked the two men from Detroit.

"We're hungry," Ennio said, "but we didn't come all this way just to eat. We're here to help you."

Baxter nodded in appreciation. "And for that you have my undying gratitude."

"I owe *you*, Mr. Baxter," Ennio said. "We both know that." Ennio was a thick man. He had thick arms, thick legs, and a thick neck. His chest was a barrel. He had worked as Baxter's chief of security during most of the eighties but he moved to Detroit to run the company's operations there back in '88 and things had not gone well. Ennio's tenure as a vice president was painfully brief. Detroit turned out to be a fiasco for Ennio Garibaldi. Within a year profits had dropped severely. Accusations of embezzlement came from back east. Baxter eventually had to intervene on Ennio's behalf. He brought in a replacement, a Jew named Goldberg, who managed to get the situation under control. Ennio was forced to make token financial restitution. He was allowed to live, but part of his penance was permanent exile to Detroit. He worked security for his successor now, a daily reminder of his failure. He felt that they didn't give him enough time to make a go of it. He *hadn't* been stealing. He was simply in over his head. He was an enforcer, not a vice president. He just had a difficult time accepting that fact. Ennio resented the whole episode, especially the shame he felt being replaced by a Jew. The fact that Goldberg had done a much better job than Ennio had only crystallized the humiliation. He wanted out of Detroit in the worst way, but the Mercantes wouldn't release him. He was in exile.

"How would you like to come back to Los Angeles on a permanent basis?" Baxter asked Ennio.

"I'd walk on hot nails all the way from Detroit to get out of that hellhole," Ennio said. His eyes were wet with the thought of it.

"You take care of this problem and I think I can square things for you back east," Baxter said.

"For you, anything," Ennio said. He was careful before he continued. "May I ask something with no intention of disrespect?"

"Why are we having so much trouble with one man?" Baxter said, anticipating the question.

Ennio lowered his head, ashamed that he would ask what was not his business. If the capo wants someone hit, you just do it. You don't ask questions. And if the hit will free you from exile, you don't look a gift horse in the mouth. Baxter did not seem upset in the least.

"Ennio, I've known you a long time. We've been through hell together. But I tell you this, my friend, we have never dealt with a situation remotely like the one I am asking you to correct. Fredrickson is a black hole. I've tossed so many men at him that I've lost count. I don't know what this guy's trick is, but it's a motherfucker. He's throwing our operation into chaos. Now I've got them coming at us from all corners—the Colombians, the Chinese, the Yakusa, the Jamaicans, even the fucking Russian Mafia—they all sense an opportunity and they're making moves. We've got to restore order, *now*. Before we pass the point of no return. I only tell you this so you can go into the business with open eyes."

"I'm proud that you are willing to give me this opportunity to prove myself again," Ennio said, emotion choking his voice. He sipped some Amerone to clear his throat.

"You're the best at what you do," Baxter said. "You just weren't cut out for middle management. I told you that before you took the position in Detroit."

"And you were right, as always. But a man must strive to improve his lot in life."

"A man must also be true to his nature. Are you better off now than you were in eighty-eight?"

Ennio lowered his eyes again. His shame was becoming unbearable. "I will find Fredrickson and I will kill him with my bare hands. These hands that have seen so much murder." Ennio raised his hands in the air for inspection. They were calloused and muscled and scarred.

"I hope you get the chance, my friend." Baxter raised his glass in a toast. Ennio and Franco drank to Baxter's wishes.

"Mr. Franco doesn't say much," Baxter said to Ennio.

"Still waters, Mr. Baxter, still waters. But he's a good man. You'll be glad he's on our side."

"Tell me, Mr. Franco," Baxter said to the quiet man, "what do you want out of this?"

Franco looked straight into Baxter's eyes. He never looked away, never blinked. It was a sign of respect and a demonstration of honesty. "I work for Mr. Garibaldi. Mr. Garibaldi works for you. I do what I'm told."

Baxter maintained eye contact with Franco for as long as he could. Franco won the contest. Baxter finally looked away to Ennio. "Loyalty. How much of that is going around these days, eh, Ennio?"

"True, Mr. Baxter. So true."

Tony Marsala entered with the antipasto and placed it in the center of the table.

"Do you know what you'd like to eat?" Tony asked.

"This will do for now," Baxter commanded. Tony skittered out of the room. He hated keeping the kitchen staff this late, but Baxter owned 51 percent of the place. He could keep them all there until sunrise if he wanted. And it had happened more than once.

"Eat," Baxter said. Ennio and Franco scooped antipasto onto their plates and dug in. Baxter stuck with the Amerone.

"There's one other bit of business," Baxter said. "Remember Ry Caulder?"

"Of course," Ennio replied.

"I put him on this thing. Twice he's claimed he killed Fredrickson. The first time was a lie, so I doubt he's good for his word about the second time. He's either in on it with Fredrickson or he's fucking with us for his own reasons. He even waved a gun in my direction this morning. When it's over I want his head."

Ennio raised his hand in a pledge. "It is done." He looked over at Franco. Franco never looked up from his antipasto, but Ennio knew he had heard every word.

"This is such bullshit," Mativich whispered to Quinn as he finished his third espresso. He could smell the puttanesca and the linguine Fra Diavlo in the back room as Baxter and his guests were finishing dinner. "These fucking guys aren't any better than us. Here we are driving them around like we're a couple of niggers. We don't even get to *eat* with them."

"We picked 'em up from LAX," Quinn said without looking away from the front door. "Big deal. They got their own car now. Anders brought 'em one of the rentals."

"Good. I'm not a fucking chauffeur."

"You've had too much espresso."

"I don't know why the boss doesn't just let us handle Fredrickson."

Quinn looked at him now. "You want that? You really want that? You want to end up like Elliot and the others?"

Mativich didn't answer. He stared at the grounds in the bottom of his espresso cup. Elliot had been Baxter's most recent chief of security—until three weeks ago. Elliot and a torture squad went after Fredrickson. None of them was ever seen again, but Elliot's pinky finger, pinky ring and all, arrived in Baxter's mail three days later.

"Well, I don't want any part of that shit," Quinn continued. "You stick our necks into *that* wringer and *I'll* kill you myself." Quinn went back to watching the door.

Mativich touched the cut on his lip that he had received in Ry Caulder's elevator. "What about Caulder? You going to let him knock us around like he did? You think *that's* okay too? You think that's *right?*"

"I've got plans for Caulder," Quinn said absently. "If he's still around after Fredrickson's out of the way I'm going to kill that fuck, no matter what Baxter says."

"At least you haven't gone *totally* soft."

Quinn looked at Mativich and considered slapping him. The cellular phone on the table between them rang, distracting him from the plan. Quinn picked up the phone and said, "Carlyle Shipping." Carlyle Shipping was the company name under which the cellular was listed. Quinn listened intently and his eyes grew wide.

By the time Baxter, Ennio, and Franco had finished eating dinner they had gone through three bottles of Amerone and it was almost one o'clock in the morning.

Quinn suddenly rushed into the room with his cellular phone. "Mr. Baxter. It's important." He handed the phone to Baxter.

"What?" Baxter asked, then listened carefully. After thirty seconds he said, "Don't let him leave . . . Do whatever you have to do, you cowardly piece of shit. He better be there when we get there." Baxter hit the OFF button on the cellular and looked at Ennio. "One of our bagmen is at Tribeca, just three miles from here. He says Fredrickson's at the bar. Can you believe that?"

Ennio and Franco were already out of their chairs. "Anything is possible, Mr. Baxter. I know Tribeca. We can be there in five minutes."

"Who do you want to take with you?" Baxter asked.

"Franco will be enough."

"You don't know what you're up against."

"He is only a man. If we cannot kill him we are not worthy of life." Ennio turned and walked out of the room, Franco on his heels.

"No truer words were ever spoken," Baxter said after the two men had left the room.

Baxter was just getting into bed when the phone rang. It was Quinn.

"Mr. Baxter? We went by Tribeca like you asked. The cops had the place cordoned off. Mativich got out and asked around. A paramedic told him a couple guys got popped in the alley behind the place. We snuck Anders back there doing his reporter act so he could get a look at the bodies. It was your two boys from Detroit. But there wasn't much left of them."

Baxter hung up the phone and turned off the lights. He did not go to sleep.

twenty-seven

Sirens woke Ry Caulder at six in the morning. They weren't coming for him. They were headed uptown. He took a couple hits off the inhaler to get his lungs working.

He felt better. The cold was still with him, but at least he was rested. He got up, made coffee, took some medication, drank some orange juice, and watched the morning news. There was no word of Fredrickson's death. Nothing.

Caulder realized that Fredrickson's location was so remote it might be weeks before the body was found. He considered calling the police and tipping them to the murder up in the Malibu hills. Or maybe sending Baxter's men out there to take a look for themselves. He thought it over while he tried to steam some of the congestion out of his lungs during a very long, hot shower.

By the time he was dry he had decided to do nothing about Fredrickson. He'd wait awhile and let nature run its course. Someone would find the body, eventually. In the meantime he was going to vacate the apartment. He packed a small duffel bag with what few belongings he wanted to take with him and left the rest, including the machine pistol under the sink. There was still one bag he needed, which was stashed in the garbage chute, but he would come back for that later. Right now he wanted to see how Stephanie and Jason were doing. He was going to say good-bye to them one last time.

When the elevator opened in the parking garage, the hairs on Caulder's neck caught fire. There was danger here. In spades. He had no gun. The machine pistol was upstairs. Everything else had been left in the trunk of the Buick, locked tight in the hidden compartment in a car registered to Richard Alton. If the cops opened that car with a warrant for someone named Ry Caulder, the weapons would be inadmissible. It was still taking a big chance, but Caulder had been too sick and exhausted to replace them in the chute. Now he was weaponless and someone was in the parking garage, waiting for him.

Caulder hit the button to close the elevator. Before the ancient doors could grind shut, two men with automatics jammed through the doorway. The first man was the ape that Caulder had met in Baxter's outer office. The ape slammed Caulder against the wall of the elevator so hard that Caulder thought his back might be broken. The second man through the door went to the elevator control panel. A third man appeared in the entrance and wedged the doorway open. The man at the panel hit the EMERGENCY STOP switch. No alarm sounded, but the door stopped trying to close on the third man's feet.

The ape grabbed Caulder by the shoulder and straightened him up. As the man at the panel turned, Caulder saw that he was wearing a thick plaster cast on his forearm, covering a broken wrist. The cast had been reinforced with steel rods all around to absorb shocks. Blanchard looked Caulder in the eyes and said, "Remember me, motherfucker?"

Caulder didn't reply, but he could feel the fear growing in the pit of his stomach.

Blanchard grabbed Caulder by the hair with his good hand and elevated his head to a desired height. He raised the cast high in the air and tightened his fingers around the plaster and steel.

"Thanks for the brick arm," Blanchard said, and he brought the cast down hard on top of Ry Caulder's skull.

When Caulder regained consciousness he found himself staring up at a canine smile.

"Welcome back, shit for brains," Baxter snarled. "Who the fuck you think you are, coming to my office, pulling a piece in *my* presence? No one pulls a piece on James Vincent Baxter and walks away." All hint of sophistication had disappeared from Baxter's manner and voice.

Caulder's face was wet and cold. Someone had dumped water on him to bring him around. He tried to focus his eyes, but it wasn't easy. His head throbbed and he felt like he was falling end over end in space. He couldn't tell where they were but he smelled oil and gasoline and he felt cold concrete on his back.

"I want you to meet someone," Baxter continued. "Ormsby, get over here."

A tall, thin man with reddish hair and a full beard and mustache came over and looked down at Caulder.

"Tell Mr. Caulder who you saw last night, Ormsby," Baxter demanded.

The red beard said one word. "Fredrickson."

Caulder stared up at Ormsby as if the man had just cut his heart out, then looked at Baxter and said, "Bullshit." He barely got the word through his raw throat.

"Midnight last night, I'm having drinks at Tribeca," Ormsby continued. "I was alone at the bar, minding my own business, and Fredrickson came in and sat down not more than ten feet away from me. I practically choked to death. I didn't even finish my martini. . . . I just packed up and got the fuck out of there."

"You're lying. Fredrickson is dead!"

"He was there . . . right there in front of me! I know what Fredrickson looks like. I've delivered pay to him. You must have hit someone else!"

For a moment that thought played with Caulder's mind. What if it *wasn't* Fredrickson he shot? What if it was a relative of his or a friend or even someone Fredrickson had doctored up to look like him? Fredrickson *had* looked different standing in the window of the mansion. If that was the case then Caulder had killed an innocent. *No*, that couldn't be it—the guy in the window was Fredrickson. No two ways about it, and the man was definitely dead. Ormsby was either mistaken or he was lying.

"Get him up," Baxter said to someone that Caulder could not see from his position on the floor.

Powerful arms lifted Caulder in the air and he was shoved up against a wall. They were in a gas station garage. The place was shuttered, abandoned. One of Baxter's laundering outfits either gone under or newly purchased. There were seven other men in the room, not counting Caulder, Baxter, and Ormsby. The ape had Caulder by the neck. Blanchard, Quinn, and Mativich were in the crowd. They couldn't wipe the smiles off their faces. The other three men were new guys. Caulder didn't recognize them. Mike Del Monaco was not in the room. He either wanted no part of this or he had not been informed at all.

Blanchard turned on a bench grinder used to cut, grind, and polish metal. There were two spinning wheels—a grinding stone and a circular brush made of sharp steel wires. The ape shoved Caulder's face close to the grinding stone. Baxter leaned in and looked Caulder in the eyes.

"Let me straighten you out on a couple of things," Baxter yelled over the grinder. "You are fucked with a capital F. We know all about your little family. The broad and the kid."

Caulder moved his eyes enough to see Quinn and Mativich. Their smiles grew wider.

"You better quit jerking off," Baxter continued. "You bring me Fredrickson's head or I'll turn that whore of yours out onto the street fucking niggers for ten bucks a pop. I'll sell the punk to a kiddie porn ring in El Monte. We'll fuck with you so long you'll get a taste of what they're going through before we take you apart."

Baxter nodded at the ape. Caulder felt pressure against the back of his neck and his head moved closer to the grinding stone. A quick shove took a piece off Caulder's forehead before he was jerked back and away from the bench grinder. Blood dripped into his eyes. Blanchard turned the grinder off and the ape leaned Caulder in a corner.

"I . . . I'm telling you, Fredrickson is d . . . dead," Caulder stuttered. "Why don't you go out and have a look yourselves?"

"We sent two guys out last night after Ormsby called," Baxter said. "Outside talent that I shipped in from Detroit. Pros . . . like you *used* to be. They never made it back. This guy's not only alive, he's barhopping and he doesn't give a fuck who knows it!" It was clear that Baxter feared for his own life. He had been hiding it well up to now, but the terror was beginning to show on his face. There was more at stake here than just business. "You keep talking shit like you can put your hands on him anytime you want. So far you've been a big zero. The question is, should I give you another chance to prove yourself? You think you can finish this? You don't, we might as well just kill you now. What's it going to be?"

Caulder looked at Baxter. He didn't have much of a choice.

"I'll get him," Caulder said through blood, congestion, and pain. "I swear it."

twenty-eight

The ape and a man with a harelip and cleft palate dumped Ry Caulder unceremoniously in the alley behind his apartment. Baxter didn't let Quinn, Mativich, or Blanchard go along for fear they might kill Caulder in an act of zealousness. Once the word went down that Caulder could be hurt it was like tossing meat to starving Dobermans. They were ready to chew each other up to get first crack at him.

The ape seemed to have more self-control. He didn't care what happened to Caulder. He was just doing his job. It wasn't personal.

Once Caulder was out of the car the man with the cleft palate said, "Gift it donfe," which Caulder took to mean "Get it done" with the speech impediment. The El Dorado left the alley slowly, as if the ape was considering coming back to finish off the job.

Caulder went upstairs. There were no signs that the cops had returned. He showered again and changed into clean clothes. Then he went to work on the friction cut on his forehead. It wasn't as bad as he thought, but it burned like crazy when he hit it with hydrogen peroxide. A large Band-Aid barely covered the wound.

He brushed his hair forward to hide the Band-Aid as much as possible.

Caulder drove out to Malibu. He passed the dirt road leading to Fredrickson's mansion twice, checking for activity. Seeing none, he found a gravel trail a half a mile farther up Kanan Dume that led to the top of a hill that overlooked the entire mini-valley. He was too far away from Fredrickson's mansion to make out much detail, even with the high-powered binoculars, but nothing seemed out of the ordinary. No police barricades warning trespassers away from the murder scene. No ambulances or coroner's vehicles to deal with the body. No forensics people scouring the place for microscopic clues. No reporters scurrying about trying to dig up the dirt. Not even a cop car parked in the driveway. Nothing. It appeared that Fredrickson's body had yet to be found, unless the authorities were hidden from view in the many clusters of trees surrounding the place, waiting to see who would show up.

Caulder checked the area surrounding the television relay tower. It was clean, but if the cops *had* found Fredrickson's body they would have calculated the trajectory of the shot and the tower would be under surveillance now.

He knew that the hill he stood on could be under surveillance too. But the panic and frustration he felt while considering the possibility that Fredrickson could have beaten death again had obscured what little rational thought Caulder had left. The specter of police suddenly circling the hill and coming in to arrest him sent chills coursing through his body, but it was too late to worry about that now. He was committed. If they were watching the hill, they already had him.

There was no sign of life in or around the house. He tilted the binoculars up and looked at the window he had shot Fredrickson through the night before. The window still had a bullet hole in it, so Caulder knew that *that* part, at least, had not been a dream, but from this angle he could not see the body, or any part of the floor itself for that matter.

Caulder stood there for a few minutes considering whether or not he should go down and climb the tower again to get a better look. Even though it was broad daylight, he felt an overwhelming desire to see Fredrickson's corpse and convince himself that the man was really dead and that Ormsby and Baxter were just a couple of no-good, cheating liars.

Caulder noticed activity on the dirt road leading to the mansion. A yellow taxicab came up the drive and pulled to a stop under the carriageway.

The sound of the taxi's horn echoed across the valley. Good, Caulder thought, some prearranged pickup call. Maybe the cab driver would discover the body. If Caulder was so sure of himself, why was his heart beating so rapidly? Why were the hairs on the back of his neck beginning to tingle? That obnoxious sixth sense of his was trying to tell him the truth about the whole affair. Trying to ease the shock of what he was about to witness.

Fredrickson emerged from the house, looking cool and crisp in a white three-piece suit. He walked casually toward the taxicab, looking perfectly happy, healthy, and content.

Caulder's eyes went wide with shock and amazement. He couldn't believe what he was seeing. This was a dead man walking. How many lives did this guy have?

Fredrickson opened the rear door of the cab and climbed into the backseat. A few moments later, the taxi started down the hill.

A panic seized Caulder. This was too much to believe! Fredrickson had tricked him again. He must have killed someone *else* last night! He had taken an innocent life. He had broken his own most important commandment.

Caulder lowered the binoculars, ran to his car, leaped in, and with a scrunch of tires spinning on gravel, took off down the trail to Kanan Dume Road.

* * *

The taxicab pulled up in front of the Sumitomi Bank of Beverly Hills. Fredrickson got out, handed some money to the driver, walked up the marble stairs to the bank, and disappeared through the entrance.

Ry Caulder's car slowed in front of the bank and then turned left into a huge parking garage across the street.

Caulder took his ticket and quickly wound the Buick up and around the six stories of parking garage to the top floor, the roof. He parked at the edge of the roof and got out. He opened the trunk and removed the duffel bag containing the sniper rifle from the hidden compartment.

Caulder slammed the trunk shut and walked, as nonchalantly as he could, over to the elevator shaft situated at the edge of the building.

There was a locked door marked SERVICE on the rear side of the elevator shaft. Caulder pulled the tension wrench and the all-purpose lockpick out of his pocket and worked the lock in three seconds flat. He couldn't have gotten in quicker if he had a key. He entered the service room and locked the door tightly behind himself, then slid a workbench under the doorknob for added insurance.

The room was small and filled with tools. The floor directly in front of Caulder opened up into the elevator shaft. Skeletal metal beams formed a barricade around the shaft so that no one would fall in by accident, but access was still allowed to the rear and sides of the elevator box for any necessary repair work. Caulder could see the elevator car down below, moving between floors. Occasionally, as Caulder went about his business, the car came to the top floor and entered the room. Only the back and the two sides of the car could be seen when this happened and none of the passengers could see into the room from the outside, so Caulder felt relatively secluded.

There was a small window in the outer wall of the room, presumably for light and ventilation. Caulder rubbed six months of dirt and grime from the window. Then he could see the Sumitomi Bank across the street from the parking garage. He turned the latch on the window and opened it a few inches. The window was top-hinged so it opened out and slightly upward.

Caulder set his duffel bag on a wooden table, opened it, and quickly began assembling the sniper rifle. He had disassembled the weapon after shooting Fredrickson from the relay tower. He thought one shot dead center in Fredrickson's face would be enough to kill the man. Obviously this was not the case.

Caulder glanced out at the bank entrance every few seconds as he worked to make sure Fredrickson didn't leave. Caulder ignored the nightscope and attached the smaller, high-powered day scope to the top of the gun. He secured the suppressor, loaded a full clip of nonexplosive shells into the bottom of the weapon, then slid the barrel of the gun through the window. He chose the nonexplosive shells in the interest of public safety and for the reduced noise factor. These bullets would fire cleaner and more quietly than the shell he had used the night before. Not only would it minimize the possibility of civilian casualties, but he might even be able to pull off the hit without being discovered. He chambered the first shell.

Caulder peered through the scope and focused on the entrance of the bank. People flowed in and out of the revolving doorway in a steady stream. He hoped Fredrickson would not exit out some door in the rear of the building.

Caulder wiped sweat from his brow. He had replayed the previous night's events through his head a thousand times as he followed the taxi to Beverly Hills and he felt certain that it had been Fredrickson who took the bullet the night before. Caulder considered all the ways Fredrickson might have tricked him, but they all seemed too far-fetched and complicated. He couldn't sell any of the theories to himself. And why would Fredrickson want to trick Caulder? What was his motivation? He certainly wasn't trying to fake his own death. If Fredrickson wanted Caulder, or anyone else for that matter, to think he was dead he would have disappeared after the limousine explosion. But here he was, still flaunting his goods out in the open for everyone to see. Bragging about Caulder's inability to kill him. Taunting him. Fredrickson's very existence had become a testimony to Caulder's ineffectiveness. That's it, he thought. Fredrickson was trying to torture him for some reason. It was *personal*.

Or maybe he was just going insane.

Caulder didn't have to think about it much longer. Fredrickson emerged from the bank and walked down the steps toward the street.

Caulder looked through the telescopic sight and focused on Fredrickson again. It was very definitely Fredrickson, looking incredibly dapper in his white suit. No weird makeup jobs to confuse the issue. At least *this time*, in the bright light of day, there could be no possible case of mistaken identity. Caulder suddenly recognized the white suit. It was a tailored job that Fredrickson had purchased on a "business trip" in Hong Kong with Ry Caulder nearly a decade ago. Fredrickson probably knew it would push Caulder's buttons, evoking memories he had been seeking to submerge for a long time. Caulder's finger found the trigger of the rifle and rubbed it nervously.

Fredrickson reached the sidewalk, turned to his left, and walked down the street. The heavy pedestrian traffic made it difficult for Caulder to get a clean shot at his target. Once again innocent lives were at risk, but he was nearly blind to all that now.

Caulder focused the crosshairs on the center of Fredrickson's back, approximately where his heart should be. If, that is, this magician had a heart. Now Caulder had to wait for Fredrickson to move clear of all the innocents.

A cold sweat soaked Caulder's face. He realized it didn't come from the fever. It came from uncontrolled tension. This was a big mistake, inspired by a series of unpredictable events. Until recently Caulder's world had consisted of two elements. There was the predictable and then there were the uncertain elements that he could manipulate to *make* predictable. What he was experiencing now fell into neither category and he was not proud of the way he was responding to the challenge. This was a panic hit. His fourth in as many days. But this was a panic hit that made his earlier forays look like textbooks of planning and restraint. This was a totally off-the-cuff panic hit in *public*. Something a slob would be attempting, not Ry Caulder.

Even that clown Oswald had had a plan, or at least he had been *part* of a plan. And Oswald, in Caulder's professional opinion, was the king of the slobs and a total sucker/sap/asshole to boot. Not only had he been played for the ultimate fall guy, but he had participated in the killing of a not-so-bad president of the United States while he was being manipulated by forces he couldn't possibly comprehend. Caulder didn't like the fact that Kennedy had ensnared America deeply in the Vietnam conflict, but he felt JFK would have handled the situation a lot better than Johnson and Nixon did, if only Kennedy had lived. Kennedy had wanted out of Vietnam before he was assassinated. Maybe Tet could have been avoided if not for Oswald.

For a brief, crazy moment Caulder blamed Oswald for the long series of events that had led him from Vietnam to this parking-garage rooftop and his current state of near hysteria. But logic returned and he realized that it wasn't *really* Oswald's fault. If it hadn't been Oswald it would have been some other dumb sucker. Oswald wasn't that relevant anyway. Even if he had missed altogether, the end result would have been the same. It was the guy in the old grassy knoll that had been the real pro that day. And you better *believe* that *he* had a plan. Not quite the one Oswald had been given, but *a plan* and a pretty damn good one at that. Yep, you gotta have a plan. Every pro knows that. But here Ry Caulder was, out on a wing and a prayer, making every mistake imaginable, with nothing in his mind other than killing Fredrickson. Plans were out the window. It was ad lib time now. And it wasn't 1963, back when only a handful of Americans owned 8mm cameras. This was the nineties. Everybody and their brother had video cameras now. If the Kennedy assassination took place today there would be hundreds of different angles showing the grassy knoll and the assassins behind the fence. Right now there could quite possibly be some jerk down below videotaping his wife's most recent jewelry purchase. Caulder could easily be featured on the six o'clock news tonight if he was unlucky. And luck didn't seem to be going his way lately.

Fredrickson moved into the clear. Caulder was about to make the shot. Suddenly the elevator car arrived in the cage next to him. Voices of the departing passengers carried from the hall outside of the service room—a group of secretaries going to lunch. Caulder held his fire. Even though he had fixed the suppressor to the muzzle of the gun, the shots would still be loud enough to hear outside on the roof. Suppressors only went *poof poof* in the movies. A real suppressor, no matter how good, would still make a popping sound, loud enough for the secretaries to hear. The main function of the suppressor at this point would be to keep the people down below from knowing where the shot had come from. Caulder's tension level rose. Fredrickson would be out of range soon and the moment would be lost. The elevator dropped out of the room and the voices outside drifted off as everyone headed for their respective vehicles.

Caulder concentrated on his target again. His finger tightened on the trigger. The moment was almost there. A man crossed Fredrickson's path and continued on, out of the way. Caulder squeezed the trigger and a small popping sound echoed around the room.

The shot hit Fredrickson in the center of his back. The bullet went all the way through Fredrickson's body and impacted quietly on the sidewalk in front of him. But the man kept walking! It was as if he didn't feel or even notice the shot.

Caulder pulled his face away from the scope and rubbed his eyes again. Was he hallucinating? What the hell was this guy made of? Caulder looked back into the scope.

Fredrickson continued walking down the street, totally unaware that he had been hit. Sometimes a person can be shot and continue to behave normally for a few seconds before realizing what has happened, but this was ridiculous. This was the longest delayed reaction that Caulder had ever seen.

Caulder focused on Fredrickson's back again and began rapidly squeezing off shots. *Pop! Pop! Pop! Pop! Pop!* Any people waiting for the elevator outside the service room would certainly hear the shots, but hopefully they wouldn't be able to identify what they were hearing. It wasn't the sound of gunfire that the general public had grown so fondly accustomed to on prime-time television.

The bullets ripped into Fredrickson's back and blasted their way out of his chest onto the sidewalk. Blood splattered out of Fredrickson's body. This time he noticed. Fredrickson stopped in his tracks, looked down at his bloody chest and the chip marks on the sidewalk in front of him.

Pedestrians on the street were beginning to realize that a man was being shot in their midst. At first there was just a lot of gawking and jaw dropping. The crowd wasn't quite sure what Fredrickson's problem was, but panic began to overwhelm them, like cattle in line at the slaughterhouse that got a look into the back room.

Caulder was stunned. Six very well-placed shots and Fredrickson was still standing! It was medically impossible, or at least highly improbable.

Fredrickson touched his white suit, now torn and smeared with dark chunks of black and crimson blood. He stuck his finger into one of the bullet holes and felt around inside his chest with what amounted to minor curiosity. He appeared to be relishing the experience.

Fredrickson turned around and looked up at the parking

garage. He judged the trajectory of the shots and looked directly at Ry Caulder.

Caulder lowered the rifle and stared at Fredrickson, dumbfounded.

Fredrickson removed his bloody finger from the hole in his chest and pointed it at Caulder like it was a pistol. Fredrickson smiled widely. It was a big happy smile. Not remotely like Baxter's faux grin that actually signaled unhappiness. No, this was the smile of a jovial man, filled with genuine humor. A drop of blood fell from Fredrickson's finger and made a small Rorschach blot on the sidewalk a few feet away from the big ones that Caulder had created.

Caulder's hands were shaking. He quickly raised the rifle and fired again, aiming for Fredrickson's head.

The shot ripped into Fredrickson's neck, tearing out a chunk of flesh and squirting a fountain of arterial spray onto a nearby woman, who screamed and tried to run away, only to trip and fall roughly to the pavement. Fredrickson himself seemed relatively unfazed. He said, simply, "Ouch."

The scene erupted into pandemonium as visions of insane snipers in towers filled the pedestrians' heads. People screamed and stampeded crazily about, pushing and shoving one another out of the way, trying to find cover from the unseen assailant.

Caulder couldn't get in another clean shot even if the area had remained clear. His hands were trembling with fear and confusion. His face was slick with a thick sheet of perspiration. He lowered the rifle and looked down at the panic scene. He was in deep now.

Fredrickson walked toward the woman who had fallen on the sidewalk in front of him. She was being trampled by the fleeing mob. Fredrickson moved through the crowd calmly, reached down, and helped the woman to her feet. She was so battered and dazed that she didn't notice she was being assisted by a man who was covered in blood and shot full of holes.

Fredrickson led the woman to the curb and flagged down an approaching taxicab. The taxi didn't look as if it was going to stop, so Fredrickson stepped out into the street in front of the speeding vehicle.

The taxi screeched to a halt an inch away from Fredrickson's body. The driver, a black woman in her early thirties, leaned out the window and yelled at Fredrickson, "Are you crazy?"

Fredrickson ignored the question, opened the rear door of the cab, and slid the dazed woman into the backseat. A frightened man in a jogging outfit tried to force himself past Fredrickson into the cab. Fredrickson slammed his palm into the man's chin and sent him sprawling on the sidewalk. Then he climbed into the back of the cab next to the woman.

The taxi driver was watching the riot scene happening all around her vehicle. "What the fuck's going on?" she asked, without looking into the backseat.

"Free samples at the bakery," Fredrickson replied.

The driver turned and got her first good look at Fredrickson and his tattered, blood-soaked suit. Skin dangled from his neck wound. When she had first seen him standing at the curb she thought he was dressed in a dark suit with light patterns. Now she realized the suit had once been white and the dark areas were of recent, involuntary design.

"Christ, honey, what happened to you?!" she asked.

"I got caught next to the cappuccino machine," Fredrickson replied, playing out his bakery gag.

A police car pulled around the corner a half mile behind them, lights flashing, siren wailing.

"Let's go," Fredrickson said calmly, as if his desire to depart had nothing to do with the presence of police officers.

"Where to? The med center?" the driver asked.

"Just drive. We're going to do some sight-seeing. My lady friend is new in town."

The driver looked into the rearview mirror at Fredrickson to see just what kind of lunatic she had picked up. Fredrickson smiled at her sweetly and capped it off with a wink. Maybe he was in shock, she thought. At least he seemed friendly and didn't appear violent. She pulled the latch on the holster that housed the .44 Special against her right calf, nevertheless.

A panic-stricken man in a Brooks Brothers suit rushed the taxi. Fredrickson locked the door and the man pulled frantically on the handle.

"Let me in! Let me in!" the man begged. "I'm an attorney! I can help you!"

The driver put the car in gear and sped away. The attorney did a spin and hit the pavement, briefcase and papers flying everywhere.

Fredrickson laughed to himself. Perfect, absolutely perfect, he thought. Fredrickson and Caulder shared similar views on attorneys. It used to be a favorite topic of conversation between them. Jameson had been an attorney. At least he had been an attorney before he went into politics. He was as crooked as any attorney or politician that had ever drawn breath. He could be bought for a steak and a martini and his word was absolutely useless. He'd sell himself to one buyer, then contradict the sale when someone with more money and a different agenda came along.

Fredrickson and Caulder had both looked forward to that job with some degree of enthusiasm. Unfortunately, Fredrickson's enthusiasm blossomed out of control. He got carried away, swept up in the moment. And when he was faced with the option of sparing or taking a life that wasn't supposed to be taken, Jameson's daughter's, there really *was* no option for him. He stole the young girl's life like an apple on a fruit stand. He plucked it away and devoured it whole and never regretted any of it for one second. It meant nothing to him. That had been the end of his relationship with Ry Caulder, both personally and professionally. Until now.

The cab sped along Little Santa Monica Boulevard, which ran parallel to Santa Monica Boulevard proper. Fredrickson sat next to the dazed woman, patting and rubbing her hand. Comforting her.

"There, there, darling ... We're safe now," he said to the woman with deep affection. She was very lovely, in spite of the bruises and cuts inflicted upon her by the frenzied mob. The abuse seemed to agree with her. It brought out the peasant beauty in the woman's features. She was suddenly Fredrickson's Dulcinea.

The woman rolled her head deliriously and looked directly at Fredrickson for the first time. The man sitting next to her, caressing her, was riddled with bullet wounds. His suit was drenched in blood and a large chunk of his own flesh hung from his neck, allowing the woman to view some of the inner workings of his throat.

The woman blinked like a raccoon. She wasn't sure she was awake. Once she realized that this was really happening, she began screaming. She was about to go a little mad.

twenty-nine

Ry Caulder, carrying his duffel bag low to the ground, rushed toward his car on the roof of the parking garage. He had taken a few seconds in the service room to remove the 9-mm Browning from the bag and strap it into the shoulder holster under his jacket in case he had to shoot his way out of Beverly Hills. Screams and sirens could be heard coming from the street down below. Luckily no one was on the roof at the time, so he got to the Buick with no witnesses. He tossed the bag in his trunk, not taking the time to put it in the hidden compartment, then drove slowly down and around the many levels of the circular garage, sucking on a fresh inhaler like it was an oxygen tank.

While there was utter anarchy in front of the Sumitomi Bank of Beverly Hills, the exit ramp of the parking garage was located on an adjacent street on the opposite side of the garage. The panic had not reached this far yet. Caulder managed to bypass the traffic deadlock plaguing the shooting area. He only had to deal with the routine traffic of Beverly Hills to make his escape. He wound up on Santa Monica Boulevard heading east. A convoy of speeding police cars going west passed by on Little Santa Monica, heading for the shooting site. It would take them a while to figure out what had happened, let alone where the shots had come from. Caulder would be long gone by then.

By the time Caulder was out of Beverly Hills his nerves were completely shot. He was having trouble concentrating on the drive and nearly rear-ended vehicles in front of him on two separate occasions. He decided to get off the street and collect himself. He stopped in at Barney's Beanery, a hip watering hole disguised as a dive in the center of West Hollywood that had three pool tables and every kind of beer, lager, and stout available as well as a full compliment of the harder spirits.

Barney's was notorious for the NO FAGOTS ALLOWED sign that had hung over the bar for as long as anyone could remember. The slogan had also appeared on Barney's matchbooks for many years, until the city council pressured the owner to tone down his advertisements. It was just about the only straight bar in the neighborhood and proud to present a haven for heterosexuals. The management had no intention of changing clientele. And the clientele had never mentioned to the owner that he had misspelled *faggot*.

Caulder found an empty stool at the bar and hunkered down. Barney's late lunch crowd packed the joint, hungry and horny. The place was filled with junior executives, has-been actors, and young, firm, wanna-be actresses. It was a poorly lit, twisted version of the old Schwab's drugstore. Caulder ordered a shot of Bacardi 151. He wanted to calm down fast. He downed the shot of rum as soon as the bartender set it in front of him and immediately requested another. The second shot he nursed along more gently. He knew 151 could get away from him pretty quick. He was there for medicinal purposes. He didn't want to go on a bender.

As the Bacardi began to work its magic, Caulder's pulse slowed to normal and his heart stopped racing. He sat and tried to understand what was happening.

It was beyond his comprehension.

He had blown Fredrickson up in his limousine. He had shot him squarely in the face with a mercury-tipped bullet. He had put six slugs into him from fifty yards off in front of two hundred witnesses. But the man still lived. The man was cruising town in a taxi with a couple of ladies while Caulder sat here shaking into his shot glass. It was unfathomable.

Caulder finally decided to try to put it out of his mind for the time being, to clear his thoughts and let his subconscious work on the problem. This was the way he usually attacked complicated situations. He would ingest the information vital to the issue and then go about the more mundane tasks of living and let it all percolate. When next he dredged up the pertinent question his subconscious would have worked things out and he would have his solution.

He decided this was his only hope and turned his attention to the smorgasbord of humanity that occupied Barney's Beanery. A lanky young brunet in a tight black skirt was shooting pool nearby with two potential suitors. She couldn't shoot for shit but she looked great bent over the table. Caulder thought she looked somewhat like Stephanie might have looked a few years back, before childbirth, an ugly divorce, and the custody battle over Jason had deepened the lines in her face and hardened her heart. He watched the girl play through a third shot of Bacardi and then he paid his tab and left.

As Caulder drove home he could feel the rum coursing through his veins. Bacardi 151 is seventy-five and a half percent alcohol and the bartender had poured with a heavy hand. Caulder was far from drunk, but he was pretty loose. He would have flunked a Breathalyzer test, but he was still driving more safely than he had been *before* the three shots of Bacardi. It was one of those rare occasions when drinking had possibly *saved* lives on the road.

With his nerves calm, Caulder became acutely aware of how

bad a case of walking pneumonia he'd been brewing. Any sane person would have gone to the hospital long before it got this bad. It was amazing that he was still moving about and functioning at all. Caulder considered, for a brief moment, going to a doctor. Then he remembered his more bizarre problem and nixed the idea. He needed some answers before he took the luxury of getting himself healthy.

thirty

When Ry Caulder got to his apartment he found the door ajar. He drew the Browning from under his jacket and approached the apartment slowly. He peered around the edge of the doorframe and took a good long look into the living room.

Fredrickson sat quietly in the old recliner, staring at the open doorway. His clothes were still splattered with his own blood, but he had no visible wounds in his flesh anymore and his face looked thinner and more "normal" than it had the night before. He obviously didn't mind sitting in the last chair that Alvin had occupied. On the small table beside Fredrickson was a bottle of Caulder's Scotch, a tall glass with ice, a lit candle, a spoon, a short yellow rubber hose, a small bag of heroin, and a loaded syringe. He had closed the venetian blinds and was enjoying an afternoon cocktail—Glenlivet on the rocks with a heroin chaser. A few small shafts of sunlight beamed from around the edges of the venetian blinds but the room was cool and dark, pleasant, in a way that reminded Caulder of a funeral parlor he had visited in New Orleans once.

Caulder aimed the pistol at Fredrickson's head. Fredrickson played with one of the bullet holes in his jacket.

"Remember this suit?" Fredrickson asked. "I bought it when we went to Hong Kong to nail that little shit Sam Leong. I always liked this suit. You ruined it. I've got a good dry cleaner, but he's not *that* good."

Caulder steadied the Browning on Fredrickson's forehead and raised his free hand, palm out, to protect his own face from the splatter.

"You're going to have to do better than that, Ry. If you shoot me again I'm going to get angry," Fredrickson said. "I'm surprised at you. It's not your style to panic."

Caulder moved cautiously into the apartment. He didn't want any of his neighbors to see him out in the hallway with a gun. He was shaking, but the rum helped him maintain his composure.

"At least the tower hit was good," Fredrickson continued. "Nice, professional job." Fredrickson held up his glass in a salute.

"What do you mean?" Caulder muttered.

"The tower last night, Ry. . . . You did well. I'm trying to give you a compliment."

"Trick glass?" Caulder asked.

"No, Ry, you hit me. Right in the head. For any other mark it would have been a lethal shot. It was a good, clean hit."

Caulder's brain buzzed with fever and rum—maybe none of this was really happening. Maybe he was already on his deathbed in some hospital somewhere and these were actually the last hallucinatory moments of his misbegotten life.

"Wh-what the hell are you talking about?" Caulder stuttered.

"High-stakes time, Ry. I've always wanted to put your talents to the acid test and now is my chance. Now we'll see which one of us is the better assassin. Pupil or teacher."

Caulder took a step closer to Fredrickson, maintaining careful aim on the center of his forehead with the pistol.

"What if I just blow you away right here?"

"Shooting me is an expensive waste of ammunition," Fredrickson scoffed.

Fredrickson held out his left hand, pulled a 9mm Mauser from his shoulder holster, aimed the gun at his own palm, and fired. The movement was so smooth and fast that Caulder didn't have a chance to flinch. Fredrickson could have shot Caulder with as much ease as he had shot himself, but that was obviously not the way he wanted to play this game.

The bullet blasted a hole directly through the center of Fredrickson's palm and imbedded in Caulder's kitchen wall. Fredrickson held his hand up and a streak of sunlight shone through the hole briefly before it filled with blood. The blood dripped into Fredrickson's Scotch glass.

People could be heard diving for cover in neighboring apartments. A man yelled, "Quit that fucking shit!" from the floor below.

Caulder looked on, astonished, as the bleeding slowly ebbed and the flesh of Fredrickson's palm begin to reconstruct itself, growing back like an accelerated version of a lizard's tail. Bone, muscle, fat, and sinew slowly filled the bullet wound and pulsed with new life.

"What's happened to you?" Caulder demanded in a shaky voice that rang foreign in his own ears.

Fredrickson smiled widely. "Magic, Ry. Sheer magic." He picked up the blood-laced Scotch and offered it to Caulder. "Sip?"

Caulder just stared at Fredrickson, who shrugged and downed the Scotch and blood in one long gulp. Caulder couldn't move. He was paralyzed with fear and confusion.

Fredrickson stood up slowly and fixed a look into Caulder's eyes that could match Caulder's most threatening stare any day of the week.

"You may think you know what the world is all about," Fredrickson said, "but you don't know the half of it." Fredrickson's smile twisted up into a cruel snarl. "Ry, my friend, it's time to go back to school!"

Fredrickson got up and went to the window. He opened the venetian blinds halfway, allowing light to flood the room. He looked down at the alley behind the apartment complex. A pack of gangbangers was working its way along the alley, looking for something to do.

"This is your flock, Ry. Your 'innocents.' You don't have to worry about killing them anymore. They're killing each other. Our profession has gone public. Murder rules the streets. America is the Vietnam of tomorrow. But the conflict isn't North and South this time. It's the rich against the poor. The poor feel they have the *right* to kill now. They've become *us*, don't you see? They've been told it's not their fault how they are. It was someone else that did this to them. It's *always* someone else. Some asshole they never saw took from them what they never had. They would shoot you for the change in your pocket and feel completely *justified*. They feel no guilt. Guilt is for amateurs. It's a war out there now. There's no room for guilt in war. The poor will kill the rich for their car stereos and their Rolexes. And you *know* the rich are willing to kill to keep their Rolexes."

Fredrickson turned and looked at Caulder as he continued. "Of course, *you* don't wear a Rolex, do you Ry? You don't treat yourself to any earthly pleasures. And why is that? Because you never learned how to *live*. You just exist. Killing time while it slowly kills you. You think I'm some kind of monster, don't you? You always have. But at least I *enjoy* myself. I bet you haven't enjoyed yourself in thirty years. You're so busy worrying that what you've done will be judged. By whom? By what? God? Society? No one gives a damn anymore! Don't you understand? What you've done is *unimportant*. The real picture is so much grander than your petty crimes. You're not even a speck of dust in God's eye. You won't be judged because you're inconsequential. You don't exist. You don't register on the cosmic scale. You've got to think *big* if you're going to get God's attention. You've got to go *global*. You can't do it by sitting on the fence. You have to decide which side you're on. Are you good or are you bad? You can't have it both ways if you want to be judged. Not unless you're Catholic." Fredrickson laughed and closed the venetian blinds. "And you're no Catholic."

Fredrickson took a step closer to Caulder. A mad light flickered behind his eyes.

"You know what I'd really like to do? I'd like to get hold of a nuclear weapon or two. Wouldn't that be something? Those babies can really get your attention. It's so much more efficient than having to pick off the flock, one by one."

"You're crazy," Caulder finally said. The sermon was wearing on his nerves.

"And you're pathetic," Fredrickson responded. "You're so limited in your thinking. You know nothing."

Fredrickson picked up his empty glass with his wounded hand and let the Mauser dangle loosely in his other hand. He went into the kitchen, opened the freezer compartment of the refrigerator, and loaded his glass with ice.

"You've had three chances to kill me and you blew it every time," Fredrickson said as he walked back into the living room. He spoke in a friendly tone, as if they were discussing the latest stock returns. "Now it's my turn. . . . I want to see how many times *you* can die."

Caulder took a few absent steps backward. The fear was coming on him again.

"Calm down," Fredrickson continued. "I'm going to give you something you never offered me: fair warning and a head start. You've got sixty seconds. Do what you want with them. That is . . . unless you want to shoot it out right here and right now." He spun the Mauser on his trigger finger like Wyatt Earp and slid it back into the shoulder holster.

Fredrickson sat back down in the recliner, placed the glass on the table, and rolled up his right shirtsleeve. He slapped his arm, trying to bring up a vein, and tied off his circulation with the rubber hose. He picked up the syringe, tapped it, forced the air and a bit of the heroin out of the tip of the needle, and plunged it into his swollen vein.

"Don't worry. I'm not hooked," Fredrickson laughed. "It's just about the only thing that gets me revved up anymore."

Fredrickson pushed the plunger, injecting the drug into his arm. "You now have forty-five seconds," he said.

Caulder was drenched in sweat. He had no idea what Fredrickson was made of, but he was no longer interested in finding out. He turned and ran out of the apartment, down the hall toward the elevator.

Fredrickson called after him, "Smart move, Ry! You always did have good instincts!"

Caulder pushed the elevator call button and placed his back against the door, waiting for the car to arrive. He aimed the 9mm down the hall at his apartment doorway. It didn't seem as if bullets impressed Fredrickson anymore, but Caulder intended to give him a few to think about if he stepped into the hallway. Fredrickson didn't come out of the apartment, but he began to laugh. It was a deep, throaty, mocking laugh that floated down the corridor and sent shivers up and down Caulder's spine.

When the elevator door opened behind him, Caulder spun and pointed the pistol into the car. No one was there. Caulder entered the elevator and pushed the button for the parking garage. He pressed his body flat against the side of the elevator as it descended. Fredrickson might wedge the doors open on the seventh floor and send a few random shots through the roof of the elevator just for fun.

The elevator door slowly opened, revealing the parking garage. Caulder entered the garage with caution verging on paranoia. He knew Fredrickson couldn't have beaten him down to the garage. At least he *thought* it couldn't be done. Of course he had also thought that he had *killed* Fredrickson on three previous occasions, yet Fredrickson still managed to be sitting in Caulder's apartment, shooting heroin and drinking his liquor cabinet dry. Anything seemed possible at this stage of the game. Thankfully, Fredrickson was nowhere to be seen in the garage.

Caulder holstered the Browning and approached the Buick. He looked under the car for bombs or booby traps, then popped the hood and gave the engine a quick check. Fredrickson had been upstairs already when Caulder got there, but he might have left an accomplice in the basement to rig the car as an ironic act of vengeance for the exploding Mercedes limousine. There appeared to be no tampering with the vehicle, so Caulder climbed in gingerly and started the engine. No big bang. The car was okay, so far at least. A hidden bomb might still be present. It could be set off a variety of ways: radio wave, like the bomb Caulder had used on the limo; it could have a timer; it could even be heat controlled and placed somewhere near the engine or exhaust, anyplace that would get hotter as the vehicle warmed up. But this was all speculation. Either the car was rigged or it wasn't, but Fredrickson was *definitely* upstairs and Caulder's sixty seconds were up. He wanted to get far away from Fredrickson as quickly as possible and that would take high-speed acceleration. Caulder put the car in gear and took off, tires squealing on the oil-slick concrete floor of the parking garage. He clicked the remote at the automatic gate barring the exit. The gate groaned open slowly and the passenger side of the Buick traded paint with the iron edge as the vehicle squeezed through the exit into the alley.

As Caulder sped down the alley behind the apartment building, something caught his eye. When he looked up he saw Fredrickson sitting on the ledge of his apartment window seven stories above the alley. Fredrickson pointed the Mauser lackadaisically and opened fire on Caulder's car.

The two tires on Caulder's side of the Buick exploded. A bullet went through the hood and played havoc with the engine. Another bullet pierced the radiator. The car rolled roughly to a stop, metal pinging against metal, steam shooting out from under the hood.

"I'd prefer you on foot," Fredrickson called down to Caulder. "Something happened to my car.... A high-speed chase is *completely* out of the question."

Caulder jumped out of his car and ran down the alley, watching Fredrickson over his shoulder as he went, thinking the lethal shot would be fired at any moment. He was a running duck out in the open like that. Fredrickson could kill him at any moment with great ease. One squeeze of the trigger and it would be over. But there would be no coming back for Ry Caulder. He knew that when *his* death occurred it would be final.

Caulder ran as hard and as fast as he could. The corner of the building lay just ahead. Once he got around it he would be safe, at least for a few moments.

Just as Caulder was about to round the corner, a gunshot went off. The sound echoed like a concussion grenade in Caulder's ears. His heart leaped up into his throat and he was sure he was dead. He stumbled around the corner of the building and fell roughly to the pavement. He lay there, wheezing and coughing, out of breath and very close to having a heart attack. A pigeon landed in front of him on the sidewalk, twitching and flailing in death throes, a gaping cavity where its chest used to be. Caulder shoved the pigeon away from his face.

Caulder took silent inventory of his body, double-checking to make sure he had not been shot. He saw no wounds, no blood. Fredrickson had just fired into the air to scare him and do a little pigeon hunting. Fredrickson's sense of humor had always been dark, but it had become absolutely opaque as of late.

An elderly lady suddenly appeared above Caulder, looking down at his sweat-covered face. "Are you all right? Would you like me to call an ambulance?" she asked.

"I'm okay ... I ... I think," Caulder stuttered. He struggled to raise himself off the ground and she helped him up. Caulder slowly rose to his feet and leaned against the building, still trying to catch his breath. His scarred, fluid-filled lungs were heaving and on fire. His energy was all gone now and he couldn't imagine continuing on. Maybe he would just let Fredrickson catch him and kill him and it would be over. But then he saw *their* faces. Stephanie and Jason. Innocent and trusting. Waiting for Caulder in some posh, overpriced museum of a hotel. Expecting him to return and explain everything and make it all right. But Caulder was dying. *No!* he thought. *Not yet!* There were still things to be done. Unfinished business that needed tending. He brought out the medicated inhaler and took a big draw. It finished the container. He tossed the empty into the gutter.

Caulder thanked the lady for her help and then stumbled down the sidewalk toward Cambria Street. The woman continued on her way in the opposite direction. As Caulder approached the corner of the building he slowed down and grew cautious again. His breathing came easier, but the hardest-working sixth sense in Los Angeles was trying to warn him again. Caulder brought out the Browning for what little comfort it supplied.

Caulder inched his way closer to the edge of the building. He wanted to look around the corner to see if Fredrickson had exited the front of the apartment complex. Caulder peered slowly around the edge of the building. . . .

"Gotcha!" Fredrickson said, trying to be funny. He was on the other side of the building not six inches away from Caulder's face.

Caulder raised and fired the Browning out of reflexive instinct and blind panic. Fredrickson's chin launched off his face and landed in a thousand pieces in the middle of Cambria Street. The elderly lady turned from her position down the block. She let out a peep of a scream and ran down the alley, having just witnessed what she assumed was a violent murder.

Fredrickson's head reeled way back on his neck for a moment, as if it were going to fall off his shoulders and roll down his spine. He put a hand on the wall of the building to support himself, then slowly straightened up and looked at Caulder. The bottom half of Fredrickson's mouth was totally gone. His face was a blood-speckled mess, his smile wide and bottomless and very involuntary. But he stood calm and still. Pain didn't seem to bother Fredrickson. If anything, he seemed to be enjoying it.

Fredrickson reached out and put his hand on Caulder's shoulder, trying to speak but no longer owning the mechanics. There was no tongue, no chin, no palate. Caulder's eyes grew wide with terror. He could tell by the look on what remained of Fredrickson's face that Fredrickson had decided the time had come. The game was over. Time for Ry Caulder to die.

Fredrickson slowly raised the Mauser and Caulder did nothing to resist. It seemed senseless to prolong it any longer. This man was relentless and unstoppable. Caulder's attempt at unconscious problem-solving had brought him no answers, only more questions. His physical actions had proven totally useless. The task at hand was too bizarre and extreme for him. He had failed and now he would be punished. Punished for all his deeds and all his failures. It was time to pay the piper.

And then the faces were there again. The woman and the child. The innocents that he had pulled into his misfortune. The innocents that might die if he didn't stop Fredrickson. Fredrickson clicked the hammer back on the Mauser and prepared to blast Caulder into the next life. He was giving Caulder time to think, time to contemplate the darkness, to wallow in his own failure. But Caulder abruptly chose survival and shoved the Browning into Fredrickson's stomach and fired continuously until the clip was empty.

Fredrickson gasped and regurgitated blood into Caulder's face. Fredrickson dropped the Mauser and Caulder kicked it out into the street. Pedestrians, who had been gathering curiously since the first gunshots in the alley, now scrambled for cover. Most of the people wanted to get clear of the shooting, but some of them actually moved closer to get a better look at the violence. This beat the afternoon *Kojak* rerun all to hell.

Fredrickson gripped Caulder by both shoulders and leaned

into him for support. Caulder held him up, thinking that maybe he had finally killed this monster. Suddenly Fredrickson's hands tightened around Caulder's neck, his grip like a hangman's noose at the end of a long drop. Fredrickson looked into Caulder's face and his eyes glistened with pleasure.

Fredrickson was crushing Caulder's windpipe. Caulder dropped his empty pistol and tried to break the grip around his neck, but Fredrickson's arms were like iron bars. Caulder punched Fredrickson in the stomach, but *there was nothing there!* Caulder's fist traveled all the way through Fredrickson's body and out his back. The gunshots had blown a hole clear through the man's midsection. Caulder pulled his fist out of the gore and tried to shove Fredrickson away, but it was impossible. No air whatsoever was reaching Caulder's lungs and he began to lose consciousness. The pressure from Fredrickson's grip on his spinal column dulled everything. It was the awareness of this pressure that triggered Caulder's knowledge of human anatomy and saved his life.

Caulder knew everything about the human body. If you were going to efficiently destroy a machine you first had to know how it worked. Caulder reached back into the center of Fredrickson's bloody stomach with both hands, shoved his way past the dangling organs that were squirting and pumping away, trying to rebuild themselves, and grabbed hold of what was left of the base of Fredrickson's spinal column. A look of shock washed over Fredrickson's face as he realized what Caulder was about to do.

Caulder tightened his grip on Fredrickson's vertebrae and jerked with all his might. The spinal column snapped in half like a tree cut for timber and Fredrickson fell backward at the waist, his hands releasing Caulder's neck and dangling free, vital information having been cut off at the halfway mark. For a moment Fredrickson appeared to be a broken doll or some Daliesque figure in an urban landscape. His upper torso was bent all the way over backward at five o'clock and his head rested helplessly on the ground, but his legs and waist were standing straight up on their own. The two sections of his body were still connected by some tissue, but only superficially. Finally Fredrickson's legs got the message and they collapsed on the sidewalk next to the rest of his body.

Caulder gasped for breath and then vomited profusely on the sidewalk next to Fredrickson. Caulder had not been able to eat solid food since the cold chicken that Stephanie had left him, so the vomit consisted mostly of coffee, orange juice, bile, and Bacardi 151, but there was a lot of it. This was, without a doubt, the most specifically disgusting thing Ry Caulder had ever done to a human being in what was admittedly a sin-filled life. Just the physical bestiality of the act repulsed him to a degree he had never experienced. Whatever evil thrill he occasionally achieved while working was totally gone now. He thoroughly purged his stomach and then looked at the two steaming heaps of flesh in front of him.

The stench rising out of Fredrickson was thick and revolting. Caulder gagged and would have thrown up again if there had been anything left in his stomach. Fredrickson squirmed about slowly on the ground. Amazingly, he was not only still alive, but healing rapidly. The two sections of his spinal cord could be seen through the gore, already in the process of rejoining each other. Flesh began to grow and extend itself in search of other flesh with which to knit.

Caulder shook the utter disbelief from his brain and started to stagger away. He knew what was happening. He didn't know how or why, but he knew what. He knew Fredrickson would soon be after him again.

The crowd on the street had gathered into a mob. They had just witnessed a man tear another man in half and they weren't going to let him get away with it. They didn't care much who the other man was. They weren't into details. Only the big picture. And the big picture called for an old-fashioned lynching, unless the cops got to them first. Mob mentality was creating little pockets of bravery in the crowd. Some of them were probably thinking about how the dozen or so folks who nabbed and beat the hell out of Richard Ramirez, the so-called Night Stalker, a few years back achieved brief fame and glory, and also shared in a cash reward. These two guys didn't look famous, but you never knew who had a price on his head. It might be worth the risk of getting shot if there was money in it. Or a guest shot on Letterman. A couple of men stepped forward hesitantly.

Caulder spun around and ran back toward the alley. There were only a few teenagers with skateboards in this direction and they were too startled to interfere with Caulder. A few of the more macho men in the mob behind Caulder gave chase, but Caulder had a good head start and he was filled with inspiration. He ran like a healthy man down the alley and headed toward Eighth Street, the shouts and screams of his pursuers hot on his trail.

Caulder smashed through crowds of angry pedestrians on Eighth. They didn't know who he was or what he had just done, but he was covered in blood and very rude in his haste. He dove through traffic, narrowly skirting an RTD bus, which slammed to a halt with an ugly screech, hurling unsuspecting passengers to the floor. The bus driver stuck his head out the side window and called Caulder an asshole.

You got that right, guy, he thought. I'm an asshole. A moron. A jerk. But get out of my way!

Caulder turned a corner and ran down another alley. He took cover in a darkened doorway and tried to catch his breath. He looked around for Fredrickson or any of the lynch mob that might still be following him. No one showed. A bum had passed out against a big, stinking Dumpster nearby. Caulder couldn't continue running around looking the way he looked. He poured the bum out of his tattered trench coat and wrapped it around his own body. The bum never stirred. Caulder couldn't even tell if the man was alive or not, his breathing was so shallow. As Caulder looked at the bum he flashed on Alvin and remembered how he had left his friend's corpse lying against the back of a liquor store.

The bum rolled over and cut a savage fart, putting the world on notice that he was *not* dead and that his struggle against conformity would be continuing.

Caulder ran down the alley. The coat was thick with filth and stank to high heaven, but it was long and reached almost to the ground. It completely hid Caulder's blood-soaked clothes. He wiped his hands off on the inside of the coat to complete his *GQ* image.

A sound came from way back in the alley. Caulder looked over his shoulder and saw Fredrickson round the corner from Eighth. Fredrickson's gait was smooth and unhurried. He too was covered in blood, but he didn't seem concerned about it. Fredrickson wore the dried gore stylishly, as if it were the latest fashion statement from Paris. He carried his Mauser at his side, having retrieved it from the street. From the calm expression on Fredrickson's face, which was, for the most part, back in place now, it was obvious he felt he could catch Ry Caulder whenever he wanted.

Caulder was no longer shocked at seeing Fredrickson return from the dead. This time he had expected it, maybe not so soon, but he knew it would happen. The question was what to do about it. There must be some way to stop him. But what?

Caulder picked up his pace and swung around another corner onto a busy street lined with stores—used furniture, Thai food, dry cleaning, and, as one shop proudly proclaimed with a bright neon sign, BUDDY'S ARMORY: A FULL ARSENAL FOR HOME PROTECTION. Caulder spotted the sign and hauled ass toward the gun store. He had abandoned the empty Browning next to Fredrickson's body on the sidewalk. He still had the little .380 Colt in his pocket, but he wanted to get hold of something with *stopping power*.

Caulder slowed his pace as he entered the gun shop. It was a small store; three long glass cases filled with handguns formed a U that separated the public from the rows of rifles lining the walls. There was only one person in the place, a fat slob in his fifties, wearing a grease-stained apron and cleaning an Elk rifle behind the counter to the right of the entrance. Caulder assumed that this was "Buddy." Buddy set the rifle aside, rested his filthy hands on his bulging stomach, and looked at Ry Caulder.

"What you need?" Buddy asked gruffly.

"The biggest gun you've got!" Caulder said, trying not to shout out of panic.

"You got money?" Buddy noted the filthy trench coat and the Band-Aid on Caulder's bruised forehead.

"Absolutely," Caulder said. He brought out his wallet and showed Buddy a thick flash of green.

Buddy reached under the counter and produced a curious-looking six-barreled shotgun.

"Jesus," Caulder said. He was impressed.

"Designed it myself. This sucker can evaporate a car. It ain't pretty, but it works."

"Just what I need."

"What in Sam Hill you want to shoot?"

"Bears."

"You shoot a grizzly with this and it's gonna take you a week to find all the pieces."

"That's fine," Caulder said. "Show me how to load it."

Buddy picked up a custom-made six-shot speed loader and cracked open the breech of the shotgun.

"Made my own special speed loader too. Just pop it in and lock it down," Buddy said. He slapped in the shells, withdrew the loader, and clanked the gun back together again. "And you're ready to raise hell."

Fredrickson appeared in the doorway behind Caulder, his pistol raised and aimed at Caulder's head.

"Bang! Point to me!" Fredrickson yelled, like some drug-addled juvenile delinquent. He was back in his playful mode. Caulder's lust for survival had renewed Fredrickson's interest and inspired him to drag the game out a little longer.

Caulder reached over the counter and grabbed the shotgun out of Buddy's hands. Caulder turned, aimed the massive weapon at Fredrickson, and let loose with all six barrels. A gigantic blast blew Fredrickson and half the doorway out into the street. The shotgun's tremendous recoil knocked Caulder back against the counter and kicked the wind out of him.

Caulder looked at the carnage he had just engineered. The entrance of the shop was demolished. Caulder handed the empty shotgun back to Buddy.

"It pulls to the right," Caulder said blankly. He turned and walked out of the gun shop, leaving Buddy shaking in his boots, too frightened to move or speak.

Caulder stepped out into the bright sunlight and looked around. The street was in pandemonium. It looked as if someone had blown up a plasma center. Blood and gore were everywhere. Blue smoke from the shotgun still floated in the air. Pedestrians were running for cover. They thought a bomb had gone off, the blast from the six-barreled shotgun had been so loud.

Fredrickson still lived. But for the first time he actually appeared to be feeling pain. Clutching his intestines with his left hand, he got up, leaned against a big blue mailbox, and examined his wounds. His midsection had not completely finished healing from his last encounter with Caulder, and now it was really blown to hell. Half of Fredrickson's body had been blasted away. There was more of him on the sidewalk than on his bones. The white suit was practically nonexistent. He still had the Mauser in his right hand, but it was useless. His right arm dangled from his shoulder by a thread of flesh. Fredrickson didn't look as if he felt well. Not well at all.

"That was . . . a good one . . . Ry . . ." Fredrickson groaned. "You're improving."

Fredrickson smiled and attempted to drag himself forward,

toward Caulder, but he had very little motor control over what remained of his mangled legs.

"A few more tries and you might actually hurt me. If I let you
live that long . . ."

Caulder could tell that Fredrickson *had* been hurt this time.
And if he could be hurt, maybe he could be killed. There was still
hope.

Fredrickson's wounds were beginning to mend. The bleeding
had ebbed and tendrils of flesh were growing and knitting with one
another.

Caulder was stunned to see Fredrickson healing so rapidly,
even though this was the third time he had seen this trick in the last
hour. The process, whatever it was, seemed to be accelerating each
time Fredrickson was hurt. Nothing stopped this man. If, indeed,
Fredrickson *was* a man.

Sirens were approaching. Maybe ambulances, maybe cops,
probably both.

Caulder turned and ran. No one pursued him this time. They
were too busy staring at the mess on the sidewalk to notice Ry
Caulder.

A crowd surrounded Fredrickson. He stared blankly at them. He
just wanted to heal enough to become mobile and get out of there.
Two kids edged forward and peered at Fredrickson's open stomach
and chest cavity. The first kid exclaimed, "Gross!" The second kid
countered with, "Intense!"

Fredrickson reached into his stomach and pulled out a mass of
blood and gore that he no longer needed. He flung the mess into
the crowd. People screamed and backed away from Fredrickson,
giving him the breathing room he desired. Fredrickson had much
more respect for Ry Caulder than he did for these people. At least
Caulder had spirit. These people were nothing but targets that
hadn't been marked yet. Most of them were so inconsequential

they would never rate high enough for a professional hit. They were meat and they deserved to be splattered.

Fredrickson had known Caulder would find it hard to cope with the exotic situation. He had been in the same position a year earlier himself and, at first, he had been just as baffled as Caulder now found himself. Caulder seemed much slower on the take than he had been. Caulder should have figured it out by now, but he wasn't even halfway there. He just couldn't tap into the creative side of his psyche. He was too much a realist, his mind too cluttered with facts to see the truth of the situation.

Though disappointed with Caulder's lack of imagination, Fredrickson *was* impressed with his pupil's ingenuity and his savage desire to kill him. Caulder was even tougher than Fredrickson had thought he would be. But of course up to now Fredrickson had only been toying with the man. Working the defense, not the offense. He could have killed Caulder a dozen times over, but that would have been unfair and boring. This kind of entertainment was hard to come by. Ry Caulder was the closest thing to a challenge that Fredrickson had encountered in the year following his change, and he didn't know when or if another opportunity like this would come along. He wanted to play as long as possible, at least until he got bored again. He would be marginally disheartened when he had to bring the final curtain down on Caulder.

Fredrickson had taught Caulder the business. Just as Caulder had taught young Nate Daniels. Fredrickson had been in his prime when they first met. At that time, Fredrickson was *the* man for the tough jobs. The number one hitter around. Sanctioned by the CIA, then let loose on the private sector. But as they both got older, Caulder got better and Fredrickson got meaner and sloppier. Their standing within the underworld community reversed and Caulder was soon considered the number-one man. The man you called when you wanted to hit a hard target and you wanted *nothing* to go wrong. Caulder's level of accuracy verged on the surgical. He worked clean. The wrong people never got hurt. And usually he could make the hit appear to be an accident. Caulder's clients had rarely been linked to an elimination, unless the elimination was meant to serve as a warning to others as well, as in the Nate Daniels case.

Fredrickson had always preferred the straight-ahead approach. If you're going to kill someone, *just do it!* And whenever possible, do it in a big way. He planned hits somewhat less meticulously than Caulder did. He wasn't choosy about who or what the targets were. He'd kill anyone for the right price and he'd get the job done as quickly as possible. But that method of operation did not suit employers who required anonymity and precision. Some of them even had patience. Fredrickson developed a reputation for being the wrong man for certain kinds of assignments.

Fredrickson had been miffed when Caulder began getting the prime jobs and he started pulling the leftovers. A professional jealousy grew between them. When they finally had to work another hit together, Fredrickson decided to teach Caulder a lesson. He killed an innocent girl. Caulder's desire to spare innocent lives was legendary in the community. He was even considered a bit of a flake because of it, but the clients didn't mind. Innocent victims usually brought bad publicity and intense heat.

The death of the girl had hurt Caulder very deeply and it had put a smear on an otherwise illustrious career. Caulder vowed never to work with Fredrickson again and he had stuck to that vow. Fredrickson didn't mind. They went their separate ways and continued to carve out legendary reputations in their individual specialties. But Caulder remained the considered number-one hitter in the land. The consummate professional. Now Fredrickson had a chance to regain his throne. Caulder's days as number one would soon be over.

Fredrickson saw two police cars approaching the gun shop. He tried his legs and found that they had regained movement. He gathered his strength and staggered through the crowd, which parted like the Red Sea. The sheep didn't want to get slopped with any more intestinal gore. Fredrickson disappeared around the corner of the building, leaving a trail of blood in his wake. No one had enough nerve to follow him. Even the two young splatter fans were unsure of what to do. The cops were coming and no one wanted to be near a wounded person when the boys in blue arrived. You might become the target of an overzealous rookie's misguided good intentions and get shot in the head.

The police cars screeched up to the curb. Two cops jumped out of the first car, saw the demolished doorway, the guts and blood splattered everywhere, but no body. The name tags on the cops' uniforms read Escovedo and Underwood. They had just come from a local hospital, where they had taken a report from a cab driver and a hysterical woman who claimed they had been cavorting with a man who was riddled with bullet wounds. They had said the man was weird, but very polite, especially considering that he was probably bleeding to death. The man had gotten out of the cab at Seventh and Union. He had even left the driver a hundred-dollar bill against roughly thirty on the meter. The two women were obviously nutcases, terrified out of their wits from having been at the site of the Beverly Hills sniper attack, but they had been a real pain in the ass and now Escovedo and Underwood had arrived on *this* blood-soaked scene, not far from where the women said they had dropped off the "weird" man. The women's story was beginning to sound less crazy by the moment.

"Hey, people! What the fuck is going on here?!" Underwood yelled.

The crowd pointed around the corner, shouting a wide variety of answers all at once. Escovedo and Underwood looked at each other with frustration. It was going to be one of those days.

* * *

Fredrickson staggered through crowds of confused pedestrians on Union Avenue. His pace was improving but he was still a bloody mess and he still had his gun in his hand. Most of the people on the street gave him a wide berth; others were so frozen with surprise and fear that he had to physically push them aside.

Fredrickson looked around for any sign of Ry Caulder. He saw none. Fredrickson usually had no trouble predicting Caulder's moves, but his senses were out of whack, discombobulated by all the efforts to kill him.

A police car swung around the corner, looking for anyone or anything suspicious.

Fredrickson ducked into a shadowy alley and the car cruised by harmlessly. Air conditioners from the tenements above Fredrickson dripped water onto his head. He looked up, studying the surrounding rooftops. He saw nothing of any interest to him. No sign of Ry Caulder anywhere.

Caulder moved far above Fredrickson, walking along the rooftops of the connected strip of tenements, from building to building, following Fredrickson's progress down the alley, crouching low beneath the lip of the roof to keep out of Fredrickson's sight. He had gotten lucky and found an elevator in one of the tenements that worked. He had taken the box to the roof, trying to earn some breathing space. Now he felt trapped, with nowhere to go but down. Caulder was watching Fredrickson so intensely that he nearly tripped over a large cinder block sitting loose in his path. The block had once been part of a dividing wall that had been torn apart long ago by energetic vandals. Caulder looked at the heavy piece of mortar and stone, then picked it up and moved quickly into position. Yeah. Sure, he thought. Drop a rock on him. If bullets and shotgun blasts and physical mutilation won't stop

Fredrickson, a big rock ought to do it. Caulder knew it was useless, but he was too crazed to stop himself.

Caulder peered over the edge of the roof. Fredrickson was a few steps away from being directly beneath him, no longer watching the rooftops. Caulder aimed the cinder block carefully, waiting . . . waiting. . . . Then he dropped the heavy chunk of stone directly over Fredrickson's head. The block made a slight whistling sound as it plummeted to its destination.

Fredrickson noticed a shadow growing on the ground around his feet. He looked up just in time for the fifteen pounds of stone to catch him full in the face. The cinder block exploded into a million powdery fragments and knocked Fredrickson to the grimy asphalt. Most of Fredrickson's teeth bounced on the pavement next to his mangled head, and he became very still. His skull crushed, gray matter and yellowish fluids oozed out of his shattered cranium.

Caulder climbed up onto the ledge of the roof and looked down at Fredrickson's comatose form, relieved that something seemed to have stopped the juggernaut, for the moment at least. Sometimes the simple solutions *are* the best. He watched breathlessly—then he noticed Fredrickson's arm twitch. It almost amused him, but he decided to save his laughter for later.

Fredrickson reached up and shoved the cinder block off his crushed face. He looked like a Picasso sculpture. The entire right side of his head had been completely caved in. His nose had been pushed over to one side and his right eye was out and dangling loose from its socket by a strand of optic nerve. Crud and blood and dust covered him from crushed head to twisted feet. Fredrickson felt around his face for his loose eye. Once he found it, he simply wedged it back into its socket. It fit loosely. His eyelid had been completely torn away and the bone around the socket was shattered. The eye didn't function, leaving him half-blind. He thought for a moment about what he had done to Savage Jack, the hapless biker, down in Mexico.

Fredrickson closed his good eye for a second to get the full impact of how the man must have felt when his eyes were plucked from his head. It wasn't a pleasant sensation to be even half-blind, even though Fredrickson had the knowledge that his vision would be returning soon. The thoughts that would run through a person's brain upon realizing he had suddenly lost his sight forever would be terrifying. Fredrickson speculated that the panic level in Savage Jack must have been enormous before he pistol-whipped him into oblivion. This knowledge gave Fredrickson great joy.

Fredrickson looked up at Caulder standing on the edge of the roof, then reached over and picked up the Mauser, which he had dropped when he was struck by the cinder block. Like a true pro, Fredrickson had managed to keep track of his gun through all the carnage.

Slowly Fredrickson climbed to his feet and aimed his pistol at Caulder, who stood paralyzed on the roof, too dazed and confused to move. Fredrickson aimed the pistol so Caulder could look straight down the barrel. Caulder seemed hypnotized, like a deer caught in the headlights. If Fredrickson pulled the trigger now it would be a kill shot.

Fredrickson moved the barrel of the gun down and an inch to the left. He fired only one shot. It hit Caulder in the right shoulder. The bullet tore out a big chunk of flesh and lodged against his shoulder blade. He fell backward, out of sight, onto the roof of the tenement.

A police car came ripping around the corner and down the alley. The car skidded to a stop behind Fredrickson, a bloody man in tattered rags firing a gun at a tenement. Escovedo and Underwood jumped out of the vehicle and crouched behind their doors, revolvers drawn.

"Freeze, asshole!" Escovedo yelled.

Fredrickson looked at them, unimpressed. He grinned wickedly and dropped his gun.

Underwood sprang forward, grabbed Fredrickson, spun him around, and slammed him facedown onto the hood of the police car. A few more of Fredrickson's teeth bounced off the hood of the car and clattered to the ground. Underwood cuffed Fredrickson's hands behind his back. Little mercy showed in the cop's treatment of his mangled prisoner. These men knew that you could get killed by anyone, no matter how damaged or hurt they were.

Another police car sped into the alley and stopped behind the first car. The backup had arrived. Two cops, with name tags reading Shaffer and Jaffe, got out of the car and approached Escovedo, Underwood, and Fredrickson.

"He was firing into the building," Escovedo told the new arrivals. "You better check it out."

Shaffer and Jaffe grumbled acknowledgment, but they obviously weren't happy about the assignment. Going into one of these buildings was akin to stepping into a lion's den. Who knew when the beasts had eaten last?

"If you don't hear from us by Saturday, send in the troops," Jaffe said over his shoulder to the two lucky cops that had arrived on the scene first.

"No problem," Underwood said with a wry smile.

Shaffer and Jaffe disappeared into the apartment building, leaving Fredrickson behind with his two captors.

Ry Caulder lay sprawled on the roof clutching his bloody shoulder. White-hot pain shot through his nervous system. A bullet that lodges in a body burns from the heat of being fired for some time, so a person who has been shot has to deal not only with his flesh being violated, but with a red-hot piece of metal suddenly living inside his skin. It is a difficult thing to endure and many take refuge in unconsciousness. Caulder couldn't afford such luxury.

Caulder crawled to the door on the roof that led down into the tenement and managed to pull himself to his feet. He staggered into the building and stumbled down the rat shit–encrusted staircase, stopping midway to catch his breath and scope out the territory. The hallway below was filled with discarded mattresses and bottles. This floor was no longer occupied by paying tenants. The homeless had claimed it for their own, but they appeared to be out. Tennis? Maybe golf?

Deep down in the building he could hear the police searching the place. They were getting a lot of vulgar responses from the leftover humanity that dwelled below.

Caulder started down the staircase again. He needed to find a hiding place before the cops got there. His foot got caught on a loose plastic stair liner and he tumbled to the bottom of the steps with a series of loud thumps.

From somewhere deep within the building a man yelled, "Hey, Jaffe, up here!" Caulder had given his position away. The cops would be on the top floor a lot sooner than expected.

Down in the alley, Underwood was behind the wheel of his patrol car, filling out a report.

Escovedo was talking to Fredrickson in the backseat of the car. Fredrickson's hands were still cuffed behind his back.

"Just hold on, buddy . . ." Escovedo was saying. "The paramedics should be here soon."

"I feel fine, Occifer." Fredrickson mispronounced "officer" on purpose, as if he were drunk. He wanted to have some fun with these men.

"Yeah? Well, you look like mashed shit," Escovedo said. He had seen a lot of mangled guys in his day, but Fredrickson was a classic. Not too many people took that kind of punishment and still walked around, let alone talked about it.

Fredrickson pulled his hands tightly against the handcuffs.

Fredrickson was strong, but the battle had sapped his energy. He didn't have what it would take to break the heavy handcuff chain. He needed another strategy. He held on to the chain with one hand and started pressing the wrist of his other arm against the metal cuff. He needed to be free, at any cost.

Ry Caulder stood at the end of the hallway, struggling to open a window leading onto the fire escape outside the tenement. The cops could be heard clumping up the stairs from below. Caulder put his weight behind his effort. White-hot pain shot through his shoulder again, but the window opened with a clatter and he climbed out onto the fire escape.

Shaffer and Jaffe entered the hallway, guns drawn. They searched the rooms along the hall, kicking doors in violently as they went, working their way toward the end of the corridor. As they progressed, the cops uncovered little pockets of human suffering huddled in the corners of various rooms. The homeless weren't out doing business, or playing tennis or golf, they were in here hiding from *the man*. Shaffer and Jaffe scoured their faces silently, looking for anyone who might be shot or might be packing a weapon of his own. No one fit the profile. There were plenty of people here who could have used medical care, a shower, or a good hot meal, but nothing dramatic enough to intrude on a police investigation. Shaffer and Jaffe made their way down the hallway, getting closer and closer to the open window and the fire escape.

Fredrickson continued to work his hand against the metal cuff. Blood began to pour out around his wrist. It was hard going and very painful, even for a man who enjoyed pain, but Fredrickson didn't allow his face to betray any emotion.

Escovedo absently picked at a small scab on his own chin and studied Fredrickson. Fredrickson's face had been slowly putting it-self back into place. It was still covered with dried blood, but be-neath the blood it had almost completely healed.

"Hey, Underwood," Escovedo said, continuing to pick at his chin. "There's something funny about this guy—" Escovedo did not get to complete his thoughts.

Fredrickson jerked the handcuff the rest of the way through his own wrist, severing his hand from his arm.

Fredrickson shoved his severed hand against the scab on Es-covedo's chin and said, "Here, pick it with this!"

Escovedo looked at Fredrickson's dismembered hand in mute horror.

Fredrickson revealed his mutilated wrist to Escovedo. Blood squirted from the severed veins and a sharp white bone protruded from the end of his arm.

Escovedo tried to scream, but couldn't force the air over his vocal chords.

Fredrickson rammed the arm bone into the center of Es-covedo's throat, pinning him against the door of the car, punctur-ing his larynx, and supplying the cop with an unwelcome tracheotomy. Escovedo gagged and struggled, but it was all over for him. His jugular vein had been severed by the movement of the sharp bone. He was choking to death on his own blood.

Underwood turned from his report to see what all the com-motion was about.

Fredrickson grabbed Escovedo's .357 Magnum with his good hand, pulled it from its holster, and blasted Underwood in the face. Fredrickson took the time to appreciate the design Under-wood's brain made on the inside of the windshield, which spider-webbed as a few of the bullets sought exit from the vehicle. The resulting collage of cracked glass and blasted gore reminded Fredrickson of the spin art that children made at fairs by dripping paint on spinning placards. He had a quick flash of nostalgia for his youth.

* * *

Shaffer and Jaffe were about to reach the window at the end of the hallway when the sound of gunfire erupted below. They looked at each other, then turned and ran back toward the stairs leading to the ground floor.

Caulder fell to the metal grating of the fire escape outside the window. He had been holding himself up on the ladder above the window in the hopes of avoiding detection. He could only use one hand and the pain was tremendous. He would never have been able to hold himself out of sight long enough to avoid detection. Fredrickson had saved Caulder from capture by killing Underwood and Escovedo. Once again they had functioned as partners, albeit unwittingly.

Shaffer and Jaffe rushed from the tenement and saw the splattered bodies of Escovedo and Underwood in the police car. Fredrickson was gone.

At the far end of the alley, just around the corner of the tenement, Ry Caulder painfully climbed down the fire escape. He reached the end of the metal ladder and had to drop the final ten feet to the ground. He twisted his ankle as he landed. Caulder stifled a scream and collected himself against the base of the building. He looked around the corner of the tenement and watched Shaffer and Jaffe deal with the nightmare in the blood-splattered patrol car as best they could. Caulder had seen Fredrickson's handiwork before, so he had a pretty good idea of what the two cops were looking at and why they were going berserk. The police academy had not prepared them for the spectacle of fellow police officers mutilated beyond recognition.

As hysterical as Shaffer and Jaffe were, Caulder knew they would still manage to call for assistance. The alley would be crawling with crazed cops within minutes. Whoever they found in the vicinity would have to be a pretty good talker. There was nothing a cop hated more than a fellow cop dying in the line of duty. Unless, of course, it was *two* fellow cops dying in the line of duty. Revenge would be the name of the game in this alley. Definitely not a good place to be. Caulder gathered what was left of his strength and limped away undetected.

thirty-one

Caulder entered a messy, but well-equipped, doctor's office. Behind the nurse's station sat a puffy-cheeked, dissipated man who had managed to fit sixty years of drinking into forty-five. The man was only half-awake, dividing his attention equally between a crossword puzzle book and a tumbler of Jim Beam, straight up. The doctor's meager staff had gone home long ago.

The doctor looked up at Caulder through glassy eyes that had very little focus and even less curiosity. He was one of the few doctors around town that you could turn to with any kind of wound and be assured of no police reports or publicity. He was paid well for his silence.

"Hello, Caulder. How's it going?" the doctor muttered.

"Thanks for coming in, Doc."

"I was just sitting around the house getting old."

Caulder looked the man over. It had been a while since he had required the doctor's services and time had not treated the man kindly.

"Hold out your hands, Doc."

"I'm fine, Caulder, honestly. . . . I've stopped using the stuff."

"Hold 'em out."

The doctor extended his hands. They trembled violently. He might have stopped using "the stuff," whatever that might be, but he was still a mess.

Caulder walked over to a filing cabinet and extracted a large bottle of George Dickel bourbon and a glass. The doctor downed his Jim Beam in one gulp and held out his empty glass. His liver would barely notice the difference between Dickel and Beam. He liked all bourbon, the nastier the better. Caulder poured the doctor a stiff drink and himself an even stiffer one.

"Let's get to it, then," the doctor said as he sipped the bourbon.

"I'll do it myself," Caulder replied.

"Horseshit. This is *my* office."

They walked into the examination room in the back of the doctor's office, bringing the bottles and glasses with them.

Caulder dug through a bunch of prescription bottles and found some Percodan. He popped two tablets into his mouth and washed them down with bourbon. George Dickel was not the prescribed chaser for Percodan, but the desired effects of both substances would be achieved quicker because of the blend. Caulder wanted anesthesia and consciousness in equal portions. The drugs and alcohol did not disappoint him.

Caulder sat down on the examination table. Beside the table was a basin of water and a tray full of surgical tools and bandages.

The doctor adjusted a mirrored surgical lamp and picked up a scalpel and cut the shirt away from the wound. He cleaned the wound with a wet rag, exposing a nasty-looking hole in Caulder's shoulder.

"It's going to take some cutting," the doctor said.

"Listen, I think I can do this," Caulder said. "You're in no shape. . . ."

The doctor raised his shaking hands into the air in front of

Caulder. Miraculously, the shaking stopped and the hands were perfectly still.

The doctor loaded a syringe with anesthetic and injected it into Caulder's shoulder. He massaged the arm, circulating the numbing fluid.

"How's that?" the doctor asked.

"Numb enough."

"You sure you don't want gas? This is going to hurt."

"No way. Let's go."

The doctor made an incision that stretched about half an inch on either side of the bullet hole. Then he pulled the flesh apart to make room for what he had to do. He picked up a pair of stainless steel tweezers and probed inside the bloody hole for the bullet. The search for the thing was more painful than actually being shot had been. The tweezers hit too close to a nerve and Caulder's arm shot out in a spasm of pain, knocking his glass of Dickel to the floor. The doctor pulled out the tweezers and caught his breath. He was going to have to make another go of it.

"Goddamn, Doc, that's not a trout you're fishing for!"

The doctor ignored him and went back to work. Caulder's face was covered in sweat and white with pain as the doctor pushed and probed, trying to get a firm grasp on the invader in his flesh. Finally the doctor yanked the tweezers from the wound and out popped the bloody slug. He dropped the flattened chunk of metal onto the work tray and leaned back with a sigh of exhaustion. Caulder shut his eyes for a moment and almost passed out.

The doctor poured himself another hit of bourbon. He surveyed Caulder and the extracted bullet on the tray.

"Lot of trouble on the street lately," the doctor said.

"What kind of trouble?"

The doctor poured disinfectant into the wound and Caulder suppressed a scream.

"I've been getting a lot of late-night business, that's all. Lotta guys coming in here all banged up, some of 'em shot to shit. I even had Dawson in here a couple of days ago." The doctor studied Caulder's face for a reaction. Caulder's expression didn't change. He had forgotten all about Dawson. He kept meaning to look the man up and find out if he had given Baxter his home address, but more important business always intervened. Now the mystery was solving itself.

The doctor assembled a stitch set and started to close the wound with heavy fiber. His hands began to tremble as he got closer to finishing the job. "Dawson was pretty messed up," the doctor continued. "Said a couple of Baxter's people had done the job. They worked him over something fierce. His face looked like they tried to resculpt it."

Caulder thought about the bench grinder that had ripped his forehead open.

"What else?" Caulder asked slowly.

"Said he was leaving town. He was certain that someone was going to kill him if he didn't. He said if I saw you I should tell you he was sorry, for whatever it was worth."

"It's worth something," Caulder said.

The doctor finished stitching and began cleaning up the blood. Caulder closed his eyes and mulled the situation. Baxter had ripped Caulder's address out of Dawson by force. He had gone to a lot of trouble just to get Caulder onto the Fredrickson job a few hours earlier than he could have by following procedure. What the hell had Baxter been so afraid of? Why couldn't he send his army against Fredrickson? Had he known even *more* than he told Caulder in his office? Did he know what Caulder was going to be up against? Who exactly was Baxter trying to set up, Fredrickson or Caulder himself?

"I'm going to give you a little blood before you go," the doctor said. "What's your type? I've forgotten, it's been so long."

"B negative."

"Oh, yes . . . I was afraid of that. That's a problem. It's a bit rare."

"I know."

"I'll call Keene over at the blood bank and have him send over a couple pints, if he's got it."

"Great, Doc. I'm feeling a little low."

"You know you've got pneumonia, don't you?"

"Of course."

"You want me to put you up somewhere? You could use around-the-clock care. I've got a new nurse named Laura. You'd like her."

"Thanks, but I've got to keep moving."

"You won't be moving at all if you push it much further. You're bad off, Caulder."

The phone rang and the doctor picked up the receiver and said hello. After a moment he looked over at Caulder and said, with some surprise, "It's for you."

Caulder frowned and took the phone. He knew who would be on the other end of the line.

"Yes?"

"Feeling better?" Fredrickson asked.

Caulder wasn't feeling better. He wasn't feeling much of anything. The Percodan and the booze had combined with his pain to create a sensation of utter nothingness. He decided not to answer the question.

"Did you really think you could hide them from me, Ry?" Fredrickson continued.

Caulder got up off the table. He couldn't have found Stephanie and Jason, could he? How?

"I know where they are," Fredrickson continued. "I even have a key to their room, courtesy of a new friend of mine at the Beverly Hills. I can have them whenever I want them. You can't protect them and you can't stop *me*. Haven't you figured that out yet?"

Caulder had been a bit slow on the uptake, but he wasn't stupid. He had been fully planning to skip town now. Fredrickson was a force that he could not reckon with and he had decided to turn tail and run. He no longer cared about Baxter or the money he was owed. He was going to leave Stephanie and the kid some more cash at the desk of the hotel and a note explaining that he had left the country. It would be rude, but it was all he could do. Now even his plans of cowardice were spoiled. Fredrickson would kill two more innocents because of their affiliation with Ry Caulder. They would have been dead already if Fredrickson hadn't suspected Caulder's thirst for vengeance was much less intense at this point than his desire to preserve innocent lives. Fredrickson was using Stephanie and Jason to keep him in the game. If Caulder disappeared, Fredrickson would kill them both just to teach him a lesson.

Caulder's mind raced, trying to find a solution to this new dilemma. He briefly considered going to the hotel and taking Stephanie and Jason with him, but he was afraid Fredrickson would intercept them and they would all be killed anyway. No, there was only one solution.

"Let's get it over with," Caulder said, trying not to reveal the fear and anger in his voice.

"You know where I live," Fredrickson said, then hung up.

Caulder slammed down the phone and looked over at the drunken doctor.

"Trouble?" the doctor slurred.

"You might say that."

Caulder pulled another glass out of a cabinet to replace the one he had broken. He poured himself more of the George Dickel and raised his drink in a toast.

"To life," Caulder said.

"To life," the doctor countered.

They clinked their glasses together and drank deeply.

thirty-two

Caulder entered the parking garage of his apartment building on foot and headed for the trash chute. There was no police surveillance outside the building and there appeared to be none in the garage. The cops hadn't put all the pieces together, despite the violence that had occurred in the vicinity earlier in the day. The Buick had been towed away from the alley and he assumed that a wide variety of witnesses had given descriptions of him to the police earlier. The neighbors might have reported the gunshot on Caulder's floor, but they probably weren't sure which apartment it had come from. Nevertheless, it wouldn't take much longer for the cops to figure out what it all added up to. Detective March had already been sniffing around before the *real* trouble had begun. This business would make the detective's job all the easier. The 9mm Browning containing Caulder's fingerprints had also been abandoned on the sidewalk in front of the building. If the police didn't have it, a citizen did. Caulder hoped whoever had the gun wanted to keep it instead of turning it over to the cops. There was also a strong likelihood that his episode in the gun shop had been videotaped. He didn't spot any cameras in the store while he was there, but they make them so small now that it was better than even odds that he had been captured on tape blowing Fredrickson through the doorway. It's a rare gun shop that doesn't have a video camera rolling. Although Buddy's could easily be the exception to the rule. Camera or no camera, Caulder suspected that he would be a wanted man by morning. Whatever he was going to do had to be done quickly.

Caulder climbed the Dumpster and crawled up inside the chute. He wouldn't have attached the convex mirror to the Dumpster even if he had it on him. He didn't care about secrecy anymore. The normals no longer seemed such a threat to him.

Caulder removed the panel on his hiding place and pulled out a very large duffel bag. He opened the bag and looked inside. The duffel was filled with hundred-dollar bills. Three thousand one hundred and sixteen hundred-dollar bills to be exact. Over three hundred grand. This was Caulder's life savings in cash. He had more in stocks, bonds, foreign real estate, and offshore accounts set up under various corporate aliases, but there would be no time to access those accounts. To many people it would seem a fortune, but to Caulder it was nothing. He knew how much blood had been spilled over the years to build this little nest egg.

Caulder flipped through the hundreds, feeling the texture of the dirty money. He closed the bag, replaced the metal panel, then slid down the chute to the edge of the Dumpster. He walked out of the garage with the duffel bag under his arm, picked up the paper bag he had stashed in the bushes, placed the bag in the duffel bag, and went out to the street to hail a cab. He had showered and gotten fresh clothes at the doctor's office. He now wore a loose pair of tan slacks, a gray sweater, and a dark blue sport jacket two sizes too large. At least the clothes weren't caked with blood.

The doctor had given him injections of penicillin, B-12, a tetanus shot, and a pint of fresh blood. He had tossed in a small dose of morphine for the pain and a couple of bottles of uppers to raise Caulder's spirits. Caulder had needed to take the drowsiness out of the Percodans and the morphine. It worked. Caulder was feeling remarkably well for a man in his condition. The trip to the doctor had cost him everything he had left in his money belt— three grand, cash—but that included the weapons.

The paper bag he had stashed in the bushes before entering the garage contained two small combat knives and an Ingram Mac 10 machine pistol, complete with three loaded clips left behind by one of the doctor's patients that *hadn't* pulled through. Caulder didn't like Mac 10s. He thought they were pieces of shit that usually jammed the first time they were fired, but his own machine pistol, the far superior Heckler & Koch MP 5, was still stashed up in his apartment and he didn't feel comfortable with the idea of going up there to retrieve it. He was risking enough by entering the garage to collect his cash. He had dropped the Browning after shooting Fredrickson in the stomach. All he had left from his original collection was the little .380 Colt, which would be okay hunting cockroaches, but he was after bigger game. The Ingram might come in handy.

The doctor was a good man to know. Not only could he help you with your bullet wounds, he could dress you and provide you with weapons if need be. All you had to do was pay.

It was after 9 P.M. Caulder considered stealing a car, but he didn't want to take any extra risks while carrying so much cash. He got lucky and caught the very first taxi to come along. It had only taken twenty minutes, but Caulder managed to walk ten blocks in that time. The taxi driver didn't look at Caulder with any hint of recognition. If Caulder's face had become famous over the last few hours, this guy didn't seem to know about it.

"Where to?" the driver asked.

Caulder looked at the man's curious face in the rearview mirror. *Where to?* Good question.

thirty-three

Michael Del Monaco was startled out of a deep sleep by the sudden awareness of a foreign presence in the room with him. His wife had left him more than a year ago, no longer able to stomach the lifestyle or the fact that every time she took a lover on the side to dull the pain, said lover would either disappear or meet with an "accident." Mike Del Monaco was supposed to be alone in the house, but he could hear someone else breathing in the dark bedroom.

"Who's there?!" Mike Del Monaco bellowed as he sat up and fumbled for the pistol in the nightstand next to the bed.

"The gun is not there," a voice said from the other side of the room. "Don't panic, Mike. It's me."

Mike Del Monaco couldn't find the pistol. He pushed his back against the headboard and tried to focus in the dark.

"Who? Who the fuck are you?"

"Ry Caulder," the voice said.

Mike Del Monaco reached over and hit the switch on the lamp on the nightstand.

Caulder was sitting quite calmly in an armchair on the opposite side of the room. The pistol Mike Del Monaco was looking for lay on the floor in front of Caulder's feet. Other than that, Caulder appeared to be weaponless.

"I took the gun so you wouldn't hurt yourself with it," Caulder said.

Mike Del Monaco's expression didn't change. "Are you here to kill me?" he asked.

"You'd be dead already."

Mike Del Monaco relaxed against the headboard. "Then to what do I owe the honor of this intrusion?"

"I want the truth about Fredrickson," Caulder said.

"I *told* you the truth."

"Not all of it. I want *details*. The guy isn't human."

Mike Del Monaco straightened up and looked at Caulder more seriously. "What do you mean by that? I mean *exactly*."

"Well, for starters, he has a tendency to grow body parts after I blast them away. I find it disconcerting."

"I see," Mike Del Monaco said. He didn't seem the least bit surprised by what Caulder was telling him. He seemed to be mulling it over like some kind of accounting problem.

"You know something about this, don't you, Mike?"

"Last year we had a little problem down in Venezuela. There was some crazy old guy down there with a coffee plantation that we were trying to buy. The guy wouldn't sell. We sent some tough negotiators down after him and they never came back. Then we started having other problems in the vicinity. All our shipping channels started drying up. People were disappearing. Just disappearing. So were our shipments. We figured it was the old guy and his family retaliating for our attempt at a hostile takeover." Even in his own home, Mike Del Monaco was a master of the euphemism.

"So you sent Fredrickson down," Caulder said, filling in the gaps.

"Yes. We sent Fredrickson. We felt the situation needed the

touch of a specialist. So we sent Fredrickson. After a few days he reported that the problem was solved. Then we started getting crazy messages from him."

"Crazy like?"

"He said the man had come back to life. Not that he was still alive, but that he had come *back* to life. We thought Fredrickson had lost his mind until . . ." Mike Del Monaco drifted off, not wanting to complete his thoughts.

"Until I started coming up with the same story about Fredrickson, right?"

"Yes. It was obviously more than a coincidence."

"Why didn't you level with me straight off?"

"I thought we had. We showed you the pictures. You knew what you were getting into. The rest was insanity."

Caulder thought about it for a few moments and realized that Mike Del Monaco was right. Even if Mike had told him everything from the beginning, Caulder wouldn't have believed it.

"How do you explain it?" Caulder asked.

"It's a little out of my line of expertise, Ry. I'm more of a numbers man myself. Do *you* have any theories?"

"Me? Christ, Mike, I'm not even a numbers man. I'm just a killer."

"I can tell you one thing."

"What's that?"

"A couple weeks after we last heard from Fredrickson we started having problems farther up the coast, but the problem with the plantation owner seemed to be a thing of the past. We sent some guys down to the place and they said it looked like a war zone. The place was leveled."

"What about the old man?"

"They didn't find him. We never heard anything from him again. But then Fredrickson began to make our troubles with the old man seem trivial by comparison."

"So you're suggesting that Fredrickson managed to eliminate the guy?"

"Perhaps. And if he succeeded, then it is also possible that *you* could succeed."

Caulder rolled that one around in his mind a bit.

"One more thing, Mike," Caulder said. "Did Baxter really want me to tag Fredrickson, or did he know it was a suicide mission?"

"Oh, Baxter wanted to eliminate Fredrickson at any cost," Mike Del Monaco said. "But, to tell you the truth, he probably wouldn't have minded if the two of you killed each other. He doesn't like you much, Ry."

"The feeling is mutual."

thirty-four

The rental car pulled up in front of the Beverly Hills Hotel
just shy of eleven. Caulder got out and handed the valet a fifty and
told him to leave the car undisturbed until his wife came down for
it in an hour or so. The man pocketed the cash and said everything
would be taken care of.

Caulder pulled a large stuffed teddy bear from the backseat of
the car. He had purchased the doll at an all-night drugstore on
the way to Hertz rent-a-car.

The lobby of the Beverly Hills Hotel was unusually busy for
a late Monday night. Caulder made his way casually through the
crowd and entered the elevator. A beautiful woman with dark red
hair got on the elevator with him. Caulder pushed three, she
pushed four. The woman leaned against the wall of the elevator as
it ascended. She gave Caulder a "fuck me" look that he would have
loved to have tested. She was just the kind of nasty piece he enjoyed ravishing. Thoroughly ornery and totally respectable. The
wedding ring on her finger told him he would have very little explaining to do afterward.

Contemplating all this distracted Caulder momentarily from the realities of his situation. For a few brief moments he didn't think about Fredrickson or Baxter or Alvin or Paul Shepfield or Stephanie or Jason, or his pneumonia, or even the hole in his shoulder. The respite was short.

The elevator stopped on the third floor and Caulder stepped out. He turned and looked at the woman. "Sorry," he said.

"I know you are," the redhead said with total confidence. The silver door slid shut and she was gone.

Caulder walked down the hall. It was deathly quiet. Cool air from the air-conditioning units burned in his congested lungs. He coughed a wheezing cough, trying to bring up some of the phlegm impeding his breathing, to no avail. He stopped in front of room 302 and knocked.

Stephanie opened the door and stared at Caulder. His face was a mess and his clothes were obviously not his. He still looked like Prince Charming to Stephanie. "I didn't think you were going to come back," she said, trying to choke back tears. She staggered forward and hugged Caulder sadly. She was dressed only in a blue robe. Caulder could feel her breasts moving loosely under the soft material. Something deep within him stirred. He tried to fight it off.

Caulder gave Stephanie a paternal pat on the back. "I'm here," he said coldly.

Stephanie took a long look at Caulder, as if she sensed a change in him. She led him into the room and closed the door.

Caulder looked the hotel room over. Stephanie and Jason had made it their own. Personal belongings were laid out as if this was their home and they were never going to leave. Caulder held out the stuffed bear. "Where's the kid?" he asked.

Stephanie called Jason's name. After a moment the boy came out of the bedroom. He smiled at Caulder and then looked skeptically at the stuffed animal.

"Gee, Ry, is that for me?" Jason asked.

"I know you're a little old for this kind of thing, but this guy is going to be a good friend to you."

Jason took the bear and seemed surprised at how big and lumpy the beast was. This was one *fat* bear.

"There's a neat movie on TV, Ry," Jason said with enthusiasm. "It's called *Commando Squad*! It's about secret agents and drug runners and it's really cool! Wanna come in and watch?"

Caulder could hear the phony gunfire from the television in the bedroom. He had experienced his fill of violence for a while.

"Maybe in a few minutes," Caulder said to the boy. "I need to talk with your mom first."

"Okay," Jason said. He wrestled the stuffed bear into the bedroom and shut the door.

Caulder led Stephanie onto the balcony. They looked out over the grounds. A beautifully manicured lawn swept down to a pond filled with ducks and swans. In a gazebo off to the left a group of impeccably dressed people bore witness to a young couple getting married. That was the reason for the crowd downstairs. A night wedding under klieg lights. Only in L.A. The Pachelbel Canon in D major wafted over the idyllic scene.

Caulder put his hands on the back of Stephanie's shoulders. It sent chills down her spine.

"You're leaving again, aren't you?" she asked, already knowing the answer.

"Yes."

"And this time you're not coming back, are you?"

"No."

"And you're not going to tell me what you're messed up in, right?"

"That's right."

A tear rolled down Stephanie's cheek. She gently scratched at the scar on her wrist.

"I should have known better than to dream again . . ." she said in a soft voice that Caulder could barely hear.

"I'm sorry, Stephanie. I wish things could have been different. . . ."

"Then why can't they be?"

Caulder answered with silence.

Stephanie turned and kissed Caulder savagely on the lips. Caulder pushed her away but she grabbed him tightly and locked her arms around him in a vicelike embrace. Caulder didn't push her away this time, but he didn't return the affection either. He just stood there, looking stupid.

"I'll miss you, Ry."

At first Caulder said nothing. And then it boiled out of him. "I'll miss you too," he said. The words were unstoppable and he immediately regretted them. It was as if he was having an out-of-body experience, watching himself from a distant corner of the room.

Stephanie raised her head and found Caulder's lips with her own again and this time he did not push her away. He responded. The kiss was long and intense. This was the moment they had both been fantasizing about for months.

Stephanie shoved Caulder into the corner of the balcony, away from prying eyes below, and away from where Jason might see them if he came out of the bedroom. She reached down and caressed the bulge in his pants.

"What are you doing?" Caulder asked moronically.

"What's it look like?"

She unzipped his pants and reached inside. He was hard and waiting. The close encounter with the redhead on the elevator had already excited him. Stephanie's advances had completed the job.

Stephanie freed his penis, slid down his body, put it in her mouth, and worked it like a pro.

Caulder's brain crackled with sensation. It had been quite a while since he had had sexual contact. And this was his little dream girl. His Madonna pulling a whore act. Stephanie licked and sucked and pulled on his cock until he exploded in her mouth. She swallowed every drop hungrily.

Caulder peered around the corner to make sure Jason had not come out of the bedroom. *Commando Squad* was obviously sufficient entertainment to keep the boy occupied.

Stephanie continued to caress Caulder's cock lovingly. The intensity of the contact after orgasm was painful for him. He pulled her up by the shoulders, pushed her against the wall, and kissed her passionately. They were both on animal autopilot. Caulder reached under Stephanie's robe and caressed her breasts. They were small, but firm and shapely. Her nipples were bright pink and rock hard. Caulder kissed Stephanie's face and worked his way south, along her neck, past her collarbone to her chest. He kissed and sucked her breasts like a hungry newborn baby. He ran his hand along her flat, firm stomach until he found the tuft of pubic hair. Slick heat greeted his rough fingers as he traced the outline and details of her lips, her clitoris quivering under his touch. He could feel her suspense build as he teased the opening beyond her clitoris, then he slid his finger up into her and probed deeply. He pried and explored her body, working the folds and crevices. Stephanie gasped with a mixture of shock and relief as juices poured from deep within her and flowed over his fingers.

Caulder kissed her belly. He wanted to devour her. He kissed lower and lower until his tongue found her waiting for him. She tasted of strawberries. His tongue played on and around her clitoris, forcing small moans out of her that she fought to suppress. She folded a leg over his good shoulder and settled in for the ride. She gripped his bad shoulder as she came and pain shot through his body as pleasure went through hers. He shifted slightly, moving her hand off his bullet wound without drawing attention to it.

"Oh my God," Stephanie gasped. "I want you inside me . . . now. . . ."

Caulder stood up, unbuckled his belt, and popped the top button on his pants. He pulled the sash away from Stephanie's robe, exposing her body in full form with the robe still wrapped around her shoulders if sudden modesty were required. Stephanie leaned back against the wall, reached down, grabbed Caulder's still-hard member, and positioned it against the opening of her vagina. The tip of Caulder's cock tingled with excitement as he felt her flesh hungrily envelop him. He leaned forward and thrust upward. They kissed each other like thirsty people finding an oasis.

Caulder reached down and caressed Stephanie's ass. Her cheeks were round and soft, but the muscles tightened as he lifted her off her feet and she sank all the way to the base of his cock. Stephanie wrapped her arms tightly around Caulder's neck as she pushed herself down on him as hard as she could. Caulder felt the back wall of her vagina brush against the tip of his penis as they thrust against each other. They fit perfectly. He could feel the warmth rising in his body again. His cock swelled and Stephanie could no longer keep the moans from welling out of her. Caulder kissed her to keep her silent. He pressed her tightly against his body, his fingers always exploring behind her. Stephanie began to orgasm intensely. Her muscles spasmed tight, a noose around Caulder's cock. Hot fluids gushed over him and he was gripped with monstrous animal desire. He pounded Stephanie against the wall repeatedly, trying to bury his entire being into her, to become part of her flesh, and then he exploded into her body, triggering yet another orgasm in her. They both stiffened up like paralyzed lizards on a rock. They were covered in sweat. Tears were rolling down Stephanie's face and Caulder was finding it hard to breathe. He moved inside her a few more times, draining himself thoroughly.

Their bodies began to relax, but they still held each other tightly. Then Caulder grew soft and Stephanie lowered her feet to the ground and stepped off of him. They slowly regained the ability to see each other with clear eyes and the total realization of what they had done began to hit them. Caulder lowered his head in shame. Stephanie laughed uncontrollably.

"I couldn't let you go without knowing what you were abandoning," she said.

Caulder lifted his pants and buckled his belt. He was embarrassed that he had gotten so carried away.

"I'm sorry," he mumbled.

"What for? *I* attacked *you*. That's the only way it was going to get done. You treat me like I'm the Virgin Mary."

"That is a myth you have just dispelled."

"I should have done it a long time ago. Maybe things would have been different between us."

"Maybe."

Stephanie wrapped her robe around herself and tied the sash, trying not to show her sudden disappointment. She stepped over to the railing and looked down into the courtyard again to avoid eye contact with Ry Caulder.

"You have to listen very carefully to me and do just as I say," he continued. "You have to leave here tonight. You have to go as far away from L.A. as you can. Do you understand?"

Stephanie turned and looked at Caulder. "Of course I *don't* understand, Ry," she said. "You never tell me enough to make me understand anything. You just tell me to pack my bags and I pack. You tell me to stay in this hotel and we stay in this hotel. Now we make love and you tell me to drive off the edge of the planet and I guess I should drive off the edge of the planet, without knowing for one minute why the hell I'm doing any of it."

"This has nothing to do with what just happened between us."

"Right," she said sarcastically.

"Your lives are in danger," he said slowly, trying to get his message across to her with emotional emphasis.

"Are they?" She was beginning to let her bitterness boil to the surface. "Or are you just trying to get rid of us? Because if that's the case you don't have to be so melodramatic about it. I don't want to be a burden to you. You certainly don't owe us anything. You don't ever have to see us again. But you don't have to scare us either."

"I don't want to scare you, but I have no choice. You *are* in great danger and it's all my fault." Caulder had to think hard for a few moments before continuing. He wasn't sure how far he should go, but considering what had just happened he felt Stephanie would need the whole ball of wax before she would believe him.

"A man wants to kill you to punish me and there doesn't seem to be anything I can do about it. That's why you have to leave. You've got to get as far away from this city as quickly as you possibly can."

"Why, Ry? Why does he want to hurt us?"

"Because he's sick and it's what he likes to do. Killing people is his job." Caulder looked at her sternly and let it fly. "It's also *my* job. It's what *I* do for a living. I kill people too."

"What?" Stephanie looked totally confused. "What did you say?"

"This man is a professional killer. I've known him for many years. He taught me the trade. We are assassins. Both of us. We kill people for money."

"Let me get this straight," she said. "People *pay* you to murder other people? Is that what you're saying?"

"That's the long and the short of it," Caulder said.

"I'm going to be sick." Stephanie clutched her stomach. She turned away from Caulder and looked down at the wedding in the courtyard.

"So, you kill innocent people for *money,*" she said without looking at him.

"No. They're never innocent," Caulder said. "But that doesn't make it right."

Stephanie gripped the rail in front of her fiercely, trying to contain her rage. "Who do you think you are? God?" she shrieked. She looked at his face and tried to keep tears of rage from marking her cheeks.

The wedding party down below came screeching to a halt. Somewhere from the shadows a man yelled "Cut!" over a megaphone. The wedding was just a scene for a movie being filmed. Caulder and Stephanie were so locked in conflict that they still didn't notice the truth behind the ceremony.

"No," Caulder said in soft, even tones, trying to calm her. "I'm just a man. I don't have any excuses for you. I'm telling you this straight so that you'll believe me and you'll understand what kind of trouble you're in. You have every reason to hate me, but that doesn't change the fact that someone wants to kill you and I want to do everything I can to prevent that from happening. Do you believe me? Do you understand?"

"Yes, Ry. I believe you. I'll *never* understand, but I believe you." She couldn't face him anymore. She didn't want him to see her tears. She didn't want to appear vulnerable in front of this animal. She felt filthy knowing that part of him was inside her own body now. She wanted to run. She wanted to cleanse herself of the wetness between her legs that had come from Ry Caulder, but she was too nauseous to make a move for the bathroom.

"I'm going to confront this man an hour from now," Caulder said. "I am going to do everything I can to stop him and I don't expect to have much luck. But at least he will be too busy to notice that you have left. Hopefully you'll be safe, but you *must* go. And you must leave no clue behind you indicating where you are going. Leave no possible trail. Will you promise me that you will do as I ask?"

Stephanie didn't answer him. She was too choked up to speak. Her legs felt as if they were going to collapse under her.

"Please, Stephanie," Caulder pleaded. "I have to know that you will be safe. I have to know that this won't be a wasted effort on my part."

It was obvious to Stephanie that Caulder did not expect to live through the night. It was just as obvious that he had more intense feelings for her than he had ever shown. Despite the terrible revelations about his lifestyle, she realized she still loved Caulder.

She also despised him now, but her love remained as well. It was still intact—cracked all over and starting to crumble in spots, but intact. She couldn't help it. If he had told her he was the bastard mutant son of Adolf Hitler and Benito Mussolini she would still be in love with him. She had to trust him. She had to do as he asked. Her life and her son's life might depend on it.

"All right, Ry," she said. "We'll leave tonight. We'll go and never see you again. Will that make you happy?"

"I don't expect you to forgive me," Caulder said. "I just want you to survive. Wait exactly one hour after I leave so that I can be sure he doesn't see you go. If I can't find him in that hour I'll call you and tell you not to move. If that happens, don't leave the room and don't open the door for anyone but me, not even room service, got it?"

"Yeah." She was not happy.

"You don't hear from me one hour from now that means I found him. Run like the devil is on your heels. He just might be. Get out of here within the following hour because I don't know how long I can keep him occupied. There is a car downstairs rented under the name Francis Sinclair. Take it and head north. When you're done with the car, abandon it. Don't return it to Hertz. The idea is that you are going to disappear, so no one can find you, get it? Everything you need to know is in this letter."

Caulder handed her a thick envelope and the rental car keys.

"This is frightening and ugly." Stephanie turned away from him again.

"I know," Caulder said, feeling foul and dirty. "I wish I had never started this with you. I knew better all along, but I couldn't stop myself. Every time I saw your face I got confused. You made me forget who I was. I tried to stay away from you, but I couldn't. You made me ashamed of myself. You made me want a better life."

Stephanie realized that this was as close to a declaration of love that she would ever get from Ry Caulder. It was too little, too late. And Caulder was no longer the man that she thought he was. That was some fantasy figure from her misty past. A dream that was drifting away into the nothingness of reality.

The couple getting married for the cameras down below had resumed their scene and were now locked in their wedding kiss. The ceremony was reaching its climax.

"They look happy," Stephanie said, not knowing how to respond to Caulder's confession, and still not comprehending what was really going on in the courtyard in the distance.

The wedding couple strutted down the runway. Their "friends" and "relatives" cheered and applauded them for making it this far. Some of them threw rice. Others just wept with joy that the night was about to be over. The director called "Cut!" again and now Stephanie realized what was really going on down below. She finally noticed the camera crew tucked away under a canopy off to the side of the ceremony. She had been duped again. One final irony for her to pack with her bags.

Stephanie turned to look at Caulder, but he was no longer on the balcony. She wiped tears from her eyes and went back into the hotel room. Caulder was gone. He had left without saying good-bye.

Jason came out of the bedroom, carrying the stuffed bear. "Mom, look . . ." he said in astonishment.

Jason held out the bear. A hundred-dollar bill stuck out of its back.

Stephanie took the bear, looked at the money incredulously, then tore open the back of the stuffed animal. Caulder's life savings, hundreds of hundred-dollar bills, twisted through the air and collected in a pile in front of Stephanie and Jason.

"Oh my God . . ." Stephanie gasped.

"All right!" Jason yelled.

Stephanie dropped the big bear on the floor and staggered speechlessly toward the door to the hall.

Jason played in the pile of cash, tossing it into the air and watching it drift back to earth.

Stephanie stepped out into the hallway and looked for Ry Caulder, but he was nowhere to be found. Tears streamed down her face. She didn't understand a damn thing that was happening.

"Why?"

Her voice reverberated gently down the empty hallway and back in a soft echo. It would be the only answer she would receive.

thirty-five

Upon leaving the Beverly Hills Hotel, Ry Caulder removed the paper bag from the trunk of the rental car and walked up Benedict Canyon. He left the empty duffel bag in the car. He wouldn't need it anymore.

Caulder stole the first car he saw parked on the street that was not protected by an alarm system. It was a 1976 Jag. The interior was ragged, but it drove like a charm. He made good time to Malibu.

It was almost 1 A.M. by the time he parked in the grove of trees down the hill from Fredrickson's mansion. He had fifteen minutes to find Fredrickson before Stephanie would be mobile. If Fredrickson wasn't in the vicinity, Caulder would have to find a phone, fast.

Caulder walked up the hill and looked at the mansion. It was completely dark. He went to the edge of the gully and looked down at the cave. Something was huddled on the ground in front of the lair.

Caulder made his way down the hill as quietly as possible. It was no easy feat. By the time he got to the floor of the gully he was completely winded. He pulled out his flashlight and approached the cave.

One of the Colombians had been caught in the big metal bear trap at the mouth of the cave. It was a woman. A Mac 10 lay a few inches from her hands. She had been dead for quite some time. Her neck was almost completely severed by the trap.

Caulder stepped over the bear trap and crawled through the artificial thicket into the cave. He was not afraid. He had a feeling that Fredrickson had already vacated the premises.

He was surprised to find light inside the cave. Two large candles flickered on a faux mantelpiece along one rocky wall. The light from these candles could not be seen from the outside.

The cave was surprisingly large and sumptuously appointed. Silk lined the floor and walls. Pillows and comforters were scattered about and there was a large wine collection stored at the rear of the cave, beyond the sleeping area.

Caulder saw something covered by a comforter behind one of the wine racks. He pulled the comforter off and found more of Varga's people piled there on the floor. Three men and another woman. They were torn to bits, their flesh hanging off their bones in red ribbons. Varga was not among them.

Caulder searched the cave thoroughly for any signs of Fredrickson, then left the place and made his way up the steep hill to the mansion. Time was running out.

Caulder stared up at the mansion and his neck began to tingle. No lights were visible in the place, but he could feel Fredrickson in there, waiting for him. The smell of sulfur and rain was in the air. A storm brewed overhead.

Light slowly began to fill the sky. Caulder looked up and saw the moon appearing from behind a mass of tenebrous cloud. The moon was fuller and whiter than the night before. It trimmed the stormy clouds with silvery highlights.

Caulder loaded a clip into the bottom of the Mac 10, cocked

the gun, and placed it in his belt under his sweater and jacket. He pocketed the combat knives and the extra clips and let the empty paper bag drift on the wind. The pain was returning. He swallowed two Percodans and walked toward the entrance of the mansion. He wasn't worried about getting drowsy now. The hairs on the back of his neck felt as if they were on fire. His sixth sense begged him not to go any farther. But something more powerful pushed him on-ward: the desire to confront the darkness and come to a resolution. *Any* resolution. And in the resolution, perhaps he could find some spark of redemption, some sense of atonement, no matter what the outcome.

The front door of the mansion stood wide open. An invitation to anyone brave—or foolish—enough to enter. Caulder stepped through the dark threshold. As clogged up as his sinuses were, he could still smell the acrid stench of death heavy in the air. Caul-der passed through the vestibule into the main hallway and came face-to-face with *Camilo Varga's head*.

The drug lord's severed head was mounted on a large wooden stake driven directly into the center of the stone floor.

A note, written in a savage scrawl, was nailed onto the stake under the head. Blood from the bottom of Varga's neck had drib-bled onto the note, but Caulder could still make out the message:

> *Hello Ry,*
>
> *Looks like Varga got a HEAD start on you.*
>
> > *Your compadre,*
>
> > *F*

The words were written in Fredrickson's ink of preference—human blood. But that was not the real horror. Upon closer in-spection Caulder realized that the message was not written on paper at all. The o in the word *Your* was circled around a human nipple. The note was made of human flesh taken from someone's chest, then stretched taut and nailed onto the stake. Fredrickson had been experimenting with some of that old Nazi technology. Presumably Varga had been the donor.

Caulder heard a stirring sound emanate from the parlor. He stealthily approached the room, the site of his confrontation with Varga and the other Colombians a few days earlier.

Moonlight and a few strategically placed candles illuminated the vast room brightly enough for Caulder to see that the place had been thoroughly cleaned. There was no evidence of the battle to be found anywhere except for the top of the baby grand piano, which was still riddled with bullet holes.

Fredrickson stood at the far side of the room. He had his back to Caulder and appeared to be gazing out of a giant bay window at the moon. He wore a loose white shirt and a matching pair of pants. No shoes. He looked ready for a cruise in the Bahamas.

Caulder was just about to say something when Fredrickson began to turn. Caulder's words froze in his throat. What he saw rendered him speechless.

Fredrickson's face was covered with a light growth of hair. His jaw was thrust forward, pulling the skin on his cheeks tight like the skin on a drum. It appeared that his jawbone had grown about four inches on either side. His appearance was similar to the way he looked in the Tomb club a few nights ago, only more exaggerated. His face had looked perfectly normal earlier in the day, except, of course, for the gunshot wounds and the dropped brick that Caulder had inflicted upon him. But those little nuisances never seemed to alter Fredrickson's appearance permanently, and whatever made him look the way he looked now had nothing to do with anything Caulder had done.

Fredrickson smiled at Caulder, revealing two yellow, curved incisors, dripping with thick white saliva. He looked very proud of himself, like he was showing off. Fredrickson was getting a kick out of how many different ways he could surprise Ry Caulder.

"Good evening, Ry," Fredrickson said, his voice more bestial than it had been any of the previous nights. It was deep and raw, as if he had been up all night drinking hot whiskey. The words came out in a staccato rhythm that indicated speech took some concentrated effort.

Caulder stood in the doorway of the parlor, transfixed by Fredrickson's metamorphosis.

"I know how you feel, Ry. A year ago I felt the same way. At first I didn't believe it either. . . ." Fredrickson paused to gather his powers of articulation.

Caulder could feel the Percodan starting to kick in, beginning to make him drowsy after all. The various chemicals in his body were fighting for supremacy. Everything began to take on a dreamlike quality. A fog was rolling across his brain.

"I want you to understand everything before you die," Fredrickson said. "You deserve to know. You've earned it. You've been a source of great entertainment. I was getting so damned bored until you popped up again. It's been a pleasure knowing you all these years and I want you to know that I consider it a privilege to kill you. But I want you to hear my story first. I think you'll get a charge out of it. I need to share it with you. I've had no one to talk to for so long. I mean *really* talk to. You know, have a *conversation* with? I've been very lonely, Ry."

"That's hard to imagine."

Caulder was overjoyed that Fredrickson had decided to turn this into a confession. It bought him time, and in turn, bought Stephanie and Jason the time required to escape. Fredrickson could talk all night long as far as Caulder was concerned. It was easier than trying to kill him, whatever he was. And Ry Caulder was in no rush to die either.

"I had been sent down to hit an old Venezuelan coffee grower that was tampering with Baxter's supply channels," Fredrickson continued with some difficulty. He wanted to talk to Caulder, but he was not having an easy time of it. His vocal cords seemed to be tightening up on him. His voice grew harsher as he spoke. "The only problem was, the old bastard suffered from a bad case of lycanthropy. You might say the guy was a werewolf."

Caulder moved deeper into the room, but he kept a lot of furniture between himself and Fredrickson. He didn't know which one of them was crazier. Fredrickson had definitely gone around the bend, but Caulder thought he must be going nuts too. He was starting to *believe* the words he was hearing. He figured Fredrickson's explanation was as good as any *he* had come up with. A werewolf? Sure. Why not?

"A werewolf, huh?" Caulder said. "That's a tough one."

"Don't patronize me, Ry, or I'll just get this over with right now."

"I'm just trying to understand." Keep him talking, Caulder thought. Keep him talking.

"No you're not. You're stalling for time so the woman and the child can get away. Do you think I'm a fool?"

Caulder stared at the beast with awe. He knew everything. He knew Caulder's plans. Was telepathy part of the package? "Whatever you are, I know you are not a fool."

"They call it *Lobis Homem* down there," Fredrickson continued. "It's actually a very rare virus transmitted through the bloodstream. It attacks the immune system, like AIDS, but in reverse. It strengthens the immune system, supercharges it to an enormous degree. Unfortunately, the incubation period is terminally powerful in most cases. Very few people survive. But the lucky one percent who live after being infected become *Lobis Homem*. God's chosen people."

"Right," Caulder said. Who was he to argue with such concepts?

"I tried everything," Fredrickson continued. "Hand grenades, incendiary bombs, mortar shells . . . nothing worked. The old bastard just kept reconstructing and coming after me. I'd hide at night, when he was strongest, then strike back during the day. The battle lasted almost a month."

Fredrickson reached into his shirt and pulled out a gold chain. Hanging on the end of the chain was a brilliant nugget of polished silver. Fredrickson fingered the shiny chunk seductively.

"Fortunately I grew up in a part of Europe where lycanthropic legends are taken more seriously than they are in this country.... I finally understood and accepted what I was dealing with and I realized that the only way to kill the beast would be the tried and true method—a silver bullet to the heart. It sounded as crazy to me then as it does to you now. It didn't matter, I was out of options. I melted down one of the old man's silver goblets while he was sleeping in the woods. I didn't have a mold so the shape was a bit off and it would not fit properly into any of my guns, but I had my bullet.

"That night he sniffed out my hiding place and ambushed me. He had me cornered and I was as good as dead unless I could find some way to make the charge go off. I was bitten many times and I lost a lot of blood, but I finally managed to grab a rock and slam it down on the bullet, aiming it at his heart, of course."

"Of course," Caulder repeated with only a hint of mockery in his voice.

Fredrickson ignored Caulder's skepticism and continued. "The explosion blew off most of my hand, but it did the trick. The old man was dead. When I awoke, I was different. I had been reborn. I was *better* than before. I had been bitten by a *Lobis Homem* and survived! I had joined a very select race ... an elite race. Side effects of the virus render the carrier virtually immortal. The old man was a hell of a lot older than I thought. You see these weapons?" Fredrickson gestured at the walls around him.

"How could I miss them?" Caulder answered.

"Most of the antiques in this house came from the old man's villa. He collected them himself. Only they weren't antiques when he picked them up. They were *new*. They aren't nostalgia, they're *trophies.* The virus slows the aging process down dramatically. You grow older, but only about one-twentieth as fast as mere humans. An allergy to silver appears to be the only weakness in the armor of the virus. If you had figured that out you could have brought along some silver bullets, but you didn't, did you?"

Caulder just stared at Fredrickson quietly.

"Of course the physical transformation that took place nightly was uncomfortable at first," Fredrickson continued. "But I grew accustomed to it. The total effects of the virus weren't apparent until the next full moon."

Caulder looked out through the bay window at the moon. The silvery orb was almost three-quarters full, but certainly didn't qualify as a full moon.

"You look pretty 'affected' right now," Caulder said.

"This is only one of the preliminary stages. Each night I go through a transformation. The degree of the change intensifies with the lunar cycle. The fuller the moon, the more severe the effects of the virus. Something to do with tidal pull, I suspect. I won't be at my full strength for another few days ... 'when the wolfsbane blooms and the moon is full and bright' as they say on the *Late, Late Show.*"

Fredrickson held up his right hand. His fingers were gnarled and sparsely covered with fur. Sharp five-inch-long talons graced his fingertips. The talons were roughly the dimension of the hole Caulder had found in the back of Alvin's neck. Caulder suddenly realized how Fredrickson had killed Alvin. He simply put a finger into his brain. The thought of it nauseated and angered Caulder.

"You should see me when I'm full *Lobis Homem,* Ry. I'm quite a sight. I'm only half as strong now as I will be then." Fredrickson lowered his head as if gathering his thoughts, deciding something. Then he looked up, directly into Caulder's eyes. "But I think I can handle you!" he bellowed in a great flurry of excitement. The time for talk was over. The bloodlust had seized him. With astonishing speed and agility Fredrickson leaped across the room toward Ry Caulder.

Caulder panicked and tipped over a heavy table to block Fredrickson, then sprang back and pulled an African spear off the wall. Fredrickson shoved the table aside as if it was a hospital gurney on wheels. Caulder slashed him across the face with the spear. A deep gash opened up on Fredrickson's cheek.

Unfaltering, Fredrickson pushed closer, his hands slashing through the air furiously. Caulder tried to block with the spear, but Fredrickson's talons raked his arm, cutting deep into his flesh.

Caulder winced with pain and scrambled backward. He threw the spear and it slammed into Fredrickson's chest. Fredrickson's body momentarily reared up from the impact, but he still advanced on Caulder.

Fredrickson looked down at the spear petulantly. He grabbed the staff with both hands and pulled it out of his chest. He touched the wound with his index finger, then rubbed the gash on his cheek. He raised his finger to his lips and licked the blood.

"Congratulations, Ry. You drew first blood," Fredrickson said with a crimson smile. "But it's not who bleeds first in this game, it's who bleeds last."

Fredrickson hurled the spear at Caulder. Caulder rolled and ducked behind a large mahogany desk. The spear imbedded deeply into the front of the desk. Caulder pulled the Ingram Mac 10 out from under his sweater, steadied himself on the desktop, and opened fire. Smoking copper rained on the floor as empty shell casings spewed out of the side of the weapon.

The bullets rocked Fredrickson's body, ripping out big chunks of his flesh, but he seemed relatively unfazed. Caulder dumped the clip into Fredrickson until he was clicking on an empty chamber.

Fredrickson shook violently from head to toe, like a dog after a dip in the ocean, causing blood to splatter the room. He grinned at Caulder, then reached up onto the wall and grabbed a Kalashnikov assault rifle.

"Now let's see how *you* like it," Fredrickson snarled as he opened fire with the Kalashnikov.

Caulder dropped behind the mahogany desk, which was immediately bombarded with thunderous gunfire. Caulder hit the release button on the bottom of the Mac 10 and let the spent clip fall from the gun, then struggled to load in a fresh clip while trying to avoid the heavy ordnance hitting all around him. A shell fragment ricocheted off a wall and bit into his leg. It was a small piece of metal and it hit the fat part of his thigh. It wouldn't stop him from moving, but it hurt like hell.

Fredrickson marched forward, firing as he walked, the bullets tearing big pieces out of the antique desk. Bullet fragments and wood splinters bounced all around the room.

Caulder dove out from behind the desk, firing the Mac 10 from ground level.

Fredrickson was taken by surprise. His body animated at the receiving end of Caulder's gunfire once again. The Kalashnikov was hit repeatedly and one of Caulder's bullets pierced the casing of the Kalashnikov's clip and impacted on the ammunition. The weapon exploded in Fredrickson's hands, knocking him off his feet.

Caulder stood up and moved warily toward Fredrickson. The weapon felt light in his hand. He sensed that he had spent the entire clip again.

Fredrickson looked up at Caulder and shook the cobwebs from his head. Fredrickson's face and body were covered with bullet wounds and powder burns but he was a long way from being finished.

Caulder got a good close look at Fredrickson in the candlelight. His features had the distinctly canine look of a wolf. Caulder's mind reeled. It just wasn't possible! Werewolves were old legend, folklore, fantasies! But whatever Fredrickson was, it was no fantasy. It was a nightmare. And the nightmare was getting to its feet for another round of play.

Caulder's mind snapped. He lost all sense of reality and replaced it with an animal fury of his own. He grabbed a mace from the wall. The mace was an iron bar connected by three feet of heavy chain to a large spiked steel ball. In medieval times soldiers would use it to crush their opponent's heavy armor. Of course, the opponent was usually a human being, not a *Lobis Homem*. Caulder spun the mace over his head and advanced on Fredrickson with a maniacal scream.

Fredrickson jumped to his left trying to avoid the mace. The spiked ball caught him on the side of his head, ripping holes in his skull and producing a flurry of blood. The impact sent him crashing into the baby grand piano. The piano had taken enough punishment. Its legs gave out and it collapsed in the middle of the floor with a jangle of clanking, plinking strings. One snapped wire lashed out and cut Fredrickson across the nose, leaving a deep gash.

Caulder advanced, raising the mace over his head, preparing to bring it down on Fredrickson's skull. Fredrickson kicked out with a hairy foot. He wasn't wearing any shoes, but his toenails were the same sort of razor-sharp talons that graced his fingers. Fredrickson's foot caught Caulder on the side of his leg, ripping out a piece of meat. Pain tore through the protective walls of Percodan and bourbon and shot into the center of Caulder's nervous system.

Caulder toppled backward onto the cold stone floor. Momentum wrested the mace from his grip and it bounced and clanged away from him across the room.

Fredrickson grabbed Caulder's foot and began to drag him closer. Caulder struggled to pull away, but the creature was too strong.

Fredrickson's yellowed incisors glistened with white froth. He growled hungrily and bit deeply into Caulder's calf. Poisonous saliva shot into Caulder's leg like hot grease being injected by giant hypodermic needles.

Caulder screamed and pummeled Fredrickson with his fists, but it was useless. His blows were no more damaging than raindrops on a windshield. He grabbed a clump of Fredrickson's hair and pulled. Fredrickson tore out a big chunk of Caulder's leg and swallowed it. Then the beast looked up at Caulder's neck. He wanted the jugular.

Fredrickson climbed on top of Caulder, gripped one hand around his throat, then raised his other hand in the air, preparing to slash his face.

"You were a good student, Ry," Fredrickson growled. "But not good enough."

Caulder reached up and grabbed the silver chunk dangling from around Fredrickson's neck, then reached into his jacket pocket and found the .380 Colt with his other hand. He fired the Colt through the jacket, directly into Fredrickson's groin.

Fredrickson grabbed his wounded crotch, leaned way back, and let out a high-pitched howl that was louder and more frightening than anything Ry Caulder had ever heard in his life.

Caulder ripped the "bullet" off the chain and tried to crawl out from under the beast. Fredrickson slashed out reflexively. His claw caught Caulder across the face, ripping open his cheek and making his mouth about three inches wider. Blood splattered everywhere. Searing pain hit him in waves, alternating with numbness. He scrambled across the parlor toward the hallway, seeking escape. Fredrickson crawled after Caulder, arms flailing, trying to get a hand on him.

Caulder stumbled into the hall in a blind panic. He had no idea what he was doing anymore, he just wanted to get away from Fredrickson. He limped toward a room at the far end of the hallway. He had lost a lot of blood and the foamy saliva that Fredrickson had injected into his leg was making it swell horribly, but he was running high on fear and adrenaline. A plan formed through the fog. A kamikaze plan, but a plan nevertheless.

Fredrickson staggered into the hallway in pursuit. He was quickly recovering from his wounds and his pace improved with each step.

Caulder made for the heavy oak door at the end of the hall, Fredrickson right on his tail. Caulder had only one chance and that was to get to the other side of that door and buy himself a few seconds' respite. It was a race to the death and Fredrickson was closing in fast. Caulder tripped and fell to the floor like a drunk. He looked over his shoulder and saw Fredrickson gaining on him. He began to think that he was going to lose the race. As Caulder grew weaker, the beast was growing stronger. Caulder got to his feet and careened forward, Fredrickson only a few feet behind him now. Caulder needed to slow this unstoppable force down somehow. He turned and fired the Colt repeatedly into Fredrickson's face at point-blank range. He knew it wouldn't stop the creature, but the flash and impact of the bullets surprised Fredrickson enough to give him pause, and that was all Caulder needed. He tossed the empty gun aside and threw himself into the room at the end of the hall, slamming the door in Fredrickson's bullet-ridden face. Caulder turned the lock on the door and wedged a heavy chair under the doorknob.

Caulder hit a light switch and illuminated the room, which was larger than Caulder's entire apartment, but served only as a giant storage closet. Weapons waiting to be mounted and furniture that had been discarded and covered with sheets filled the space. Packing crates were stacked unopened in one corner. Caulder had been in this room the night he and Alvin fought the Colombians. In here he had found the LAWS rocket launcher that had frightened the Colombians off.

Fredrickson bashed against the heavy oak door. Caulder shoved more furniture against the door. He had to buy time. Time to regain his composure. Time to assess his wounds. Time to figure out how to save his own life, or at least the lives of Stephanie and Jason Taylor.

Caulder stumbled over to a workbench used to place the weapons on their mounts. He examined the chunk of silver that he had ripped from around Fredrickson's neck. The "bullet" was simply a ball of silver that had previously impacted on something very hard. One end had flattened out like a flower. It was difficult to judge the caliber of the original shell, but it looked close to a .44.

Fredrickson continued to smash against the door. The lock was holding, but the heavy wood door itself was beginning to splinter. The walls and the floor vibrated with each crash as though the "big one" had finally hit California.

Caulder searched the storage shelves frantically for an appropriate weapon with which to discharge the "bullet." He found a .44-caliber Magnum under a pile of smaller-caliber pistols in a packing crate under the workbench. Caulder got the distinct sensation that this was a fresh collection of local weapons. Fredrickson had begun to collect his *own* trophies. Caulder pulled the Magnum out and found it, like most of the weapons in the house, was fully loaded. Loaded weapons are dangerous things to leave out in the open, but Fredrickson had nothing to fear from them. He kept all his weapons loaded and ready for action.

Caulder emptied the Magnum onto the workbench. He picked up one of the shells, pulled out one of the combat knives he had gotten from the doctor, removed the bullet from the casing, then crammed the piece of silver into the case on top of the gunpowder. It was a snug fit, so it should be functional, but there was no way the awkward chunk of silver would slide back into the Magnum. The "bullet" was much too wide at the top. Caulder would have to shape the silver or find another way to set off the charge, as Fredrickson had bragged he had done with the old Venezuelan.

Caulder couldn't believe he was so caught up in the bullshit story that Fredrickson had fed him, but the myth was the only thing he had left to hold on to. That was probably what Fredrickson had meant when he said he had run out of options while combating the old coffee grower. Desperate situations sometimes call for desperate resolutions. Fredrickson was not the kind of man who would make up a cockamamy story like that, even bragging. If there was anything to the story at all it might be the key to killing him.

No matter what happened next, Ry Caulder was going to die. He now realized his wounds were terminal. No amount of medical help could save him. He was bleeding out. He would be going into shock at any moment. Death would soon follow. All he wanted before he headed into the abyss was to make sure that Fredrickson got there first. Caulder didn't mind dying, as long as he could die last.

The banging at the door ceased. It appeared Fredrickson had given up. A new fear gripped Caulder. The fear that Fredrickson might *not* get through the door. Fredrickson didn't have to do anything to kill Caulder now. All he had to do was wait for nature to run its course. Caulder would be a dead man in the next few minutes. If Fredrickson didn't make the effort to come after him, the game would be over. Caulder certainly had no strength left with which to pursue the man. He stared at the door for what seemed an eternity. The room was beginning to spin and he could feel unconsciousness nibbling at his brain. He was growing very sleepy. The fog was thickening. He just needed to close his eyes for a few seconds, that's all. . . .

The door suddenly exploded off its hinges, splinters flying like shrapnel as Fredrickson crashed into the room. The report the door made as it tore open sounded like a lightning bolt striking a redwood. Hurling the heavy furniture out of the way as if it were cardboard, Fredrickson lumbered through the debris toward Caulder.

The noise brought Caulder out of his stupor. He backed away from Fredrickson, holding the now useless "bullet" between his teeth. He was cornered and running out of time, but he had gotten his wish. Fredrickson had come to him. Now what?

All human intelligence had disappeared from Fredrickson's

eyes, replaced by an atavistic glare of brutality. Drool foamed out of his mouth and matted the thick fur on his chest. He was hungry.

Caulder spotted the LAWS rocket launcher that he had threatened Varga with on one of the upper shelves. He grabbed the launcher, armed and fired it all in one crazed move. He barely took the time to aim.

The rocket exploded with a fantastic blinding white light and a sonic crash that deafened Caulder. The entire room lit up with fire. Fredrickson was blown through the wall into an adjoining room, one of the mansion's kitchens. Half of Fredrickson's body evaporated instantly. His whole left side formed a Jackson Pollock on what was left of the crumbling wall of the storage room.

The heat from the exhaust of the LAWS rocket bounced against the wall of the storage room behind Caulder and flooded around, engulfing Caulder's back, scorching him terribly. He screamed in unholy agony. Gunpowder ignited in some of the weapons stocked on the shelves, discharging the bullets. The room began to look and sound like a fireworks factory that had caught fire.

Caulder tossed the rocket launcher aside and pulled his flaming jacket off, dropping it to the floor. Part of his sweater had melted onto his skin. He stumbled over the antique furniture into the main hallway. He didn't want to die in this house.

Flames flared up in the storage room and a few more bullets fired from the heat. A sprinkler system kicked on and began working on the fire. The sprinkler system was the one piece of modern technology that Fredrickson had added to the mansion. He treasured old things and old things were usually flammable.

Caulder staggered down the hallway toward the front door. As he reached the stake in the center of the floor he had to stop for a moment and lean against Varga's head. Caulder was losing consciousness. He could feel the cool night air coming from the open front door but he wasn't going to make it out of the mansion. He was out of juice and about to die. But before he died he wanted to know whether or not he had stopped Fredrickson. He wanted to believe that it had not all been in vain. Somewhere deep within the fog, his sixth sense tingled a vague response. Caulder turned slowly and looked down the hallway.

Fredrickson was crouched in the splintered doorway of the storage room! Even though he was missing quite a bit of his body, he had managed to drag himself out of the kitchen, through the storage room, and back into the hallway. Fredrickson was a twisted mass of bloody flesh and hair. His face was crimson and black. Part of his forehead was missing, exposing his brain. Broken bones protruded from all over his body. He had one complete leg and part of one arm left. Muscles hung from meat threads and arteries dribbled and squirted blackish fluid onto the floor. There wasn't much left of Fredrickson, but what was there was still smoldering. He hovered under the sprinkler system, trying to extinguish the last of his flames. Acrid white smoke filled the air. The smell of scorched flesh and burned fur wafted down the corridor and violated Caulder's nostrils.

Caulder stared at Fredrickson in near-religious awe. "You are *one tough motherfucker,*" he said to the smoking monstrosity.

A snarling smile played on Fredrickson's mangled mouth as he dragged himself closer to Caulder. A black trail, like that of some diseased snail, marked Fredrickson's wake. Fredrickson's flesh and bones were regenerating, but he was in no mood to wait. The bloodlust was up. He wanted to tear Caulder apart and eat the tender parts while Caulder was still alive.

Caulder realized through the fog in his brain that the silver bullet was still clenched between his teeth. A lot of good that was going to do him now. Maybe he could spit it into Fredrickson's heart. He scanned the hallway walls for something, anything, that might help him. He noticed an ancient crossbow hanging a few feet away. Caulder had lost most of his basic motor skills but he shoved himself away from Varga's head toward the crossbow and fell against it, knocking it off the wall onto the floor. The metal quarrel that had been loaded in the firing groove bounced a few inches away from the weapon. Caulder allowed himself to fall next to the crossbow. The shock of his scorched flesh touching the cold stone floor almost made him pass out, but then it began to feel good to him. He lay on the cool floor for a few seconds, unsure whether he had the strength to continue. Caulder stared at the weapon, a fully operational medieval crossbow. The metal quarrel was a replica. It looked much newer than the bow itself. Caulder managed to sit halfway up and get hold of the crossbow. He scooped the quarrel from the floor and let the bullet drop out of his mouth into his palm. Then he jammed the bottom of the shell against the end of the quarrel. He almost pressed it on too forcefully. He thought for a moment that the primer pin might go off in his hand, but it didn't. The shell stuck precariously on the tip of the metal quarrel.

Fredrickson was healing rapidly and closing in on Caulder. The knob that had once been Fredrickson's left arm was beginning to extend, growing with new life. A dangling piece of dead muscle dropped to the floor, no longer needed. He struggled to stand upright and move forward on his reconstructing legs.

Caulder made a Herculean effort and managed to load the quarrel back into the crossbow. Luckily the bowstring, already cocked, had not fired when he knocked the piece off the wall. He would never have been able to pull the bowstring back far enough to make the weapon functional. Caulder was running out of time and strength simultaneously. His legs were useless and his arms were practically paralyzed. Fredrickson was only a few feet away from him now. Caulder tried to focus as he stared into Fredrickson's psychotic eyes. The eye contact sparked something in the beast. Suddenly filled with a burst of enthusiasm, Fredrickson lunged. . . .

Caulder fell flat onto his back and fired the crossbow. The quarrel hit Fredrickson dead center in his chest. There was an explosion as the impact on Fredrickson's sternum forced the tip of the quarrel sharply against the back of the shell, activating the primer pin, firing the gunpowder, and blasting the silver chunk outward in a hundred small fragments into the screaming beast's body.

Fredrickson landed on top of Caulder, clawing and scratching at him with animal fury. Caulder tried to get out from under the snarling blob of flesh, but it was impossible. Fredrickson bit deeply into Caulder's charred neck. Caulder jammed a thumb into Fredrickson's eye, trying to dislodge him. The two men pulled and strained against each other until they both slowly collapsed and lay still.

The hills outside the mansion were starting to come alive with nature's scavengers, alerted by the sounds of violence and attracted by the scent of cooking flesh. A coyote appeared at the entrance of the mansion and sniffed the dead meat in the offering.

The heavens opened up and a heavy rain began to fall. The coyote stepped into the house. He moved closer to the two men on the floor, sniffing them curiously.

Suddenly Fredrickson's back moved. His shoulder lifted up, as if he was struggling to sit up or turn over. The coyote skittered back into the rainy night, unwilling to fight for its meal.

Fredrickson's body rolled limply over and landed back on the stone floor with a meaty splat. The remnants of the quarrel protruded from Fredrickson's open chest cavity, which had been blown apart by the exploding silver "bullet."

Caulder looked over at Fredrickson's face. The beast's eyes were open, but Caulder could not tell if he was dead or alive. Fredrickson seemed to be speaking. It was but a growling whisper and his lips did not move, but it sounded like he said three words to Ry Caulder: "I created you."

Caulder wasn't sure Fredrickson had said the words. He thought he might be hallucinating. A sound came from Fredrickson's body. The sound of air being let out of a tire. What dim light there had been in Fredrickson's eyes was now gone.

Ry Caulder sat up. Bloody, burned, bitten, and beaten, but the victor. He looked down at Fredrickson. The beast was not breathing. He had no pulse. And most importantly, there were no signs that his body was regenerating. Fredrickson was dead. At last. The silver had found its mark. Nothing like a little late-night mythology to rid yourself of your troubles.

The victory was a hollow one. Caulder realized he would not live to enjoy it. He'd been bitten and torn in too many places. He had lost more blood than anyone could and remain alive. First-, second-, and third-degree burns covered his body. His legs had puffed up twice their normal size. His chest was filled with fluid and his head was pounding and ringing and clouding over.

Caulder had finally completed his assignment, but the price was going to be his life. It was proper justice, he thought to himself. He had been responsible, in part or in whole, for a lot of death in his lifetime. He had seen the Reaper's handiwork often in his day and now he would get to meet him face to face.

Caulder's only regret was that Baxter and his mob weren't dead as well, their body parts strewn around the mansion like his and Fredrickson's. Now Baxter would have it all. He wouldn't even have to kill Caulder. Caulder had done Baxter's dirty work for him in total, including his own demise. If only he could have gotten to Baxter, if only he could have ended that bastard's life, he'd feel more complete. He wouldn't feel like he was leaving so much unfinished business behind.

Caulder realized he should have tagged Baxter before trying to kill Fredrickson. He had known his chances of surviving the encounter with Fredrickson were slim to none. He should have taken care of the easier business first, but there just hadn't been time. Caulder had let his concern for Stephanie and Jason cloud his judgment. He had wanted to eliminate Fredrickson at any cost.

Baxter had threatened to hurt Stephanie and Jason, but there was nothing that led Caulder to believe that Baxter knew where they were. Caulder had moved them before Baxter realized they could be used as bargaining chips. They'd already been relocated before Caulder got his face carved in the garage, and Baxter had given no indication that he knew they were gone. Baxter wouldn't take the time and trouble to find and kill them now. Not with Caulder dead. There would be no point to it. Fredrickson had been the greatest threat to Stephanie and Jason. With him out of the way, they would be safe. If Caulder's speech and the letter he left her had frightened and informed Stephanie properly, Baxter would never find her, even if he tried.

Still, Caulder regretted leaving Baxter alive. It had been selfish, considering the greater harm that Baxter represented to society in general, but Caulder couldn't save the whole world. Just two small pieces of it. Besides, there would always be a Baxter. That mold would never be broken, just updated.

He had only one other regret as he contemplated the eternal—the innocent that haunted him always. The Jameson girl. But there was nothing he could do about that. Nothing he could *ever* do about that. That was ancient history. No matter how many women and children Ry Caulder could have rescued from the darkness, the Jameson girl would remain there. At least he and Fredrickson would no longer be around to commit any more such atrocities.

Caulder stared down at Fredrickson's body for as long as he could, fearing that the man might start breathing again, that he would start growing flesh and bone before Caulder's very eyes, that he might jump up and spit a horrible laugh right into Ry Caulder's face before he bit it off; but Fredrickson didn't stir. Caulder had confronted the incredible and come up a winner. He had attempted the impossible and succeeded. What more could he ask for? Life?

Caulder had very little time to think about what it had all

meant, about how strange a death it would be for him. No one would ever know what really happened here. Nobody would have believed the truth anyway. The fog in Caulder's head thickened and suddenly he didn't believe it either. Maybe that was the secret strength of myths. The reason why people who considered themselves logical never truly believed in werewolves and vampires and ghosts and UFOs. There must be some shred of truth behind every myth, some fire within the smoke, but the media mavens had made farce of such things. When and if the extraordinary were to occur, most people would react the way he himself had reacted. They would deny the contact. They would convince themselves they were dreaming. They would come up with "logical" explanations. Any excuse to avoid the truth. Maybe these experiences weren't as rare as they seemed and society merely rationalized the truth out of the myths until they became just another news story about some crazy guy tearing up a bunch of coeds. Sure, he thought, this kind of thing probably happens all the time. All the fucking time.

Caulder had enough energy left to snort out a blood-laced chuckle, and then his strength was gone. He collapsed back onto the stone floor and stared up at the ceiling. Strange images were painted there. Gargoyles. Beasts. Nymphs. For a moment Caulder thought they were moving. His vision blurred and grew dark. The curtain was dropping. He could hear the rain coming down outside the mansion. He wanted to crawl out onto the lawn, to feel the rain splash on his face one last time, but he had absolutely no energy left. He was drained.

Caulder closed his eyes and an image came to him. A face. The face of a woman whom he used to love. A woman whose life he had saved, hopefully. The woman was smiling and reaching out to him, but it was too late to reach back. Caulder's lips parted, but he could force no air through his blood-clogged throat to articulate her name.

And then Ry Caulder drifted off into the ether.

thirty-six

The moon shone full and bright. Pollution cast a blood-red haze over the giant orb and it loomed large over the city. Dark pink clouds punctuated the sky like dirty cotton candy. Behind the clouds the firmament was a brilliant, clear blue. It seemed to glow, as if light was shining through it from some distant star of unknown origin.

A lone figure stood silhouetted against the glass walls of the big conference room, staring out at the angry moon. Waiting . . .

Almost a week had elapsed since the confrontation. A week to explore new possibilities and contemplate alternatives. A week to draw up battle plans. Life plans. *Death* plans. He was ready to gambit.

Three heavily armed men burst into the room. *It's about time,* the figure in the window thought. He had placed the phone call over an hour ago.

One of the men yelled, "Freeze, motherfucker!"

The figure didn't move. Not because the man told him not to, but because he didn't *feel* like moving yet.

James Vincent Baxter entered the room and stared at the hulking shape in the window.

"Caulder?" Baxter asked, his voice only slightly above a whisper. It had sounded like Caulder's voice on the phone earlier, but *this* certainly didn't look like Ry Caulder. Baxter had assumed that Caulder had skipped town with the girl and the kid. None of them could be located in the last week. Quinn and Mativich had also disappeared, but the trouble seemed to end there. The rest of the week had been relatively uneventful, until now.

A low snarl came from the silhouette in the window. The snarl slowly formed into beastly words. "You may think you know what the world is all about," the shadow said. "But you don't know the half of it!"

The figure in the window turned and faced Baxter and his men, allowing them a better look at their destiny.

There was something majestically hideous about the creature. Its entire body was covered with silky, clean, brown fur. Its limbs were taut, revealing sharply defined muscles underneath the fur. Talonlike claws extended from what passed for its fingers. The talons were long and each one tapered to a sharp point. Its face was more beast than man. Its eyes were a luminescent yellow, as big and round as the moon outside, but brighter. Its mouth was more of a snout than anything resembling a human mouth. Its teeth were large and canine. They glistened in the moonlight and saliva frothed from the beast's lips and formed white pools on the floor.

Baxter was all out of nasty smiles. His bodyguards were frozen to their spots, their machismo melting like wax under a blowtorch.

Mike Del Monaco was not among the men, which was just as well. The beast had bigger plans for him. The ape was not there either. He too might prove useful in the future.

The beast tilted its head back and howled at the moon. The sound sent a wave of terror through the gangsters.

The howl built to a nightmarish roar as the creature leaped toward Baxter and his bodyguards. The men made some small, but useless, attempts to defend themselves from the horrible monstrosity. Brief, deafening gunfire was soon replaced by the sounds of screams and tearing flesh.

Baxter watched in utter terror as each of his men was torn limb from limb. Blood splattered the conference room as the monster bit, clawed, and ripped the life from the three thugs with bestial fury. The last of the three was wearing a cast on his arm. It was Blanchard. The creature grabbed the cast and yanked hard enough to pull Blanchard's arm completely from his body. Then he beat Blanchard over the head with his own arm until the man's neck broke and he stopped breathing. When the beast was finished, it turned and approached Baxter.

Baxter's legs were jelly. He collapsed to his knees in front of the towering behemoth. "Please, don't ... please ..." Baxter begged. He was so frightened that he lost control of his bodily functions and soiled himself.

The beast stood over James Vincent Baxter's cowering form and snorted with a mixture of human and animal indignation. Baxter was no better than a common criminal. A flea on civilization's ass. An insult to this magnificent creature's very existence.

The beast turned its head from side to side, studying Baxter, considering which part of him he would devour first.

Business was about to trade hands.

epilogue

It was a small house nestled high in the hills of Encino. Three bedrooms, one and a half bathrooms, a functional kitchen, a fairly spacious living room, a tiny den. It was more than adequate for a single woman and her young son. A palace compared to where they had lived before.

Stephanie Taylor paid for the house with cash, and even though Ry Caulder had given her a lot of money, more money, in fact, than she had ever seen in her life, it had taken almost all of it to buy the place. Even a *small* house in Encino was expensive these days.

The hurriedly written letter on Hertz rent-a-car stationery Caulder had left her that night explained many things. Mainly survival tactics. How to properly set up an alias. How to move about relatively unnoticed. How to handle cash transactions and avoid unsightly tax situations. Basically, how to most efficiently utilize what he had left them in the stuffed bear. There was no mention of what Caulder's motives were for leaving such a generous gift, just facts and figures and strategies. Ry Caulder was cold and hard to the finish.

Stephanie had considered staying out of the Los Angeles area permanently as Caulder suggested, but she couldn't bear the thought of never seeing him again. As long as she was in the vicinity there would always be hope.

Stephanie and Jason stayed in a hotel in Santa Barbara for almost two weeks before returning to Los Angeles. They lived in a small apartment in Hollywood for a few months, waiting to hear from Caulder, hoping he would find them somehow. Stephanie eventually took what was left of the money and bought the little house in Encino.

Purchasing the house was a direct violation of a number of Ry Caulder's rules of finance. He suggested strongly that they always rent, never put down roots, never tie up capital. He wanted them always prepared to leave at a moment's notice. But Stephanie couldn't live that way. She couldn't make her son live that way. They weren't gypsies or circus people or hit men. She craved a sense of stability and she knew that it was important for Jason as well. She refused to live a life of uncertainty and dread. Even if normalcy was an illusion, she wanted to embrace the concept and play by its rules. What if the authorities found her, pierced her new identity, and somehow managed to seize her house? She and Jason would be no worse off than they were before finding the money in the stuffed bear. In the meantime they could live the *Ozzie and Harriet* lifestyle, although "Ozzie" seemed to be away on a permanent vacation.

Stephanie scrutinized the news closely in the weeks following their escape from Los Angeles. There was a Mob war raging in the city and the death toll was high. She watched intently for any mention of Ry Caulder, sensing somehow that he was a part of it all. She was always greatly relieved when his name was not listed among the deceased, but somehow she felt he was there, somewhere, between every line in the announcements. She saw Detective March interviewed a number of times. His words and manner revealed that he had become a bundle of frustration. He looked haggard and worn, as if he had been chasing phantoms down blind alleys, coming up with nothing.

Then, as mysteriously as the Mob war had begun, it was over. The city settled back into the patterns of random violence and anarchy that everyone had grown accustomed to. The police and the media were baffled as to the specific nature of the Mob war. All they had to go on was a mountain of dead gangsters, drug dealers, attorneys, and businessmen. Anyone who knew the motives for the murders was either dead or keeping a lid on the details. The streets were unusually silent on the issue. Of course there were rumors— bad craziness about some wild beast terrorizing the night. No one bought that nonsense for a second. No one that mattered at least. Besides, the crime rate had dropped dramatically, or so said the statisticians.

A few months after Stephanie and Jason settled into their new home, Stephanie found a job as a receptionist for a legal firm on Ventura Boulevard. She had changed her name to Gloria Caulder in the hope that it might help Ry Caulder locate her. Her savings were down to under twenty thousand dollars. With expenses and the private school that Jason was attending, that would be gone in less than a year. It was time to earn a living again. The money she *did* have allowed her the luxury of a sitter when she couldn't be with Jason, and her job paid well enough that they were soon not only keeping their heads above water, but saving some new money every month as well.

And then there was the mail. Every few months they would find an envelope in their mailbox containing a thousand dollars or more. There would be no return address, just Stephanie's address typed on the front of the envelope. The post office stamp said simply LOS ANGELES. It could just as easily have come from the moon for all they knew. It was a gift from the gods and it came in handy on more than one occasion. Between it all they made out quite well. It was a new standard of living. No more than people deserved, but times were tough in America, and many folks were far less fortunate, out on the streets with nothing. If not for their guardian devil, Stephanie and Jason could have easily numbered themselves among the homeless.

The Portland-based custody battle for Jason was eventually dropped. Alexander, Stephanie's ex-husband, stopped pursuing the case. In actuality the man simply vanished from the face of the earth. Even though he cleaned out the safe at the used car lot that he owned before he disappeared, the police thought there was more to his departure than simple midlife crisis. Foul play was suspected. Stephanie was thrilled. Experience had hardened her to the degree that she felt no sympathy for her ex-husband. She blamed Alexander indirectly for all that had happened to her and Jason in Southern California, and she hoped he was burning in hell.

Stephanie didn't date for over a year. Around the office she earned the nickname "Frostbite," but she didn't care. She owed Ry Caulder and she was willing to wait for him. Finally she started going out again, but never with anyone connected to the law firm. She didn't like lawyers any more than Ry did. And she knew he would never approve of her dating one. She kept her romantic affairs to a minimum. She joined a gym and would occasionally accept a date from one of the many men there who asked her out. Once in a great while she would go to bed with one of these men, but never at her place. She allowed no men in her house, even for a casual visit. It wasn't only out of respect for Jason, but also for Ry Caulder. She didn't want to give him the wrong impression. Stephanie had lost grip on reality when it came to certain issues. Ry Caulder was at the top of that list.

Stephanie had worried when she and Jason first moved back to the city. She didn't know who the mysterious man was that Caulder said wanted to kill them. She was afraid he might still be around, even though she suspected that he was one of the many men mentioned in the nightly body count on the news. Stephanie believed that Caulder had survived his conflict with the man that night, and if Caulder had survived, the "evil" man had not.

Stephanie's initial fears drifted away after a few months. Soon she became very relaxed. She came to feel that they were not alone. She could sense a protective presence nearby, especially at night. It was always close.

Stephanie hung a hammock in her backyard and she would lie there late into the night, listening to the sounds in the darkness. There were a lot of coyotes up in the Encino hills, but on bright shining nights when the moon was particularly full there was something else out there as well. Something that dominated the hillside and ruled the night. Stephanie would sit listening to this thing move about in the darkness and she was never frightened, even when it would howl its inhuman song to the moon and whatever gods it praised or cursed. For Stephanie it was as if she was back in the old tenement downtown. She was filled with the same sense of security she had known in those days. The feeling that, in spite of the obvious dangers all around them, she and Jason would be safe. Their dark angel was invisibly guarding them from all harm.

As for Ry Caulder, she never saw him again. But she knew he was out there, keeping a protective watch over her and her young son.

And somehow she sensed he was content.

Certain technical specifics concerning explosives and automatic weapons have been altered or omitted in the interest of public safety.

Creative license was occasionally employed in the physical description of Los Angeles.

No attorneys were injured during the creation of this work.